THE STRANGE ANGELS

LAURA KALPAKIAN

buried
river
press

Buried River Press
Clerkenwell House
Clerkenwell Green
London EC1R 0HT

www.halebooks.com

Buried River Press is an imprint of Robert Hale Ltd

2 4 6 8 10 9 7 5 3 1

Typeset in Palatino
Printed in Great Britain by Clays Limited, St Ives plc

This book is for Juliet Burton

What is the knocking?
What is the knocking at the door in the night?
It is somebody wants to do us harm.

No, no, it is the three strange angels.
Admit them, admit them.

Song Of A Man Who Has Come Through
D. H. Lawrence

Does the Eagle know what is in the pit?
Or wilt thou ask the Mole?
Can Wisdom be put in a silver rod,
Or Love in a Golden bowl?

The Book of Thel
William Blake

PART I

CHAPTER ONE

THE JUNIOR PARTNER

SHIVERING IN THE bitter January chill, the very air grainy with soot and fog and exhalations of the quietly desperate, Quentin Castle left his home near Tavistock Square and hurried towards Russell Square tube station. One among many men huddled under black umbrellas, alike as an army of weekday beetles, Quentin joined this undistinguished throng descending into the bowels of the city. Every morning he was reminded of the story his father loved to tell of Sydney Thaxton, the great novelist. The story had smoothed and grooved over time, become amusing so that the bitter little nugget at its core was undetectable. His father, Albert, clothed the story in charm, but Quentin thought he missed, misunderstood its poignance.

Sydney Thaxton was among the earliest of Castle Literary's clients, a difficult, brilliant writer whose mercurial star had risen in the early twenties, and never quite set, even after his death in 1934. On his last visit to the agency, Sydney Thaxton had wheezed up three flights of stairs to Castle Literary Ltd. He was a man of middle years, the celebrated author of modernist fiction, but lax in matters of personal hygiene, generally unshaven, and usually unwashed. He smoked three packs of fags a day, and his fingers were brown from nicotine, and black from so often changing typewriter ribbons. Thaxton hulked there in Albert Castle's office, wafting the obnoxious odour of wet genius. He had come to lash out at the critics who had savaged his latest novel, and Quentin's father, Albert Castle, as befits the literary agent, agreed all critics were dogs, which wasn't enough for Thaxton, who blathered on, inspired invective describing them as spineless, puling, gibbering, frogspawn in stained underwear; he blasted their morals, their mating habits, their teeth, their flabby shanks and filthy hands, their minds, if they had any, which he likened to darkened sewers, their general sense of self-congratulation, a habit they shared with pigs living in shit. (This last bit Albert Castle left off if there were ladies present when he told the story.) Albert soothed the author with cups of tea sweetened with whisky, and at last, worn out by his diatribe, the genius rose, and was about to leave, commenting on the beastly weather, rain sluicing down. He ranted on a bit about the English weather too, speaking of it in that odd combination of nostalgia and loathing, which, after all, were the signature features of his work.

Albert Castle took his second-best black umbrella from the stand, and gave it to the writer. 'Here, you must take it.'

Thaxton declined.

Albert insisted, adding, 'I should like to think of you huddled under a black umbrella like the rest of us.'

Thaxton replied, 'You wish to compromise me, then?'

Albert always gave himself some witty riposte when he told the story, but in truth he was flummoxed and without the least idea what to say, or what Thaxton meant. When Sydney Thaxton left, he did take the umbrella, but without a word of thanks, nor promising to return it, or any such conventional palaver. He died a week later. His wife found him slumped over, his face in the typewriter.

Albert Castle, in his genial fashion, always ended the anecdote with the observation that one could not part with one's best umbrella, even for a genius.

But Quentin understood what Albert had not. In cowering under a black umbrella, Thaxton had become indistinguishable from the narrow, priggish people he detested. Under a black umbrella no one would know the great genius from the wheezy clerk, the soaring eagle from the burrowing mole, the peacock from the sparrow. Quentin Castle sympathized with Sydney Thaxton though Quentin personally had no genius and nothing to compromise, no gifts spurring him to rebellion, much less achievement. He was nearly twenty-five, tall, lanky, like his mother's people, near-sighted. Thick glasses over his hazel eyes gave him a studious air. He had the usual sallow colouring of a Londoner, a mass of brown hair, a thin nose, high cheekbones in a rather gaunt clean-shaven face. Quentin Castle hunched under a black umbrella nearly every day.

Quentin emerged into the air again at Oxford Circus. He glanced idly at the kiosks with their peeling bills promising Michael Redgrave as Hamlet and other more garish entertainments. Vendors hawked headlines from the newsstands, 31 January 1950, a new year – a new decade, 1950 – but the headlines only chronicled pallid political bits, Mr Wilson and the Board of Trade, how to make the Germans pay their debts, to keep the Soviets from boycotting the UN, the future of Jerusalem, the brutal weather closing roads in the north. All of it merely grim in a grey way. Not like during the war when one read even the bleakest articles eagerly, anxiously, almost savagely, religiously, desperately seeking any information that might shed light on the fate of people one loved, soldiers far away. Now one endured because one must, had stamina because one must, lived with ongoing austerity because one must, but utterly without the glory or sustaining solidarity of the war years. Quentin, with all the other men – black flotsam in an ocean of post-war grey – made his way up into the street where grit and litter blew against his legs, clung there like the beggar children of Rome.

He marched on towards Mayfair. Sleet-needles stung his face as he pulled his Burberry close. Like everyone else's, Quentin's overcoat was old; the lining had been replaced three times, and he had lost more than one coin in the hole in the pocket. He could sometimes hear the shillings rattling in the hemline. His suit was newer, though it had still seen a couple of years' wear. It had been fashioned by the same London tailor patronized by his father, though his father habitually wore a bowler and Quentin chose a fedora. The hat did not make him jaunty or debonair, but at least he didn't look like his father. His tie reeked lightly of benzine used to remove an unfortunate mustard stain. His white shirt was freshly laundered and ironed as befits a newly married man.

He came to a quiet, narrow street in Mayfair, where the buildings had Regency flair though that flair and the street itself were enveloped in a hundred years of effluvia from coal fires, smoke penetrating the stone, and even now the light snow hung like grey granular curtains. Castle Literary's offices were not near the great hotels or ambassadorial residences of Mayfair, but they had a Mayfair W1 address just the same. The rent was exorbitant, but Albert Castle was a firm believer in appearances, and even in the earliest days of the firm, 1920, he justified the cost with the Mayfair cachet. The street had been spared both German bombs and neo-Gothic enthusiasms of the 1890s; it had hardly been touched or changed since the 1840s. Quentin passed solicitors' firms dating back fifty or sixty years, and a few newer firms, architects and accountants, and even something called Public Relations. Street level were small upscale art galleries, a new travel agency and an old stationery shop. The buildings, three or four storeys tall, had marble steps and brass plaques by the doors, the steps and plaques kept polished by night-working charladies.

Opening the door to Number 11's large, airy foyer, Quentin shook out his umbrella. Once there had been a hall porter who would have taken the umbrella. Quentin remembered him from childhood visits to his father's office, a Mr Jobson, maimed in the Great War, lacking the fingers on one hand, and the sight in one eye. Jobson deferred politely to everyone who entered the building, even the boy, Quentin. Jobson had held the door, taken the umbrellas, collected the post and delivered it to each office. He barely made a living wage and received bonuses at Christmas. But by the time Quentin came to work at the agency, neither Jobson nor his job existed at all.

A noisy fluttering overhead caught his attention and he stopped at the second landing, and looked up. A sparrow caught under the high skylights flung itself against the grey, wired glass. Time after time the bird swooped and twirled and hit the ceiling with the barely audible thud of its tiny body against the high grey glass. Again and again it dove down and flew up, as though surely, surely on the next try the heavens would open to him. The bird made no sound, no frantic cries, but as Quentin ascended the stairs, he watched each swoop lose energy and momentum as the sparrow darted, trying for the light. By afternoon the sparrow would be dead. Once Mr Jobson would have removed its carcass from sight immediately. But now its feathered remains would lie in ignominious state on the ground floor till the charwoman, Mrs Rackwell, came at night to sweep it out to the dustbins.

At the top of the third floor, Quentin came to the door of Castle Literary Ltd with its distinct castle logo. He walked in, and amid the typewriters clanging, the bells, tapping keys, ringing phones, he greeted Miss Marr, the fierce, didactic secretary. She ran the office with an iron hand. Her fingertips were blue from carbon paper.

'Your father would like to see you in his office.' Miss Marr spoke as if Quentin were a child called into the headmaster for a thrashing in which she would secretly delight. 'Not at the moment, however. He's on the telephone.'

He hung his coat on the ornate brass coat rack by the door and put his hat there at a rakish angle. 'Good morning, Monica,' Quentin called out over the typing and bells of carriages crashing. Monica, the typist, waved, but kept her back to him. All that he saw of her was a high, untidy bun atop a brown cardigan. Her desk was up against the grimy window and bookended by tall, grey filing cabinets with papers stacked atop, creating a sort of cavern. (After thirty-plus years in the literary business, paper, the storing of paper, was something of a problem for the agency.) In these utilitarian offices, Miss Marr had a rather more spacious desk behind the low gate separating the working space and the office foyer, which is to say the line of four chairs and the coat rack. Miss Marr's desk protected the door of Albert's office. Above Miss Marr there hung a galaxy, perhaps a hundred, framed black and white photos, most of them signed: Castle Literary's many clients, some illustrious, some not, some living, many dead. Sydney Thaxton's grizzled portrait was in the centre.

'My father wants to see me with regard to …' Quentin had an ingrained, reflexively deferential habit of letting others finish his sentences.

'I can answer that,' said Enid Sherrill, bustling in from her own office, a cigarette in one hand, a sheaf of handwritten letters in the other. She deposited the letters on Miss Marr's desk to be typed. 'Selwyn and Archer have declined Louisa Partridge's latest book, and you will be the one to tell her.'

Monica's typewriter fell silent, and she turned round in her chair, mouth agape. 'You don't say!'

'I do say,' replied Miss Sherrill. 'It will be a dreadful blow to her pride. She was expecting, well, her hopes hardly matter at this point. But you, Quentin, will handle her with tact and decorum.'

'But I have never dealt with Mrs Partridge before,' Quentin protested. 'She'll expect to hear the news from you or my father.'

'She has been advised by Miss Marr to come in tomorrow lunchtime.'

'To see me?'

Enid paused. 'Not exactly. However, she will see you. We will be out. Deal with her you must. Do not send her round to us.' Miss Sherrill often spoke of herself and his father in this way, as though they were yoked in a testy but durable marriage, and in some ways, that was exactly what they shared. 'You are a partner, are you not?' she inquired with her usual condescension. 'You must accept a partner's responsibilities.'

Quentin nodded or shrugged, or some self-effacing combination. He was a partner by virtue of nepotism as everyone well knew. In fact his father had actually given him the partnership as a wedding present six months before. Everyone (in what was, after all, a small, sniping, close-knit world of agents, authors and publishers) considered Albert's foolish mingling of the professional and the personal to be evidence that he was losing his grip, that age or alcohol was eroding his judgement. Enid Sherrill certainly thought so. Enid Sherrill was a partner. Enid had earned the title, fought for it, threatened to leave him in 1935 unless she was granted a partnership and her name on the letterhead. She had given her entire working life to Castle Literary Ltd, and though a partner, she was not quite Albert's equal. She had her own strong client list, mostly women authors. (Certainly all the unattractive women authors, the young and lovely, if there were any – authors are notoriously plain – belonged to Mr Albert Castle.) Enid detested Quentin for his easy ascension, and had scant respect for his abilities or insights. If he had any.

Miss Sherrill blew out a long, indignant banner of smoke. 'Your father has the returned manuscript and Bernard's letter in his office. He'll give it to you. You will have a look through the manuscript and give Mrs P. some ideas how to revise it.'

'But they've declined it. They don't want it revised. We should just send it out to another firm. After all, Louisa Partridge is a well-known cookery writer, and her books ...'

'This is not like her other books.'

'In what way?'

Enid raised her eyes to the light fixture overhead, as if seeking divine guidance. Monica's machine fell silent. Miss Marr lit up a cigarette. Finally Miss Sherrill said, 'Consider the books of your mother-in-law, Rosamund Phillips.'

Behind his heavy-framed glasses, Quentin kept his gaze studiously blank.

'Rosamund Phillips is the doyenne of British garden writers: roses, perennials, garden design, formal gardens, English gardens. Fearless, with a spade in one hand and a pen in the other, wouldn't you say?'

He nodded. His wife's mother was the sort of authoress – and that was what she called herself – Quentin secretly detested.

'Then just imagine if she suddenly took herself to Siberia or some such place, and started writing about potato farming there. Would anyone publish her? I think not.' Miss Sherrill spat out these last three words, as if

18

aiming for an unseen spittoon. She was a spectrally thin woman who sometimes seemed to wobble with suppressed emotion. She always wore a navy-blue suit and white blouse. The skirt was long to cover her thin legs, the jacket cinched tight at the waist, and her gaunt cheekbones were laying siege to thin, compressed lips.

'What's wrong with Mrs Partridge's book?' Quentin offered reasonably.

'I'll tell you,' said his father, flinging open his office door and joining them. 'She's forgotten how to preach to the choir, and she's gone off to convert the heathen! Like most of the heathen, they don't want it, don't want to hear it, don't want to read it, and Selwyn and Archer most assuredly don't want to publish it.'

The three women regarded Albert Castle with rapt admiration. He had this gift, had Albert, for aphorism and pithy replies, a gift he had augmented over time with considerable practice. His glib charm endeared him to those who, like bluebottle flies, preferred to skim over the surface of things and watch their own reflections flicker below.

Quentin followed Albert into his office, which (in contrast to the rest of the Castle Literary premises) was a gracious room, like the chambers of an Oxford don, bathed in lamplight, warm against the grey rain pelting down the window and the view of London rooftops and sooty chimneys. Splotches of pigeon dung ran white in the deluge, and brown sparrows huddled under eaves. But inside, leather-bound books glowed on the floor-to-ceiling shelves. The wheeled library ladder served as an informal open file for current projects; manuscripts tied in string or black ribbon lay on the steps. No one ever used it as a ladder because the books on the shelves were unread, part of the traditional ambience, as were the polished wood cabinets with shining brass handles, the inlaid rosewood side table with three crystal decanters, sherry for the ladies, single-malt Scotch and a fine old brandy (not so very fine in truth; it was mainly for show) and six clean crystal glasses. Framed prints and awards dotted the walls and mementos from thirty years dotted the shelves.

'Well, there it is,' said Albert, wagging his finger towards the small fireplace. On the mantel was a short, framed letter from Sydney Thaxton, dated 1922, and filled with obsequious gratitude for his dear agent, Albert Castle. Alongside it sat a photograph of Quentin's brother, Robert, and a rock from Kilimanjaro given to Albert by the famous climber and adventure writer, John McVicar. 'Go on, have a look.'

Quentin sat in one of the four leather chairs that faced each other on either side of the fire. On the low tea table in between sat Mrs Partridge's rejected manuscript, wrapped in brown paper, like a parcel, and tied with string, the rejection letter on the top.

30 January 1950

Dear Albert

Best of the new year and new decade, and sorry to be the bearer of bad tidings. S&A must decline Louisa's *Apricot Olive Lemon*. Please do tell her we'll be happy to read anything else she cares to write, but these are difficult times, with paper hard to come by, and libraries not buying as they used to, and readers short of funds. In short, we publishers must make difficult choices and bite the proverbial bullet. Austerity rules the waves, I'm afraid.

Yrs etc, etc. Bernard

PS Ordinarily I would publish it just to keep dear Louisa in the S&A fold, but I cannot. Whatever was she thinking? Louisa Partridge, the Mrs Beeton of Our Time, embarking on a book like this? Where's the beef and beer? The fish and chips? The bacon and eggs? Where's the reassurance to British women that if a man's home is his castle, the wife is queen? Please tell Louisa I would welcome a revised edition of her immortal 1935 classic, *The Book of British Housekeeping*. I'd be willing to pay her a lovely advance (though not, I'm afraid, up to our pre-war standard) but this book I cannot print. We have to think of our reading public and this is not what they want to read.

PPS When are you going to get Francis Carson back into harness to write another novel for us?

Sitting behind his desk, Albert called out, 'Dangle the bit about the advance for revising her old book in front of Louisa. She'll like that.'

'Will she? I shouldn't think she'd like anything about this letter.'

'Don't be daft! You won't show her the letter! It's too candid. You'll rephrase it.'

'Rephrase it? How?'

'Think of something.'

'You mean something that doesn't ask if she's basically barking mad?' Quentin instantly wished he had not asked this question. 'Mrs Partridge has been your client, or Miss Sherrill's, for fifteen years. Why …'

'You haven't dealt with a difficult author yet, have you?'

'They're all difficult in one way or another, some more than others.'

'Quite right. Louisa is one of the worst.'

Quentin thought it a strange remark. He actually suspected his dapper father might once have had a *petite affaire de coeur* with Louisa Partridge. She would not have been the first, nor the only. Discretion was the cardinal virtue in a literary agency. Discretion of every sort.

'This will be good for you, my boy.' Albert rose, took a pipe from his pipe stand, and walked to the grate where he began the elaborate process of filling it. First, a pinch of tobacco from the Chinese jar on the mantel. 'You'll learn from this.'

'You know as well as I that means it will be disagreeable.'

'Part of the trade. Any trade. You're the junior partner here, after all. But, think of it, one day you'll be the senior man here, and you too can take Francis Carson to lunch, and listen to genius in its cups.' Albert often took these long, jovial lunches with the impressive and expensive authors, often not returning to the firm till nearly four. His mood could be judged from which of the Gilbert and Sullivan repertoire he sang on his way up the three flights. The ladies in the office always remarked on how well he sang; however, after these lunches, an invisible coalition of Miss Marr and Enid Sherrill kept him from signing anything important, or taking phone calls with clients until the next morning.

'In the meantime,' his father continued confidentially, 'let me offer up a little professional guidance. Authors are like children. Like children, authors are meant to be read, and not seen and not heard. Like children, they can be ill-mannered savages, and your job is to keep 'em in line, keep 'em happy and satisfied with themselves. People always think authors must be such a deep lot, suffering and all that. But they're not. They're simple creatures, really. They're not interested in power, only praise, and a little honey for their bread. A real writer can live for years on a small advance and the mere repeated words that you loved their book, you cried, you laughed; whatever you

22

were supposed to do, you did. They will love you.'

'I don't want them to love me.'

'You are unkind, sir! Who else will love them if not the agent? Their spouse? Ha. The spouse is the last to love an author. The spouse is always suspecting the worst, and quite right too. The parents? All that nasty stuff coming out about the past? What parent will love that?'

'They don't all write nasty stuff, Father. Mrs Partridge is a cookery writer,' he said, trying to bring the conversation back round to the topic at hand.

'Bernard thought it was nasty.'

'He did?'

'He declined, didn't he? That's nasty in my book. What about yours, Quentin?'

'I don't have a book. I'm not a writer.'

'God, you are so literal sometimes! Just like your mother!'

'I'm a literary agent. Like you.'

'Quite right.' Albert regained his jovial stance, and smoothed his hair, quite grey by now, but distinguished. He had always been florid, and the veins across his nose testified to indulgence, but like everyone else, even the solid Albert Castle had thinned, diminished in the last decade. Still, his fundamental bonhomie remained unimpugned; he could have passed for an eighteenth-century country squire (which is what his forebears had been). Albert differed from them perhaps in that he had an underlying shrewdness, and a finely tuned instinct that passed for literary taste, the sort of gift that makes a great hostess, knowing intuitively who will go well with whom. On this he had built a distinguished literary agency, one of the earliest, its reputation now somewhat diminished in a crowded field.

'What can I possibly tell Mrs Partridge?'

'Treat writers like children, Quentin. Praise them, pat

them on the head, but if they sulk, give them a good rap on the palms now and then, and send them back to their desks.'

'Do you ever cane them?' Quentin asked, irony intended.

'I'd often like to,' Albert replied with a straight face.

'Am I the nanny, then, standing in for you and Miss Sherrill, the parents?'

'Good analogy. But mind you, be the firm nanny, not the old pillowy bosom little children cry on.' He stuck the pipe between his teeth, and then tamped it down.

'My nanny, as I recall, was a complete witch who believed in purgatives.'

'We got rid of her, Quentin, as soon as we found out. You know we did.'

Quentin paused briefly. 'Mrs Partridge will be insulted to hear such dire news coming from me. The junior partner.'

'Believe me, if I had the choice of Louisa Partridge or that …' He pointed vaguely towards his desk where a thick stack of paper was held down by a brass paperweight '… I'd take Louisa.'

'You do have the choice, Father. Please take Mrs P. and give me whatever that is.'

'Oh no. That …' He laid regal emphasis on the word '… requires the hand of experience, the superlative blend of tact, decorum and firmness.'

'What, or who is that?' asked Quentin, genuinely curious.

'Francis's American wife in Oxfordshire. Francis calls her the BEB, the Blue-Eyed Beauty. She may be a beauty but she's certainly foul-mouthed, presumptuous and demanding. Well, I haven't actually met her, but she writes a mean letter. I personally think of her as the FMB. The Foul-Mouthed Beauty, or perhaps another word beginning with B. She is, without doubt, a harridan wife.'

Quentin suppressed a chuckle. His father had an ingrained animus against the spouses of the authors Castle Literary Ltd represented. Wives, especially, were meddlesome; they inevitably got in the way of production. 'He ought to provide for her, Father. She's his wife.'

'She's an American. I loathe Americans. Always expecting to be entertained and looked after, everything made jolly for them just because they're Yanks. Here she is, American nobody, an orphan, I believe, married to the most brilliant British novelist of his day, and now she's writing to me – to me! – demanding, complaining that she's stuck in a run-down half-timbered rotting ruin in Oxfordshire with half a dozen brats. She just kept pumping them out! There are some women who know no restraint.'

Quentin wondered if his mother had restrained his father. Quentin was ten years younger than his brother, Robert. Sometimes Quentin thought of Robert more like a father than a brother. In his own marriage to Florence, restraint seemed to be Quentin's burden, though he was not the one with the calendar under the bed. He brought himself back to his father, who was still ranting against the FMB.

'She seems to think I am her banker, or her husband, or that I ought to send her money. She writes me these dire notes; begging, demanding letters which I send on to Francis. It's not up to me to support his family.'

'His royalties come through our firm.'

'Yes, and she should know that the last book, *Hay Days*, failed outright, commercially and critically.'

'The reviews weren't all bad.'

'No, and that's because it was dedicated to Lady Sybil Dane. All of the papers her husband owns, they were respectful, but not more than that. All the other critics savaged the book, low-minded dogs. They poisoned the public against him.'

'He was a conchie during the war, Father. Who can blame readers? It was hard to forgive in '47. Impossible to forget. Perhaps if he'd done some kind of war work, like those conchies who went about digging up unexploded bombs, but he didn't. He sat out the war at Sir Sanford Dane's estate, living in a Georgian mansion while everyone else slept in the Tube stations, worked in munitions factories and slogged every day through rubble. And after all that he publishes *Hay Days*, a pastoral description of life with the Land Girls working the manor? Whose bad judgement was that? One can't expect people who lost their sons and ...' He did not go on. Neither wished to speak of Robert, dead at the battle of El Alamein, enshrined in memory, handsome in his officer's uniform in the photograph on the mantel. Robert had their father's robust sparkle, his outgoing instincts, his good humour, a great smiling grin that women loved and men admired. Quentin admired it.

Albert struck his match but did not light the pipe. The carpet around them was pocked with little marks where matches and embers had fallen from Albert's fingers. 'Francis saved his hide during the war, and ruined his reputation, and it's a shame, really, since he never had any politics. So many other writers gnashing themselves into mince over socialism or fascism or Trotsky or Stalin! Francis, all he cared about was being able to write, being able to drink, being able to ... well, you know.'

'Do I?'

'Francis Carson, writer, drinker, lover, tenor.' He lit his pipe. 'And not always in that order.'

'Father.'

'What?'

'He is a father too. You said he had half a dozen brats.'

'More's the pity.'

'Well, perhaps his next book will do better,' Quentin offered. 'It is a new decade.'

'Yes, if only he'd come back and write the bloody thing. Francis Carson is the jewel in the Castle Literary crown. At least among the living.' Albert blew out the match and lowered his voice. 'Don't tell Francis I said that. His conceit is already intolerable.'

'I'm not likely to tell Francis Carson anything, Father. You deal with him exclusively.'

'Don't tell Enid either.'

'You said nothing of the sort,' Quentin assured him. Like his mother, Margaret, Quentin Castle instinctually kept the peace. Like her, he was not given to outburst. He was a listener, never one of those crisp, demanding men so beloved of fiction and film, the sort who stride forth and take action, like Robert or his father.

'I warned Carson against going to California,' Albert grumbled. 'If he wanted to write for films, why not stay right here, go down to Ealing and work for Arthur Rank?'

'*Passport to Pimlico* doesn't much seem like Carson's cup of tea. I read *The Moth and the Star*, and *Some of These Days* and thought them lovely but …' He thought perhaps Albert would finish the thought, but he did not. 'Rather hyperbolic. All that sex and ecstasy, as though love had transcendent meaning that somehow imbued one's character forever.'

'You are a young man. What would you know?'

Quentin resented this as a slur on his masculinity. 'Carson reminds me of Lawrence, all that lyricism and emotion, that poetic intensity.'

'Your point?' Whatever one might be obliged to say among one's peers, Albert deemed it disloyal, within the confines of Number 11, to speak well of any authors Castle Ltd did not represent.

'That was a very long time ago. People now aren't ... well, passion and intensity, all that's passé now. People just want to get on with their lives as best they can. Mend and make do.'

'The problem is—' Albert's voice was that of an irritated schoolmaster '—not what Francis is writing but that he isn't writing at all. I've written to the FMB suggesting if she needs money, she ought to bring him home and have him writing books!'

'Isn't there a lot of money in films?'

'Oh, Francis is rolling in American dollars, having a fine time! He lives in a place called The Garden of Allah. A brothel, I'm sure! He spends his days beside swimming pools, and his nights, hmmph.' This sound was Albert Castle's all-purpose evasion or dismissal, depending on the situation. He finally lit the pipe. 'Castle Literary gets not so much as a sixpence for his writing films.'

Quentin felt obliged to soothe. 'He'll be back. He's a novelist after all, Father. That's what they do. Besides, you said his wife was here, in Oxfordshire.'

'What makes you think he'd want to come back for his wife? He's in Hollywood, after all!' Miss Marr knocked on his door, entered without waiting and put in Albert's hand a telex. He read it, rumpled it and tossed it across the room where it landed by the brandy decanter.

'Bad news. John McVicar's gone.'

'Hasn't he been in Nepal for a while?'

'Yes, Quentin,' Albert growled, 'he has been in Nepal, but now he's dead! He fell. Oh, God! Can you imagine? The premier mountaineer and adventure writer of his day, and he fell! Fell to his death!'

'Perhaps that's how he might have wished to go,' Quentin volunteered, wondering at his father's vehemence. McVicar was a longtime client, and friend, though when the author had remarried, relations had cooled. Mr and (the new) Mrs McVicar had not been invited to Quentin's wedding last June.

'It will be a bloody mess.' Albert gave the pipe a few puffs, and then it went out. 'Authors are more trouble dead than they are alive. No sooner does the poor sod croak, than all the family swims in like eels, fangs bared.'

'Eels don't have fangs.'

'Don't be literal.'

'Sorry.'

'And who do they go after first? The agent,' Albert spluttered.

'Why would they come after you, Father? You always treated him fairly. You treat all your clients fairly.'

'Do you truly not see? The agent is the only one devoted to protecting the author. Their families, survivors, whoever they are, they are out for themselves. They tear each other to pieces in the courts and everywhere else. They don't give a damn about the author! Or his reputation! They want the rights to his work! They want to get rich off work they didn't do! Books they didn't write! They are stoats and weasels! Bloodsucking parasites! And the agent must keep on the good side of all of them! They're not obliged to stick with us, you see.' Albert plopped down in a leather chair that squealed in protest, 'If we don't keep on everyone's good side, then whoever wins – and in McVicar's case, there's the new wife, the ex-wife, the children, the sister, oh, and the mistress, don't forget her! – they can say, they will say, "Fie on you, Castle Literary! I'll take dear old McVicar's estate, and his royalties, to another agency." At least Sydney Thaxton had no children, and the only party to be placated is his widow, dear uncomplaining Constance.'

'Hasn't she remarried? A much younger man?'

'She has, and she lives in Nice.' Albert sighed, and puffed, but the pipe had gone out. 'Give me a living author any day. Give them a lovely lunch in London once a year, and they'll go back to their little corner of Cornwall, or wherever they hide, and write their hearts out if only you feed them a nice steady diet of praise and quarterly cheques. Everyone's happy. Once they die, the estate becomes like a great, gaseous bag that can float off at any minute.' His father took the pipe from his mouth and regarded it sadly. 'To hell with the past! I want to move forward with the new!'

'The brave new world?' Quentin ventured.

'Good title. Silly book.' Huxley was not their author.

'Well, Father, by that measure, then, you should be happy to be dealing with the FMB. At least Francis Carson is alive. '

'Yes.' Albert turned to a nearby bookshelf that held Carson's three novels, *The Moth and the Star*, *Some of These Days* and *Hay Days*, and smiled fondly at a signed studio photograph made to look casual. Francis Carson wore an expensive double-breasted suit, but the tie was loose, as though he might at any moment undress. He was tall, with big shoulders, suggesting strength, a round-faced young man with a shock of dark hair rakishly adrift across his forehead, a cigarette in hand, half-hooded pale eyes brooding, an enigmatic smile, as though some lively secret beckoned that only he could see. 'Now, if only he'd come home and write another novel like *Some of These Days*.'

'Yes,' Quentin offered in sympathy, 'and if everyone would forget he was a conchie.'

'*Some of These Days* is a brilliant book!' his father shot back.

'Is that the one they're making a film of?' asked Quentin, placating.

'Yes. The main character, Elsie Rose, is played by none other than Linda St John herself!'

'The name means nothing to me.'

'Then you, my son, must be living on a rock in Scotland. Linda St John is the most famous American film star since Vivien Leigh.'

'Vivien Leigh is British.'

'Why must you be so literal!' Albert rose and wandered back to his broad desk. He eased his bulk into the chair, his back to the window. He sifted idly through the stack of papers from the FMB, then pushed them aside. 'You and Florence and Rosamund are coming to Sunday lunch, I hope. Your mother expects you.'

'Of course. Why upset the planets in their orbits?'

This bit of humour escaped Albert, who made his *hmmph* sound again.

Leaving his father's office, with Mrs Partridge's rejected manuscript under his arm, Quentin paused at Miss Marr's desk. He pointed to the galaxy of black and white photographs dotting the wall above it. 'Which one is Louisa Partridge?'

Miss Marr regarded them with characteristic gravity, pointing to a photo near the epicentre of that galaxy. 'That's from her glory days, 1935. Her *Book of British Housekeeping* has never been out of print since.' Miss Marr sat back down, her hands poised over the typewriter like Liszt at the keyboard.

'My wife got a copy for a wedding present.'

'From Mrs Partridge?'

'I don't know. Florence did the thank-you notes. But I don't think so. Mrs Partridge didn't come to our wedding. I wonder why. She's been an author with us for years.'

In her portrait, Louisa Partridge rested two fingers against her left cheek, but unlike the other authors, she did not look world weary, nor did she wear a hat at a jaunty angle, nor did she hold a cigarette. Marcelled curls rippled down one side of her head and her beautifully manicured hand sported large smooth rings. Opal? Jade?

31

The black and white photo made it impossible to tell. She had a direct, dark-eyed gaze, and a confident smile with surprisingly good teeth. She was one of the more attractive women authors.

'Her hair is longer now. Everyone's is. It's the New Look,' said Miss Marr in an authoritative voice which Quentin found odd on a small, narrow woman whose brown skirts were silvered with cat hairs, whose collars had frayed, and whose lank hair was twisted in a knot at the back of her neck. Rimless spectacles rested atop her long, restless, pointed nose, and her brown eyes were close-set.

'Yes,' Monica added, lighting up and turning round from her typewriter, 'but New Look or old, Mrs Partridge is still a fearful old battleaxe.'

Miss Marr chastised Monica for disrespect to a client. 'What if we had another client in here, and they heard you? Why, they'd never come back.'

Monica shrugged. 'I don't see 'em lining up, do you?'

'Nonetheless.' Miss Marr was firm, the pillar of propriety. 'Quentin, I have contracts for you to look over, and I've put your post on the desk in your office, and I shall need to know your schedule for the rest of this week.'

'It takes all the running I can do to stay in one place,' he said.

'Do not quote poetry at me, Quentin. I shall need the schedule.' Quentin ducked into his own office, and closed the door behind him.

Quentin Castle found himself sometimes bedevilled by random lines of poetry. Carroll, Donne, Blake, Byron, Yeats, Auden, Shakespeare, Eliot, Lawrence, Hardy, assorted others battered his brain like that sparrow flinging itself against the ceiling. One line fell away and another would take its place. Always bookish, an eclectic reader, the literary agent's profession – linking the lone author scribbling away and the vast reading public – suited him. Fortunate, since his life's work was settled as surely as if he'd been born to a family of nobles, or rabbis, or miners. Quentin had no other path than following his father. Indeed, his whole life seemed rather like a chess game in which he was made to move in predictable patterns. He had no reason to complain. He did not complain. He had a university education (an undistinguished third from St John's, Oxford), and he was happily married to a beautiful girl. He was comfortable in a country where many lived in want and soul-killing misery. (He knew this from reading George Orwell, not from experience.) Quentin Castle was no T. S. Eliot labouring for Mammon at the bank by day, and serving the god of poetry by night. No, he was content to toil in the agency aspect of literature's vineyard, though his authors were mostly inherited from Albert and Miss Sherrill, frowsy female mystery writers, ageing historians whose theories had been rendered obsolete by the Cold War, the dull, the passé, authors Albert and Miss Sherrill could no longer be bothered with.

Rather like Mrs Partridge, he thought ruefully, untying the strings that bound her rejected book.

CHAPTER TWO

THE AFRICAN VIOLET, THE ASPIDISTRA

QUENTIN CASTLE WAS an inveterate early riser, and this created something of an ongoing domestic dispute. In general, Florence and Quentin's newlywed difficulties were tempered by their love for one another, and eased because they had known each other all their lives. Too, they both subscribed to a certain code of civility. But in this small matter, Quentin could be stubborn. He rose early and observed his small solitary morning rituals: to bring in the milk, make a pot of tea and drink it while reading *The Times* in the kitchen. Florence maintained that Quentin should not be in the kitchen at all. It wasn't suitable: Effie, the maid-of-all-work, should see to these things. He smiled and agreed with his bride, soothed, but persisted in rising early, bringing in the milk, making tea and reading the long grey columns of *The Times*, so he was there, at the kitchen table, when Effie slunk in through the back. Quentin nodded, though he did not speak.

Effie hung her coat and hat on the hooks by the door. 'I would've got the milk,' she said, tying on an apron. 'I always tell you that.' She was eighteen or nineteen, sullen, not very bright, with bad teeth, much-gnawed nails, lank hair framing her face like a greasy helmet, though inoffensive otherwise.

'Never mind.' He did not like Effie. By simply arriving, being, taking up oxygen, she intruded.

'Missus won't say no never mind. She'll think I'm shirking.' Effie always spoke in a tone that suggested an unspecific grudge against the universe. 'I might lose my position cos of you.'

Quentin did not dignify this with a reply. Effie's wages were his mother-in-law's wedding gift to them. It seemed to Quentin undemocratic, stuffy, pretentious and Edwardian to have the luxury of a servant when so many were making do with so little. Oh, a charwoman to come in now and then, shine the brass, that sort of thing, fine, but Effie, the maid-of-all-work? Quentin assumed that Effie herself resented the title since she did all the work badly, like a music-hall parody, lacking only the feather duster and the good looks of a music-hall maid. Once she had lit her first fag of the day, as she did now, Quentin folded the paper and took it to the bathroom with him. His wife would not yet be awake.

They had been married about six months. Florence was the daughter of the doughty garden author, Rosamund Phillips, a client of Castle Literary since 1928 when she had published the first of her successful series of garden books. Rosamund was herself once a sort of garden nymph in her heyday, but she had grown enormously fat, despite wartime and post-war privations, despite rationing, and shortages of sugar and butter and eggs and meat. By 1945 her bulk had become an impediment to movement itself, and so her pretty daughter, Florence – aptly named for the child of a garden writer – acted on her behalf. Florence typed her mother's manuscripts, and personally delivered them, usually to the Castle home which was not far from their own. Margaret and Rosamund were good friends, and the two families sometimes took holidays together, especially after Rosamund was widowed. As Florence and Quentin were much in each other's company, it was no surprise – not even to them – that they should court and wed. Everyone said it was a perfect match. Their wedding at St George's, Hanover Square, on a beautiful day in June, 1949, had seemed to Quentin rather like a reunion of many old people rather than the union of two young people.

The daughter of a writer, the son of a literary agent, their honeymoon was a fittingly literary pilgrimage to the Lake District where the weather was uncooperative, and their walks were rain-sodden and generally unromantic. Florence finally declared she wouldn't take another step outside till the weather changed. He offered to go alone, but she laughed and reminded him they were married now and they would do things together.

Sex, for instance, making love, they would do that together. Married, there would be no more furtive relieving oneself by hand, no more furtive groping on the occasional drunken evening – or on those two occasions in Quentin's university days, something more. On the first, a lively girl he had met at the Anchor took him, after a few drinks, to her nearby bedsit. Afterwards she asked for money. Quentin hastily paid, embarrassed that he had mistaken the encounter for something else – not love, he was not stupid or mooning – but something at least good-natured; he had not guessed that the rollicking and her squeals would come at a price. On the second occasion, the girl, a student at Lady Margaret Hall with whom he had romped in a secluded spot near the river, collected herself afterwards, plucked her knickers out of the grass, nodded, said something trivial and bolted. Quentin had not thought that was love either, but he was disappointed that she never spoke to him again and always studiously looked away from him, even when they were in the same overheated rooms for tutorials.

Still, he had some quiet pride at coming into the marriage with experience, though Florence early on whispered wasn't it nice that they were both pure, and he agreed that it was. She hoped he would be tender and gentle and he promised he would be, and was. She blossomed under his touch, and she always murmured, *'Wasn't that nice?'* And he agreed that it was.

By the time they had returned from their Lake District honeymoon, however, Florence made it clear that she regarded making love as a charming necessity but hardly an outright pleasure. She likened it, using her mother's garden imagery, to digging a furrow in order to plant. Not a pleasure in itself, necessarily, but pleasant just the same, part of a process. Quentin was about to laugh, but he saw she was serious. He thought her attitude bloody strange. Then she let it be known they would only be digging their furrow – so to speak – two weeks of every month. One week, of course, she had her monthlies, and couldn't be expected to comply with his demands. He had not thought they were demands, but he listened anyway. Listening was the one thing Quentin excelled at. And, she went on, one week per month, well, one had to be careful, didn't one? It was called the rhythm method. Quentin had never heard of it. Florence laughed – she had fine, rippling laughter – and called him naive, which he disputed without actually saying that he was not a virgin when they married. Florence kissed him lightly, and said when she was ready to have a baby, it would be different. She kept a calendar under the bed with certain forbidden dates marked with Xs. If he rolled towards her, swung his leg atop her thigh, caressed her breast, she leaned over the edge of the bed and consulted the calendar before she responded. Or not. Last night was one of those marked with an X.

This morning, as usual, by the time Quentin had

finished his morning ritual, bathed, shaved, and dressed, Florence was in their small dining room with the tea. The drapes opened to emit a grey wedge of morning light spilling over the purple African violet on one windowsill, and the pale aspidistra in the other. Workmen were already at their jobs across the street, rebuilding a structure that had been bombed.

Quentin gave Florence a swift kiss on the cheek, and *The Times.* She again reminded him that Effie ought to be getting the milk bottles, and he ought not to be in the kitchen. He listened, nodded. He noticed that her dressing gown fell slightly open; it was a lovely shade of peach, and the rounded mounds of her breasts reminded him of scoops of vanilla ice cream. Pre-war scoops. Everything was bigger and finer and richer in the past.

'Mother read somewhere that Orwell asked to be buried in London, but there's no room for him. More likely no one wanted him in their churchyard. He was such a scoffer.'

'What great writer isn't?' Quentin had felt Orwell's death in a drab London hospital some ten days before as something of a personal loss. Quentin admired his books, his stringent, precise writing, his tempered passion, the deeper and more intense for its being so tempered. There was no thrashing splashing emotion in Orwell; Orwell's passions were coolly put. But Quentin did not defend the author to Florence. Their minor differences of opinion extended to literature, films and music, though in films and music he easily acquiesced to her superior taste and knowledge; he had a tin ear and little interest in films.

'Lucky for you Orwell isn't your client. He married some woman just days before he died. That'll be a right jolly old mess! Oh, and look, here's a notice of John McVicar's death. Margaret called Mummy yesterday afternoon and told her the shocking news. It says here he died from a fall in Nepal. What was he doing in Nepal?' she asked.

'I expect he was scouting new climbs. Looking for new challenges.' Quentin borrowed the first page of *The Times* and immersed himself in its endless litany of the dreary. Someone selling a dinner jacket, like new, hadn't been worn since 1939....

'Yes, well, the high altitudes must have addled his brains.'

'What, dear?'

'McVicar. Wife, ex-wife, mistress, and estranged adult children. He certainly left a mess for the Old Family Firm.' She often referred to the Castle Literary Ltd in that fashion, as though they had some sort of royal patent. 'I thought Albert was great friends with him. Didn't you spend one summer at his place near Montreux?'

'It wasn't a summer. It was a winter holiday. He taught me to ski. I wasn't very good at it.' As a child Quentin had dutifully learned to ski. He had learned to swim. He had learned to race, and play cricket and lawn tennis, but he had never been any good at any of it. If he had any latent talents, they were perhaps in amateur theatrics. Useless.

'What about the wife and children? What about the mistress?'

'What about them, Florence?'

'What were they like?'

'I hardly think my father and mother and I would have been introduced to the mistress. It was a long time ago. I was just a boy. I think McVicar was married to the first wife then, and his children were all experienced skiers and nasty bullies.'

'Well, it seems they haven't changed.'

'McVicar and his warring family are my father's concerns. Thank God. I could not bear to deal with all that.'

'You're too modest, dear. You are an excellent literary agent. One day you will be the best. Better than your father.' She leaned forward to pick up the teapot and her dressing gown opened over her breasts like a theatrical curtain. Florence exuded a kind of fleshy opulence. One day that opulence would expand to obesity like her mother (she would out-flesh Rosamund before she was fifty) but now Florence's rosy skin seemed to testify against the grey and grainy world all around them. Quentin thanked her, though whether for the tea or for embodying an antidote to rubble, to rationing, the retreat of Empire, all that he could not say.

'Two lovely lumps of sugar, dear. The Black Market Lady made her weekly stop yesterday at the back door. Aren't we lucky? And you heard they've upped the bacon ration from four ounces to five and the sweets ration from four ounces to four and a half.'

'I hadn't heard.'

'Well, no reason you should. The housekeeping is my job.'

Effie came through the door bearing two plates of scrambled powdered eggs enlivened with bits of Spam. She plopped them down with a snap in front of Florence and Quentin and returned to the tiny kitchen where she had left a cigarette burning.

'I'll be going to Mother's later, naturally, to type for her,' said Florence. 'And then Mother and I might go to the pictures. Linda St John's new film. Why not meet us there, Quentin? Do you good to get out of the office a bit. Albert works you too hard.'

'I'm not much for American pictures, Florence. They're too … too loud. Too noisy.'

'Yes.' Florence gave him an affectionate smile. 'One could never say that about a book, could one?'

'Some books are loud. Noisy. It's possible.'

'Didn't I read somewhere that Linda St John is starring in some film they're making … one of the agency's clients, dear, you know who I mean.'

'Francis Carson's *Some of These Days*.'

'She is so beautiful, so very glamorous.'

'That's odd, since the main character, Elsie Rose, is an old bawd with a great voice.'

Florence laughed her fine rippling laughter. 'Anything special on today at the office? Any bright new literary lights to be discovered?'

He shook his head as he put a dab of marge on a slice of dry toast. The scrape of the knife sounded ominous. He could not bear to discuss Louisa Partridge who, in any event, was neither bright, nor new, nor literary for that matter. He had only barely skimmed her book. Thumbed through it. *Apricot Olive Lemon* seemed to him an unsettling mix of exotic place names and cooking gibberish. The thought of meeting Louisa Partridge today drained his appetite, but he applied himself to the powdered eggs, eating quickly.

'Your mother and father expect us for Sunday lunch,' said Florence.

'Yes. The planets in their orbits.'

'Oh, Quentin, you are always so irreverent.'

'Hard to be reverent about my mother's cooking. Do you think she cooks the cabbage in dishwater?'

She was about to laugh when Effie brought the post in on a china saucer, which annoyed Florence. Effie fled to the kitchen before she could be chastised.

Quentin rose and said he must be leaving. He brought his lips swiftly to Florence's and longed to move down her pearly throat, to that tiny little lake formed by her clavicles, or run his hand over the silky robe to reveal the apricot glow of her breast, but it was morning and time to be about one's tasks.

Unlike his father's spacious, gracious domain, Quentin's office was narrow, spare, spartan; grey filing cabinets, a fraying wing chair and a rug that had long ago given up

41

the ghost of blue. A struggling African violet, a wilting aspidistra, gifts of Florence, sat atop the radiator, the only bit of colour. His view, too, was grimy and looking across the roof into the brownish brick building next door. Sagging shelves high and on either side of his desk held manuscripts which originally he had kept in alphabetical order by author, but those good intentions had long since been superseded by the general higgledy-piggledy mentality of Castle Literary Ltd, which relied on eccentric memory and gnomic cues. In contrast, Quentin's desk, his own little acre, was neat, not slavishly so, but had a pleasing order about it. He disliked hodge-podge. Unlike Albert or Miss Sherrill, Quentin had his own typewriter, and typed his own letters which he signed with a fountain pen, gift of his father when he had joined the family firm.

Sorting through his post, he was pleased to see a letter from a novelist, a man of his own generation, whose work Quentin had championed. Castle Literary's cachet rang with the names of great writers of the twenties and thirties, but Francis Carson's meteoric *Some of These Days* was a long time ago, 1939, and the halcyon heyday of Sydney Thaxton long before that. Castle Literary needed a new shining light. Quentin was looking for the next Orwell, and he had had high hopes for this new voice. But after one novel, the writer turned querulous, prickly and, worse, unproductive. Now he wrote nagging Quentin to seek foreign sales for his one minor novel. 'Humph,' Quentin snapped, knowing how like his father he sounded. He put a sheet of creamy agency letterhead in his typewriter and was about to reply when he glanced at Louisa Partridge's parcel.

The rejected manuscript seemed to scowl at him, to remind him almost audibly of the very few hours between now and Mrs Partridge's arrival. There wasn't time to take the typescript to the London Library to read. Miss Sherrill often chided Quentin for not staying in the office to do his reading; she reminded him that every minute Miss Marr spent taking messages for him was time deducted from Miss Marr's other important work. Miss Marr, too, always made carping demands when he left: *Where are you going, Quentin? How might you be reached, Quentin? How long will you be gone?* Her grip on the workings of the agency was firm and not to be trifled with.

He glanced at the framed photo of his brother Robert on the shelf, and felt a surge of unworthiness. Would Robert sit here wondering if he could evade two old spinsters? No. Robert would simply take the parcel, tip his hat and say *I'm off to the London Library, Miss Sherrill! Cheerio, Miss Marr!* But then, Robert did not allow himself to fall into the family firm. Robert had insisted on being a journalist, and Albert finally capitulated, even using his literary contacts among the firm's American authors to get Robert a place on the Paris *Tribune*. Robert went to Paris, to a life that promised raffish company, experienced women and uncertain hours. Adventure. When war came, Robert, with characteristic panache, resigned from the *Trib*, and joined the tank corps with half a dozen of his best friends. They were a lively lot, Robert and his cadre of fine companions, and Quentin, the bookish boy, had admired them immensely. He had kept a map on his wall following their exploits in the desert. He wrote them weekly letters. Robert and all his friends were so vibrant, so alive. And then they were not. Not vibrant, and not alive. Each death seemed to young Quentin a sort of knell, the whispered conviction that Quentin himself might be alive but he would never be vibrant, that the obliteration of Robert and his generation had left the world somehow singed and forever ashen. Quentin turned away from Robert's photo, and succumbed to the imperative demands of *Apricot Olive Lemon*.

CHAPTER THREE

APPETITE, NOT SUSTENANCE

IT WAS NOT a voice one could ignore. Behind his closed door, Quentin overheard her words, and felt the sting of her indignation. 'Quentin Castle? You must be mistaken. The call came from Albert.' Louisa Partridge's voice was unmistakable, cawing, raspy: the voice that, through nine editions in fifteen years, had admonished the women of England to revel in work well done and, indeed, how to do that work better.

'The call came from me, Mrs Partridge,' said Miss Marr in her schoolmarmish way. 'And it's Mr Quentin Castle who wishes to discuss your book with you.'

'Did he read it?'

'He loved it.'

This was the standard Castle Literary Ltd response.

Quentin put down his fountain pen and smoothed his hair. Meet this like a man, he told himself, as he opened his door and strode towards her, offering his hand.

Mrs Partridge had thickened since the photo on the wall above Miss Marr's desk. Solid rather than stout, she might be said to be arresting, but no longer attractive. She wore a hat with a long, gorgeous feather, and earrings in the shape of snakes. She carried a handbag of enormous proportions, and made of some strange substance like snakeskin or alligator, now the colour of dusty rouge. Many bracelets bangled on her gloved wrists. She wore a mannish suit. Her nose was red from the cold, and her greying hair was straight, and dry, cut evenly at the chin-line.

Quentin rattled on how delighted he was to meet her, and that he had indeed loved her book, though he hadn't had the chance to savour all ...

'I insist on seeing your father, young man. Or Enid Sherrill.'

He opened the low gate for her, asked Miss Marr for tea, and showed the reluctant Mrs Partridge into his narrow, utilitarian office. She put her handbag down on the floor with a thud, and removed her gloves the way a prize-fighter removes his robe. She sat in the well-worn wing chair across from Quentin's desk and plucked at its arms, which were threadbare, then applied her gimlet gaze to the whole place. The African violet seemed to wither even more under her scrutiny.

'What is the problem with my book?' she asked, folding her gloves. Her hands were very different from the photograph too. Ringless, veiny and strong. 'I wouldn't be here if there weren't a problem. I'd be lunching with Bernard.'

'Well, there is a bit of a problem, Mrs Partridge,' he said after he had cleared his throat several times.

'Just spit it out, my lad. I've no time for this sort of shilly-shallying.'

Quentin considered his father's instructions to soften the blow, to paraphrase Bernard's outright rejection. Perhaps Albert Castle could mollify her, jolly her along, but Quentin certainly could not. He handed her the publisher's letter. She scanned it quickly, then went back and reread it without any haste. Then the redoubtable author of *The Book of British Housekeeping* burst into tears, sobbing into her hands.

Quentin was shocked to his core. A bad beginning. Should he rise and pat her shoulder? Should he sit it out? Leave? Should he go get Miss Marr? What would Miss Marr think? That he had offended this important client? This was his first weeping author. Should he commiserate and call the publisher a hack? Should he offer his handkerchief? It was clean and neatly ironed by Effie, though, as he shook it out, it smelled of Effie's fags. Mrs Partridge took it, but she wept on for some moments more. She sniffed a little at the handkerchief's odour.

'So, this is what it's come to.' She composed her body, back straight, shoulders squared, before she could compose her features. Her lip still trembled, her hands too, as she opened her handbag and took out a cigarette case and a silver lighter. 'Bernard wants me to revise again a book that has been left behind, in the dustbin of another time, another era, and rejects my ... my ...' *Masterpiece* hung in the air. Mrs Partridge did not say it because she did not wish to seem too egotistical. Quentin did not say it because even after a brief glance, he thought the book unsaleable.

'Bernard is a throwback, a dinosaur,' she went on, 'a complete dodo bird, flapping around in the second half of the twentieth century. What an ass.' She lit up, the silver lighter making a sharp snap on closing, like a pair of shears coming down, snipping Bernard's testicles. She smoked in short puffs. 'Does he not know there is no going back? No lovely little pre-war dream, no Edwardian child-hood, no flappers, no Bright Young Things. All that is finished. Over. Ended. Look at the world as it is!'

'But that's exactly what your book doesn't do,' said Quentin reasonably. 'Don't you see? Readers will expect that Louisa Partridge will tell them how to better their immediate lives.'

'What do you think the book is trying to accomplish?'

'Mrs Partridge—'

'Louisa. You must call me Louisa. I could count on one hand the number of men who have seen me cry. I cannot possibly have wept in the presence of a man who calls me Mrs Partridge.' She looked around for an ashtray.

'Louisa, with all due respect to your housekeeping expertise ...' Quentin dug in a desk drawer for an ashtray; he did not smoke, and he did not often entertain clients in his office.

'Sod housekeeping expertise.'

'No one in Britain today is going to be making ...' He leafed idly through the manuscript. 'Figs? Honey? Butter? Liqueur? Meringues?' He flipped through the typewritten pages. 'Olive oil? Almonds? Oranges? Limes? These might as well come from the moon.'

'They are not from the moon, young man. However, you won't find them delivered with the milk! We can no longer live insular on this isle, however green and pleasant, and if you ask me, it is certainly not green, and no longer pleasant.'

'I meant only that they are not here.'

'*Here* has changed altogether, young man!'

'Please call me Quentin.' He took the saucer from under the African violet, and passed it to her.

'We must accept that we are more connected to the world. And let us begin with our diet. You are what you eat! Isn't it ghastly to think so? Tell me, what did you have for breakfast?'

'Powdered eggs and Spam, toast and tea.'

She gave a distinct snort and asked after last night's dinner.

'Whatever I ate last night, it is a dim and dreary memory.'

47

'Best remembered by your bowels, which are no doubt constipated.' He did not reply to this.

'You see, the effect, the overall effect of the way we eat is not nourishing. It's deadening. It's killing us from the inside out!'

'There are shortages everywhere, Mrs Partridge, rationing. What would you have the British housewife do?'

'Will you please stop talking about housewives and housekeeping! Don't you see? I am talking about something much, much larger.' She stood, strode up and down, as though she could not suppress her own sheer vitality, and this narrow office could not confine it. 'Who has not buried someone in a land we will never see? Who would ever have believed that their loved ones would be buried in Burma, or Egypt or Crete, or Dunkirk for that matter? Remember your Rupert Brooke! "If I should die –"' She cast her gaze dramatically to the drab ceiling '"– think only this of me: That there's some corner of a foreign field that is forever England!"'

'My brother and his friends died at El Alamein.'

'Then you know whereof I speak.'

He didn't, but it seemed unwise to say so. Quentin sought to bring the conversation back to the book. To the rejection of the book. 'Selwyn and Archer are happy to give you an advance on a revision of *The Book of British Housekeeping.*'

Louisa sat down and tapped her cigarette in the saucer. 'And I am happy to give them the kiss-off. That's a lovely, vulgar expression, don't you think? I learnt it during the war. An American phrase.'

Miss Marr knocked and brought in a tray with a small, chipped brown pot, two cups and saucers, a jug of milk that was a curious yellow colour, and a tiny dish of sugar. Two spoons. She retreated as soon as Quentin took the tray from her. He brought it to the desk. Mrs Partridge picked up the milk jug and sniffed it. Her nose wrinkled.

'Have you nothing stronger, Quentin?'

'Stronger?'

'Oh God, the younger generation. Do you not drink?'

Albert Castle had three crystal decanters and six crystal glasses on a silver tray in his office. Quentin had a bottle of Dewar's White Label stashed in a cupboard. He had bought it ten months after joining the family firm, to privately commemorate, to congratulate himself on the first author whose work he had actually selected and successfully put forward. Since then he had returned to the Dewar's for perhaps three other small triumphs, and a half-dozen instances when courage was called for. From the dark cupboard he withdrew the half-empty bottle and a single glass. 'Not very clean, I'm afraid,' he said. She was, after all, the Queen of British Housekeeping. In reply, Mrs Partridge handed him his own handkerchief, and he wiped it out then set the glass on the desk.

'Where's your glass?' she asked.

'That is my glass.' He poured her two fingers full of whisky.

Her bangle bracelets jangled as she took a short swig. 'As I recall of the contract with Bernard, they have the right of first refusal. They have refused. I shall never publish with Selwyn and Archer again, no matter what they offer.' Clearly she wanted him to congratulate her on her spirit, but he merely nodded. 'And I will never again write a book like *British Housekeeping*. What was that book but a soothing bit of tripe, telling women, live as you always have, dearie, keep your feather duster in one hand, and your knickers tight. Fear everything you don't understand, embrace nothing but convention.' She took another swig.

'I don't think that's how readers saw your book. I think many women saw that book give dignity to what they were doing, especially since no one had staffs of servants by the time you wrote it. Or now,' he added, thinking of Effie. 'My mother always said your book seemed like having a friend in the house. A wise friend.'

'Really? Margaret said that? I never thought she liked me.'

Margaret had never said that, and he had no idea if his mother liked Louisa Partridge or her book. Actually, he thought not.

'I only wrote *The Book of British Housekeeping* because I couldn't do anything else. If I had been able to teach, I would have waded into a schoolroom. If I had been able to preach, I would have got up into the pulpit. I had no decent education, no special skills – I taught myself to type! – no training, no real imagination. All I had was all this ... this ... this unseemly energy!' She opened her arms, her ringless fingers, to the file cabinets and bookshelves, the radiator, the African violet. 'I had energy, even ambition, but what could I do? After I'd cleaned the bloody house, and done the bloody shopping, prepared the bloody meals and looked after the whining brats, what was left? Well? I suppose I could write a book about doing just that. And that's what I did.'

He was surprised at her shameless use of the vernacular. She was middle-aged after all, and her reputation was that of the most proper housekeeper in the British Isles. 'I'm surprised to hear you speak so harshly ...'

'What? Finish your sentence!'

'To disparage the kind of work you were famous for.'

'I didn't always feel that way,' she confessed, nodding towards the glass. He poured her some more. 'The book changed my life. It got me out of the house and into the world. I was feted and respected, and the magazines were forever giving me lovely assignments. I travelled everywhere. Met important people. Did you ever see my series on the wives of British ambassadors?'

'When would that have been?'

'Oh, before the war.'

'I was a schoolboy.'

'Oh.' She put out the cigarette and its last plumes of smoke serpentined in the air above them.

'I'm not surprised that you became a household name,' Quentin went on. '*The Book of British Housekeeping* did very well. It made money. For everyone.'

'Spoken like a true agent.'

'I include our firm, naturally.'

'It might surprise you to know your father took me on as a client at some risk. I was determined to have an agent, not trotting my book around to London publishers like the Little Match Girl. I hardly dared hope that Castle Literary, with their great reputation – Sydney Thaxton, and the dreary rest of them. That Francis Carson for instance! Unreadable! – would take me on. Nonetheless, I brought my manuscript to the agency, and the great Albert Castle himself asked me to lunch.' Her sharp features momentarily softened. 'Soho, all those years ago. When he told me he would represent a book of housekeeping, well, I was flattered. Thrilled, in truth. It was the happiest day of my life so far. Truly. I was a nobody then.'

Quentin nodded, thinking of Mrs Partridge in the picture above Miss Marr's desk. Her good looks might have had something to do with his father's taking a literary chance. And the *affaire de coeur*? No doubt.

'I have remained a loyal author to this firm.'

'Indeed you have.'

'And to Selwyn and Archer. Those dogs. After all the money I made for them! They decline? Telling me I must plough the same furrow!'

Unwillingly Quentin thought of Florence and her digging the furrow in order to plant. He agreed that Selwyn and Archer were thankless wretches.

'But I am not that same woman,' she explained. 'After what I have been and done and seen, would I ever – ever! – again want to sit with the wife of some ambassador or another and talk about native servants? The gorge rises! No,' she continued, gathering steam and passion, 'I am not the same woman, and I would venture to say readers are not the same. No one is the same! Neither men or women. How could we be? We won the bloody war, and what have we to bloody show for it? We've lost the bloody Empire. There's rubble everywhere! Unexploded bombs. Queues for the simplest necessities! Not enough coal or butter or eggs. Children evacuated for six years who returned, and did not even know their own parents. Men who will never be coming home. And those who did, well, they're not the same, are they? We must see ourselves beyond the confines of our island. We must regard with some respect those immigrants washing up on our shores. What might they have to teach us? Let us begin with our diet! Let us eat beyond fried fish and chips in newspapers, the sweets that rot our teeth, the tea that serves for every purpose. My book is not about sustenance, it's about appetite!'

He leafed through the rejected typescript. *Apricot Olive Lemon*. Appetite? His eye fell on words he could not begin to imagine: *saffron, basil, pomegranates*. Appetite? He raised his gaze to the solitary light fixture, and pondered her words. 'What kind of woman are you now?'

'Pardon?' She looked more quizzical than offended.

'You say you are not the same woman who wrote *The Book of British Housekeeping*. Tell me about the woman who wrote *Apricot Olive Lemon*.'

Her expression changed and a smile lit her lips, as though she suddenly forgave him his grim office, his waning African violet, his dirty glass and smelly hand-kerchief. 'Cairo, summer 1939. I was on assignment for *The Lady*, interviewing the British ambassador's wife. You can't even begin to imagine what Cairo was like. Oh, never mind the cries from the minarets, the flies, the heat, the stench, the unthinkable squalor.' She spoke of these things with positive relish. 'The place was mad with rumour and innuendo, a great broth of intrigue everywhere, everyone terribly tense, drinking too much and falling into bed. Every day that passed, people grew more nervous, frightened, one day closer to the brink. Everyone knew it was coming. When it finally did, war declared, I think people were actually relieved, but then, suddenly, everyone was scurrying about, panicked, packing, getting visas, passports, booking tickets, hurried goodbyes, English women and children to be evacuated immediately. There were only so many ships leaving for home. Home.' She glanced into the bottom of her glass as if it might reply.

He replenished it, but he waited for her to speak. He was a listener.

'You have no idea, Quentin.'

'Enlighten me.' He leaned back in his wooden chair, hands behind his head.

'Home for me was back to Mr Partridge. Herbert is a good sort, an honest man, a total bore to whom I was married off before I had any idea what the world might hold for me, or how I might navigate its shoals.' She paused as though noting the phrase for future use. 'I was nineteen when we married. I didn't exactly love him, but I didn't not love him, if you know what I mean. He was well-to-do, good prospects, house in Chiswick, which, truth be told, he had actually inherited from a spinster aunt. Mummy and Daddy approved. Herbert's politics were respectable, his religion strictly C of E. He worked in insurance. He still does, for that matter. He was too young for the Great War, so he didn't have any of that beastly shell shock that other men carried round. I was a beautiful bride, and we had one of those lovely weddings that girls are supposed to cherish all their lives. Their one big day. Really, Quentin, I ask you! One big day out of fourscore and ten years? Well, never mind. Herbert and I married and had three lovely children in very short order, all exactly like their father. Three out of four is rather good for odds.'

Quentin frowned.

'You know perfectly well what I mean.' She drew a short sharp breath in through her nose. 'I was in Cairo, September, 1939, quayside with all the rest of them, shuffling forward among the tearful women and children, loading on ships to return to England, everyone having their papers and passports and tickets checked, their names on rosters, and passenger lists, everyone so anxious and afraid of what the future would bring. War was about to engulf everything. I looked up to that hard sky, like a pitiless bowl of blue, and I could all but see an enormous wave cresting overhead, about to splash down, and carry everything we knew with it, to crash down, to kill some and leave the others beached wherever they might be. And if I got on that ship, that wave would crash down, and I would be beached sitting across from Herbert Partridge. And I thought, if I am to die – everyone does – then let it be in Egypt.' She took another sip. 'I gave the ticket to a girl who had been a nanny for a rich family – they were prepared to abandon her there – and I went to British headquarters and said, "Put me to work. There's nothing I can't do."'

'You have a supreme confidence, Louisa.'

'Hard won,' she replied, finishing off the Dewar's.

'You were gone the entire war, then?'

'I spent three years in the Middle East and when the Americans came into the war, they made me the liaison with the staff of an American general, a colonel in particular. I will not say which one,' she added with a cryptic smile. 'I lived all over the Mediterranean in those years.

I lived deeply, fully, richly. I know I ought not to say it, but the war unshackled me, don't you see, not just from Herbert, but from *British Housekeeping* altogether! I was, am, forever changed. And then it was over. My American colonel returned to Tallahassee, Florida. Really, what kind of name is that? Tallahassee? He returned there. To his wife. I returned here.' Mrs Partridge looked from the glass in her hand to the grey-brown bricks outside the dirty window where a pigeon huddled at the sill. 'The cab left me off in front of the house in Chiswick. My key still fit in the door. I opened it, and Herbert was exactly where I had left him. As if nothing had changed. He asked if I'd like a cup of tea and some bacon and eggs. Powdered eggs, but he had been saving the bacon for my return. I said yes. What else was there to say?'

'One might say you were still beached there with him, as if you'd used the ticket.'

She clearly gave this some thought. 'The children had been evacuated during the war, so Herbert hardly knew them. They were certainly all strangers to me, and I to them. How could I go back? I was utterly changed.'

He was curious if she were still married to Mr Partridge. She wore no rings, only bracelets. However, to ask such a question was unthinkable, and in fact, divorce itself was unthinkable, the act of the brave or foolhardy, the desperate or demented. Quentin rested his hand atop the rejected manuscript. 'None of that is in here in this book. It's as though you've pared away all your experience, and left only the food, the cooking.'

'That's sufficient. Everyone has to eat, after all.'

'Perhaps if you enlivened it with some personal reminiscence.'

'Oh no. I told you I would be perfectly willing to teach or preach, but not to stand up on the stage and wave my knickers about.'

That isn't exactly what he had meant, though he could see why she would think so.

'Besides,' she went on, 'writing isn't like a recipe, you know, where you can prescribe a bit of this and that, a pinch. Once you start writing, once you open it up, open up your actual experience, then you've got the whole imperial pound, or nothing. No—' Her lips pursed '—I saw, experienced things and people I shall never forget, things and people I shall cherish always, no matter what, no matter that we are parted forever. I saw such cruelty, such crass, swaggering stupidity that will haunt me as long as I live. I saw heroism too, not the lofty sort, not that vainglorious sort, the quiet, ongoing sort, the more heroic for its being so unsung. If I'd been a different sort of writer, braver, smarter, I would have addressed all that, met it with clarity. If I'd been George Orwell, for instance, poor sod. But I am not. Indeed, I have been uncharitably described as a housemaid with a pen rather than a feather duster. Perhaps that's true. I may be a writer with more energy than talent. But this book? *Apricot Olive Lemon*. This book is unlike any other. This book should shake up all the dear old things!'

He paused, as though her words, like the smoke from her cigarette, needed time to dissipate. He did not think the book a masterpiece by any means, but he would follow her lead. 'All right, then. It's Bernard's loss. We'll send this out and find another publisher for your book, though I have to warn you, you probably will not get the sort of advance you might like. It will be a risky proposition, to publish a book like this in the world we live in.'

'It is risky not to.' She rose and pulled her gloves back on. 'Then we are in accord, as the French say.'

'We are.' He rose too. 'Oh, and do you have any more copies of the manuscript? Other than your carbon. I'd like to send it out to more than one publisher, I think.'

Mrs Partridge beamed at him 'I do indeed. I have two others. You shall have them tomorrow. Give your father my regards, but tell him I shall expect in future to deal with you and you alone when I come to Castle Literary. I feel confident that you are a man of understanding, and not a literary grubber, pushing print from a barrow, and crying in the streets of Gomorrah.'

'Indeed not,' he replied, a little alarmed at the image.

'No need to see me out. I know my way round.'

The following day Enid Sherrill happened to be talking to Miss Marr when the redoubtable Louisa flung open the office door. Enid braced, expecting a tongue-lashing for having fobbed her off on the junior partner. However, Mrs Partridge was cordial, or rather, crisp. She carried a shopping bag and declined to take a seat. She asked for Quentin.

Miss Marr alerted him via the intercom. The office was not that large, and the intercom was simply a gesture towards modernity.

'Louisa,' he said, emerging.

Mrs Partridge's face lit and she took his proffered hand warmly. 'How good to see you, Quentin.' She followed him through this door without another look back at Enid Sherrill and Miss Marr, who exchanged puzzled glances.

He showed her again to the wing chair, but she did not sit. From the shopping bag she took out two solid manuscripts tied up in brown paper. She put them on his desk. He began to speak of his thoughts on the letter he would write, but she waved all that away.

'I have complete trust in you, Quentin, complete faith. I'm sure you will write a lovely letter, and I have no doubt you will find me a wonderful publisher. I have something for you, a gift, a reward, if you will, for your understanding, for I feel certain that you do understand.' She smiled and reached into her enormous alligator bag, and pulled out a shopping bag. From this she drew several fluttering thin pages, and a small bottle containing an amber-unto-golden liquid. 'Pure Sicilian olive oil.'

'It's beautiful.'

'It's not to be looked at, Quentin! It's to be used! It's a gift. My gift to you.'

'You're too kind, Louisa.'

'And!' She pulled from the bag a half-dozen soft black orbs, greenish at the tip, which he stared at. 'They're figs, Quentin! Have you never seen a fig?'

'I don't know.'

'Well, I got them off the black market, of course. Don't tell your father. He can be such a prig.'

'Thank you. My wife will be ...'

'Not your wife. Do not hand this to your wife and expect her to understand. You understand. She does not. Mind you, I'm casting no aspersions on your wife, whom I do not know. I heard you married Rosamund's daughter. I'm sure she's charming, but this experience is for *you*.' Beneath her hawkish nose, Louisa's lips curled into a conspiratorial smile. 'I'll leave the bag with you too. Keep it close to the vest, Quentin, but once you try this, you will understand what my book is trying to do. And don't tell them, out there.' She nodded, perhaps to the outer office, perhaps to the great world. 'This is our secret.'

The six figs sat on the windowsill all that day and the next, fat little black apostrophes signifying nothing, save that they looked entirely out of place, utterly foreign, and a little forlorn to find themselves in the draught. The occasional pigeon eyed them through the glass. The jar of Sicilian olive oil Quentin put in the cabinet alongside the Dewar's White Label. He did not take it home. He didn't quite know why. Nor did he mention the olive oil and the figs, though he certainly told Florence about his conversation with Mrs Partridge. Florence applauded him for his acumen, reminded him that he was good at his job, excellent at handling difficult authors. Quentin accepted her praise, but he knew that all he had really done was listen well, and agree with Mrs Partridge that Selwyn and Archer were thankless wretches.

Before he could undertake the letter to send *Apricot Olive Lemon* out on its new quest, he had to read the whole of the book, a task he found complicated, especially difficult when Mr Weedon appeared after lunch. Twice a week he shared the office with Mr Weedon, the bookkeeper. Quentin found it hard to concentrate not simply because the bookkeeper punched his numbers into the Exacta adding machine, but because he also percolated resentment. Once this had been Mr Weedon's office alone. Now he did his work in what amounted to a closet while Quentin had the big desk fronting the window. Quentin took Louisa's typescript, and informed Miss Marr (in a tone he hoped worthy of a partner of the firm) that he would be at the London Library, and he left before she could object.

His father belonged to an exclusive club where he could go to be undisturbed, to drink or eat or read or think in peace. Quentin had no wish to join that club. To read, to think, for peace in general, the London Library in St James's Square was his retreat, his favourite place in the whole city. The ambience was studied, cultured, rich in a dry and unpoetic way, and Quentin always imagined the people working around him to be great writers and scholars, men (and a few women) unearthing secrets, writing books that would illuminate the past, the present and the future. He liked the knowledge that he, Quentin Castle, had been admitted to this sanctuary, a place where great minds had once worked, and would work again. He pleasured in the quiet, the occasional cough, the rustle of paper, the scrape of chairs, and the fact that absolutely no one could reach him here. Oh, perhaps if his father fell over dead, someone could insist that the librarian find Quentin Castle and advise him of these dire events. But barring that, the London Library seemed to Quentin like Keats's unravished bride of quietness. Here he seriously read *Apricot Olive Lemon*.

On truly diving into the book as a whole, rather than sampling, he found Louisa wrote with such colour and vivacity, such crisp, tart prose that he had to remind himself that just outside the door, even in elegant St James's Square, people sank under the weight of yet another frigid, austere winter. The wartime Mediterranean life Louisa Partridge had lived (complete with adulterous affairs, cruelty, crass stupidity, quiet heroism, danger, deprivation, folly and death) was nowhere present in these pages. The war had vanished. All that remained was the sun and the sea and the sky, the golden stones, the narrow streets, the calls from nearby mosques, the bells of ancient churches, unsubtle voices haggling in foreign markets, coloured awnings and doors where beads sufficed for curtains. Mrs Partridge spoke of an undifferentiated 'we'. We went here or there, we found lemons glowing in the marketplace; we peeled the oranges and breathed in their damp brightness; we poached a silvery fish in briney water. Quentin also better understood how writing the book, minus the war itself, must have seemed to Louisa like the chance to relive all the best of it. And to have done so while the indelible experience was still fresh, and before time had eroded or buried it. The book left him hungry, an unspecific kind of hunger, perhaps more a sense of being unfilled. Appetite, not sustenance. Isn't that exactly what she had said?

When he finished it, dark had descended. He left the London Library and walked to Hatchards, browsed there till he was quite certain nearly everyone at Castle Literary would have left for the day. Having just read *Apricot Olive Lemon*, he could not endure the thought of talking to the narrow-nosed Miss Marr.

He climbed the three flights and let himself into the Castle Literary Ltd premises. In his own office, he lit the gooseneck desk lamp, rolled paper into the typewriter, and considered how best to write his letter. More fundamentally still, to whom? John Murray? Faber? The Bodley Head? Jonathan Cape? Wherever the book went, it would already carry with it the odour of failure. In the small, gentlemanly world of London publishers, everyone would ask: why had Bernard declined? What could Quentin say to a new potential publisher? Should he describe her book as a travelogue with recipes? Should he say it was a clarion call for a new and better British diet? Calling for courage and change and boldness was utterly out of step with the times. People had had enough of change and courage and boldness. Mend and make do while the Americans contemplated making a hydrogen bomb.

Drafting and re-drafting, he found no satisfactory words. He paused and spied the six fat figs on the windowsill. He reached for one, snipped off the stem, and sliced it clumsily with a letter opener. He put one half in his mouth. The tiny seeds scattered over his palate, and the soft parts dissolved, yielding to his tongue. Eyes closed, he savoured it, and did the same with the second glorious fig. He had no experience to parallel what the taste did for him, no metaphorical connection to make. How could he possibly convey the experience in a letter? To a jaded publisher. A jaded public.

He opened the cabinet and took out the jar of Sicilian olive oil, unscrewed the cap and sniffed it. Again, he had no parallel. He dipped his finger in and licked it. Honey? A single-malt Scotch? It wasn't like either of those. He had no words to describe it. He returned to his letter. Paper littered the floor; the hour grew late, and still his typewriter clattered away, but he had no satisfactory draft.

He heard a broom and bucket banging in the front office. 'Alloooo, anyone 'ere?' the charlady called out. Mrs Rackwell was certain that Regency ghosts remained in the building, and that they were not respectable.

'Hello, Mrs Rackwell, I'm back here.'

She opened his door. 'Oh, young Mr Castle,' she said, her hand going to her scrawny bosom. She wore a headrag and a dirty apron. 'You gave me a fright.'

'I always do when I'm working late.' He winced to see that Mrs Rackwell's pallid cheekbone bloomed in a greenish-blue, a bruise, a serious bruise probably delivered some days past. Mrs Rackwell, lacking both the funds and expertise for make-up, sometimes dusted flour over her face to hide the bruises after Old Rackwell beat her.

'Not many works as late as you, sir. Very dedicated, you must be.' She smiled and her ramshackle teeth heightened the garish impression, the greenish-white of her face and the gash of red lipstick across her mouth. Her eyes were full of pain, old, ongoing, ignoble pain.

Quentin stood and struggled against the urge to touch the woman's shoulder, to say she oughtn't to let Rackwell vent his rage and ugliness on her, to commiserate with her in some basic human fashion, but he could not. Some combination of reticence, chagrin, fear stopped him. Instead he said, 'The bird the other day, the battered bird who got trapped, did you find it?'

'I did. I put it in the bin, but 'oo'd ever notice one drab sparrow more or less?'

'I guess not,' he said, wondering if she were referring to herself.

'They say it's an omen, a bird caught inside. They say it means a death. I dunno 'oo says it, but it makes sense, don't it? Someone's always dying, aren't they?' She paused, as though awaiting an answer, but Quentin didn't know what to say. She turned to leave. 'I'll start with your father's office. Cheerio, young Mr Castle.'

He could not bring himself to say cheerio to a woman who, along with her broom and bucket and bruises, her talk of the certainty of death, had filled the narrow room with inchoate misery. He was about to put the bottle of olive oil back in the darkened cupboard to keep company with the Dewar's. But first he took another sip. He ran his tongue along his lips, and again words eluded him, but his feeling of hunger sharpened, broadened, till it gave the sensation of sadness, the impression of a vast, unfamiliar emptiness that could not be assuaged.

CHAPTER FOUR

FIGS AND THISTLES

L IKE A DINGHY alongside the *Titanic*, Quentin took Rosamund's arm and helped her out of the taxi. Florence took Rosamund's other arm as they aided her, in baby steps, through the garden gate. Rosamund had a horror of falling; she made little short gaspy sounds as the gate squealed open and clanged shut behind them. With Florence's soothing encouragement, they negotiated the few broad stairs to the landing where Albert flung the door open. 'Ah, Fair Rosamund!'

Albert had been greeting Rosamund Phillips as Fair Rosamund, that ill-fated beauty of legend, for twenty-five years, though her mountainous flesh bulged out of her shoes and tested the seams of her second-best dress.

'Dear ones! How lovely to see you!' Quentin's mother placed a fleeting kiss on each of their cheeks, and ushered them inside quickly. Margaret Castle was broadshouldered and lanky as her younger son. She wore her grey hair marcelled in the style of twenty years before. A bit of fallen lining peeked at the hem of her tweed skirt. Her long, loose cardigan over a grey blouse smelled tired. Her face was the image of Quentin's, save for her continual expression of vacant beatitude. 'Come into the sitting room where it's nice and warm.'

The sitting room was one of those timeless places, at once comforting and cloying, as is family in general. Quentin's parents had moved here in 1924, before he was born, but it seemed much older, overstuffed, everything padded with a profusion of small pillows to muffle every sharp edge. Blue-veined marble framed the fireplace and mantel and topped the tea table that sat before deep wing chairs. The wireless was the newest piece of furniture, handsome in its impressive oak cabinet. The walls swarmed with heavy-framed pictures, watercolours all executed by Margaret. She had painted most of them the summer of 1920, in St Ives when Robert was just a little boy. Over the mantel there hung a watercolour of little Robert in a sailor suit and St Ives sunshine. Beside it another watercolour, Robert in his officer's uniform taken from the photograph. The telegram announcing his death had stayed atop the mantel till 1947. Quentin had no idea who had taken it down, or where it had gone, and he had never had the courage to ask. The war had been over for five years, but the blackout curtains remained up, unused, but there.

The room was warm, well lit, the gas fire and wainscoting providing insulation against the thrash of rain and wind, and snow, and the velvet drapes were half drawn. Quentin brought in a fifth chair for himself, upright and unyielding, while the others sat in the wing chairs, sipping pale sherry with a plate of stale biscuits. Margaret had also cut the crusts off thin ribbons of Hovis bread, smeared them with prawn paste, and put them out, dignifying them with her best china. All this was as it should be. The planets-in-their-orbits Sunday lunch began with sherry at one and lunch at two.

The ladies chatted amiably about household matters,

the costs, the queues, about Rosamund's longtime gardener thanklessly demanding higher wages for his services, and how they all hoped the working classes would not be calling a General Strike as they did after the first war: no longer the Great War, just the first. Albert and Quentin talked shop, much as they might have at the agency, including new and more urgent demands from the FMB. Albert railed against Francis Carson's irresponsibility, not in leaving his wife without funds, but in failing to respond to Albert's telegrams and telexes.

'Oh, I know what he's doing out there in California. Oh yes, it doesn't take a great imagination.' Albert's eyebrows did an expressive dance around his forehead, indicating that his imagination was certainly equal to the task, but nothing could be said in front of the ladies.

A useless bit of chivalry since Rosamund remarked, 'He is a totally unpredictable drunk, given to singing sentimental songs, reciting poetry, and being rude to the women.'

'Wherever did you hear that, Mother?' asked Florence. 'He hardly travels in our circles.'

'I did not hear it. I saw it with my own eyes. So did you, Florence. He was invited to my book-launch party a year ago, simply because we share the same agent.' Rosamund shot an evil look to Albert, who shrugged and smiled, guilty-as-charged, and muttered something about having inadvertently mentioned it at lunch when both he and Francis were wonderfully afloat on a sea of cocktails. 'He came with a woman not his wife.'

'I think he came with Lady Sybil Dane,' said Albert. 'She's something of a patron of his.'

'Oh yes,' Rosamund remarked, 'a woman utterly outré, all her flowing peacock robes and her beady, narrow eyes, dark and darting, always as though she is looking for ...' Words failed Rosamund.

'For something to eat,' offered Quentin, who had met Lady Sybil Dane at the launch party. They all three regarded him quizzically.

'I remember Francis Carson now,' said Florence. 'Not exactly handsome, but full of—'

'Drink.' Rosamund quaffed her sherry in one bolt. 'Drunk when he got there, drunker when he left, and he seemed to think he'd been invited just to sing music hall ditties and recite lines about daffodils.'

'"I wandered lonely as a cloud",' offered Albert. 'He does a fine Wordsworth.'

'He offered to kiss my golden toes,' said Florence, giggling.

'What!' Rosamund and Margaret said in unison.

'Yes. He actually asked me to take my shoes off!'

'Cheeky beggar!' snorted Rosamund.

'Yes, Mummy, but I told him I was engaged to Mr Castle's son, and there was an end of it.'

'Authors are a pesky lot,' said Albert sagely.

'That may be,' Florence replied, 'but Quentin handled that Louisa Partridge so well. She was tame as a kitten when she left his office.'

'I never said that.'

'Oh yes,' Albert said, 'how did that go?'

'Not as you'd expect,' said Quentin.

Albert looked alarmed. 'I wouldn't know what to expect from Louisa Partridge.'

'Louisa Partridge,' Rosamund scoffed, 'is nothing but a housemaid with a pen rather than a feather duster.'

Quentin looked up swiftly, the strip of shrimp-paste Hovis hovering at his lips.

'She can be very outspoken and unpleasant,' said Margaret.

'Is that why she wasn't invited to our wedding?' asked Quentin, feigning both ignorance and innocence, the bread going limp between his fingers.

'We didn't think it necessary to invite her, did we, Rosamund?' asked Margaret. She fretted a pearl necklace at her throat, and glanced at her husband, who studiously regarded a watercolour depicting a palm tree at St Ives.

Oh yes, thought Quentin, Albert and Louisa. The *petite affaire de coeur* was an absolute certainty. This seemed as good a moment as any. Quentin brought a bag out of his pocket, and the four figs tumbled out across the marble-topped tea table. 'Louisa Partridge brought me these. She said if I tasted them, I would understand her new book.'

'Figs!' cried Margaret. 'Wherever did she get figs this time of year?'

'She's resourceful,' said Quentin.

'They look positively ...' Florence faltered. 'Positively.'

'I thought we should share them,' said Quentin.

'There are only four,' said Rosamund.

'I ate mine.'

'How does one eat them?' asked Margaret.

'One peels them. With a fruit knife. On a saucer,' said Rosamund, somehow impugning Quentin's having put them on the table, bare naked.

'I don't think so,' he disagreed. 'You can slice them, of course, or just pop them, squash it in your teeth. Really. That's what she says in her book. Or you can peel the thin rind back and see the pink and green flesh, or slice them and see the teeming insides.'

This odd statement convinced Rosamund to pop hers without slicing; the bulge in her cheek was especially comic. Margaret followed suit; her expression was distrustful. Albert chomped three times and swallowed. But Florence peeled hers in tiny black ribbons, using her fingernail; she nibbled the pink-and-green flesh, visibly allowed herself some sense of pleasure. That made Quentin happy. 'That's what her book is about,' said Quentin.

'Figs?' said Margaret.

'About opening up your life to imagination,' said Quentin.

'What on earth does that mean?' asked Rosamund.

'I have no idea,' Quentin confessed.

'Did you get her to revise it?' asked Albert.

'No. She refuses. I shall send it out as it is.'

'When will this dreadful winter end?' asked Rosamund, in her whining way.

'Good luck getting it published,' said Albert.

'If anyone can, Quentin can,' said Florence loyally.

'My bursitis is acting up again,' said Rosamund.

The conversation then meandered down the usual paths: Rosamund's pout assured, Margaret's sympathies expected, Albert's good nature heightened by drink, and Florence's girlish laughter enlivening talk of the weather, and small domestic fracases. At quarter to two Quentin and Albert escorted the obese Rosamund into the dining room where they placed her close by the gas fire. At Margaret's request, they said a long prayer. In the years since Robert's death, Margaret had become progressively more devout, going to church weekly and without fail, and erecting a small shrine in his room, which remained as it was when last he had slept there. When Quentin had moved into the Bloomsbury flat, three months before his wedding, his room was instantly given over to the sewing machine.

Prayers finished, his father ladled up the consommé; that's what his mother called it, but really the soup sprang from a cube and hot water garnished with chopped leek. Margaret had a hired cook right up until 1940 when the old girl quit to make more money in a munitions factory. She had not been replaced. Margaret's own cooking was as usual: a shrivelled joint of beef, baked potatoes with marge, cabbage. The awful food too was part of the

Sunday tradition. Quentin thought of Louisa's book, as he looked up from his plate to the window where ice hung from the branches of the copper beech. He wondered idly what would happen if one planet plunged or lunged or whatever planets do. Would the others go on in their orbits without it, or would they fall too?

That night as soon as Quentin and Florence got into bed, his wife turned to him, brushed her lips to his, smiled and turned out the light. They made love; long, fine, easygoing love leading up to moist little cries that Quentin had never heard from her, and her cries unleashed from him a torrent of words wrapped in sounds he did not know he could make.

Afterwards, enjoying a fine sense of physical peace, and the warmth of her arm flung over him, her breath sweet and even, he lay awake, pleased. How wonderful that she had come to him, wanted him, expressed desire, and revelled in affection. He kissed her forehead and she murmured, turned to him, brushed her lips along his bare chest.

'Lovely, darling,' she whispered.

'Yes, it was.' He smoothed her hair.

'Are you happy, Quentin?'

'Of course, dearest.'

'I am too.' She kissed his chest again, her lips lingering on his nipple, and her body yet willing and eager again. As was his. A deep, complex surge of peace and excitement overtook him, of contentment and connection, a sense of what marriage should truly mean. He wondered, before he fell into a deep well of dreams and sleep, if he could somehow fasten a ribbon to that insight, and keep it always as one might a key to open a secret door.

The telephone's ring pierced his dream, again and again, and in the dream he answered it – *Hello, hello* – but it continued to jangle. *Hello, hello.* Quentin awoke, but Florence groaned and turned away from him. He fumbled by the bedside for his glasses, and reached into the drawer for the torch he kept there. Shivering, he lit his way to the small hall table where the telephone continued to burst in noisy volleys till he picked it up.

'Quentin!'

'Father? What is it? Mum? Is it—'

'No, no, worse than that – no, not worse, excuse me, Margaret, no, I didn't mean that at all – oh, damnation, Margaret! Leave me alone, will you?'

'Father?'

'Quentin, I've just had a call from California. Francis Carson is dead. The stupid sot!' spluttered his father. 'A whole brilliant literary career ahead of him, and he …'

His father rattled on, heaping invective on Francis Carson, on McVicar the mountain climber, and careless writers in general. Quentin, naked and freezing, shone his torch on the mantelpiece clock. 'I'm very sorry to hear about Francis Carson, but it's four in the morning, and what can I do about it?'

'You have to go to Oxford. You have to get there before the press. You have to tell her.'

'Go where? Tell who?'

'The FMB! Don't you listen? Didn't I just get through telling you? She has no phone. She can't hear this from the press, and they'll all be up there as soon as they get wind of it. I asked them to hold off a public announcement, but I don't trust them.'

'Who is them?'

'Whoever called me from California. Roy someone from Regent Films. Don't you see? We have to protect her.'

'We do?'

'Oh. you are dense, Quentin! We have to protect ourselves! As soon as they announce his death—'

71

'Who is they?' he asked again.

'How do I know!' Albert shrieked. 'Francis is dead and now we have to answer to her! Oh, goddamn that goddamn Francis. No, Margaret, no I will not apologize! You must go to Woodstock, Quentin. Protect our interests. You must be the one to tell her. On behalf of the firm.'

'Why me? He was your client.'

'You are the junior partner and you will do as I say. Get dressed, get to the station and take the first train to Oxford.'

'This is ridiculous. You should go. You are the—'

'It's not ridiculous if I tell you to do it.'

They wrangled some more, but it was a foregone conclusion that Quentin would obey. He woke Florence briefly to kiss her goodbye, tell her he was off, and why, promise to be home soon. It was all but ordained that in the brutal predawn cold, he would shave and dress in his first-best suit, befitting the sombre occasion. As he was about to turn out the bathroom light, some fleeting second thought made him take his toothbrush from the glass and put it in his leather bag before snapping it shut with emphatic finality.

CHAPTER FIVE

THE FOUL-MOUTHED BEAUTY

THE METER TICKED off the miles merrily away as the cab lurched and rattled over country roads in the sluggish winter dawn, skidding on the ice, getting lost time and again as the driver sought out the vague Harrington Hall nr Woodstock. It was all Albert had by way of an address. Quentin, flung from side to side in the cab, fought off both nausea and hunger. His watch said nearly half eight when finally the cab chugged in front of a wooden slatted gate, surrounded on either side by high, ivied rock walls, and a tiny brick inset with letters that read, cryptically, Ha ngt n H l. The driver grumbled, got out and tried to open the gate, but it was locked. Shivering, he got back in the cab and pointed to the outrageous fare, adding that there ought to be a fat tip for all the petrol he had wasted.

'You're the one who has blundered all over Oxford-shire,' retorted Quentin.

'Oxford, mate. I picks 'em up at the Oxford station just like I picks you up, and I takes 'em round Oxford. See? Not out here in the bloody back of nowhere.' He nodded curtly and roared away. Quentin stood there in a swirl of exhaust and bad feeling, the trousers of his first-best suit splattered with mud. He cursed the driver, and then regretted dismissing him. Beyond the gate a lane led to a half-timbered house, only part of which could be seen. Smoke rose from one of the many chimneys. A milky fog lay over all, swathing, softening, rendering everything around him indistinct. He heard scuffling in the underbrush behind him. What if this were not the home of Francis Carson? And even if it were, he knew for a fact the FMB had no phone. How would he get back to Oxford? Back to London? He was a confirmed urbanite and the surrounding countryside – its naked trees and icy ruts, its eerie quiet, save for the wind knocking bare limbs one against the other – struck him not as pastoral, but empty and ominous. He rattled the gate, called out, 'Hello, the house!' but it was at some distance, and no one emerged. The high walls on either side cut off his view, but the gate itself was only chest high. He climbed up and over the wooden slats, and started towards the house.

A dog tore out of nowhere, racing down the path, barking furiously, fangs bared. Quentin hustled back to the gate, climbed up and perched there while the dog yapped at him. Quentin was still there a few minutes later when a boy of perhaps ten came out of the house and called the dog off.

The boy wore a much-patched jacket and a cap pulled low over his ears. The dog continued to bark, and the boy patted his head.

'What you want? Who are you? You look bloody strange up there on the gate.' The boy started to laugh raucously, as though he and the dog were being entertained.

His pride stung, Quentin called out, 'Is this the home of Francis Carson?'

'My question first.'

'I need to speak with your mother, Mrs Carson.'

'My question first, you sod.'

Shocked at the boy's coarse language, Quentin reached into his breast pocket and took out his card. 'I'm from Castle Literary. We are your father's literary agents. Give this to your mother.'

'Stay here,' said the boy. 'Sit, Pooh.'

He left, and the dog sat, never taking his suspicious gaze from Quentin who felt miserable and cold and ridiculous perched on a fence in the middle of nowhere, clutching a leather case, watched by a snarling cur named Pooh. Thank God no one at the agency could see; he could well imagine how his father would chortle. And Miss Sherrill? Miss Marr? Quentin chased their supercilious images from his mind.

Finally the boy came back. 'All right. Come up the house. No, Pooh! No, it's all right. Come on, then.'

Gingerly Quentin got down from the gate. The dog sniffed him all over, thrusting an especially intrusive canine nose into his groin. He followed the boy up to the half-timbered house, a portion of which, not visible from the road, looked to have caved in on itself. Chickens and ducks clucked amiably in a broad, cobbled yard, and he heard the occasional grunt which he assumed to be a pig.

A pig then crossed his path, paying him no mind whatever, as did a slow-moving dappled nag, its hooves clomping on the stones. Coming on the house itself, Quentin could see the roof was a patchwork of styles and materials; there were Georgian touches and neo-Gothic crenellation. Icicles hung down from the outbuilding eaves, and from the upper, unheated reaches of the house. The place was enormous, a Jacobean monstrosity to which later generations had added or ignored as they saw fit. Old renovations embraced even older elements, like the drunken hug of someone who then went to sleep for hundreds of years.

The boy pushed open a heavy door, and called out

to his mother, 'It's Mr Castle!' leaving Quentin in a mud room which truly deserved the name: thick crusts of dried mud on the floor, wellies lying everywhere like fallen sentries, coats and hats, an armoury of umbrellas, a baby's battered pram. There were shelves with jars and crocks and garden tools, saucepans and lanterns. The boy pushed another door that led into a kitchen so vast that the daylight eking in through small windows was seemingly swallowed up. Thick beams, dark with the smoke and soot of years, striped the low ceiling. As Quentin's eyes adjusted, he could see the place was a jumble of contradictions: a massive hearth, tall as a man, as well as a new Aga, a big soapstone sink, an old-fashioned washing copper beside a new wringer washing machine. Children's clothes and tea towels lay stiff and dispirited, hanging over a clothesline strung from a pulley above the hearth. Against one wall a battered upright piano with yellow keys stood, and atop it a huge typewriter and stacks of papers. Scattered about on the dressers, the counters, the floor, like detritus from a departing fair, were toys, dolls, clothes, books, jars of pens and paintbrushes, assorted envelopes marked 'overdue', and clothes pins. The boy and two suspicious-looking younger children sat at the long wooden table, illuminated by a single light fixture overhead. The dog barked.

The tall woman at the sink mopped her hands. Her face flushed with steam, and a damp lock of wheat-blonde hair, fallen from a loose knot atop her head, clung to her cheek. Alarm lit her face. 'Oh! Forgive me, Mr Castle. I'm just surprised, I mean, I expected someone much older. I always thought of you, I mean, Frank always said you were, well, ancient. No offence intended.'

'You're thinking of my father. He founded the firm in 1919. I'm only lately come into it. Quentin Castle.' He took off his glove and extended his hand. She had a strong grip, and her features, though not regular, were pleasing. The mouth was large and mobile, the nose straight, the wide-set eyes clear as Highland lakes, the blue deep enough to drown in. Tiny creases fanned out beside her eyes. Clearly she had grown out of her youthful beauty and into something else, though quite what Quentin could not say. By any standard he had been taught to admire, or even recognize, she was not especially attractive. There must be something wrong with the standard, he thought fleetingly, because he knew for a fact he had never beheld a woman quite so unexpectedly beautiful.

'I guess my last letter did the trick.' Her throaty voice still had flat American intonations. In one smooth, economical gesture, she swept some books and dolls and letters from the settle, letting them fall to the floor. One of the smaller children swooped up the doll, and clutched it. Mrs Carson beckoned Quentin to sit near the warmth. She wore a faded apron over a long blue sweater and a long black skirt. 'How good of you to come and bring the money.' She sat across from him, her face imbued with warmth and light.

'The money?'

'Well, I've been writing to the firm for weeks now, telling them, your father, I guess, that Frank hasn't sent any money from America in, well, in a very long time, and I'm getting desperate here, and I need an advance on his royalties. I know that *Hay Days* didn't sell that well.' She took off the apron, and flung it over a nearby chair. The blue sweater was pocked with ember burns. 'But he's working on another novel – he is – and you know how successful he is really, and what a fine writer.'

'I haven't come with the money,' he said, kicking himself for not insisting that his father cough up something for the FMB. No. The wife. The widow. Right.

'Then what?'

'Could we speak alone, Mrs Carson?' He glanced at the boy who hovered nearby, suspicious, ready to leap to his mother's defence if need be.

'There is some problem?'

'There is.' Quentin removed his coat, feeling rather like a surgeon with a particularly nasty incision about to be made. No anaesthetic.

She told the boy to leave, and to take the girls upstairs; she shooed the dogs as well, Pooh and Tigger, vicious-looking beasts despite their innocent names. Quentin rose from the settle, and took a seat at the large, rough-hewn table before a yellow bowl filled with mottled green apples. He wondered how she managed out here alone. He wondered why the boy at least was not in school. He wondered how she'd take the news, and then he wondered how, exactly, he would put it. He regretted being bullied into this. His father ought to have done this dismal deed. His father ought to have dealt with Louisa Partridge too. Filial resentment churned his already upset stomach.

She returned, sat down across from him, work-rough-ened hands clasped in front of her. Her only jewellery was a thick gold wedding band. Her brilliant blue eyes were troubled, but her gaze was bold.

'Mrs Carson, I'm afraid I have some very bad news. Your husband, Francis; I'm afraid he has died in California.'

'Died?' Her face fell, like a child who has failed an exam. 'What do you mean, died?'

Quentin took a deep breath. How much plainer could he be? 'I'm sorry, Mrs Carson, to be the one who has to bring this sad news, but your husband, Francis, has died. He's gone. They called us from California, from Los Angeles, early this morning—'

'Gone? Frank? You mean he's—'

'We did not want you to hear this news on the wireless,

or hear it from the press. It seemed only—'

'He can't be dead. Not like that, just gone. Dead?'

'I'm sorry, Mrs Carson. Truly.'

'Frank? I can't believe it. Frank? Frank is the alivest person … alive.' She seemed to reel, like a woman unexpectedly struck, slapped across the face, and falling, unbalanced.

'I'm sorry, Mrs Carson. We, our firm, thought it best that you should hear, that we, that I should …' He could all but feel the news throttling through her bones, her blue eyes darting about the dim room, and he remembered the sparrow trapped in the upper reaches at Number 11, unwilling to believe itself trapped even as its strength flagged, and it thumped against the unyielding roof and its inevitable fate.

'How?'

Quentin considered. The lame truth – that he knew nothing – would clearly not be sufficient, or kind. He knew, from Robert's death, that something – anything – was better comfort than nothing. Given Francis Carson's reputation, it could well have been from drink, but such a death didn't usually happen that quickly. Did it? He had no idea. Could he say, 'I have no idea'? He suddenly remembered Sydney Thaxton's unexpected death.

'Heart attack.'

'Oh, and was he out, drunk, with some Hollywood tart? Some whore or another?' Her face contorted and she burst into tears.

Confronted for the second time in a week with a weeping female, and just as dumbfounded, more so, Quentin took out his clean handkerchief, and handed it to her.

The smell of Effie's fag did not deter her in the least. She wiped her eyes, her nose, and wept some more, all the while murmuring *Oh Frank Frank no, no no dearest sweet sweet* … 'All right,' she gulped after a while, knotting the handkerchief. 'All right.' She took a deep breath. 'How did it happen? Tell me.'

'I've told you.'

'Tell me more.'

'They found him late at night. Alone, working, slumped over the typewriter. Into it, actually. He fell over into it.'

'Who? Who found him?'

'The people who clean. Charladies.'

'They found him, and then what?'

'Well, they called us. I mean, the charwomen called the studio people and the studio people called us.'

'Who?'

'Well, my father. I'm the junior partner. I came immediately. We couldn't let you hear it from a stranger. Though I suppose I am a stranger.'

She put her head down on the table and wept with abandon, shoulders shaking. One of the dogs came back and whined piteously by her feet, sitting with his nose on her shoes. She kicked him away. Quentin felt as ungainly as when he had perched on the gate. He might have reached out and touched her shoulder, but the same instinct, that innate recoil against emotion, that forbade him to comfort Mrs Rackwell, forbade him now, but neither could he look away. He had never seen anyone sob so openly. When news of Robert's death had reached the Castles, Quentin had been at home. His father had walked outside without a word, stepped into the garden, and walked into the garden shed. His mother had stood in front of Quentin, brushing imaginary lint from his lapels, stroking his shoulders, her eyes empty, almost blinded; he had not dared to move as she stood brushing, murmuring, *There there, that's better, there, that fixes it, there there* for twenty minutes, perhaps half an hour or half an eon, until she finally wobbled away, and collapsed to the floor. When at last they had got his mother settled, and Quentin was alone and could cry for the death of his brother, he had fought off tears. And won. He had thought himself manly. Now he wondered, why had he not simply heaved and shuddered like Mrs Carson? He wanted to place his hands atop her blonde head, but folded them instead, like a parson, pleased after a particularly stirring sermon.

'Ma,' came the call from somewhere unseen. The boy's voice. 'Ma.'

Her head came up off the table. 'Shut up. Go away. I'll talk to you when I'm ready.'

'Ma, is it Da?'

'Close the door, I tell you!' The door closed.

'Can I get you a cup of tea?' Quentin asked. That he could do.

She rubbed his handkerchief all over her face, and bit her lip. 'A drink. I need the pain dulled. I don't care that it's morning. Over there.' She pointed to a bureau that held some heavy plates and cups on hooks. In the cupboard below he found a bottle of Dewar's White Label, nearly full. He saw no glasses, so brought two teacups to the table and poured them each a splash. She lifted her chin, her cup to his, her eyes still moist. 'To Frank.'

'Francis Carson. Rest in peace.' The sip of alcohol burned all the way down and into his empty stomach.

Claire finished hers in one gulp. 'There'll be no peace, Mr Castle, no more than there was in life. I know Frank. I know him like no other. I loved him like no other.' She wiped her nose with the handkerchief, strangled it fiercely. 'We were always for good and always, Frank and me, even when we weren't. We loved each other, even if, well, there were rows, of course. But I loved him, and he loved me. I was lightning to his thunder.'

Quentin had no idea what it meant to be lightning to someone's thunder. He took another burning sip.

'Oh, Frank, it can't be. Can it?' She seemed to look

far away, beyond the confines of this kitchen, to some horizon he could not see. 'Can it be that I'll never see him again, never hold him, never love him, or lie beside him, or fight with him, or prod him in the ribs, smell his armpits, or kiss his roughened cheek, or look at his fine, handsome backside when he comes out of the water?' She moved both hands through her thick hair. 'Oh, Frank, it means you'll never slap me on the arse, or come up and put your lips at the back of my neck and send my knees weak like jelly. He knew how to touch, oh, he knew what it was to caress a woman, and he knew how. He always did. Shall I never watch him shave again or hear him snore, or sing "Kathleen Mavourneen" till I cry my eyes out? Or "Mistress mumbo jumbo jimmy-bob-jay-O'Shea" till I laugh myself sick? Shall I never hear him curse? Oh, he was eloquent at that! Or recite poetry, or tease the children, or declaim Shakespeare? I'll never read his drafts? I read everything, Mr Castle. From the beginning, from Broadstairs, from the rooms we had in Brixton, or the Chelsea flat, or the cottage we took after the war, I read all his books when they were still just scrawled in his unreadable hand. I typed all but one of them.' She frowned. 'What was he doing over the typewriter? He couldn't type.'

'He had to learn. Anyone can hunt and peck,' Quentin added, hoping he had not said too much, lied with too much detail. 'No one writes by hand any more.'

'What else did they tell you?'

'Who?'

'These studio people from California.'

'He'd been feeling unwell.'

'Who told you? Who called?'

'Someone from the studio. Someone important. I don't remember the name.'

'Did they tell you what they were doing to his picture? To *Some of These Days*?'

'They didn't tell me anything.' Which, he reflected, was the most honest he had been.

'Not even that he was slumped over the typewriter?' Her blue eyes blazed with indignation.

Perhaps Albert Castle could have lied, patted her back and somehow made the falsehood noble. Quentin could not. He had bollocksed everything. The whisky pulsed through his veins, and he felt rather sick. 'I don't have any idea how he died, Mrs Carson. They didn't tell us anything except that he is dead. I'm sorry. I will not lie to you again. Forgive me.'

'I suppose you were trying to be kind.'

'I was, but I ought not to have lied. Shall I leave you?'

'No. Please don't.' She reached for his hand. 'Don't leave me. How can I tell them?' She nodded towards the deep stairwell. 'The children? Until I've taken it in? What it means. He's been gone to California for such a long time, last April or May. It was just supposed to be for a few months, but look at all the time that's passed. Look at it!'

She spoke as though that time might be in this very room, shimmering somewhere, and Quentin dutifully looked, but could see nothing but the mottled apples, the drying clothes, the battered upright piano. The yellow, broken keys reminded him of Mrs Rackwell's teeth.

'We've got used to living without him, you know? We've had to, but not … this. Not living without him *forever*? That he won't be back at all?' She sipped again, and slumped. Her lip trembled, her voice too. 'What shall I do?'

'I don't know.' Quentin thought about Robert, so vibrant, so alive, so lost forever. 'Endure?'

'Oh, Frank!' She bolted the Dewar's. She took a deep, painful breath and steadied her voice. 'He wrote me every day in the beginning, when he first went to California. He wrote the way he used to talk. He knew he could fume and rant and ramble and I'd understand everything,

everything his heart meant to say, no matter if he scribbled just a few lines, or page after page after page with The Garden of Allah across the top! Can you imagine?'

'The Garden of Allah? I don't suppose I can,' Quentin admitted.

'He was writing this wonderful script for *Some of These Days*! It was marvellous to be there, working. So many talented people at Regent Films! Oh, Frank was full of them, and he had notes for a new book, a novel about all these Hollywood people. It was all lovely and exciting. And then—' She wiped her nose with the back of her hand '—it wasn't. Time went on and they were gutting his beautiful novel like a fish. Blood everywhere. Metaphorically. They were philistines. Bloody philistines.' Her flat American voice trailed off, and she put both hands over her face. When finally she laid her hands in her lap, and gazed at him, her eyes were full of truth and anguish.

'I'm sorry for your loss,' he said, hating the convention, not knowing what else to say.

'He is a free spirit. Was. The world loves them, and needs them, and applauds them, but someone always has to smooth the path before them, and clean up the shite behind them.' She regarded him as though she expected a thought or response, and he could not oblige.

'My father says you haven't heard from him in a while.'

'Since Christmas. No matter how often I wrote, time again, begging him not to leave me in darkness, he'd scarcely reply – a postcard, perhaps, as if he were a tourist, and I some mere acquaintance.' She drew herself up with dignity that was clearly painful. 'I guess we were at the end of our tether, Frank and me. Do you have a cigarette?'

'I'm sorry I don't smoke.' And he meant it.

'I'd kill for a fag. No money, you see?' She started to stand, trembled, braced herself on his shoulder, and crumpled back into her seat, her palms digging into her eyes.

'What'll I tell the kids?'

'I can't help you with that. I'm sorry.' He meant that too.

'You have kids?'

'No.'

'You married?'

'Yes.'

'Then you know how devastating this is, how the whole world crumbles beneath you, as if the bricks and beams have been pulled out of my life and the whole thing come crashing down, like one of those homes hit during the Blitz and the dust and destruction is so terrible I can hardly breathe.'

Imagining such ruination was beyond him. Perhaps he had not been married long enough.

'Frank was feckless, and shiftless and brilliant, and a sodding alcoholic. I knew the drink would kill him one day. It might have killed me too, you know, but three kids, well, that's enough to sober you up, isn't it? But I loved him. Always. And he loved me, and I knew, we both knew, from the time we met, from the time we first kissed or made love, there was never anyone else, not really ... Well, the occasional—' She shrugged '—you know ...'

He did not, but he nodded just the same.

'He could drink the Roman army under the table and still be brilliant, recite poetry, Shakespeare, so there wasn't a dry eye in the house! Hardy's "Convergence Of The Twain"? Oh! You'd think the sea had washed over you right there in some low, smoky pub. And all those silly music-hall songs, and sentimental ballads.' She burst into tears all over again. She mopped her face, and raised her chin. 'He had the tenor voice of an angel. We used to sing duets.' She gulped, but she could not immediately speak. 'And of course, he could write like no other, living or dead. He could take a September afternoon, or a crashing wave, or an old tart caterwauling "Some Of These Days" and turn them into words so beautiful, you'd have to close the book for a bit because you couldn't stand to read on for the beauty of it.'

'He was a very great writer.'

'Do you really think so?'

'Yes,' he lied, though he had promised he wouldn't. 'I admired his work profoundly.'

'I loved him so! Oh, this is so awful, and now, all this grief, I'm so alone with it. It's so shocking, as if I'd been singled out for something dreadful. Not like the war. Everyone lost someone. During the war, there was such a great pool of grief that everyone shared in it. Like we were all splashing about in sorrow. Now there's just this little puddle, and I'm alone in it.'

'You're not alone. You have me. Us. The agency. People will mourn with you. He was a very great writer.'

'I can't take that to bed, can I?'

Quentin murmured something inadequate.

'Let us drink to Frank; dear, dear Frank. Bottoms up, Mr Castle. What is your first name?'

'Quentin.'

'I'm Claire.' She touched her cup to his. 'Bottoms up, Quentin. We might as well drink now and believe we won't die.'

Her round blue eyes crinkled, and perhaps it was the whisky so early in the morning, or the lack of sleep, but she looked to him altogether luminous. That image of Claire Carson – her tragic blue eyes deepened by the blue sweater that clung to her throat, her tousled blonde hair, her pale, sad mouth – he thought he might carry that to his grave. And he did.

CHAPTER SIX

ON BEHÁLF OF THE FIRM

CLAIRE WENT UPSTAIRS to tell her children the dire news. Quentin went to the lav which had been built on, added to a small hallway off the kitchen perhaps fifty years before.

The toilet was a huge ceramic bowl, *Ottley and Sons, Banbury* in Gothic lettering, set in an enormous box of polished wood. The overhead chain was brass, and when pulled, the sound rumbled with an operatic echo. He took off his coat and glasses, splashed his face with icy water; the lavender-scented soap pleased his memory in some wordless way.

On his return to the kitchen he winced to hear distant childish wailing. He moved to the huge hearth that once had clearly served many purposes. The fire had burned to mere embers. He stoked it with some nearby logs, sat in the rocker, loosed his tie, and fell into a dreamless sleep.

Claire rattled his shoulder and woke him.

'Sorry,' he said. He wiped his lips, and wondered if he'd snored. He had no idea how long he had slept. The light in the kitchen had shifted.

'I've told the children. They're busted up, but they're

tough. They'd have to be to be our children. They know it's not your fault.'

'How could it be?'

'They're only children. You brought the news.'

'Yes. Sorry,' he said again.

She turned to the children, who had straggled into the kitchen. 'Children,' she said, 'this is Mr Quentin Castle, Daddy's literary agent. These are our children. Michael, Catherine and Mary. Say something, children.'

The three children mumbled and murmured. They wore rough clothes and their hair was mussed, their faces none too clean, and streaked with tears. Quentin couldn't tell the girls apart.

'I'm very sorry about your father,' he said.

One of the girls marched up to him, and stood, arms crossed, before him. 'I hate you.'

'Hush, Catherine,' said Claire.

'I'm sorry,' he said again. Feeling foolish and useless, he asked if he could help.

'Firewood. Show him, Michael.'

The surly boy bade him follow back outside, across a cobbled yard with crusts of frost that crunched under Quentin's city shoes. He had to step gingerly to avoid assorted piles of animal excrement. They rounded a corner and came to a shed where logs were neatly stacked under a protective shelter. Michael picked up one that looked to weigh as much as he did.

'I'll do that,' said Quentin.

'I don't need your help,' snapped the boy. 'She don't either. She's got me.'

Regardless of his best wool suit, Quentin bent, filled his arms with firewood; the scent that pitched up off the logs was musky, moss or something, wild and sweet. He followed the boy inside where they found Claire in the rocker, a small girl in her lap. She rocked back and forth, soothing the child, singing softly, something about a mockingbird and a diamond ring. Her hair swirled at her shoulders, falling forward, obscuring her face. Quentin stacked the logs as best he could beside the fireplace. The boy stoked the fire, and the immediate vicinity warmed.

Claire put the child down, donned the dirty apron, and picked up a massive fry pan. 'I hate you too,' said Mary, kicking Quentin when her mother's back was turned.

Quentin was ravenously hungry, and perhaps that's why he could not remember a breakfast this wonderful. Not in ages. Before the war? Perhaps his grandmother's house in Cornwall? That long ago.

Though the tea was weak, heavy on the milk (no sugar, Claire said, she'd used her ration on a birthday cake for Catherine last week), the eggs, scrambled, were fresh and fluffy. There was no bread, but smaller biscuits, she called them, soft inside with crispy tops. 'Not your sort of English biscuits,' she said. 'Idaho biscuits. Easy to make in small batches.' There was no butter, just the usual oleaginous marge, but plenty of fruity jam that contrasted vividly with tender, salty ham.

The little girls whimpered all through the meal. Claire finally hoisted the youngest on her lap, and fed her like a little baby while she hiccupped tears. The meal finished, she made no effort to clean up the empty plates that sat in dirty profusion. Finally she asked Michael to see to the animals and take the girls with him. She gently lifted the youngest to the floor. 'Go on, then, go with Michael.'

Claire and Quentin sat together in companionable, contented silence. Perhaps he ought to look at his wristwatch and say how the time had got away from him. But he didn't. He rose and fed the fire, which crackled happily. A house cat darted after a mouse, or a rat.

'It was all going to be grand, this house,' she sighed, and a wan smile escaped her lips. 'Frank thought this place was

Blenheim Palace. He never noticed that it was a Jacobean dump. When Frank was going to the bathroom, he'd turn to us and announce: "I'm going to sit on the throne!" Little Frankie Carson, the schoolmaster's asthmatic son, suddenly lord of the manor, squire to his own great pile of golden stone in Oxfordshire. He believed that we would have fine parties here. He saw teatime in the grand garden, and string quartets in the folly, Noël Coward and Cole Porter at the grand piano. Oh, not that upright thing over there.' She pointed to the battered instrument with yellowed keys. 'I insisted on that old thumper. I said to him, just until we could have the salons redone, Frank, and the grand piano lowered in through the French doors opening off the balcony.' She scoffed. 'Can you imagine? He really thought that's what it would be like.'

'He was a fiction writer, after all.' This was all he could offer.

'Yes. Frank saw what he wished. That's why they call it fiction. I saw what you see.'

Quentin glanced round the kitchen. 'The Aga's very nice.'

'That's new. You should have seen what was here when we moved in. Frank bought the place outright. Didn't even tell me, just drove us all out here, opened the gate and says, "Welcome home, Claire," happy as if he'd got the deed to Eden, this great barn of a place.' Her arm swept out. 'First thing, he had a folly built, like Woodlands, only ours was a little wooden gazebo, and theirs was a marble shelter by a willow tree. Oh, our place would be better than Woodlands one day! He was certain he'd be knighted, or lorded or whatever you Brits call it. He would be Sir Francis with his own grand house and gardens. He used up the whole *Hay Days* advance to buy this house, and then the book was a crashing failure. No one would forgive him, not for writing a mediocre book – look how many of those there are! – but that he didn't live the war like everyone else.'

'The book was badly timed,' said Quentin diplomatically.

'And now look at us. What shall I do?'

His earlier answer, endure, was inadequate now. He sought something more concrete. 'Is there anyone you'd like me to call or contact when I get back to London? Family? Friends?'

The breath seemed to exit her body in a gust of fatigue, and she wept all over again. When finally she looked up from her hands, she said, 'Like Frank's high-flying literary friends? Only too happy to jolly him along. The rich, the well born, well educated, men and women alike, Lady Sybil La-di-da Dane? Those friends?' She seemed to want an answer.

'I know nothing of his friends.'

'Lucky you. These people—' She shrugged '—there'll be a great flying of sympathetic fur, and then it will all be over. They will be indifferent in a week. Frank will be forgotten.'

'I'm sure that's not true.'

She scoffed. 'All the sodding literati. They loved to dish it out. "Oh, Francis! You're a genius!" And Frank loved to hear it.'

Quentin remembered his father's advice, that authors needed only a bit of praise and a bit of brass to be obedient. Perhaps that was true.

'They'd drink to him. They'd buy him drinks. Or he'd buy theirs. He was dead drunk in Soho when Michael was born, thank you. The boy was almost born in a taxi. Catherine was born at Woodlands, and God knows what he was up to while I was up there on the fourth floor popping out this baby with only the housemaid to hold my hand.'

'No midwife?'

'She got there later. I'd kill for a fag.'

'Sorry.'

'I hated every day at Woodlands. Sometimes I had to tell myself, at least Frank's not being bombed or burnt or shot at or trekking through some godforsaken jungle. He's here beside me every night, no matter who he slept with in the afternoon. Sybil, of course. You won't hear me calling her Lady. He was safe from the war, but everything he wrote there was tripe; worse, shite. Sybil Dane would type his every bloody word – not me, not that book – and every evening, she'd hand him his pages like they were the fecking Magna Carta, and Frank would orate and declaim in the library, reading aloud, and they'd all swoon, and baste him with praise like a prize goose at Christmas. Fawning toadies. To them he was nothing but a minstrel tarted up. They used him for their amusement. He lost his head. *Hay Days*—' She snorted audibly '—dedicated to Lady Sybil Dane. Yes, he really put her bloody title in there. He was …' She glanced towards the mud room as though the word might come through the door. 'Besotted. Not so much with Sybil, but with the flattery she fed him. He did not listen to me. You can see what it cost him. It undermined his reputation.'

'He saved his hide and lost his reputation,' said Quentin, quoting his father, though he did not attribute the thought.

'Yes. At first I don't even think he knew it, but after *Hay Days*, that's when the fear started to come on him. He was afraid that his gift would run out, like a roll of twine or string that would unfurl, that he'd lose his talent. He was desperate to get everything on paper before that happened. Instead his life ran out.' The kitchen clock on the shelf ticked in the silence. She bit her lip. 'We'd drifted apart, you know?'

Quentin didn't, but he nodded just the same.

'He bought this great wreck of a house, and loved it for a while, but then he drove the car into the ditch and sat there all night, dead drunk, singing and snoring and sitting in his own filth. That was the beginning of the end, now that I look back at it. After that, he was restless, off to London or somewhere, constantly, and after Sybil gave him the key to her London flat ... well, he'd take himself and his suitcase full of manuscripts, and say, "Oh, just a day or two, Claire, I have to meet with Albert Castle, or Bernard at Selwyn and Archer." But a week might go by before he'd come home. I knew where he was, and who with.' Her lip trembled, and she fought tears. 'We might have been at the end of our tether, and yet—' Her blue eyes were mirrors of pain '—I can't believe that he died without me. It seems so unfair. We should have gone together.'

'Then who would look after your children?'

She glanced around the room, as if surprised that Mary, Catherine and Michael weren't there.

'Is there some family you can turn to?'

She shrugged. 'The Carsons? They're gone. They broke Frank's heart with all the abuse they heaped on *The Moth and the Star*. His father, the schoolmaster, and his nasty Quaker mother and his prig brother wrote him horrible, accusatory letters and then said don't darken our door. The brother, the last of them, died in a motoring accident in '46. Even if they were alive, they'd not lift a finger for me. The American whore.'

'What about your own people?'

'In Idaho? I haven't had a word from any of them since I left in 1935.'

Quentin tried in vain to place Idaho in his vague geographical sense of America. 'How on earth did you meet Francis Carson?'

'A long story. Stranger than fiction, truly. We were just kids. We met at Broadstairs. We fell in love. Frank would go swimming, naked, in the mornings before he taught school. I would sneak out and meet him down at the beach. Can you imagine how cold that surf was? He was such a strong swimmer. He'd run up on the beach, naked, and I'd help him get warm. He was a wild, poetic presence, unlike anyone I'd ever known, or ever will know, and certainly not like the rest of the English, prim little aspidistras, happy in their tidy little pots behind lace curtains.' She added hastily, 'Present company excepted, of course.'

Quentin nodded, though he knew the description fit him all too well.

Both dogs perked up their heads and barked ferociously. Quentin looked at his watch. It was past noon. 'That might be the press. They would have heard by now. Shall I deal with them? I can do that much. You needn't.'

She nodded, suddenly, clearly exhausted. 'Thank you. I mean it, Quentin, thank you.'

'Perhaps I ought to leave with them. It's getting late and I've got to get back to London.'

'Must you leave? Couldn't you stay? Just tonight. You've been such a comfort to me. Tomorrow I can drive you into Woodstock. I can't use the petrol to go all the way into Oxford, but there's a bus out of—'

'I'm happy to stay. Of course.'

Quentin put on his coat and gloves, and followed the sound of the dogs' fierce barking. The sky had thickened with clouds foreboding snow and it fell in flurries. On the other side of the gate where lately he himself had perched, he could see perhaps half a dozen men and three or four vehicles. Bulbs popped, questions too. Michael stood there, telling them to sod off, calling them bastards.

'I am Quentin Castle,' he announced. 'Mr Carson's literary representative. It's true that the novelist Francis Carson has died in California where he was working on a film to be made of his novel, *Some of These Days*. I will answer your questions, but you've no right to bother Mrs Carson. Go inside, Michael, please,' said Quentin. He waited till the boy had turned the corner before he interrupted their clamouring questions with a simple statement. 'Mrs Carson and her family are grieved beyond words and ask for your understanding. They need privacy. Anything further you need, contact my father, Albert Castle, at Castle Literary.'

'Was he drunk when he fell in?' one demanded.

Quentin wanted to ask where and what Carson had fallen into, but he dared not betray his ignorance.

'What else would he be?' another laughed. 'Francis Carson spent whole days spreadeagle drunk, pissing himself blue.'

'He could certainly write rings around any of you. That's why he was in California and you're out here in the cold.' Quentin paused to let the insult penetrate. No more bulbs flashed and they started towards their cars. 'Hey, you!' Quentin called out to a man who had a cigarette between his lips the whole time he was jotting with his pencil. 'Do you have any more cigarettes?' He rummaged in his pocket for some coins, and without counting, held them out.

The man put a half-pack of Player's in his hand, and offered in music-hall Cockney, 'Wot! A poor scribbling bloke, the likes of me, givin' you a fag?' He spat for good measure, in case Quentin might have missed the derision.

'Sorry. Could I ask you one more favour? Could you send a telegram for me? Sorry.' Quentin proved it with a pound note, borrowed his pencil and paper, wrote down the Castle Literary Ltd address and scribbled: *Needed here. Home tomorrow. Send money immediately to Mrs C.*

When he turned back to the house, the snow was coming down in earnest. The brown and dun and grey landscape he had beheld this morning had all been transformed into white shapes, sparkling, the path back to the house softly delineated, pocked with the tracks of the dogs' paws and the horse's hooves. Quentin stomped his feet in the mud room and came into the kitchen. Claire had not moved from where he had left her.

'What did you tell them?'

'I told them that Castle Literary is handling all the arrangements.'

'And are you?' Her pale face was tragic in dim light. Tears gleamed in her eyes.

'Of course. If you like.' He struggled with the strange, discordant impulses Claire Carson roused in him, the conviction he would do anything to earn and keep her favour. He handed her the cigarettes.

'Oh, thank you!' She put a match to the hearth and it flared. She lit the cigarette, and inhaled deeply, smiling. 'I should quit. Bad habit, and bloody expensive, but there are times a fag's a great comfort. Where'd you get them? I thought you didn't smoke.'

'I bought them off a reporter. They always smoke. Let me be of some use. Why don't you get some rest? Send your children in here. I'll read to them,' he added in a moment of inspiration.

'Frank always read to them. Oh, he was a marvellous reader.' She started to cry again.

'I am not a marvellous reader, but I can do this.' He rose and went to the bookshelf in the corner, and took down the *Yellow Fairy Book*.

'You needn't read to Michael. He has chores. I rely on him. Too much. He's just a boy. He can be gruff. Always so anxious to be the man, is our Michael. What will I do with him when he is a man? He'll be quite the lad, won't he?'

'Like his father?'

'Michael will never be a free spirit like Frank. Truth is, he reminds me of my old Dunstan grandmother.'

'Go to your room, and get some sleep,' he said tenderly, as if she were a child.

She started up the stairwell and turned back to him. 'My old dad used to say, no rest for the wicked and the righteous don't need it. I know what camp I'm in.'

'And I'm with you,' he lied. At that moment Quentin actively regretted not being among the reckless, the daring and colourful, the flamboyant, the witty, the wicked and adventurous, the freewheeling and free-spirited. Like Robert. Like Frank. Still, someone had to be righteous, upright, orderly and responsible. Perhaps Michael would grow up to be that.

The children, of course, would have nothing to do with him. He put the book back on the shelf. Gloved, hatted, his scarf round his neck, he took a wintry stroll round Harrington Hall in the late afternoon sunshine that peeked out from under heavy-lidded clouds. Chickens, ducks and the pig roamed in the cobbled yard near the stone barn. He wandered further, out to where once there had been a formal garden, now run to ruin. In what had been the grand front of the house, the windows on two of the three storeys were boarded-up doors and a massive lock clung to the door. Snow settled over a dry fountain in the middle of the drive. Clearly, the Carsons only lived in a small portion of the place; the rest was completely shut up. The house was, in fact, a Jacobean dump. The work required to make it right would have bankrupted a lord.

Quentin could hear the children calling, hooting to one another, and he guessed they were playing a game, themselves as the spies and allies, and himself as the enemy. He came upon all three on the back of the dappled nag, clinging to each other. They rode on without speaking to him, and he turned in a different direction. In the distance he could see the skeletal structure of a folly, an eighteenth-century bit of fol-de-rol, a frothy gazebo set in what was meant to be a garden, and was now a ruin of naked black-berry bushes and blackened ferns. Where he stood, there was a crudely hand-lettered sign: *Footpath to Folly*. The story, inasmuch as Quentin could tell, of Frank Carson's life, and judging from the reporter's question, his death as well.

Claire was awake, back in the rocker, gazing at the remains of the fire when he returned to the kitchen. Quentin fed the fire, prodding it till sparks flared up and flames crackled. They sat across from each other, their hands extended towards the warmth. The kitchen clock ticked.

At last she spoke. 'I've never dealt with a death. I don't know what happens next, and all this is so ...'

'Overwhelming. Sudden and unexpected,' he offered, thinking it odd that he should finish someone else's sentence instead of the other way around. 'Did Frank have a will?'

'Oh yes. I made sure of that. I insisted. After he wrecked the car and I could see that one day he'd step over some line or another, and God would say, "Enough!" Though I never thought it would be so soon.' She ran a hand over her face. 'I can't remember where the will is. I'm not very organized. I'm sure there must be a thousand things I ought to do, but I can't think what they are.'

'There's the question of burial.' That lingered between them; the fire popped and Quentin picked up the poker and pushed the log back. 'You will have to decide what you want.'

'He has to come home. I won't have him buried in California. Not by those philistines.'

'Oxford?'

'Oh, I don't know. I don't know.' She rose and took a cigarette off the mantel, lit it, plucking a bit of tobacco from her tongue, looking into the fire. 'He liked to pretend he was lord of the falling-down manor out here, but he was happiest in London. He loved London.'

'I don't know if there's a place for him in London. The graveyards are filled. The papers said that George Orwell wanted to be buried in London, but they had to take him to Sussex or somewhere. But perhaps my father can arrange something. He's very persuasive. We looked after Francis's interests in life, and we'll do so now. I speak on behalf of the firm,' he lied. He was speaking wholly and completely for himself.

'I'm hungry,' said Mary, bursting in, flinging her sturdy little body against her mother. 'And Michael is being mean.'

'We'll have our tea after I put the chickens away, and the animals in the barn. It's getting dark.'

'Would you like me to help?'

'Oh, Quentin, have you ever in all your life chased a chicken into the henhouse? You stay with Mary.'

'No. I hate him. I'm coming with you.' She put her hand in her mother's, and Quentin wondered if she feared her mother, too, might vanish, as her father had, though he reminded himself, Francis Carson had been gone for almost a year. Since April or May.

By the time they ate, the lamp over the table whose light had been so wan in the morning shone brightly; its beams stretched unsuccessfully towards the far reaches of the room, dancing on the pans hanging overhead and the irregular panes of glass in the windows. The little girls clamoured, and cried, and whined, clinging to their mother in ways that Quentin found appalling, even intolerable. Though he knew nothing of children, he could neither remember nor imagine himself clinging to Margaret in that bratty and demanding fashion. Margaret would not have stood for it. Claire seemed not to notice. Michael pounded upstairs, refusing his mother's request that he should light a fire in the room where Quentin would sleep. Quentin hastily assured her he did not want a fire in his room; he would not be indebted to the testy Michael Carson for anything if he could help it.

Finally, the girls, one by one, wore themselves out and fell asleep, one of them on the floor with her head on the unprotesting dog. Claire roused the eldest gently and guided her upstairs. Quentin lifted the youngest, Mary, off the sleeping dog and followed. In his arms, she was all sweet repose. A child in his arms was an altogether new experience. The narrow stairwell was lit by only one uncertain bulb at the landing, and the steps creaked like old bones. The hall was draughty. The room was cold. The little girls shared one room. Michael had another.

Claire lit a flickering lamp. Following instructions, and Claire's example with Catherine, Quentin took off Mary's shoes, leaving her stockings on for warmth. Claire tossed him a small flannel nightgown and when he had got the little girl, protesting, out of her clothes, he put it over her head, struggling as well with an odd rush of affection for a child who hated him. Claire pulled the bedclothes up over the girls, who instantly rolled towards each other for warmth.

Quentin and Claire finished the bottle of Dewar's and talked late into the night, as she told him the Stranger Than Fiction story of how she had met the gifted but difficult, the mercurial Francis Carson, their early life together. Quentin listened, his forte. The unusual surroundings, her voice, the rapt attention of this beautiful woman all combined to rouse in him unlikely, even foreign, impulses, not even emotions, but odd crackling combinations of lust and tenderness, of ease and arousal, of having his every sense sharpened, heightened, and at the same time relaxed. No doubt it was the whisky and the late hour, but he had the sensation that somewhere deep inside him some new alchemy was transforming the ordinary straw of his life into gold the same colour as her hair.

CHAPTER SEVEN

STRANGER THAN FICTION

THE STORY CLAIRE told him over the bottle of Dewar's that night suggests that life or destiny, or even God, must enjoy irony. The Broadstairs beaches that Claire Dunstan and Francis Carson had frolicked on were well known to her father, John Dunstan, though it is unlikely that any of the Dunstans ever frolicked at all.

John Dunstan was one of four sons in a dour maritime family. Leaving school at fourteen, he went to work at a chandler's shop for a few years then left home for Brighton, for reasons he never made clear. There he was swept up by the fervour of a couple of Mormon missionaries whose zeal (to say nothing of their stirring stories of biblical battles, glorious rendition of the afterlife, and belief in earthly patriarchal blessings for men) appealed to him, a scrawny young man with few prospects. He converted, went under the waters of baptism, and in 1910 took passage with a group of newly minted British Mormons to America to populate Zion, the mountain stronghold of the Latter Day Saints in Utah.

John Dunstan always believed that God Himself had intervened to spare him the fate of his brothers in the Great

War. One ended up a rotting corpse on some bit of barbed wire in northern France. One brother died in Gallipoli. One brother, William, survived; that is to say that by 1919 he was still warm, and more or less upright, though one-armed and nearly deaf. John Dunstan, by contrast, was a whole man, a sterling pillar of the Mormon Church, confident in his eventual accession to the Celestial Kingdom where he would inherit, as befit the meek, many celestial wives and vast tracts of heavenly property.

On earth his lot was less splendid. John Dunstan eked out an often impoverished seasonal living in the sugar-beet fields of Idaho, that and anything else he could find. He had married young, and his bride Alice was younger yet. They had six children, of whom Claire Catherine, born 1919, was the eldest girl. Claire's earliest recollection, she told Quentin, was following her brothers along the train tracks not far from their house, picking up coal that had fallen along the tracks. She thought she might have been four or five. The Dunstans routinely ate rabbits that her older brothers trapped. They couldn't afford the bullets to shoot them.

The Dunstans couldn't afford to feed their children, and so parted with them whenever possible. The boys went to live with Alice's relatives, dry farmers who needed their brawn. At sixteen Claire too was parcelled out, but to another branch of the family, to John's people in Kent. Word came that John's mother had had a stroke. His one-armed brother William could not look after her, and there was no money for a proper nurse. If John could spare one of his daughters, the Dunstans would pay her third-class ticket and give her room and board in Broadstairs.

For an imaginative 16-year-old girl who had grown up in frontier Idaho, the journey by train, rattling across the open plains of the Midwest, and passing through the cities of the east, was full of wonder. In New York she was met by an elder of the Mormon Church who escorted her to the ship, and saw to it she boarded with no chance to experience the city. The great ship, even travelling third class, thrilled her, whetted her appetite for adventure, convinced her that great things lay ahead. Full of hope and high spirits, good health, good looks and native intelligence, Claire Dunstan stood on the deck and looked fearlessly ahead, certain that life in England would live up to the Sir Walter Scott and Brontë novels she adored: mysterious castles, great houses, noble families, verdant streams, rolling meadows. She imagined her grandmother a lovely old lady with pink cheeks, white hair and a lace cap, living in a charming cottage near the sea.

She was met at Southampton by her uncle, William, who was bitter that his brother had converted, emigrated, and escaped the war where William had lost an arm, and much of his hearing, from an explosion on the Somme. William lived on a pension, and could no longer afford the occasional prostitute. He looked at his tall, blooming niece, her fair hair, fine posture and bright mouth with something other than avuncular affection. On the train to Broadstairs he rode in silence, though she chattered away. With his good arm he carried her carpet bag as they walked from the Broadstairs station to the Dunstan house. He stopped before a grey brick rowhouse with a single narrow downstairs window framed in lace curtains shielding an aspidistra in a ceramic pot.

This was not the seaside cottage she'd imagined. William ushered her into the stale, sour-smelling parlour to meet her grandmother, and Claire knew that the adventure was over.

Mrs Dunstan, who insisted on being called Mrs Dunstan, was perhaps sixty-five, and in an alarming state of physical decay. A stroke had robbed her of mobility, and her mental faculties were equal only to rants against the government, her late husband, and the son who had abandoned her to join the bloody Mormons. She and William attended no church whatever.

Claire hoped at least Sundays would be free, but her duties were unending, seven days a week. She was the fetch-and-toter, fire-maker, grate-scrubber, pot-emptier, bootblack and laundress, ironer, cook, cleaner, and all-round slavey. Additionally Claire had to perform nursing duties for the old woman, whose days were divided between a wheeled chair and a bed in the parlour. Claire changed her daily, bathed her twice a month, fed her three times a day and saw to her toileting needs.

Mrs Dunstan also required Claire to read aloud to her for hours at a time, three-decker Victorian novels, not just Dickens and Thackeray and Trollope, George Eliot and the Brontës, but Rhoda Broughton, and Mary Braddon, and George Meredith, Samuel Butler. The books had all been left in the house by a previous tenant, their pages stuck together and odorous with mildew. These long reading sessions fed Claire's imagination and engaged her heart. She sometimes took the books to bed with her to read ahead, and then, eager to move on to the next book, she made up the story the following day for Mrs Dunstan, who didn't seem to know the difference as long as everything ended in a tidy fashion, the wicked duly killed off and everyone else married; in short, a happy ending.

Claire's was a tiny room at the back of the kitchen, a narrow bed, a chest instead of a bureau and a rag rug. She took her meagre meals alone. William mostly kept to his upstairs room, his good ear turned towards his wireless, while he built model airplanes. Claire could sometimes hear William's heavy tread coming down the stairs at night. She put a chair in front of her bedroom door, and a teacup and saucer on the chair to alert her if it were to be opened. He sometimes paused at her door, but went on to the privy at the back. Brutally homesick, she wrote imploring letters to her parents asking to come home. They did not reply. Their defection pierced her heart, but within a few months, Claire knew she must fend for herself. Without friends or funds (they paid her no wages), Claire could imagine no way out, save for the old woman dying. And at that, the thought of being alone in the house with William was too terrible to contemplate.

She managed to pinch, hold back tiny bits, tuppence here and there when she was sent out to the shops, but she did not attempt outright thievery. She was certain Mrs Dunstan and William would send the law after her. Her American accent, her height, even her beauty was against her. Mercifully the old woman went to bed early, slept like the dead and snored like a rattling pump handle. William played his wireless loud to compensate for his hearing loss. Claire took to making tiptoeing escapes from her small room, out the back gate, and down the alley.

She went to the Oak and Crown, a pub she had noticed on her rounds of the shops. The air was turgid with cigarette smoke, but the voices were loud and lively; there was often singing, and beer splashed. She didn't know that a girl alone oughtn't to wander into pubs, and she didn't care. As an American she was already an anomaly in town. Claire, who had never tasted beer or liquor of any sort, found it to her liking, that it loosed her voice, her bright soprano trained in the LDS church choir. She and the schoolmaster, one Francis Carson, both had a good ear and could sing any song having heard it only once. They did duets of music-hall tunes. Francis Carson was only one of many young men swarming around the tall American girl with pale hair the colour of raw sugar and crystalline blue eyes. Men vied to buy her a drink, vied for the honour of walking her back to the Dunstans'; not all the way back, mind you, she would not risk that, just to the alley. Claire took up smoking to cover up the smell of smoke in her hair and her clothes after these escapades.

Francis Carson was a few years older than Claire Dunstan. A solid, broad-shouldered young man, with a thick mop of curling dark hair, half-hooded grey eyes, a slow smile, and fingers stained with nicotine, he was well known in Broadstairs. He was a schoolmaster, after all, his university education cut short by his father's death. His students feared him. He had a fierce roar and was not afraid to use it. When he was not terrorizing schoolboys, Francis knew well how to charm women. As the schoolmaster, he was much sought as a matrimonial prospect for the young ladies, and on more than one occasion provided afternoon amusement for their mothers.

His way with women was not lost on Claire. Within a few months he was the only man walking her home. Frank Carson did not deign to stop at the alley, fearing William. He walked her all the way to the back gate where he held her tight, his lips to hers, his hands to her breasts and buttocks and told her she was driving him mad with desire. He had to have her.

Francis and Claire recognized in one another the kind of heedless hunger that would characterize their union for a long time. For over a year they rousted and wrestled, rolled over one another like puppies, and made love, meeting early mornings on the beach at Broadstairs, on warm evenings behind fences, along the hedgerows. Their choices were limited since Claire had no place of her own and Francis lodged with a nosy widow. They were ardent lovers and they had ardent rows, occasioned by pregnancy scares, by his roving eye, by her demands. He gave her books to read, books he loved and many she didn't, and they argued about those as well. Her uncle knew she was running wild, and raised his hand to her. However, he struck her only once. *Touch me again, and I'll leave you alone with your old mum forever,* she threatened. In the meantime, she was making plans to bolt in any event, to leave with Francis, not simply that she should be rid of the Dunstans, but to free Francis to write. She fostered Francis's fine, high idea of himself as a writer. As she told Quentin Castle over the bottle of Dewar's that night, when she read Frank's book, the still unfinished *The Moth and the Star,* she had cried into her hands because the work was so lovely, so moving, the characters so heart-rending, the language so poetic.

The Moth and the Star, like many first novels, was a re-imagining of Francis Carson's youth. A schoolmaster, rather like Frank's father (or, rather, how Frank had conceived of his father) was a man with the wisdom of Samuel Johnson, a man of moral magnitude, with fine abilities and literary ambitions, cast into wretched circumstances by unkind fate. This character had a carping, penny-niggling Quaker wife, an elder son, pious and dutiful, and a younger son, intelligent but rebellious, whom the father tries to break but secretly admires. The father's hopes for the son are dashed when his wild ways oblige him to run away to sea, leaving a local girl in the proverbial family way. (The lovers' passion described in lush prose, more lush and lyrical after Frank ran off with Claire.) The girl's own family casts her out and the schoolmaster – to the bitter ire of his wife and pious son – takes her and her bastard brat in. The son returns, and to the father's everlasting sorrow, takes the girl and the child away with him. Not a happy ending.

Claire believed in Frank's genius, just as she believed escape was essential if he were to fulfil it. Francis, for his part, was not altogether unhappy there in Broadstairs. Left to his own devices, he might have stayed, teaching school, bedding the local ladies, but Claire insisted. Train fare was out of the question, and so one spring dawn they hitched a ride with a market gardener going into London. Claire carried only the carpet bag she'd brought from Idaho. Francis never did learn to travel light, and he had three suitcases (one full of manuscripts). They were prepared to pose as man and wife to rent a tiny set of rooms in theatrical digs, but the Brixton landlady didn't care if they were Wallis Simpson and the King as long as they coughed up the rent. First. The place had a lumpy bed, a wardrobe, a washstand and cupboard and table that faced the window to serve as a desk.

Claire made a bargain with Frank: on the promise that he would not drink, nor idle, nor diddle the oversexed landlady, Claire would free his time to write, to finish *The Moth and the Star*. She would get a job and support them. Claire's good looks, long legs and choir-trained soprano landed her a place in the undistinguished chorus at the Brixton Odeon. By 1936 the music hall, that venerable British institution, was then in its twilight glow, but audiences still flocked there for the beer, the pretty girls, the songs that everyone could sing.

The young couple's days assumed a kind of rhythm. They laughed, they loved, they fought, they stayed out late, they stayed up late, they rose late the next day before starting all over. When she woke in the mornings, Claire took what Francis had written the day before out of the suitcase by the door, and read it. She offered praise, and made suggestions, and if scenes proved difficult or the characters recalcitrant, she acted them out for him. Claire and Frank were in love, their health and high spirits and affection, their hopes for the future were a daily tonic against the otherwise constricted circumstances of their present life. They shared a sense of destiny.

The writing and rewriting, the revisions of *The Moth and the Star* moved forward, and Francis kept to his part of the bargain (or at least to the spirit of it: the oversexed

109

landlady was too good to pass up). After writing all evening, Francis would walk to the Odeon in time for the late acts. He had a few drinks at the bar, applauded the girls in the chorus, heckled the comics, laughed at the dog act, and joined in enthusiastic choruses to all the songs. One act, however, left him spellbound: the blowsy, ageing mudlark Rosie Evans belting out her trademark 'Some Of These Days'.

Rose Evans' rendition of 'Some Of These Days' did not have the usual uptempo conviction – the singer certain that her erring lover would soon be back in her arms. On the contrary, in Rosie Evans' delivery, the singer knew that those days would never come again, that she had been utterly forsaken, abandoned, left clutching cold pride and defeated dreams. Rosie's grandeur, her tawdry beauty, were allied to her being old and blowsy and still having the strength to break hearts every night in a place where broken hearts and broken hopes and dusty dreams were strewn on the floor like once-lit matches The deep parentheses of her cheeks, caked with stage make-up, were accentuated by the harsh electric light ringing the proscenium. Her voice, still clear and strong, though wavering on the long-held notes, rang all the way up to the gallery while the rouge ran down her face, and her lipstick fanned out into a delta of lines round her mouth, and the wattles of her thick neck shook with emotion. She wore a long, lacy gown, the lace gone sepia and the bright yellow satin faded in patches. She carried herself with tragic aplomb. Rosie Evans stood till the last bit of applause fell away in the gallery, then she left the stage.

In Rosie's youth, thirty or forty years before, it was said that she had brought down many a thousand-seat Empire theatre up and down Britain with her spirited, sensual delivery of music-hall standards. She could sing even the Victorian saccharine-sweet 'Come Into The

Garden, Maud' so that men got erections and women prickled happily between their thighs. She fell desperately in love with a man who refused to share her with an adoring public. She disappeared from the stage for a time, perhaps a dozen or so years, and in that time she lost her lover, her looks, and two children. When she returned, far from playing the Empire music halls, she was reduced to this backwater Brixton Odeon. *Some of these daaaaaaaaaaays you're gonna miss my lovin' ... you're gonna miss my kissin' ... you're gonna miss me, baby, when I'm faaaaaaaar away ... I feel so lonely ...*

Francis Carson was easily moved to emotion. Routinely he gulped back tears at her every performance. And he was not alone. At the Odeon bar, gruff men surreptitiously wiped their noses with the backs of work-stained hands. Stout matrons and experienced tarts blubbered outright.

After the last act, and the curtain came down on the chorus, Francis waited for Claire at the Odeon stage door. Rosie Evans usually exited first, still wearing the gown she had performed in, a hat, a coat, long, soiled gloves, her stage make-up still smeared about the eyes. Francis always removed his hat and greeted her respectfully, but she never spoke to him. She spoke to few people, though she might occasionally tell the stage manager to sod himself; certainly she never bestowed any camaraderie on the giggling gaggle of chorines that Claire belonged to. But her character fired Francis's imagination and some years later he would fashion from Rosie Evans his immortal character Elsie Rose in his second and most famous novel, *Some of These Days*.

But first he struggled to finish *The Moth and the Star*. When he did, Claire rented a typewriter from a Brixton shop. She put it on the table and by day taught herself to type. Then she went to work, transcribing his spidery, Spenserian hand into typescript. Her fingers were stained

111

blue from the carbon paper. There was much pounding on the door and floor and ceiling, cursing on the stairs from the other lodgers: her constant tapping was keeping them awake; these were theatre people and they needed to sleep by day. Claire typed on.

When she finally finished, Claire got some brown paper and twine from the butcher down the street, both gratis (a pretty girl is like a melody, after all) and wrapped up the typescript, tied it as though the twine were satin ribbons. She told Francis to take it into London and get it published, to make her proud. She kissed him on the lips and he slapped her on the backside.

Francis Carson had his heart set on having *The Moth and the Star* published by one of the great literary houses, as befits the work of a great writer. However, as he wandered London that rainy afternoon in the autumn of 1937, and faced the doors – John Murray, The Bodley Head, Chatto and Windus, Jonathan Cape, Selwyn and Archer – his nerve failed. He needed a drink to fortify himself. And then another. And a third for the road, though he did not leave, and in fact, had a fourth. He gathered courage in pub after pub as he worked his way towards Mayfair. Such was his strong constitution that his only awareness of alcohol tingling in his veins came with the impulse to recite Shakespeare or Byron, Shelley or Yeats, or his latest enthusiasm, Auden.

When the pubs closed for the afternoon, he found the autumn weather had turned blustery, and rain pelted down. He opened his umbrella and made his unsteady way down the street. A sudden gust of wind snatched his open umbrella and blew it away; he ran after it, but he tripped and dropped the precious parcel in a filthy puddle. He scrambled to snatch it, and continued after the umbrella, comically staggering, splashing, finally nabbing the runaway umbrella in front of a doorway where the wind again had at it, and turned it inside out. He pushed into the building to get out of the rain until he could right the umbrella.

A Mr Jobson, the hall porter, eyed him dubiously, summed him up as a writer, and said he'd hold the umbrella, fix it even, while the gentleman (Jobson used the word loosely) kept his appointment with the literary agents on the third floor.

Francis thanked him, shook off his wet hat and started up the stairs. There indeed, stencilled on the glass along with the distinctive castle logo, he read:

CASTLE LITERARY LTD. AUTHORS' REPRESENTATIVES.

Miss Marr gave him the gimlet eye. She was less forgiving than Mr Jobson and had scant patience with those authors who looked so seedy and disreputable, in short, so authorish. Moreover this one was wet and wafted an unpleasant combination of odours. She asked his business.

'Here to see Mr Castle, madam. I have a book for him. A novel.' Francis drew the parcel out from beneath his wet jacket, and brushed it tenderly.

'Is he expecting you?'

'I don't know.'

'Well, I do. Mr Castle's not in, so he couldn't possibly be expecting you.'

'I'll wait, madam,' said Frank, flashing her a good-natured grin that used to slay them in Broadstairs.

Miss Adeline Marr, however, was made of sterner stuff and returned to her typewriter. Moreover, Miss Marr knew that Albert Castle was lunching with Mrs Partridge, and these lunches were always long, lubricated with alcohol, high spirits, beefsteaks, a rich dessert, and no doubt some forbidden fruit for the finale. Miss Marr was no fool. Miss

113

Marr said none of this to this Mr whatever his name was. Let him wait.

Francis had nothing else to do. Outside the rain was still pouring in buckets. He opened his typescript and read it with audible pleasure, shaking each of the top pages dry, blowing on them when necessary. Francis's personal, raffish odour, intensified by cigarettes and beer, did not improve on drying, but drifted towards Miss Marr, whose long nose wrinkled.

Earlier than expected, Albert Castle could be heard on the stairwell singing, each staccato syllable from *Princess Ida*. 'While Love, the housemaid, lights the kitchen fire ...' booming the last as he opened the door, and tipping his hat, and popping through the low gate that separated Miss Marr's desk from the unwashed author, who rose to his feet.

'And how was your lunch with Mrs Partridge, sir?'

'Excellent, Miss Marr! Excellent. Between ourselves—' And here he bent towards her, balancing his tipsy self on her desk '—we have our literary cachet to uphold, but the wheels are greased by *The Book of British Housekeeping* while we await the next Sydney Thaxton.'

'Sir,' said Francis, rising. 'Mr Castle, I presume.'

'This man has no appointment,' said Miss Marr.

'But I have this book,' said Francis, extending his parcel, open now, the creamy sheets of paper glowing like a pale flower in wet brown leaves. 'This novel. It's ... it's very good.'

As a literary agent Albert Castle was often pressed to read novels that their authors thought very good. Wasted time was an occupational hazard. He gave such books fifty pages, and not a dot or comma more. If, in fifty pages, he was compelled to page fifty-one, there was perhaps something to be said to the author. At this moment the bedraggled Francis Carson did not inspire confidence,

114

but the smell he exuded was somehow familiar to Albert Castle. What was it? He frowned and scrabbled after memory. *Wet genius. Thaxton and the second-best umbrella.* 'Leave your manuscript and address with Miss Marr, and I'll have a glance at it and get back to you.'

All the way back to Brixton, *A glance at it and get back to you* rang in Francis's ears, and with these words he heard as well the rush and rustle of turning pages exuding the sweet smell of fresh print. Success! The editor's delight! Publisher's pride! Booksellers beaming happiness, as *The Moth and the Star* flew off the shelves, so swiftly it had to be plucked from the front window of Hatchards to satisfy demand. He stood in front of Hatchards and imagined this very scenario. After a stop or two for a celebratory drink, Francis also heard waves of delighted critical acclaim, noisy as the waves washing up on Broadstairs beach, the ripple of readers' laughter and tears, rapture, excitement, delight, second and third editions, translations, oh, it all lay there before him, fuelled by the same capacity for fiction that allowed Francis Carson to see a grand manor in a Jacobean dump.

Castle Literary Ltd had two form letters that covered the swathe of their experience with potential authors. One, signed simply *Castle Literary Ltd*, said, in a florid and roundabout fashion, replete with good wishes, nothing doing. The other used words like 'delighted to read your ms' and 'looking forward to meeting with you at your earliest convenience'. Albert Castle or Enid Sherrill signed these personally. This latter short letter, postmarked 30 September 1937, signed and with a cheery postscript by Albert Castle, launched the lifelong (and the afterlife-long) connection between the firm of Castle Literary Ltd and Francis Carson, their agreement solidified by a hand-shake, nothing more. Albert Castle's nose for genius was truly vindicated. Selwyn and Archer published *The Moth and the Star* in 1938, and critics hailed Francis Carson as the best writer since Thomas Hardy, or D. H. Lawrence, or Compton Mackenzie.

Even before publication, on the strength of the modest advance, and convinced that bright days lay ahead, Francis and Claire left Brixton and moved to a chic flat in Chelsea they could ill afford. Their insular love affair opened up to include many friends who sought Francis out. They took up with – or rather were taken up by – a fine, fast crowd of people who flocked to toast Frank's success, laud his genius, supply him with drinks, dinners and soirées in artists' ateliers and country homes, in cafés, and restaurants. These were smart, lively, arty, educated, confident people; most of them were privileged, a few, like Lady Sybil Dane, still rich, despite the Depression.

On the buoyant tide of this acclaim, and with Rosie Evans still fresh in his mind, Francis set to work on what would become *Some of These Days*. His own discipline was not always equal to this task, but Claire's was. Claire recognized the central conflict of Frank's life, his very nature: the struggle to balance the discipline to write and the energy to live. Claire put herself between Frank and noisy interruptions, no matter who rang or came to the door. She read, she acted out the scenes, offered dialogue; she wept and typed and lauded. He finished it in an inspired eight months.

On publication in June 1939, *Some of These Days* was widely regarded to be one of the great English novels. In retrospect, though it was not *Brideshead Revisited*, or *Women in Love*, it nonetheless represented the final flowering of a romantic tradition. Francis Carson, in his heart, subscribed to all those old values that made such novels possible, values which would be deemed cloying, stultifying, that would require rebellion from later twentieth-century writers. Carson's reputation never quite rose again to the heights accorded *Some of These Days*, and suffered setbacks, notably the failure of *Hay Days*. But by the 1990s the tide had turned in his favour. On the basis of *Some of These Days* and two posthumous novels, *An Inconvenient Wife* and *September Street*, he was considered a major British novelist, thus making even more poignant his premature death by drowning in 1950.

CHAPTER EIGHT

THE VOW

IN THE PREDAWN darkness Quentin put on his glasses, lit the candle by the bed, and consulted his watch: quarter past six. He was conscious of an encroaching hangover.

Despite the drinking, he had slept only fitfully. Wind whistled at the window panes, and scooted in draughts and intermittent blasts, and the hot water bottle, as a substitute for human warmth, was insufficient against the cold. He dressed hurriedly and made his way down the dark staircase towards the kitchen. There he found lights on but the fire out. He busied himself making up the fire and putting the kettle on. He used the lav down the hall, glad he'd brought a toothbrush.

The kitchen had barely begun to warm when he returned, and heard the door open. He went to the mud room and found her there, a lantern in one hand. She blew it out and handed him an apron full of brown, speckled eggs. She wore a man's heavy coat, a scarf round her neck. Her cheeks were flushed with cold, and her eyes too were red-rimmed, ringed with fatigue. 'I'm hungover,' she confessed. 'I feel like shite.'

'It'll pass,' he said with the voice of experience, though

he could not actually remember when he had last had a hangover, or had gone a day without shaving, or had done anything but drink tea and read *The Times* in the early morning.

He took the eggs into the kitchen, and she followed, chatting inconsequentially, as though they had between them an easy understanding, a bond forged in the long night they had spent talking. She held her hands out to the fire, then wandered around the table, picking up the occasional toy, or doll, or shoe, placing it here or there, distractedly and without imparting any sort of order. 'I tell you, Quentin, some lovely bright light, a beacon, has gone out of the world. Frank ought to have written a dozen more books, and we ought to have laughed and had rows and made up and made love for years yet. And now he'll be shipped home in a box, like so much crockery or furniture, a tag attached, a destination. A beautiful man no longer. A thing. Freight. I can't bear the thought of it. Oh, dear God, how will I ever deal with those people? How can I even bring him home?'

'I could do it,' he offered.

'What?'

'I could go to California. On your behalf,' he said in a spasm of chivalry. 'I could accompany the body home.'

'You'd do that?' she marvelled. 'Go all the way to California?'

'We, I, would be honoured,' he added, though he could hear his father protesting against the expense, ranting against the FMB and demanding to know if Quentin were absolutely daft to make such an offer. Quentin decided he wouldn't say he'd offered, but rather that he'd been asked. He knew how his father felt about keeping on the good side of the late author's heirs.

'Oh, Quentin, would you?'

'Yes. I would be honoured.'

119

'Really?'

'Really.'

'Oh, thank you. For everything.' She crumpled onto the bench across from him. 'You tell them for me, in London and, yes, in California too, it has to be you. No one else fetching Frank, or judging him, or bringing him home but you. You and no other.'

'Of course.'

She rumpled her hair and fought tears. 'Frank would have liked you. He was easily led by flattery, especially if it came from some sneaky tart, but he prided himself on recognizing the good in people, in recognizing other poetic souls.'

'I am prosaic, I'm afraid.'

'You do yourself an injustice. I'm sorry you didn't know him.'

'I'm sorry too.' This was a sudden truth to Quentin.

She put her elbows on the table and rested her chin in her hands, pulling the blue sweater up towards her face. 'Will you bring home the suitcase too? Please.'

'What suitcase?'

'Frank always travelled with a suitcase full of manuscripts, some of them half written, some even abandoned, sometimes just notes he was keeping towards books he thought he might write, but he put everything in the suitcase. Every night, no matter where we lived, from those Brixton digs, to this place, when he finished working, he'd put that day's work in the suitcase and put it by the door, so if there ever was an emergency, a fire, say, he could grab it, fast, on his way out, he'd never lose his work.' She smiled. 'I remember sitting on that suitcase in the back of the market-garden truck the day we ran away from Broadstairs. Even when we could afford new suitcases, Frank wouldn't part with that one. He was superstitious about it. The new book will be in it. It's almost finished.'

'I don't think my father knew of any new book.'

'Your father doesn't know everything.'

'Ah. What's it about?'

'It's about me,' she said with injured dignity, 'about our marriage being tattered and banged up long before he left for America. I'd have grabbed his ankles and crawled to keep him from going. I was like Elsie Rose in *Some of These Days*, a woman willing to give up everything to hold on to a man who didn't want her. I was ready to burn for him, you see?' She picked up a cigarette, struck a match and lit it, watched the smoke waft away. 'Not like this little match, but like a fiery torch, like a lighthouse beam, like a Roman candle lighting up the sky. But finally all he wanted was just the useful little Lucifer to shine on his face for a single moment while people around him, women mostly, swooned. I had no pride by then. But when you're ready to sacrifice everything, and everything has no value, what's the point?'

Quentin was confused, and his face must have shown it.

'I was an inconvenient wife.' She blew out a plume of smoke. 'The woman who still loved and needed her husband, but he has tired of her. He wants to move on. That was me. That's what he was calling the book.'

'Didn't you mind? I mean, to be written about. It sounds so unflattering.'

'Oh, it was unflattering all right, but what's the use of protest? It's like that with writers. They use what they want from people. They never ask. When I read his drafts, typed them, it was *déjà vu*. I read what I had lived just a few months before. He made no excuses. My life belonged to him. Everything we burnt up in our path became fodder for his writing. Even our marriage.' Her blue eyes were unflinching, though her lip trembled.

Bewildered, and having no experience with the sort of love, the passion and rancour she described, Quentin could

121

not offer even understanding. He felt rather like a tourist, in the midst of grandeur to which he had no connection.

'You bring him home, Quentin,' she spoke fiercely, gulping tears, 'and you tell them there in California, tell them I won't have any pious blather, or crocodile tears, or Hollywood tarts throwing themselves over the coffin. There won't be any of that shite for Frank Carson. Nothing. You tell them for me. You bring him home and we'll say goodbye here.'

'You can trust me. I promise. You have my word.'

This seemed to Quentin a solemn vow, sacred as his marriage vows. One made one's wedding vows knowing – everyone did – that one could not possibly live up to the letter of those vows, sickness, health, richer, poorer, every day of their lives. It was enough to promise to try. But this vow to Claire Carson? Quentin would keep this promise. He must succeed, whatever obstacles his father might put in his path.

Michael clomped down the stairs, pale and sulky. The girls followed him, moving instantly to their mother, clinging to her embrace. Michael hunkered across from Quentin, playing with his knife, flinging it, time and again, against the wooden floor, trying to get it to stick upright.

'Stop!' cried Claire at last. 'The sound will drive me mad! Stop that, and do something useful for humanity.'

'What do I care for humanity?' The boy closed the knife and put it in his pocket. 'My da is dead.'

The girls burst into tears.

'See to it the dogs are fed,' Claire snapped.

'That's not humanity.'

'It'll do.'

All through breakfast Quentin tried to remember the workday morning at Castle Literary. Miss Marr and Miss Sherrill and Monica, and his father, all bustle and business, and paper and people, ringing phones, pinging bells as the typewriter carriages came to the end of one line, and crashed back to start another. Though he had only been here twenty-four hours, he felt as though days, weeks, whole seasons separated him from his old life. Still, once the children scattered, he said, 'I suppose I should be going.'

'Yes, I know you must,' she replied. 'And I shall have to face everything alone.'

'Not alone. You have us. The firm will not desert you,' he said, feeling like a fool for citing the firm when what he meant was himself, that he would not desert her. 'And tomorrow, certainly by tomorrow, there will be money in your account. I shall see to it personally. Against your husband's royalties, naturally.' The mercenary thought came to him that with his untimely death, Carson's book sales would doubtlessly rise. He was starting to think like his father. That thought gave him pause. 'Perhaps you should write me a letter.'

'A letter?'

'A letter in your hand with your wishes. I may need some sort of authorization. If I should have any ...'

'You're right. Of course. Typed?'

'I should think not. Handwritten.'

She went to the large bureau and brought paper and pen to the table. The cream-coloured paper was beautifully engraved with *Harrington Hall nr Woodstock* at the top. This letterhead too, it turned out, was a luxury Frank Carson had insisted on.

This letter later turned up, inexplicably, in the effects of Miss Adeline Marr on her death in 1991, amid a vast trove of valuable literary memorabilia relating to Castle Literary Ltd clients. (And a few non-clients, including a whimsical exchange between Albert Castle and H. G. Wells, and a testy exchange with Virginia Woolf.) Miss Marr's nephew, her only heir, offered the whole for auction through

Sotheby's. The literary curator at Sotheby's – a friend of Quentin's and fellow former London Library trustee – was a man who believed in discretion. He alerted Quentin to the contents, adding that some of the letters were rather ordinary, some lively, but some were passionate, even beautiful love letters signed CC as well as short epistles from Roo to Kanga, erotic promises conveyed in the code of longtime lovers.

Quentin's solicitors sent Miss Marr's nephew a letter saying these letters had been systematically stolen over years, and he had no right to sell them. The nephew maintained Mr Albert Castle had given Miss Marr all this memorabilia in return for her many years of unsung service and low wages, and that she deserved some compensation since, after all those years of service, Miss Marr had been summarily sacked in June 1965, without cause, without references, and forced to retire on a pittance. Quentin's solicitors ignored this plea. They pointed out that many of the letters were dated after Albert Castle's death in 1959, thus they could only have been stolen. The nephew, forced to settle, asked to keep at least the H. G. Wells exchange, but Quentin was adamant. Everything was returned to him. When he opened the box, this letter, handwritten, dated 7 February 1950, was at the top:

7 February 1950

To Whom it May Concern

I hereby authorize Mr Quentin Castle to represent me in all things dealing with my late husband, [Frank, scratched out] Francis Carson. Castle Literary Ltd. represents my husband's work, and Mr. Quentin Castle himself is acquainted with, and prepared to carry out

124

my wishes regarding my husband's remains, his effects and his manuscripts. Mr. Castle has my full confidence. Please show him every courtesy, and consider his requests to be my own.

Signed
Claire Carson

She blotted the letter with a tea towel, and called for Michael to mind the girls, that she would drive Quentin into Woodstock. She put the scarf round her neck and slid her arms into a heavy jacket, and Quentin, also muffled against the cold, and carrying his leather case, followed her outside.

One of the dogs came too, but then tore off, chasing some creature in the underbrush. The snow lay all around, transforming everything in its path, democratic as death. Their breath frosted in the cold as they struggled with a sliding door in an outbuilding that sheltered the car, a battered Humber.

'I hope it will start,' she offered, coaxing it with the choke. 'It's not very reliable after Frank drove it into the ditch.' As if to disprove her point, the motor coughed to life.

He reached into his jacket, took out a money clip and pulled out what he'd need for the train and cab fare. He gave the rest to her. 'To hold you over. Just for a bit.'

'Thank you.' She took the money. 'You can't imagine ...'

'I can imagine, actually.'

Her eyes filled with tears. 'Why couldn't you have been Frank's agent? How he would have liked you.'

'Did he not like my father?'

Claire shrugged and backed the car out. 'It was a business arrangement.'

Quentin gave a definitive nod, like final punctuation.

To have said anything more would have been disloyal to his father.

Michael stood at the unlocked gate, holding it open for the car to leave. Quentin raised a hand in farewell as he passed the boy, whose face remained stony, impassive.

She navigated the icy, narrow roads carefully. 'Would you have just rung me up if there'd been a phone? Not come all the way out here?'

'I would have brought you this news myself no matter what,' he said, knowing this to be a lie. 'Will you get the telephone reconnected? My father will need to talk to you. I could ring you too.'

'It's not worth it. I'll be leaving here. Soon.'

'Where will you go?'

'I don't know. But we could barely eke by here while Frank was alive and sending money. And now? I will sell this place as soon as I can, even if it's at a loss. But where we'll go? I can't think that far ahead. I'll let you know when I see you again. I will figure out everything by then; well, maybe not everything. There's too much.'

He smiled to himself as she drove towards Woodstock. He would see her again. 'I'll come as soon as I return from California.'

'Will you bring my letters too? I wrote to him all the time, replied to all his letters. I wrote to him even after he quit writing to me. I don't know if he saved them, of course. But if he did—'

'You can rely on me.'

She stopped at the Woodstock bus stop by a news-stand where stout matrons in headscarves and carrying empty shopping bags awaited the bus into Oxford. The car idled and she reached out a cold, rough hand. 'Thank you, Quentin. Thank you for bringing him home. For everything.'

Quentin took off his glove. Took off both gloves. 'Put

them on. They'll keep you warm.'

'I can't take them.'

'Of course you can. You need them.'

'They're too fine,' she said, stroking the soft leather.

'I have others,' he lied.

She put the gloves on her hands. The bus throttled up, spewing an excess of exhaust upon the already dirty snow. He started to open the car door.

'Would you do me one more favour?' she asked.

'Anything,' he said. Then he cleared his throat, and added, needlessly legalistically, 'In my power.'

'My name.'

'What?'

'You haven't said my name once.'

'I haven't? That seems astonishing, doesn't it? Claire. Claire Carson.'

She nodded, smiled. Her eyes were blue and bright, gleaming like votive candles, and suddenly the small cold confines of the car felt like sacred space, suffused with significance.

'I will come back,' he said.

'Good.'

They got out of the car together, and she leaned against it, smiling. He joined the line of matrons, and got on the bus, taking a seat at the back where he could see her, waving in farewell. He returned her wave until the gears ground into first, and the bus rattled away and turned a corner. Under that drear winter sky, her warm brightness highlighted by the cold snow, she seemed to him like a slender flame.

Before he died in 2007, just as he clutched his chest, and fell to the ground in the Oxford Circus Tube station, Quentin Castle thought he saw her waving to him again, not wavering as a ghost, but brilliant, warm, tangible as she looked against that snowy background. In that last moment he would cry out her name: *Claire!* The crowd gathering round him, mobile phones frantically dialling, thought he was crying out for air, and respectfully stepped back. *Claire!* he cried again while his heart attacked him, beat wildly, wildly till someone knelt and asked him what he wanted. Too late; death had taken him.

In this regard Quentin Castle the literary agent, a man temperate, shrewd and circumspect, shared a fundamental connection with Francis Carson, the garrulous drunk, reciter of poetry, singer of duets, erstwhile genius, renowned lover whose flame had beckoned hundreds of women into his arms. As death exploded in his chest, Francis Carson too had tried to cry out *Claire!* and though he could not speak, hers was the last image, that face, those blue eyes, wavering before his vision, blurring underwater.

PART II

PART II

CHAPTER NINE

THE POST-WAR MODEL

QUENTIN CASTLE FINALLY arrived back at Number 11 to find the agency in an uproar, Monica physically putting herself between Miss Marr's desk and a half-dozen gentlemen of the press, demanding to speak to Albert. Miss Sherrill sat in Miss Marr's chair, talking on the phone, saying curtly, 'Lady Sybil, I am not in the habit of dealing with wailing women. You must contain yourself and be reasonable. Call back when you are lucid. No, I am not putting you off, I am merely ...'

As she spoke, Miss Sherrill waved Quentin into his father's office, and when he opened the door, Miss Marr greeted him in a shrill voice of pure outrage. 'Did you have to send the press to us? Look at them!'

'Now, now, Miss Marr.' Albert rose and came to her. 'Quentin was quite right. Who else can speak for poor Francis? He's our client, after all. Was.'

'I shall never get any work done today.'

'Of course you will,' Albert soothed. 'Bring us a nice cup of tea, will you?' He closed the door behind her and leaned against it. 'She sometimes makes me feel like I work for her, and not the other way round. Well, lad, you look like hell, if I must say.'

Quentin wanted to protest that he was no longer a lad, but held his tongue. He had bigger bones of contention. He brought out Claire's note.

Predictably Albert reacted by going red in the face and insisting there was no need for Quentin to go to California. Shipping the body back was a mere matter of forms, international forms, fine, but mere paperwork that did not require the junior partner's actual presence. And all the expense that would entail. Quentin lied without a single qualm, saying Mrs Carson had asked him to go, and that the firm must now stay on the sunny side of the FMB or stand to lose Francis as their client. Albert saw the wisdom, especially after he was promised a new and almost finished novel in the second suitcase that Quentin would bring back. Besides, Albert reasoned aloud, Castle Ltd could eventually deduct Quentin's expenses from Carson's royalties.

Quentin went home to pack, where he lied to Florence as well, that Mrs Carson had asked him to escort her husband's body home. This lie too was easier than he would have thought possible. Certainly easier than saying that Claire Carson's plight and dignity touched his heart. That he had never met a woman, anyone really, so freely open with her sorrows, her troubles, her love, her fears and failures; he had never before breathed the air of such candour. He could not say that though it was winter, Quentin had found Claire Carson warm, refreshing as a spring rain.

Late that afternoon he took a cab back to Number 11 where the immediate tumult had passed, and Miss Marr, in a great flurry of efficiency and telexes, had procured tickets, and reservations, rail, ship and plane; she exchanged pounds for American dollars at Lloyds Bank. Albert had dealt via transatlantic cables with various parties in California, including Roy Rosenbaum, president of Regent Films where Carson had worked. Albert conveyed Mrs Carson's wishes that her husband's body be returned to England, that there be no services of any sort in California, that the firm's junior partner, Quentin Castle, would arrive there to act on her behalf. Mr Rosenbaum personally assured Albert they would take responsibility for the body, and see to the necessary paperwork so that all would be in readiness when Quentin arrived. Moreover, Regent Films would absorb all Quentin's expenses while in Los Angeles. This last offered Albert a good deal of relief.

From the *Queen Mary* Quentin sent Louisa a telegram that *Apricot Olive Lemon* had gone out to Chatto and Windus, John Murray, and The Bodley Head. He would discuss everything with her on his return. Louisa's reply said simply, 'Have every faith,' and he could not tell if that was her advice or her conviction.

Cunard Lines advertised that 'Getting There Is Half the Fun' but Quentin's four-day crossing to New York, tourist class, was not. He socialized little, walking the decks till cold drove him inside. He had brought four typescripts to work on, but mostly he whiled the time with paperback mysteries, and crashed through the newspapers. All of them, from the stately grey columns of *The Times*, London and New York, to the juicy gossip sheets, served up the same information about Carson's death, how gardeners found the body of the novelist, Francis Carson, in the Garden of Allah pool Sunday morning. No witnesses saw him plunge or fall. The American press's breathy coverage included splashy photos of the late writer squiring beautiful women around Hollywood, and a photo of the glamorous Linda St John getting out of a taxi, captioned 'Film Stops Production for Author's Death'. There were long, laudatory, literary appreciations from London critics, from New York editors, and prestigious book reviews, from Hollywood illuminati, including Roy Rosenbaum of Regent Films, all of these people attesting to Carson's genius.

Quentin regretted bringing the four heavy typescripts once the *Queen Mary* docked in New York and he realized he would be carrying all this. He stood in the long lines for Customs, passport in hand, and pushed his bags along the floor with his foot. A few questions, a few rubber-stamp thumps, and he was pushed through the bureaucratic bowels, and thence through revolving doors, out onto the street where the weather was brutally cold. A huge yellow taxi pulled up at the kerb, Quentin got in, and the cabbie drove like a madman, swearing at other drivers, 'Go backta Joisy, yamoron!' as the urban canyons and bridges of New York flashed before Quentin's eyes on his way to Idlewild airport.

Quentin had never before flown. He followed the instructions of smiling young Pan Am women offering choices and directions in vaguely colonial accents. The entire flight his eyes were wide with fear, and he gripped the armrest, deafened by the roar. He took his glasses off, too terrified to look out the tiny window. The plane touched down and he was about to bolt, only to be told they were refuelling. More lay ahead. Finally the plane's wheels skidded on the tarmac while the dulcet voice of the stewardess welcomed him to Los Angeles.

Quentin rose unsteadily to his feet, retrieved his hat and stepped out into the aisle with his Burberry over his arm. His heavy leather case in hand, he obediently followed the man in front of him towards a wheeled stairwell they had rolled up to the door. The air that blew in was a strange brew of fog and salt water, petrol fumes, and something else that eluded definition. The light blinded him as he followed his fellow passengers down the stairwell and across a swathe of twinkling asphalt that glittered under the merciless sunshine which touched his cheek with a caress that felt at once seductive and dismissive. He came into a terminal where squawking public address systems blathered in raspy American tones. He eventually collected his two heavy bags. Everyone in the crowd wore dark glasses, and milled about, greeting one another, noisy reunions conducted in voices that were extraordinarily loud and harsh. The women looked especially strange. Few wore hats and gloves; many wore trousers. Quentin wished he hadn't worn his winter underwear and a vest with his second-best suit. He wished he could rid himself of the totally unnecessary Burberry hanging on his arm, and that he didn't have four heavy manuscripts in his leather case and a suitcase. Perspiration beaded his forehead. His mouth was dry.

Crowds thinned, and people moved through broad double doors and into the sunlight. Quentin followed like a lemming. Across the way, lining the sidewalk, flowers, bright, fresh, yellow flowers, bloomed in profusion on short woody shrubs. The sunshine spilled down, and though it was cool in the shade, the brilliant light hurt his eyes. He understood the ubiquitous sunglasses. He stood there under an awning, unmoving as a figurehead on a ship. He had no idea what to do.

'I'll just bet you're Mr Castle,' said a voice behind him, a girl's voice.

He turned to her. 'I am.'

'Well, amen for that! You're the fourth guy I've said that to, and they all looked at me like I was crazy,' she said in between snaps of her chewing gum. 'See, no one had a picture of you, and they just told me, oh, he'll look British. Fine and dandy, but what does that mean?'

'I don't know,' he confessed. She was like no one Quentin had ever seen up close, much less spoken to. She had auburn hair, unbecomingly short. She was petite, and wore loose, cream-coloured trousers, belted at the waist, and a short-sleeved blouse with a garish print of tropical leaves in a colour Quentin could not name. Her face and arms were the colour of warm sand. Her toes, sticking out of high-heeled espadrilles, glowed in a bright shell pink. She wore no hat, no gloves, carried no handbag. She took off her sunglasses and rested them atop her head; she had bright brown eyes. He asked, 'And you are…?'

'I'm your ride. Roy bought me the MGT on the condition that I'd be your chauffeur and all-around dogsbody while you're here.'

'I meant your name.'

'Oh, sorry. I'm Georgina Fischer, that's with a "C", but you can call me Gigi. Everyone does. Come on. You got all your stuff? Are you ready? Oh, sorry again, I should have said right away I'm sorry for your loss. That's what people always say. Frank Carson was your friend.'

The fiction was easier than the truth. Quentin said yes, thank you.

She snatched one of his suitcases and started walking with the springy tread of the natural athlete. 'Let's go! The car is swell!'

The car was indeed swell, a sporty MG, racing green, top down. 'This is the post-war model. Just like me,' she added with a wink. He couldn't imagine why she would wink at him. She caressed the fender of the MG. 'They only made ten thousand of these little gems altogether.' She put one suitcase in the boot and tied the other to the luggage rack.

He got in the passenger's side, astonished that they would be driving with the top down in February. He had to remind himself it was February. He felt as though he had travelled a great distance not merely in miles but in time, as though hurled into the future, a distant summer for a time-torn man.

'You'll notice the steering wheel's on the wrong side.'

She opened her own door. 'Roy thought that would make you feel more at home, but believe me, I had to learn how to drive like this. Not easy! Do you have a car?'

'Afraid not,' he replied, emphasis on the afraid as she fearlessly pulled out into traffic. 'I don't know how to drive.'

'Well, I do! Take off your hat. Unless you want to lose it. I cut my hair to go with the car. With short hair, I can drive fast and it doesn't matter. I just love this car! I fell in love with the MG when I went to London with Roy and Doris last spring. We were there for two weeks. What a dismal place. Pinched. You know? Everything just seemed pinched and nasty. And all that destruction everywhere. Everywhere you look, almost everywhere, there's a bunch of rubble and destruction, houses cut in half like mouldering slices of cake.'

Quentin's jaw tightened on behalf of his native land, and unwillingly Sir Walter Scott's poem rattled through his aching head: *Breathes there a man with soul so dead* … Finally he said, 'They dropped a hundred thousand pounds of bombs on us in one night, the Sunday after Christmas, 1941. Bound to be a lot of destruction, don't you think?' He was instantly sorry he had spoken. It seemed to make her drive more recklessly. She made a blind pass that nearly drove the car up on the sidewalk. Enormous American cars with thick, high fenders lumbered on every side of the little MG until Gigi tooted the horn, pulled out and passed them. She clearly loved to use the horn. She was very young, Quentin thought, or perhaps she just seemed so, so energetic, so unencumbered with any kind of … what? The word hovered somewhere beyond the reach of his numb, unwilling brain.

'The English people were fine,' she said, ignoring his comment about the bombs. 'Roy was working, of course, meeting after meeting – that's where he met Frank and convinced him to come to California. And there were all kinds of people who wanted to show me and Doris, that's my mother, around and invite us to tea. Tea! I never drank so much tea in all my life. I was constantly having to say, "'Scuse me, I have to pee," and people were just going pale. What am I supposed to say, baby? All that tea? It goes through you just like a sieve. It does me anyway. Pee. Pee. Pee.'

Quentin, unaccustomed to discussing bodily functions with young women he had just met, with women at all, could only nod.

'Doris was happy as a clam in Harrods, but me? I fell in love. Twice.'

'Twice. In two weeks?'

'First there was this lord or earl, something like that. He had a nice title, the Something of Something. Everyone, and I do mean everyone, called him sir. I called him Eddie. Roy thought he had lots of moolah. He didn't, but he was certainly agog for the picture business. Really, positively agog. Isn't that a great word? Eddie taught it to me. Eddie introduced me to the MG.' She patted the steering wheel and flashed him a winning grin. 'He let me drive it. I was smitten!'

'More with the car than with Eddie.'

'Well, you don't see Eddie here, do you? Eddie had a lot of titled flash, but not a lot of cash. He was looking to marry a rich American girl. I'm not looking to get married at all. I'm working now, baby. You are my first job.'

'I am?'

'Roy said to me, "Gigi, I have a job for you." I said, "Great, baby! When do I start?" I thought I'd at least be a script girl, or something, but no. He said a Brit is coming to visit, on important business, and how would I like to take care of him, to see to his needs? I told Roy, "Sure. It wasn't the job I'd hoped for, but I'll do it. I need to be paid, though." And Roy said, "Gigi, go out front and have a look in the driveway." And there it was. This car. He knows me all too well.'

'The car is your wages?'

'Yes! And you are my job. So I hope you'll want to go lots of places I can drive you. What do you think about Mexico? The Rosarito Beach Hotel. Baja? It's not so very far, and they say they invented the margarita there.'

'I do not know Margarita, and I could not possibly go to Mexico with you. I am not a tourist. I'm here on sad business, Miss Fischer. I am escorting the dead.'

'I already told you I'm sorry for your loss. What else is there to say?'

Quentin considered this. 'Where are you taking me?'

'Well, Roy and Aaron figured you'd be a mess, I mean, tired, so you'd want to rest, or something. You can meet them later. Drinks. Dinner. Right now I'm taking you to the Garden of Allah, a great place, or at least it used to be. Legendary way back when. It's where Frank was staying, and we – that is, Roy and Aaron – figured you're a friend of his, and that's where you'd like to stay. The Brits especially loved it. Very Noël Coward, Charles Laughton, Laurence Olivier, pip pip cheerio, I say, old chap. You know how they talk. I mean that in the nicest way,' she explained. 'Probably that's why Frank asked to stay there. In fact, they've put you in his old place. I mean, after all, the rent's paid for the rest of this month. You don't mind, do you? Do you think it's too creepy because he died there? I mean in the pool, not in the room.'

'So I read.'

She frowned, tooted the horn, and zipped around another car. 'Usually there's just dead mice in the pool, but I'd take bets there hasn't been so much as a ripple in that pool since they found Frank Carson there. Oh, sorry, again. I know he was your friend.' She swung a left;

another motorist honked at her and she raised her fist to him. 'Outta my way, you geezer! I love that about convertibles. You can let everyone know exactly what you think of them.' Her short hair blew light in the stiff wind. 'Can't drive a convertible at Vassar. Not on your life, baby. I don't even care about getting kicked out.'

'Of?'

'Vassar. College. I got kicked out in January.' Quentin's instincts as a listener stood him in good stead as Gigi spun a long complex tale around a not very convolute subject, namely that Vassar was a very high-class snooty college back east, where the eastern girls thought they knew everything, but they were bores in tight girdles, and her roommate – a bore, and a prig as well – had said she was going home to Westchester to see Daddy and Mummy one weekend, but then she came back early, Saturday night to be precise, without telling Gigi – and Gigi was certain it was on purpose because she must have known (everyone did) that Gigi had already had two curfew infractions and was on social probation – and this *slut* walked in on Gigi and her Beau of the Moment (she talked like that, as though certain words were titles, like the Earl of Oxford) when they happened to be in bed in her dorm room which was on the ground floor. She was in a dorm rather than a sorority because she was Jewish. Vassar could put their sororities up their prim tight keesters. Anyway, getting the Beau into her room was no problem, but there wasn't time to get him out, not when they were both of them naked as the day they were born. After this terrible infraction, Vassar kicked her out.

He held on tight to the door. Her driving was not only fast but spine-tingling fearless as they passed oil wells, patient as nodding dinosaurs, and the sports car merged into noisy traffic traversing broad streets lined with white buildings and splashed with stout, feathery palms and blinding sunlight. 'Roy could have bought me back in twice over but he wouldn't do it. He said I screwed up my one chance to be something other than a Hollywood brat. My mother's distraught. That's her favourite word. Distraught.' Gigi held a hand to her forehead, covering her eyes for one terrible moment. 'I'll have to go to UCLA or USC in the fall. I don't want to go to college, but they tell me that I have to.'

Quentin remembered the university women he had known at Oxford, girls from Lady Margaret Hall and St Anne's, all so serious, so intent on their studies, so humourless, competitive and lax with their looks. Gigi too was lax with her looks, but in a different way. No careful coif, no make-up that he could discern, just a tan and ebullient health and high spirits. She wore them like a costume. He said, 'I should think college would be a wonderful opportunity for a girl.'

'I suppose. I might as well go. I'm not doing anything else. Roy and Mother won't let me work. Won't even let me hold the clapper.'

'The clapper?'

'Never mind, Quentin. I can call you that, can't I? I hate being all formal. Call me Gigi.'

'Gigi. Did you know Frank Carson?'

'Oh, sure. But not biblically.' Her laughter was easy and bountiful. 'He was at my parents' house a lot last summer. The last time I saw him was at my parents' Christmas party.'

'Can you tell me about his death?' he asked, wondering about the 'biblically'.

'What's there to tell? He was drunk. He fell in the pool. It was late at night and he drowned. They found him there in the morning.'

'They?'

'The guys who clean out the pool, or the gardeners,

141

someone like that. He'd been at a party Saturday night. I heard he was just his usual self. Pour a few drinks into Frank – easy enough, as I'm sure you know. You're a friend of his – a few drinks, and he's off! Reciting Shakespeare like we're all supposed to stand rapt and speechless, just dazzled because Frank can do Prospero and Ariel and Miranda without taking a breath, and throw in Byron, Yeats and Auden and whoever else pops up into his mind, and off his golden tongue. What light through yonder window breaks? Then he gets all angry and morbid because no one appreciates him, calls us philistines. What did he think! This is Hollywood! They're all actors! They all stand around and spout other people's lines. He was nothing but a writer. And they're a dime a dozen. Sorry. Again. Anyway, I wasn't actually at the party, but I can imagine. I don't get invited to the Vernons' parties.'

'Too young, I suppose.'

'It's not that. They're afraid I'll tell Roy what goes on.'

'Your father?'

'Stepfather, though Doris has been married to him for so long now he might as well be my father. I like Roy. I even respect him. It's nice to have someone to look up to, you know?'

'I do,' he replied, thinking of Robert.

'Roy always says he doesn't care what his people do as long as they don't frighten the make-up girl, though that's a total lie. He cares. Oh yes. And why he should mention the make-up girl is beyond me. I've seen make-up girls who would do it with the cavalry and the Indians, all in the same day. No class, no morals whatever.'

'Was Frank doing it?'

'Not with cavalry or the Indians. Though don't get me wrong, baby,' she added quickly. 'I personally don't care who you go to bed with. I'm very broad-minded, but not everyone is. Just so you know.'

Her meaning clarified slowly in his sleep-deprived brain. 'Are you asking if I am homosexual? In Britain that's a criminal offence.'

'Really? Here it could ruin you, but probably not jail unless they catch you with your pants down on Wilshire. Of course, you could be ruined with Roy for a lot less. You could be ruined with Roy Rosenbaum for adultery or drugs, or orgies, falling down drunk at the Cocoanut Grove, talking to Louella Parsons. Roy's strait-laced. Caesar's wife all over again. He drinks, sure, but you'll never see him get fuzzy. Lose control? Never. And any of that other stuff, the powdery stuff or the weed, or any of that, the weird sex stuff? Not on your life. *Tsk tsk*. He's been married to Doris for twelve years and I bet they still do it in the missionary position. But you – not meaning you – but anyone under contract to Regent in any capacity, you better watch yourself! He hears about anything scandalous, and Roy'll put your tit in the wringer, if you have one – a tit, not a wringer – and if you don't, well, he'll put that—' She pointed to Quentin's penis '—in the wringer too. No joke, and they all know it. Everyone knows there's stuff goes on at the Vernons' parties that would curl your hair. All your hairs, the short and the long. I'm Roy's stepdaughter so I don't get invited. I'll always be an outsider while Roy's in power. And then,' she sighed deeply, dramatically, 'when Roy's not in power, I'll be a nobody.'

'You could be a somebody in your own right, couldn't you?'

Gigi's laughter pealed behind her like a banner. 'You slay me. What could *I* ever do?'

'By the way, I'm not.'

'Not what?'

'Homosexual. Just so you know. I'm a married man.'

The wind blew over them and the February sun pinked his pale, gaunt face. He clung to the side of the car as she drove recklessly along palm-lined Sunset Boulevard, the small, swift MG darting among the massive American autos like a bluebottle fly navigating through a herd of hippos in the zoo.

At last she came to the Garden of Allah. Quentin knew this because of the sign. He sighed with relief as she parked the car. As he stepped from the MG he saw a large central building, white stucco, red tiled roof, fronted with a flagpole, a fountain, tall shrubs and the street flanked by other buildings, also white and roofed with cinnamon-coloured tiles. No muted greys, or the grubby ecru of London, but as though everything had been dusted in the last hour and would be dusted again shortly. The shapes were all rounded: rounded doors, rounded arches, rounded red tiles overlying one another sloping down the roofs. The very shrubs were rounded; pale, fat hydrangeas drooped drily. Only the palms stood tall, feathery at the top, and the grass under his feet seemed brushy, stiff, as though it might exhale rather than collapse under his weight. The greenery was dazzling. The light was golden.

'Come on, I'll take you to Frank's villa.' She reached behind the driver's seat and lifted out a shopping bag, took his one suitcase off the luggage rack and handed it to him.

Carrying his Burberry, his suitcase and the heavy leather case with the four manuscripts, he followed her, struggling to keep up. They walked down uneven flag-stone paths flanked by exotic plants and slender grey trees with tiny hard fists of yellow blooms. Mimosa: the word came to him from a long-ago, pre-war Provence holiday with his parents. Robert had come down from Paris to meet them at the home of who was it? Some author or another.

'Are you listening to me?'

'Yes. Sorry. Carry on.'

She nattered on how no one stayed in the main hotel

at the Garden of Allah. The service was terrible, and the food – she turned to him and made a face, and a retching noise, turned back around and kept walking. However, Schwab's was a five-minute walk, and there was a deli, and a grocery store nearby too; you could do your own cooking if you had a mind to. Gigi personally had given up cooking. Gigi liked to drive, to play tennis, to swim, to dance. She wasn't good at anything else. He followed her past woody hedges that bloomed with red and yellow flowers like velvet stars with tiny black hearts.

'Hibiscus,' she told him, 'and don't eat the oleanders.' She waved towards pink and white flowering shrubs. 'They're poisonous. Here's the pool,' she said, as they came upon a jewel-like expanse, a blue-sculpted gem twinkling in front of a rounded arcade with white pillars and cool, darkened recesses, surrounded by banana trees with elephantine leaves. 'They say it was designed in the shape of the Black Sea,' Gigi offered, 'but I don't know what that means.'

'Is this the pool where ...'

'Yes. Follow me.' The path led between small separate buildings with the windows open, and from some there came the sound of tinkling pianos, or radios, or voices, a few raised, laughter; the screens over the windows were dark and the sounds free-floating. She put her key in the lock of a rounded door and stepped in.

'You say this was Frank Carson's flat?'

'Villa, Quentin! The Garden of Allah has villas!' She put down her shopping bag, and went about opening the windows so the breeze obligingly stirred the long gauzy curtains. 'Just in case Frank's ghost ...'

Quentin could not imagine any self-respecting ghost lingering in this threadbare, dispirited place. It was compact and cool, and shabby. The smell of tired ciga-rettes, like mourning, clung to everything, despite the open windows. The carpet was stained, the colour sun-bleached in patches near the windows, perhaps once burgundy, now faded to a shade of rust. The furniture was dark, heavy wood, mahogany, or oak, and everything had burns around the edges where cigarettes had been left too long. The cushions were a sallow olive colour, also stained; even the *plein air* paintings on the walls were yellowish with old cigarette smoke.

Gigi threw the keys on the desk that fronted the window. On the desk sat a large Royal typewriter, a stack of plain white paper, a brass paperweight holding it down. A pen-and-ink set sat off to the side. 'Sorry there's no television, but Roy never lets any of his writers have a television. Roy likes his writers to write. So they always have a typewriter.'

'Frank couldn't type.' Quentin laid his leather case beside the typewriter.

'Well, who cares?' She stopped in front of a heavy-framed mirror, reached into her pocket and pulled out a tube of lipstick, applied it with a flourish, puckered up.

'I won't miss the television,' he confessed. 'I've only ever seen television once.'

'Really?'

'Yes, at Selwyn and Archer's Christmas party last year at Bernard's home. He had one. We all stood and watched, at least while there was anything to watch. It was rather dull.'

'Good. Tell Roy that. Roy loves to hear people say that television is dull. He's afraid television will kill off the movies.' She took her bag into the kitchen, painted a pale cabbage-green and the walls and counters stained and blotched. She turned on the tap and advised letting it run before he actually drank the water. She opened the fridge, which seemed to Quentin enormous. 'If you run out of ice, just call the bar. They'll send it over. I'll be back around

146

seven and get you for drinks and dinner with Roy and
Aaron and Mother, and the Lotus.'

'The Lotus?'

'Aaron's wife. Roy's daughter from his other marriage.
She's insufferable, but men seem to like her. Be careful.
She bites. You need to be nice to her because she tells old
Aaron what to do. Make no mistake of that. Not Roy. No
one tells Roy what to do.'

'Will you be there?' he asked.

'Nope! After I deliver you, my job is over for the
evening. I have a date with a beautiful, brainless boy.
We're going dancing. Roy's driver will bring you back here
tonight, but after that, whatever else you have to do, or go
while you're here, I'm your driver, baby, your guide, your
all-round Girl Friday. Yours to command.'

'Did Francis, Frank, have a car when he was here?'

'He did, but he wrecked it. Really, totalled it, even
though he walked away. He was drunk, of course, and
driving on the wrong side of the road. So after that, they
just sent one of the fleet for him when he needed to be
somewhere.'

'One of the fleet?'

'Oh, you know, the studio has a fleet of cars.' From the
bag she carried she spilled out a dozen oranges onto the
table. She paused, looked up. 'I wonder why they didn't
send a studio car for you. They're mostly all big Packards,
and the drivers are all silver-haired gents. Roy thinks
silver-haired gents inspire confidence. I think they're
boring as hell. Lucky you, baby, you got me.'

'Lucky you,' he corrected her. 'You got the MG.'

She laughed and put half a dozen beer bottles into the
fridge, which, as though made suddenly happy, burped
and buzzed to life. 'There's a bottle of gin here. I specially
asked the Garden to have a bottle of gin for you. Brits like
gin. I learned that from Eddie.' She took from the fridge a

plate with a sandwich and a scoop of something nubbly. 'A ham sandwich, and potato salad, courtesy Schwab's famous soda fountain.' Her face fell momentarily. 'We were assuming you're not Jewish. You can eat ham, can't you?'

'I'm not Jewish.'

'You're not Jewish and you're not homosexual. How will you get along here in Hollywood?' She batted her eyelashes at him, and laughed. Her mirth bubbled from some unseen opulent well. 'Adios,' she said on her way out.

Quentin walked round the flat, eating the ham sandwich and drinking the beer from the bottle, listening as the sound of a trumpet from the next bungalow free-floated in, scales. Other than the typewriter, and the blank paper beside it, nothing suggested that Francis Carson had lived here for months; no books, no notes, no photographs or letters lying about, only endemic smoke caught forever in the voile curtains. He rested his hand on the typewriter, wincing to remember his lie about Frank falling face forward into the typewriter. Quentin would not lie to Claire again. Not ever if he could help it. He rummaged through the drawers. They were empty save for some stationery emblazoned with *Garden of Allah* at the top. Where were all the letters that Claire had written her husband? Or the letters from Albert at Castle Literary Ltd, for that matter? Where was the cheque book or matchbooks, or receipts, the pencil stubs and postage stamps, the ordinary detritus of any life, especially the life of a writer far from home?

In the bedroom he stripped off his wintry clothes, and hung them in the closet. He noticed a dark suitcase at the back. He opened his own suitcase atop the lumpy bed, and smiled to see Florence's ornate Valentine.

The bathroom was lavish, tiled in bright blues with painted peacocks. He turned on the hot water (there was

148

no meter) and stayed in the tub for what seemed like hours, refilling it happily whenever the water cooled down. Towelling off, he cranked open the bathroom window, and again the unfamiliar air wafted in along with the trumpet player, in full swing now. Quentin shaved, again with as much hot water as he wanted, but he was so exhausted his vision blurred. He half feared going to sleep; perhaps he would wake in London. Perhaps he was truly at Number 11 reading some tremendously compelling novel that had brought this place alive.

He opened his eyes to darkness, and a banging on the door. Electric light flashed overhead and he beheld in his bedroom a girl wearing a strapless, clinging gown of sea-foam green, a lovely light silvery shawl around her shoulders, and long white gloves over brown arms. Now he knew he was dreaming.

'Why aren't you ready?'

'What time is it? I fell asleep.' He raised himself on his elbows.

'Well, you better chop-chop because Roy's a great stickler for on time. You know what they say in the picture business?'

'I'm afraid I don't.'

'Time is money, baby. They say money talks and everything else walks, and if you're not young and beautiful, baby, you better be rich. Get dressed, and let's get going. I have a date, and you have Roy waiting.'

'Does one wear evening clothes here?'

'Who do I look like? Edith Head?' She went to his closet and ruffled through the clothes he had so carefully hung. 'Is this all you've got? This stuffy old tux and that awful morgue suit you were wearing today? Let me tell you the truth, Quentin, you don't want to be meeting Roy and Aaron in any of that.'

'Why not?'

'Because you'll look like the poor old grasshopper in *The Grasshopper and the Ant*, all gaunt and tattered, legs and elbows. Style, Quentin. It matters here.'

'I'll have you know my father and I get our suits from Savile Row.'

She gave him a withering stare.

'You look stunning, by the way.'

Pleased, she offered him a wry smile she had learned from Lauren Bacall in *To Have and Have Not*. She turned back to the closet and her eye fell on the suitcase, which she hauled out and opened. Everything was perfectly packed as for a journey. Shirts pressed, suit jackets of a fine, lightweight material, trousers, socks folded neatly, and a gaudy tie. In the little pockets lining the divider, a straight razor, toothbrush and comb. 'Frank's clothes.'

'Is that all that's there? There ought to be a second suitcase. He always travelled with it, and he would have received a lot of letters and … that sort of thing.'

'Don't ask me. I'm the driver, nothing more.' She shook out one of the shirts. 'Oh, good, this is all cleaned. Frank could get kind of ripe, if you know what I mean.'

'I hope you're not suggesting that I wear Francis Carson's clothes.'

'Just for tonight. We'll go shopping tomorrow and get you something decent.'

'My own clothes are quite decent.'

'Decent here equals dreary, the kiss of death. Please don't make me explain everything. We don't have time.' She pulled out the trousers and a light suit coat. 'Get out of bed and put these on.'

'I don't think my wife would approve of my being in my underwear with a strange woman.'

'I'm no stranger than most women, and your wife isn't here, so get out of bed.'

He got out of bed, but he said, 'I can't wear Francis

Carson's clothes. It's disrespectful, as though I were trying to impersonate him.'

Gigi looked studious. 'Let's see … are you going to tell the world what a genius you are, one of the greats, and shouldn't we all kiss your rosy red ass? Does that sound like you?'

'Don't be daft.'

'Well then, you're not impersonating Frank. Look, I know he was your friend, and he might have been brilliant on the page – I don't know, I never read his books – but in person? He was somewhere just west of awful. I mean, he wasn't even that good-looking, kind of bug-eyed and pale and a little bloated from all that drinking, but the women here fell for him like flies. Like flies!'

'How could he?' said Quentin. 'He has a beautiful wife.'

'Don't be stupid. What's he going to do? Play with Little Mary Five Fingers for months? He must have slept with dozens of women.'

Hollywood tarts. Quentin winced on Claire's behalf.

'And that was before Linda.'

'Linda?'

'Linda St John, the star of *Some of These Days*. She and Frank were hot and heavy, and everyone knew it because after he took up with Linda, he quit propositioning other women. Linda wouldn't stand for it. He was her slave. No joke. She would have cut off his prick, pardon my *Française-touché*, if she caught him looking at another woman. She put Frank in his place. It was actually pretty comic. He was abject with love for her, and she was agog for him.'

'But doesn't she have a husband?'

'Gilbert Vernon. Yes. Doesn't Frank have a wife? What of it?'

'Didn't the husband … Surely he …'

'You don't get it, baby. She's Linda St John! What Linda

wants, Linda gets. Only, really, she's not. She's really Mavis Ryan. All that crap you hear about her, that story of how she was discovered in a ballet studio, it's all a great big glittering lie. The studio created her, Roy, Roy actually created her! But Linda doesn't have a speck of gratitude. Oh no, she thinks she is Regent Films. Linda gets what she wants, even if it means the whole world, including her husband, looks the other way. Besides, Frank certainly wasn't her first. But Linda and Frank forgot … oh, what's the word I want? Decency? I don't know.'

'What are you trying to say? An extramarital affair is itself indecent.'

She gave him a look of consummate pity. 'Don't be silly. But Frank and Linda were so hot for each other, they'd chase her maid out of her dressing room, and lock the door on set, between takes! Of course if Gil was around, they couldn't do that, but what they had going on between them, you could feel it in the air. Like a thunderstorm.'

Quentin's mind returned to Claire. Lightning to his thunder.

Gigi held the shirt up to his back, and the pants from his waist to his ankles. 'You're a lot thinner than Frank, but it'll just have to do, for tonight anyway. Wear the pants low on your hips, and wear your own tie,' she called out as she left the room. 'Frank's was godawful. And hurry up. I'll call the house and let them know we'll be late.'

As he dressed, Quentin's heart was filled with rancour. Frank Carson, you bloody fool, he thought as he slid his legs into Frank's pants and buttoned Frank's shirt, you ought to have begged Claire's forgiveness and come home, and stayed home. The clothes lay loose upon Quentin and he buckled the belt as tightly as he could. The lapels of the jacket were wide, flash unto garish. You stupid, conceited ass, Frank. You fool.

'Hurry the hell up, will you?' Gigi yelled. 'You're late.

Roy won't like it.'

As he followed Gigi outside into the night air, he was accosted by a fleshy, tipsy girl who clapped her arm around his shoulders and said they were all bastards, and he shouldn't take it personally. Gigi told the girl to scram, and she disappeared into the darkness like a perfumed ghost.

CHAPTER TEN

ILL OF THE DEAD

THE MG RACED up a long, palm-lined drive and approached a Moorish monstrosity complete with towers and balconies and bougainvillea clinging to the reddish walls, the gardens lit by floodlamps and fountains contrapuntally splashing. A black man in a crisp white jacket emerged from the house, and stood framed in the enormous doorway.

'I call our house the Moroccan Mausoleum,' said Gigi. 'I hate it, except for the pool and the tennis courts. Some silent film star built it in the twenties, but Roy and Doris moved in here when they got married, and it's been home ever since. I'll pick you up tomorrow at ten.' As he got out of the MG, she added, 'They won't bite, except for the Lotus,' and sped away.

'Mr Rosenbaum expects you in the conservatory,' said the man, taking Quentin's hat.

Quentin followed him dutifully through cool, high-ceilinged halls with finely polished floors and elegant Persian rugs. They came to double doors that opened into a verdant jungle dominated by huge split-leaf philoden-drons, towering ficus, rubber trees and masses of brilliant orchids in pots. Lounges and thickly cushioned chairs were set at companionable angles surrounding a low bamboo table with a drinks cart to the side. So tropical, Quentin thought, Peter Lorre might have lurked behind one of the palm fronds.

A tall, casually dressed man with silver hair rose, took his hand, and introduced himself as Roy Rosenbaum. 'My wife, Doris.' He pointed to an older, thinner, version of Gigi who wore an expression of practised serenity. 'My daughter, Lois, and her husband, Aaron Reichart. We are so sorry for your loss. We were all devastated. What a talent he had. Never have I met anyone with such creative flair. What are you drinking?'

'Gin and tonic,' said Quentin, surprised to have an icy glass instantly thrust into his hand. 'Thank you.'

'We are ready for you,' said Roy with a sad smile. 'We know what you need.'

The two women were languid; they seemed to mirror the orchids that dangled pendulously nearby. They wore sleek clothes in pale orchid colours, and like Gigi they were tanned, though they had none of her careless candour. The men were brisk, their movements economical, as though constantly weighing the outlay of energy or charm or goodwill against some imagined cost only they could tally. Roy Rosenbaum was a good deal older than Doris, perhaps sixty, slim, unstooped, and authoritative. He wore a camel-coloured sport coat, double-breasted, of elegant material, a pale shirt and a fine tie. His gaze was benign.

'I hope you're finding our Gigi amusing,' he said.

'Charming.'

'And her driving?' asked Aaron, a man whose receding hairline and ample torso announced impending middle age.

'Her driving is ... remarkable.'

'You should have never given her that car, Daddy,' said the Lotus, a woman perhaps thirty-five, her face dominated by a brilliant mouth, cherry-red lips and white teeth. 'She's wrecked two cars already. And three speeding tickets last year.'

'Not altogether wrecked,' said Doris on her daughter's behalf.

'The Packard cost more to fix than it was worth.'

'Was it a gruelling journey, Mr Castle?' asked Roy. 'Did you fly?'

'I came on the *Queen Mary* to New York, and flew from there.'

They all agreed that the big airplanes were bad for you, that they took your body and put it down in one place when your mind was still in another. The only truly refined travel was on the great ocean liners. Doris went on at length about the Cunard liner they had sailed on last spring. She waxed eloquent about the amenities until Roy coughed, and put a fresh gin and tonic in Quentin's hand. 'I've always wondered why Arthur Rank or one of those producers didn't do *Some of These Days*. It's such a quintessentially English story.'

Quentin found himself thrashing through the joyless explanation that though he couldn't answer for Arthur Rank, during the war, a story of an ageing music-hall warbler wasn't sufficiently heroic, and after the war, Francis Carson and his work had suffered somewhat of an eclipse due to his having been a conscientious objector.

'Sad, the way people must sometimes pay for the past,' said Doris. 'We're going through that now, here, with the House of Un-American Activities. They call people to Washington, and grill them about their past and—'

'Why shouldn't they pay for the past?' snapped Aaron, lighting up a Chesterfield. 'They did it, didn't they? Whatever it was.'

'But it was so long ago,' Doris maintained. 'Almost twenty years. The world was different then. People got caught up in all sorts of political enthusiasms, and to take people now at the height of their careers and make them pay for youthful indiscretions, it seems so—'

'I'm sure Quentin doesn't want to hear about American politics,' said Roy. The finality in his voice put the topic to rest. He turned to Quentin. 'As his friend, you must be devastated by Frank's death. He was a remarkable talent. A great writer.'

'Perhaps he was a great writer,' said the Lotus with a sniff, 'but he could be very abrasive. He propositioned all the women, and if they didn't go to bed with him, he'd sing dirty songs at parties, and use their names in the lyrics. Really, Daddy, I don't know why you tolerated him, all that bad behaviour. You wouldn't put up with it from anyone else.'

Beneath his tan, Roy flushed slightly. 'He wasn't like everyone else.'

'It's sad,' Doris mused, 'but perhaps his death will spark new interest in his work.'

'Undoubtedly,' Quentin replied. 'My father says Selwyn and Archer will publish a new edition of *Some of These Days* within a week. It was a huge success in '39, the last great book before the war. Elsie Rose, and all that lyricism and emotion, struck a chord of nostalgia even before we needed it. During the war, it was printed on such cheap paper that copies of *Some of These Days* would go from hand to hand until the book itself dissolved, the very pages. People wept for Elsie Rose. They loved her.' He sipped the unusually icy drink. 'English literature lost three great authors in as many weeks: Orwell, McVicar and Carson.'

'Did George Orwell die?' asked Aaron.

'January 21st,' Quentin replied.

'I don't believe I know the name McVicar,' said Roy.

Quentin described the great climber's exploits, books that had filled the British reading public with vicarious adventure. Roy and Aaron agreed such books were unsuited to pictures, too expensive to produce. Orwell's work was too grey and grim, but Carson! All those headlong love affairs! All that opulent sex! Their talk then turned to a string of American pictures, American names, discussed in a jargon that reminded Quentin of a conversation he had once tried to have with a Scotsman while on a walking tour in the Hebrides where they both spoke English, but neither could understand the other. Quentin felt the foreigner in every imaginable way, even foreign to his own skin, or perhaps that was Frank Carson's clothes.

'I'm afraid we're boring Quentin,' said Roy.

'Not at all.'

'When do you leave?' asked Aaron.

'Tuesday I fly to New York. I'm booked for the *Queen Mary* next Wednesday, the weekly return to England.'

They all agreed once again that the great ocean liners were a far more civilized way to travel than the airplane. Doris reiterated how pleasant was their last sailing to England, their first trip since the war, and sadly, they had found England … She sought some elusive description.

'Austere,' said Quentin, hoping he would not again have to hear his country described as pinched and nasty. 'We live in an age of austerity.' The very word seemed to waft over them like the pale smoke from their cigarettes. Quentin added that they had won the war – he included their American allies, naturally – but in England, memory lingered amid the losses and the ruins. His having evoked this unhappy past lay uneasily upon people whose faces were resolutely towards the sunlit future.

The white-jacketed black man arrived and announced dinner was ready. Doris rose in a rustle of chiffon and took Quentin's arm. She led him to the dining room, chatting all the while about Harrods, and the hotels and the country houses where they had stayed last spring, the titled people they had met, none of whom Quentin knew, not even the names.

Fatigue, disorientation, two drinks on an empty stomach, his wine glass constantly refilled, the unfamiliar food (a salad served first followed by a thick steak still eerily red in the middle and mounds of golden butter melting on the potatoes), unfamiliar voices, unfamiliar topics of conversation all heightened Quentin's sense of being somehow tested and found wanting. He felt he was failing to grasp some essential underthread of the conversation, not simply what was being said, but what was being implied, or elided. His understanding rose and ebbed. He struggled to assess his hosts. Roy seemed much as Gigi had painted him, a man who held his power reined in, never parting with more than was necessary, who remained astute, alert, even when practising being at ease. Quentin's sense of Aaron was not as flattering, but for reasons he couldn't altogether identify. The Lotus with her bright red mouth did seem to bite and carp. Doris seemed bland, but scattered, a woman accustomed to being ignored. Quentin chewed reflectively on what seemed to him nearly raw meat, thinking of T. S. Eliot and do I dare to eat a peach?

Roy returned the conversation to Frank Carson and his gifts. Roy had also loved *The Moth and the Star*. *Hay Days*, though a lesser novel, had much to recommend it. Roy was sad Frank wouldn't write any more novels.

'He was writing a novel!' said Quentin, rousing. 'He had almost finished it.'

'I'm quite certain he only worked on our film while he was here,' said Roy. 'Aaron, do you know of anything else?' Aaron shook his head.

'His wife told me about it,' said Quentin. 'He had it with him. Here. I'm sure it's in his other suitcase. Where is it, by the way? The second suitcase.'

'Was there some problem with your luggage?' inquired Doris.

'Francis Carson's second suitcase. He never travelled light. Mrs Carson says he always took a battered old suitcase full of drafts of his work. He was never without it.'

'We had everything in his place cleaned and pressed and packed,' said Aaron.

Quentin hoped they had not noticed he was wearing Frank's clothes. 'And what of his personal effects? His letters? His receipts, bank statements, the post he would have received. Where is all that sort of thing? I will want to return everything to Mrs Carson.'

'The Garden of Allah people would have cleaned up the place after his accident.' Roy turned to Aaron. 'Call there tomorrow, will you, and ask after all this for Quentin?'

'Sure.'

They repeated that they would take care of all the dreary bureaucratic work. It would all go smoothly, though no one quite specified what it was, and Quentin, mindful of his manners, did not wish to seem ignorant or rude, though he did ask what would be the protocol for bringing the remains home to England. Roy assured him they had everything he needed, that he should come to Aaron's office tomorrow after lunch to collect what he needed.

'It seems very odd to me that Francis Carson would drown in a swimming pool,' said Quentin. 'He was a strong swimmer. He used to swim in the English Channel.'

'The coroner's report came in. We have it for you,' said Aaron. 'Accidental death by drowning. He was very drunk when he fell in the pool.'

The Lotus said, 'Everyone treated Frank well, and that's how he repays us?'

160

'Are you referring to his dying?' asked Quentin, certain now that he too disliked the Lotus.

'Francis Carson was a great loss to us, a great personal loss to all of us,' said Roy, sounding like a parson delivering a sermon to sinners.

But the Lotus continued, headlong. 'He was always scribbling on this or that, papers sticking out of his pockets, pencils behind his ear. Don't you remember, Daddy, at the Christmas party he stood by the mantel, writing away, and when I asked him why, he said he was taking notes, and he'd return to England and write a tell-all novel about us.'

'I doubt that,' said Roy. 'He was well treated here.'

'Very well treated,' said Doris.

Roy turned his full attention to Quentin. 'He was at the prime of his artistic life, and his death will be long felt. We loved his book, and he loved our movie.'

'That's true,' said Aaron.

Quentin nodded, by now resigned to the nearly raw steak, and actually, with lots of salt, rather liking it. He was enjoying the never-ending Bordeaux as well. Everyone except Roy drank lavishly, and empty bottles vanished at the hands of invisible servants, and new ones took their place. 'But I keep wondering,' Quentin went on, 'I mean, why did Francis Carson go into the pool? Did he just jump in? Did he fall in?'

'It was an accidental death,' Roy reminded them. 'No matter what sort of tripe and innuendo the press offers up. We, movie people, are always the objects of scandalous speculation. We have to be more circumspect than most. Reputation is everything.'

'Caesar's wife,' offered Doris.

'He was alone,' said Aaron, 'so no one knows the answer to your question, Quentin. There weren't any witnesses.'

'Gigi said he was at a party the night he died,' Quentin

persisted, the wine fuelling his curiosity.

'There was a birthday party for Gilbert Vernon,' said Doris, 'the director. Linda St John is his wife.'

Quentin's breath came in short piercing stabs, as if, like John McVicar, the altitude had robbed him of thought and oxygen. 'The party was at her house? Her husband's house?'

'Frank was very drunk,' said Roy. 'He was often very drunk.'

'More drunk than usual,' said Aaron. 'The party was over and they found him sprawled and asleep in one of the servant's bedrooms.'

'Who found him?' asked Quentin.

'The servants,' said Aaron, 'of course. When they went to bed.'

'Someone drove him back to the Garden,' said Roy drily, 'and left him off.'

'Who? Who drove him?'

'Do you remember who, Aaron?'

'Their chauffeur.'

Roy made a gesture with his hand, and from a doorway hitherto unseen persons emerged, cleared the plates, and laid clean forks for dessert. 'I so wish Frank had gone home to England when he had the chance.'

'The chance?' Quentin gulped from his water glass, thus far untouched. He resolved to clear his mind. To focus.

'After he finished his draft of the script, we told him, thank you, Frank, you've done a great job and we're grateful. We'll have someone have another look at it, and you can go home now.'

The Lotus turned to Quentin. 'It's not like writing a book. Lots of people contribute to a script. It's really a collective work, but he insisted it was his book, and he must be part of the picture.'

162

'Yes,' said Aaron, 'he went around shouting something like, "Play up! Play up the game!" What exactly does that mean, Quentin?'

Quentin (casting about for some explanation that didn't involve hundreds of years of inbred education, classical training, caning, banality, brutality and Flanders Field) was spared this Augean task because the dessert arrived, a beautiful confection of creamy colours.

'Ah, our cook is famous for her almond cheesecake,' said Roy. 'Do you like cheesecake?'

'I hardly know.' He did like the cheesecake. It was even better with the liqueurs that magically appeared, each in small crystal glasses.

'His death has upset everything,' said Doris, her voice moist with the cocktails, the wine, and now the liqueurs. 'It's all so unseemly, and everyone here was so distraught, so unnerved, they had to shut down production. Linda left town. She was so devastated, she couldn't even—'

'Yes,' Aaron snapped, 'and because of that we've got a lot of people standing around collecting paycheques for doing nothing while the star and the director nurse their wounds.'

'Why can't you just give people a chance to grieve, Aaron?'

'We did, dear,' said Roy. 'Now it's time to go back to work. Tomorrow. Cameras roll again tomorrow.' He dabbed his lips with his napkin. 'Everybody back on their heads.'

At this all tension evaporated, as Roy laughed heartily, as Aaron chortled and the two women giggled irrepressibly, and good spirits seemingly totally restored. Quentin, bewildered, couldn't see anything funny. He applied himself to the almond cheesecake, and Roy said that Gigi would be his personal driver and guide, and he should feel free to ask her for anything.

'Anything within reason,' said Doris.

Roy put a stopper in each of the liqueur bottles. He said again how sorry they were for Quentin's loss, and literature's loss. Their collective level gaze rested upon him, and Quentin did not need the refined social sense of a peer of the realm to know the evening was at an end.

The car that took him back to the Garden of Allah reminded Quentin of a yacht. He hadn't much experience of yachts, but one of his father's titled authors had taken them on a cruise off the Isle of Wight once when he was just a boy. The Rosenbaums' car was vast, huge like a yacht, the purr of the motor like a yacht, and by the time he got out, Quentin thought he might be a trifle seasick.

Certainly he was disoriented and he could not remember the path to his own villa. He wandered the Garden of Allah, occasionally accosted by some roistering drunk or another, asking directions or offering inebriate wisdom. He brushed them off. The night air had a light chill, not seriously cold, as if the weather were merely decorative, though women in fur coats walked past him, and men wore scarves. Like actors, Quentin thought, like actors playing Chekhov on stage, pretending to be Russians bundled against imaginary snows. Around him, from the open windows, there came the sounds of music, domestic quarrelling, social gatherings, tinny applause probably from a radio or television, and the unmistakable high-pitched squeals of a couple in sexual throes. Probably not connubial throes, Quentin thought, pausing briefly to listen. He could not imagine Florence and himself making such unguarded sounds.

His wandering brought him to the swimming pool where underwater lights twinkled in the depths. He stopped and watched, momentarily mesmerized. Had Francis Carson been drunkenly enchanted by these rippling lights, somehow mistaking this pool for the beach at Broadstairs, and thrown himself in? Had he thought, oh, nothing like a little dip to sober one up? Or had he simply stumbled, fallen in, drunk as he was? Too drunk to swim to the shallow end? To swim to one edge or another? Would Frank have cried out, and was there no one to hear? Quentin thought of Rupert Brooke and wondered if the Garden of Allah qualified as some corner of a foreign field that would be forever England. The lights in the pool went out and the water went dark.

CHAPTER ELEVEN

GUTTING THE FISH

GIGI COLLECTED HIM at ten as promised, knocking lightly, letting herself in without waiting for him to open the door. 'Ta-ta! It's me,' she called, as he came out of the bedroom rubbing his fresh-shaven jaw. She wore a dress of bright-red flowers on a white background with a tightly cinched waist, a full skirt, long sleeves. Her legs were bare, her feet thrust into high-heeled sandals. She was peeling driving gloves from her hands. 'Why are you still in those awful clothes? Frank's fit you fine. Well, not fine, but all right.'

'I am not wearing his clothes, and there's an end to it, Gigi.'

'Look, I'm one of the few people who actually tells the truth, and the truth is, I personally cannot be seen driving around town in my smart little British sports car with you looking like a funeral director.'

He righted his tie in the mirror. 'I am here on account of a death.'

'So?'

'I am British. I could go along with your car.'

'Nice try.'

'I am who I am, Gigi. Can't you understand that?'

'No, I can't. I like people who are what they want to be. By the way, we have the whole day today. Aaron called, and said there was some kind of snafu, and I should bring you by tomorrow morning.'

'A what?'

'Snafu. Situation normal, all fucked up. Oh, don't look so shocked. He'll have everything you need tomorrow. We'll go then.'

'What do I need? What exactly is going to happen? Will I need forms to collect Frank's body? Will I—'

'Look, talk about the dead with Aaron tomorrow. We can do something fun today. Go somewhere. Let's walk to Schwab's for breakfast. I'm famished. You?'

The dappled sunlight, the effulgent green, the slashes and splashes of colour all seemed foreign, as foreign as expressions like 'all fucked up', or everyone referred to as baby, or Gigi's breezy dismissals of anything that displeased her. But then, he thought, in the last three weeks, three women – Claire, Louisa and Gigi – had all left him shocked and amused, provoked and pleased. He was equally shocked when they came to Schwab's.

'But this says pharmacy,' he protested. 'Isn't that like a chemist?'

'There's a lunch counter. Grand Central, baby. Everyone comes here because everyone else is here. It's crawling with people.'

Crawling was the correct description, he thought, as they walked into a smoke-laden haze, loud voices, phones ringing in the booths, people jumping up, jostling. Gigi swept in as though she expected to be the centre of attention, and indeed all sorts of people came up to her while they waited for seats, everyone making small talk, offering comments, inquiries that somehow seemed to involve or invoke Roy Rosenbaum. These people, most of them

167

young, regarded Quentin with undisguised curiosity. On hearing that he was Frank Carson's literary agent, come from London to escort the body, conversations were cut short. In this animated place, no one discussed the dead.

Two stools at the counter opened up, and Gigi dashed and held them both. 'Let me do the ordering,' she said, snatching the greasy menu from Quentin's hand. 'I'm happy to say there's none of those nasty little fish the English eat for breakfast. They stay on your breath all day long!'

'They do?'

'Take my word for it. Remember Lord Eddie? His breath was positively putrid with those little fish.' Gigi ordered them two coffees, eggs, over easy, bacon, hash-browns, and a new bottle of ketchup. She doused the eggs and potatoes on her plate with ketchup. She chatted all through breakfast about her date last night, dancing at the Cocoanut Grove with Walter, tanned and handsome, but otherwise dull. 'But what do I care? He's good at tennis and dancing, and that's why I date him. However, I don't sleep with him. I'm not sleeping with anyone at the moment. Interested?'

'I am a married man.'

Gigi burst out laughing. 'You are so ka-razy-serious! Want a chocolate soda for dessert?' Quentin, bravely trying ketchup on his eggs, said he wasn't sure what a chocolate soda was, and breakfast did not have dessert. Gigi was undeterred. When it came, he sipped it and gave himself up to the pleasures of her voice and her stories, to ogling the noisy throngs and enjoying the eccentric energy all around him.

'Hello, Brat,' said a young man, tapping Gigi's shoulder.

'You know I hate being called Brat.'

'Gigi, then. I hear they're going back to work on *Some of These Days* today.'

'What's it to you, Don? Meet Quentin Castle, Don. Don calls himself a screenwriter, but he's really a first-class hack.'

'I like the first-class part.' Don tipped his hat, and then turned back to Gigi. 'They'll need a rewrite. They might need me. You know, someone who can actually write.'

'Quentin is Frank Carson's literary agent, Don. He's come all the way from England to take Frank's remains back to England. The least you could do is offer your condolences.'

'My condolences.'

'Frank Carson was a real writer. He wrote novels.'

'Yeah, well, from what I've heard, *Some of These Days* is a fucking disaster. Sorry, mister. They're three weeks into shooting, and the script is still a mess. I could fix that. You could put in a good word for me with—'

'Tell it to the marines, Don.' Gigi picked up the tab, nodded to Quentin, slid off the stool, sailed past Don and headed towards the door.

As they meandered back to the Garden of Allah, she told a lively story, strewn with expletives, about Don. 'He'd do anything to get back in Roy's good graces, but he screwed the wrong girl. I refer, of course, to myself.'

'You mean ...'

'Yes, Don was two-timing me, the bastard. Probably three-timing.'

'So you told Roy?'

'Don't be stupid. I simply told Roy I thought the last picture Don worked on was putrid. Writers are a dime a dozen. Roy'll never hire him. Honestly, though, Don's not that bad of a writer. Not great, but better than some. He's finished now.'

'Because of you, what you said to Roy?'

'Yes. Go ahead, say it. I'm a hard-hearted, small-minded bitch.'

'I try not to say such things.' Then lest he seem even

more judgemental, he asked, 'How long did your affair with Don go on?'

'Affair! You make it sound like Rhett and Scarlett. I don't know.' She shrugged. 'A couple of months maybe. It was a long time ago, two years.'

'But you must have been a child!'

'I'm almost twenty-two.'

'You seem younger.'

'How old are you?'

'Almost twenty-five.'

'You seem older.'

'I have a profession. I'm married. You're still looking.'

'For what?'

'A husband?'

'Not on your life.'

'Looking for a career, then. You're a very bright girl.'

'I'm not very bright. And what kind of career could I possibly have? I can't even type, and I haven't any talents, and it doesn't matter anyway. They won't let me work.'

'Maybe you should be a literary agent. You read, don't you?'

'Yes, but I'm easily bored.'

'That might be useful. You're certainly very persuasive. Otherwise I wouldn't have worn Frank Carson's clothes last night.'

'Did that go well?'

'Well, I hardly know. I'm not sure I can judge. They all seemed to be having a sort of joke at my expense. They all laughed at any rate. Something about standing on one's head.'

'Oh, that's nothing, Quentin, and it wasn't at your expense. It's an ancient joke, and Roy thinks it's funny, so everyone else does too. They laugh when Roy laughs.'

'I see.'

'It goes like this. This sinner dies and goes to hell. The

devil meets him there and says, "OK, you have your choice of three rooms in hell, but whatever room you choose, you have to stay there forever and ever, for eternity." So the devil takes him to the first room and there are all these sinners in the fire and there's lots of little devils poking at them with hot irons and there's flames everywhere and lots of screaming. The sinner says to the devil, "Hmmm, that doesn't look too good, show me the next room." So the devil takes him to the next room and there are all these people and they're having hot oil poured over them and they're screaming and, well, you get the picture. The guy says to the devil, "I don't think so. Show me the next room." So the devil takes him to this room where there are all these people and they're standing there, drinking coffee, knee-deep in shit.' Gigi's eyes widened with practised alarm. 'And the guy thinks to himself, well, this isn't too bad, and at least it's better than the other two choices. So he says, "OK, Devil, I'll take this room." He wades on in, and no sooner has a cup of coffee been put in his hand than the devil says, "OK, coffee break's over, everybody back on their heads."' She burst out laughing. 'So it's sort of an everyday saying now. Everyone back on their heads when you have to go to work. Hey!' Her face lit. 'They're starting back to work on *Some of These Days* today! Hey, let's go and watch. If we stay out from underfoot, no one will even notice we're there. Let's go!'

Quentin found her driving less knuckle-gnawing scary than he had yesterday. He wondered if this reflected on Gigi or on himself. 'There was something else they said last night that troubles me. Perhaps you can explain.'

'I'm here to help.'

'Your sister asked Roy why he tolerated Frank's bad behaviour, and he said Frank wasn't like everyone else.'

'The Lotus is not my sister.'

'I beg your pardon.'

'Fine. OK. Just remember that.' She drove a while in silence, which, feeling her rebuke, he did not try to break. After passing a fat-fendered Chrysler, she went on, 'Probably Roy meant that Frank didn't need anyone, not Roy or Aaron or Regent or any of them, to make him a writer. He was already what – who – he wanted to be. There's almost no one in this town who can say that. Everyone here in Hollywood, even the best and most beautiful, inwardly they cower and fret and need to be loved. But Frank was never like that. He was confident in his own talent. He thought his novel was holy writ, and when they started to screw around with his story, he got really mad, like he blew a gasket! And he didn't give a good goddamn who knew it.'

'He had genius,' said Quentin, surprising himself.

'Well, maybe he did, but when you work for Regent Films, you follow Roy's rules, and Frank broke them, and I don't mean his drinking, or the drugs—'

'Drugs!'

'Oh, reefer and a little cocaine, nothing to speak of. No, Frank was already out of control, and then he took up with Linda, and no one could touch him, even Aaron couldn't rein him in. That doesn't happen on one of Roy's pictures.'

'You make Roy sound like God.'

'No, God's not in it for the applause or the power or the money. Roy is. Really, he's more like a master chef. You know, those men who stride through the great kitchens of Europe, making all the decisions, their white clothes absolutely unspotted while all the other people slice and chop and stir and boil and gut the fish and slice the onions, and weep and bleed and dump the garbage, and finally when the beautiful meal goes out into the restaurant, who gets the credit? I mean, does anyone ever say, "My compliments to the poor schmuck who beat the egg whites till his arm fell off, and please, pass my compliments on to the guy nursing a third-degree burn on his right hand."'

'How do you know so much about kitchens?'

'I attended the Cordon Bleu in Paris last summer. Yet one more thing I wasn't any good at.' She leaned on the horn and passed a delivery truck.

Perhaps she had failed at the Cordon Bleu, but Gigi Fischer had many enviable skills which she put into action when the MG pulled up to the broad, impressive gates at Regent Studios. She breezed her way past the guard with little more than a baleful stare and the words *Roy Rosenbaum*. She asked where they were filming *Some of These Days*, and tootled off with a wave of her hand, though the guard called after her to get a pass.

They drove along avenues flanked on either side by vast buildings that reminded Quentin of airplane hangars. Assorted cranes and lights and trucks hauling lumber or whole trees were parked on the sides, and people pushing racks and riding motor scooters and what looked like little milk floats zigzagged among them. The MG got stuck behind a huge truck towing a log cabin on wheels, and the driver of that remained impervious to her shouts, or her laying on the horn. 'If that driver knew Roy is my step-father, he would pull aside, get out of the truck, lie down on the street, and let me drive over him.'

Finally she parked near another airplane hangar blindingly white like everything else. Quentin got out and followed her through a small door. They slid into a vast, dim space, the ceiling barely visible; an eerie gloom rose to heights filled with cranes and catwalks where men aimed lights with the precision of navy gunners sighting hostile shores. On the ground perhaps two dozen people milled round the set, mostly men, along with a wardrobe woman, and a make-up girl.

Gigi warned him to watch his step amid the cords and cables. 'They're not filming anything now. They're just setting up the shot.'

Quentin was puzzled. The scene did not look at all the way he had pictured the dingy, comfy, beery, smoky music hall from *Some of These Days*. Everything was bright. He leaned over to Gigi. 'We must be in the wrong place. This isn't a Brixton music hall from the thirties. This is—'

'San Francisco the night before the 1906 earthquake. See that make-up girl. She's the one I was telling you about. One of them. Morals of a—'

'How can that be? The novel's got nothing to do with San Francisco and the earthquake! *Some of These Days* is the story of an ageing singer in a Brixton music hall, about her life and—'

'OK, so they took a few liberties. It's a movie, baby, not a translation. They had to make a few little changes.'

'But this is a kind of blasphemy! How could Frank have agreed to this?'

'He didn't! I already told you that. When they screwed with his story, he had a shit fit. But I ask you, who is going to give a good goddamn about a bricked music hall or an old whore who's been around the block once too often?'

'But that's what made it tragic *and* beautiful!'

'Well, in a Regent film there is no tragic and beautiful. A little misty moment, fine. But tragedy? No one goes to the pictures to cry their eyes out nowadays. They want to be amused.'

Quentin turned back to the set. The wholesale ransacking of *Some of These Days*, the total corruption of the book that he beheld before him made him burn with indignation, outrage and loyalty, not simply for Francis Carson, but for the novel, any novel. Francis Carson's very bowels must have roiled when he saw what they were doing to his story. Now he understood Claire's remark that Frank had written her that philistines were gutting his book and turning him into the fishwife. Gigi's image of the vast kitchen came to

174

mind, the poor sod gutting the silvery fish. How could Carson bear to watch this? Even sleeping with Linda St John, the star, how could he endure this? 'This is appalling.'

'Miss Fischer,' said a prim-looking woman in severe clothing, clutching a clipboard to her narrow breast, 'you are not supposed to be here.' She spoke in a low tone so that her voice should not echo in the high vaults.

'I'm supposed to be anywhere I want.'

'Mr Vernon won't like it. No visitors are allowed on set.'

'I'm hardly a visitor. I was born on this lot.'

'That is a legend you'd like me to believe. Now, where is your pass?'

'This is Marjorie Deeds, Quentin. Marjorie, this is Quentin Castle. He's—'

'He could be Alan Ladd for all I care. You do not have permission. You'll have to leave. Mr Vernon will insist that you leave.'

'Fine. Let him take it up with Roy.' Gigi turned and winked at Quentin as the woman walked away. 'What a prig. Come with me. We'll have a better view from over there.' She took his hand and led him in an arc around the set itself. Several people regarded her grimly and a few muttered, *Mr Vernon won't like this.* Gigi shrugged, or made rude kissing noises at them. She found a place for Quentin and herself in the shadows, looking at the saloon set from the side.

'Hello, Brat. I heard you got dumped from Vassar. What brings you here?' said a woman's voice coming up behind them.

Gigi jumped. 'You startled me! You know I hate being called that.'

'If that's all you've got to hate, count yourself lucky, ducky.' She was a voluptuous woman, full breasted, her silky robe cinched at her small waist. She wore a fantastic wig in a 1900 pompadour. Her face was a study in fierce contrasts: red mouth, green eyes, heavy black brows, pale white skin. 'Do you have a cigarette?'

'I don't smoke. I play tennis. Remember I beat you last summer.'

The woman turned to Quentin. 'Cigarette?'

'Sorry. I don't smoke.'

'This is Linda St John,' said Gigi.

'Run and get me a cigarette, will you, Gigi?'

'Who was your slave last year?'

'Please, Gigi.' Linda spoke as though bored. 'They're in my dressing room.'

Gigi's eyes narrowed, and Quentin felt sure she would tell Miss St John to kiss off, but she didn't. She went to get the cigarette.

Miss St John looked him up and down dubiously. 'What role are you playing? There are no Brits in this picture, though God knows there was meant to be.'

'I am not in the picture. I am Frank Carson's literary agent.'

Her contemptuous expression altered instantly, and something of interest, possibly even tenderness, took its place. 'You're a lot younger than I thought.'

'Oh, you're thinking of my father. My father, Albert Castle. I'm Quentin Castle, here on behalf of the firm. I've come to escort him home. To take his remains back to England. To his wife, and three children,' he said, adding, to inflict more hurt, 'Frank was a strong swimmer. He used to swim in the English Channel. How could he have drowned in a swimming pool?'

Her full red lips trembled till she pressed them tightly. 'What does it matter? He's gone, isn't he? Gone forever. It's devastating, you know? The loss. I'll never get over it. I'll live, but I'll never get over it, over him. The phone call that morning from Aaron nearly killed me. Frank drowned? Dead in the Garden of Allah pool? And I'm supposed to be all poised and answer all these awful questions? Roy even called. Roy says, "You can do this, Linda, you're an actress." But I'm not acting! There's the police and the press, everywhere, popping their little flashbulbs and trampling on the grass, and acting like they had every right to poke, and pry, and ask all sorts of nasty questions. I had to get out, to get away. We went to Santa Barbara. I'm destroyed.' She carefully ran a fingertip under her eyes to spare her mascara. 'I called Roy yesterday, and begged him for a few more days, just a few more days, but he said time was up. The show must go on. Frank's dead and they want business as usual. Everybody back on their heads. It never stops. Damn them all. What do they want from me? He's dead. Drowned.' Her voice caught.

She raised her green eyes to his face, and beneath the thick, fake lashes, they were full of tears and truth, and anguish, an old ignoble pain. She reminded him of someone. Mrs Rackwell? Mrs Rackwell, the charwoman, with her thin chest, her dirty hands and dusty headrag, her floured bruises and garish red mouth? How can that be? The eyes. The hurt in her eyes, ongoing, without mitigation. Such hurt was unmistakable if one has once recognized it in another. Again, Quentin had the urge to touch her shoulder, to offer some physical, ineffectual palliative. But his instincts would not permit it. He said instead, 'I guess one simply endures.'

'Endures? Like for the rest of my life?'

'I can't say. I don't know. I am unequal to the grief people feel for Francis Carson.' This was certainly the truth. 'Can you help me, Miss St John? I'm looking for Frank's suitcase full of manuscripts. He was never parted from it. No one seems to know anything about it. Do you?'

'Where is that girl with the cigarette?' Linda glanced behind Quentin, and when she turned back to him, Mrs Rackwell's pain was gone from her eyes, and she had total control of herself, confident in her imperial self, her imperial beauty. She moistened her lips with her tongue. 'I have no idea about anything, Mr Castle. No idea at all. I say no lines that are not given to me. I have no emotions that can't be dictated by a director. I have no feelings whatever, and I never shall again.'

Gigi returned with the cigarette and thrust a matchbook at her, and asked in her jaunty, snotty fashion, 'Did you give Frank the kiss-off, Linda, so he just had to jump in the pool and drown his sorrows?'

Linda lit a cigarette, blew out the match, dropped it on the floor. 'You really ought to go back to Vassar, Gigi. Learn something besides how to drive and how to screw. You really are the stupidest girl on two feet.' And with that she walked away.

'Bye, Mavis!' Gigi called out, laughing as Miss St John flipped her an obscene gesture.

Gigi turned to Quentin. 'She's a bitch and Gil's a fraud. They owe everything to Roy.'

The man who strode towards the set could be none other than Gilbert Vernon. Tall, well built, bald, with a hawk-like nose, Gil Vernon barked out instructions. Around him, like flocks of swooping birds, people congregated, collected, moved into their respective places, and assumed their respective duties. Linda St John dropped her robe and someone whisked it off the floor. She was wearing a floozy costume c.1900 that showed off her long legs and full breasts. She handed her cigarette to the make-up girl who powdered her face, and walked into the moment, 1906, and the centre of the scene.

'Let's get out of here,' said Gigi.

Quentin agreed. He turned back to look, however, when he heard a clapper come down with a short snap. 'Earthquake scene!' a voice called out. The lights on set went up.

178

'It's just before dawn,' Gilbert Vernon announced. 'Everyone, look alive, and remember, the earthquake is coming any minute now.'

She drove to the Santa Monica pier, which the women of his family, Margaret, Florence, Rosamund, would have deemed utterly vulgar, but Quentin suspended such judgements and walked in the sunshine beside Gigi, determined to enjoy the rides and booths and cheap games of skill to win tawdry prizes. Gigi won a gaudy bear which she left on a bench. For lunch she suggested the hot dog stand, and afterwards the Ferris wheel. Both were firsts for Quentin.

Was it the Ferris wheel, or the hot dog, or the briny-tar smell of the pier (or perhaps an incipient ulcer) that made him nauseated, cramped and woozy? They left the pier and he sat in the cold sand feeling miserable and sick until finally he chucked the whole thing up. Gigi held his head. The last woman who had held Quentin's head while he vomited was the much-maligned matron at his school. He felt stupid and disgusting, but Gigi said it was nothing. She threw up all the time. She said he needed to walk, and took his arm. They strolled along the shoreline, talking, till the wind and tide rose.

'All right,' he said as he got back in the MG. 'I'll get some new clothes. I can't possibly deal with Aaron Reichart tomorrow wearing a suit that's full of sand.' He could not bring himself to mention he had also thrown up on his trousers.

'Very wise,' said Gigi.

She took him to the May Company on Wilshire, a place she likened to Selfridges, and she personally chose everything, a double-breasted suit, wide lapels, and new shirts, new socks, and a tie that seemed to him absolutely dreadful. The old clothes were boxed up and he wore his new self out of the store, and onto the broad, palmy

Wilshire Boulevard.

'I look like an actor trying to play an American,' he grumbled, as they got back in the MG.

'What's so wrong with that? You look a lot better than you did. I mean, you're no Bob Mitchum, don't get me wrong, but you're a handsome guy.'

For dinner she took him to a place in Chinatown where they knew her by name, Miss Fischer. After his experience with the hot dog, Quentin demurred, but she assured him she wouldn't order squid or hundred–year-old eggs or bird's nest soup. Seeing his face pale, she laughed. She taught him how to use chopsticks, not well, but adequately. He found the experience exotic, and not unpleasant.

Gigi and Quentin opened their fortune cookies in the Garden of Allah bar where they had a drink. Perhaps it was the dim light and the dark panelling, or because this crowd was a good deal older than the people thronging Schwab's, but no one seemed to recognize Gigi. Quentin had never had a fortune cookie, so he was disappointed that his fortune said only *Expect Great Change*. He said that was true for everyone, not him in particular. It wasn't specific enough; what kind of change? Gigi laughed and called him a cynic. Gigi's said *Follow the Undiscovered Path*. Gigi put it in an ashtray and lit it afire. Quentin tucked his in his pocket. She kissed his cheek before she got in the MG. He watched her drive off, and returned to his bungalow, this time avoiding the pool.

Once there he washed out his old socks and hung them up; he hung up his old shirt and coat and brushed the bits of foul stuff from his old trousers, damped them down, and lay them over the shower door. Through the thin walls some neighbour or another played the piano, three or four bars over and over, pausing, playing again, pausing. Enough to drive one mad. In the small sitting room he rolled a piece of Garden of Allah stationery into the Royal.

The Garden of Allah

Thursday 16 February 1950

Dear Florence,

   I missed you all day on Valentine's Day, and I have your lovely card here before me. I have thought of you

All lies. He had not thought of her at all, except when he woke up alone and erect this morning. Her card remained in his suitcase. What could he possibly say to Florence? The sun-splashed California weather and some lovely little botanical bits to share with Rosamund? The lakes of butter, the steaks nearly raw, ketchup on eggs, chocolate ice cream for breakfast, Chinese food which they eat with sticks, and hot dogs? Should he say he had met Linda St John, or that his driver was a petite American beauty who drives like a race driver and walks like a racehorse? Who lives at the centre of her own little universe, a place where she can act like a duchess in an Edwardian novel and swear like a sergeant major? Should he say Gigi considers the English nasty and pinched, and suffering from bad breath?

Loud knocks sounded at his door. Quentin got up to be confronted by a paunchy man with an incredibly beautiful girl clinging to him, her arms round his thickset middle, her head tucked against his armpit. The man asked if he had any ice. The girl was clearly underage. Quentin could not decide if she clung to him from drunken affection or if she could not stand up. Quentin told the man to sod off and closed the door.

He returned to the desk, pulled the paper out of the typewriter, and wadded it. How could he possibly share with Florence the turmoil he felt? His own agitation with regard to Francis Carson's life, his sudden, unseemly death, his butchered-up work. Florence only read Barbara Cartland novels, Georgette Heyer, perhaps, a bit of Agatha Christie, and enjoyed them for their assured endings. She never read novels that plunged the reader into either great joy or great sorrow, and certainly nothing as turbulent and demanding as the work of Francis Carson.

In life Francis Carson meant nothing to Quentin, but in death...? Quentin certainly could not write to his wife that in coming here, he found himself embroiled in the very squalor that Francis Carson created and clearly relished. A free spirit, Claire had called him. And now, Quentin too was one of those cleaning up the shite Francis Carson left behind. And yet Quentin could not shirk nor shake a feeling of responsibility to Francis. Quentin felt keenly that Francis Carson was a fellow Englishman to be protected against the Americans. An author to be protected from the philistines, even a friend to be protected from people who would harm him, who had gutted his work and made a 1906 San Francisco burlesque out of the sufferings, the grandeur of *Some of These Days*, Carson's masterpiece. He was dead and would never write another.

Quentin put another sheet of paper into the Royal.

The Garden of Allah

Thursday 16 February 1950

Dear Claire,
    Everyone I have met here is desolated
by Frank's death. He had many friends and
admirers.

182

All too many. He tore that out and tried again.

The Garden of Allah

Thursday 16 February 1950

```
Dear Claire,
    I hope you are well, and that the
agency is looking after your interests and
seeing to it that money is deposited in
your account, offering support in your
```

Quentin put his aching head down on the Royal. It was like being asked to write *Anna Karenina* on flypaper. He pulled that sheet of paper out of the machine, wadded it as well. Whatever he had to say to Claire, he would say in person. Even in person, how would he tell Claire about the Hollywood tarts? No doubt she had seen the same newspapers that Quentin had read. She would surely have known that women had – what was Gigi's phrase? *They fell like flies.*

And Linda St John … Was she just another adulterous Hollywood tart? The look in her eyes told Quentin she had loved Frank. At least he thought so. He was not a man accustomed to reading women's eyes. Would Linda St John have forsaken her director husband? Was Frank so besotted with the actress that he would abandon a wife and three children? Leave Claire for Linda St John? Preposterous. And yet, Gigi swore that Linda had turned the philandering Frank into her faithful slave.

'Hmmph,' he said aloud, distressed to sound so much like his father. 'Would that have stood the test of time?'

In reply to himself, he went to the fridge and got out the bottle of gin, poured two fingers' worth. But really, be honest, he chided himself, is it even remotely possible that a gorgeous woman like Linda St John, a screen goddess, would actually fall in love with a drunk and disorderly author? Unthinkable. Any more unthinkable – came the nagging voice after the first swill of cool gin – than that Frank Carson should actually fall in love with the woman at the very heart of the evisceration of his novel? The woman who embodied the total corruption of his work? Maybe Frank bedded the lovely Linda for revenge. That was possible. A nice, slow turning of the screw. Literally. *You disembowel my novel in front of my eyes, I screw your wife, your star, in front of the world.* Had Frank loved Linda? Everything Quentin knew of the late, lamented author suggested he loved no one but himself, that he was an omnivorous sponge for the affections of others, that he would soak them up till he was bloated and people who loved him were empty, and still he would demand more, and expect to be loved. And he was. Claire loved him still. Linda loved him still.

Quentin struggled with an ice-cube tray. He understood why Americans used so much ice. It was so damned dry here. From outside his window a noisy argument escalated, two men, a woman coming between them, someone else yelled for them to shut up for Chrissakes.

What had Roy said of the night Frank drowned? The Vernon servants had found Frank asleep in one of their rooms, and he was asked to leave. Why not let him stay? Find another bed for the poor girl whose narrow bed he had taken, and let the drunken author stew in his own aromatic juices till morning. Unless Frank had been in one of the beds – servant's or not – with Linda St John herself.

Quentin paused with the drink to his lips. He could see the whole, like a flickering film in front of his eyes. Gilbert Vernon had come upon Linda and Frank. Gil probably yanked her out of bed, and pushed her against a wall. Maybe Frank tried to intervene. Maybe he did intervene, and maybe they argued all the way down the stairs, Gil yelling at Frank to get out, never darken my door, etc. etc. Maybe the argument extended to the outside, to the pool. Surely a famous director and a famous actress had a swimming pool. Maybe Gil pushed Frank in, or maybe Frank just fell. The two men fought in the pool. But not the Garden of Allah pool. No, Quentin thought, wandering back to the Royal. There was no fight to the death in the Garden of Allah swimming pool. There would have been spectators. Quentin felt certain that any fracas at the Garden of Allah pool, spectators would have emerged from their villas, taken sides, cheered them on, probably selling tickets. Outside Quentin's windows, the argument escalated, and someone threw a bottle and it shattered.

He brushed his teeth, went into the bedroom and got into his pyjamas, turned out the light and lay down. He could not sleep, no doubt because of headache, and still-unsettled digestion, fatigue, foreign peoples and their strange tribal practices. He lay in bed, semi-sleeping, alternately waking from bizarre dreams, only to find himself confronting bizarre thoughts. Had Frank and Linda rolled around in this very bed? No doubt. *They fell like flies.* He was uncomfortable with desire. He got up, made his way to the living room where he sat on the lumpy couch, his head in his hands. Quentin missed home. He missed Florence. What was she doing? He missed his ordinary routine, his office, his father, Miss Marr, Miss Sherrill, Monica. What were they doing? He glanced at his watch. Two in the morning. What was the time difference? Eight hours? It would be tenish, in London. Tenish in Oxfordshire. What was Claire doing? Lines from a Hardy poem came unbidden: *Was it not worth a little hour or more/To add yet this: Once you, a woman, came/To soothe a time-torn man ...* like me, he thought. He focused on his watch, willing his time-torn mind to clear. The call about Frank's death had come to Albert at around four in the morning, London time. Eight at night here. Francis Carson, found on Sunday morning, had been dead for hours and hours. They had waited for hours before calling London. Why? Why would they not have phoned England shortly after the body was found in the pool? What had happened to Francis Carson here in California? What was happening to Quentin Castle?

He returned to the Royal at the table, turned on the light. At last the altercation moved on, and it was quiet. He put some paper in the machine.

The Garden of Allah

Thursday 16 February 1950

Dear Louisa,
A writer such as yourself can put paper in
the machine and write, but I cannot simply
put my thoughts in some sort of free-
form expression, I must write TO someone.
A letter. So I shall write to you, as,
of my acquaintance, you alone, a person
who has felt her life upended more than
once, I should think you might understand
what I am trying to convey, my thoughts,
unsettled as they are, confused and contradictory, in a word,

But that word, and others, eluded him, and he stared at the dusty *plein air* watercolour on the wall: a small child in an orchard of pear trees in blossom, 'Saratoga, 1882' written in deep-blue paint in the corner. His unknown neighbour returned to the piano, and again and again thrashed out the same intricate patterns, chords that continued to resist any happy alignment.

CHAPTER TWELVE

THE EARTHQUAKE SCENE

THE MISS MARR of Aaron Reichart's office was a Mrs Lindstrom, known informally as The Swede. Gigi informed Quentin on the drive to the studio that morning that the Lotus herself had chosen Mrs Lindstrom for the job, and anyone could see why. Yes, he thought when he met her, The Swede, a tall, full-figured, middle-aged woman with a jaw like a coal scuttle, exuded inflexible authority. In a business where one's husband is likely to be surrounded by lovely young women, hungry for notice of any kind, Mrs Lindstrom counted as a marital insurance policy.

Mrs Lindstrom informed them that Mr Reichart was engaged, and they could have a seat. He would be available shortly.

'But he said ten, and here we are,' Gigi protested. 'We are even on time.'

'Nonetheless, you must wait. He won't be long.'

They took two chairs across from The Swede, who returned to her typewriter. Quentin, who had been up most of the night before, bristled with nervous energy on an empty stomach. The confusions he had confessed in his letter to Louisa the night before remained unresolved, but Quentin was determined to act on behalf of his client. If Aaron Reichart wanted to know what *Play up! Play up the game!* meant, he was about to find out. He put his hat on his knee, and looked straight ahead at The Swede.

Gigi, beside him, fidgeted, crossed and uncrossed her knees as she leafed through *Life* magazine. She coughed and sighed and cleared her throat. She was wearing smart grey trousers, the material in a subtle pinstripe, and a matching jacket cinched at the waist, but open enough to reveal a blouse of ruby-red silk. She flecked a bit of imaginary dust from her red high heels. She closed the *Life* with bored finality. Quentin smiled to himself; he knew she was up to something.

'Who's he with?' Gigi asked at last.

'I believe he is on the phone with Mr Vernon.'

'Well, then …' Gigi raced for the door. The Swede was on her feet in an instant, but she could not vault over the desk, and Gigi victoriously led Quentin into Aaron's office. 'Hello!'

'Sir!' cried The Swede, bursting in behind her, but Aaron waved her away.

Gigi pushed a couple of chairs up to the desk, sat down, Quentin beside her. The office was bright beyond belief, utterly uncluttered, furniture low and sleek. Except for Aaron's dark suit, a pen set and chocolate box on the desk, all the reflective surfaces were pale: beige walls hung with pale-wood bookshelves, a sand-coloured couch and low chairs, the television a squat box in a blonde wooden cabinet. The sunlight streaming through the windows further bleached the room.

Aaron hung up the phone, lit up a Chesterfield and glared at Gigi. 'As I recall, you were asked specifically not to take Quentin to the set of *Some of These Days*.'

'Wait! Was I? Oh well, I just never was very good with

rules, baby.' Gigi gave a coy smile. 'By the way, Quentin was appalled – that was your word, wasn't it, Quentin, appalling? – to see the changes you made to *Some of These Days*. I told him, don't be silly. Frank was fine with it, wasn't he?'

'He was,' said Aaron, his broad forehead furrowing.

'It was to be a short, lucrative stay,' declared Quentin, 'but for the last few weeks Mrs Carson has had no money at all. So I'm wondering what became of Frank's accounts.'

'We paid him,' said Aaron. 'What he did with it is his business.'

'What is the name of his bank? Where is his chequebook? Where are his papers?'

'I have no idea about his banking habits or anything else. Regent Films paid him by cheque. Look, Quentin, I'm sorry all this has happened, but there's no need to get pushy. It's simple, sad but simple. Last year Roy read *Some of These Days*, and he was intrigued with it. He talked to Frank Carson last spring when he was in London, and they got along fine. Frank agreed to sell dramatic rights. Your firm got their commission from that. Roy thought it would be prestigious to have the big literary author's name on the screen, you know, like they got Faulkner to write on *To Have and Have Not*. He invited Frank to come out here and write the screenplay. That fee was separate. That's not your business.'

'This is not about our fee. It is about Mrs Carson's money.'

'Well, then.' Aaron shrugged. 'Take it up with her.'

'Who drove him back to the Garden of Allah the night he drowned?' Quentin demanded.

'The chauffeur.'

'And he just left him there?'

'He's a chauffeur, not a nursemaid. He dropped him off at the Garden of Allah and drove away. What else should he have done?'

'Why has no one asked why he went in the pool?'

'There's no one to ask. He was alone.'

'That place never sleeps. Someone must surely have seen him.'

'Read the papers if you want to know the tawdry details,' Aaron snapped. 'I thought we were here to deal with—'

'He was a strong swimmer,' Quentin said stubbornly. 'Are you telling me a man who swam in the English Channel couldn't get to the shallow end of the pool?'

'I am not telling you anything at all. I can't answer for what passes for hopeless drunk in England, but your friend was never sober.'

'After what you did to his story! Who can blame him? The earthquake scene?' inquired Quentin, not bothering to conceal his contempt. 'The earthquake scene was the best part of the novel. I'm so looking forward to seeing it.'

'We never intended to let him write more than one draft. When he read the script we revised, he acted like he was Shakespeare, and we had Romeo and Juliet get married and move to the San Fernando Valley. He swore and blustered, and yes, threatened. He threatened Gil, and he threatened Roy.'

'Can you blame him!' Quentin repeated, trying to conceal the fact that he was trembling. 'You've made Elsie Rose thirty years younger than she is in the book. You've made her glamorous. You've completely upended, destroyed the novel! Your picture is a travesty!'

'Frank was deluded.' Aaron stubbed out his cigarette. 'He was deluded and naive and an egocentric blowhard who thought the artist, the writer, was somehow sacred. Writers here are spawned like litters of kittens. They're everywhere. Just ask Gigi's friend, Don.'

Gigi made a face.

'Everyone will be happy when we've finished with this

goddamned picture. Especially Roy.' Aaron laid his hand on a large manila envelope. 'I have everything for you right here. The death certificate is here, and the coroner's report, all the other paperwork.'

'I have questions.'

'It's all in order here.'

'Why did you wait so long to call my father? It was the middle of the night, almost four in the morning for us. Frank was found in the pool that morning, your morning. You waited almost a whole day, endless hours before you rang us.'

'We were looking for the wife's number. We couldn't find it. We remembered the agency, but that's not a number that a man like Roy Rosenbaum will keep at hand. If you know what I mean. And it was a Sunday,' said Aaron calmly. 'Your offices were closed. We had to find your father's home number. We could have waited till Monday morning, but we didn't. We telephoned as a courtesy. We behaved admirably.'

'What else was happening in those hours?'

'What do you think was happening! All hell was breaking loose! Any whiff of scandal brings the press out like cockroaches, especially to a place like the Garden of Allah. We had to deal with those maggots. And the police. Frank had to be hauled out of the water, taken to the coroner's office. It was a regrettable accident. We did our best, Mr Castle.' Aaron brought his hand down on the envelope. 'You can read the report. He was drunk. He fell in the pool. You've seen him when he's drunk.' Aaron paused. 'Haven't you?'

'My relationship with Francis Carson is not under discussion.'

'You're creating scenarios that don't exist. I thought we business types—' He gave a small insincere laugh '—left that to the writers.'

'Sod off, you supercilious Yank.'

Gigi suppressed a giggle.

Aaron's lips curled. He thrust the manila envelope at Quentin. 'There's one more thing in this envelope. The life insurance policy for ten thousand dollars. Regent Films takes out a policy on all the important people connected with any film. When the film is finished, the policy lapses. Roy took one out on Frank. Why do you look so strange?'

'Life insurance?'

'To protect our investment; if the worst should happen and we have to start all over again, we are indemnified. Regent is always the beneficiary of these policies, naturally. Roy has very generously assigned this policy over to Mrs Carson. His lawyer has made certain everything's in order. Twenty thousand is a lot.'

'Twenty? Thousand?' said Quentin, still stunned. 'American dollars?'

'It doubles if the death is due to an accident. Which Frank's was. See –' Aaron lit up again '– we're decent men here. Twenty thousand is a goddamned fortune.'

'Indeed,' said Quentin, hating his own stupidity.

'Now, please, take Frank and leave.'

'Take him? Where shall I collect the body? Where—'

'Take him.' Aaron pointed to the black velvet chocolate box.

'Where? What are you talking about?'

'His ashes. Frank Carson was cremated.'

'Ashes! Ashes?'

'We thought the box would be easier for you than an urn. Though if you'd prefer the urn—'

'Cremated?' Quentin's throat closed, like the hand of Frank Carson throttling him, like the voice of Frank Carson crying out from the black velvet box. *See what they've done to me! Help me! Help me!*

'We took care of everything, just as we promised.'

With some difficulty Quentin eked out, 'You had him cremated without talking to his wife?'

'She has no telephone.'

'You should have asked us, asked my father, asked … someone!'

'We knew you were coming, of course, and thought this would be easiest for you.'

'But what if … how could you?' Quentin blustered, his breathing erratic, his chest tight. He feared he was having a heart attack. 'By what right, on whose authority did you make that decision?'

'Everything's in order here.'

'You haven't answered my question.'

'Regent Films did everything properly.'

'By cremating a man's body without asking permission? Cremation is … It goes against custom and religion. It's not what we do!'

'We would have buried him here, and paid for everything, but Albert Castle wired Roy, and specifically said Frank's wife wanted no services of any kind here. She wanted him returned to England. We honoured that.'

'But to cremate him without permission! It's unthinkable that you should have done this.'

'But it is done,' said Aaron. 'And I am a busy man.'

'When?' cried Quentin. 'When did you do this?'

'After he died,' said Aaron. 'That's when cremation usually happens.'

Quentin turned to Gigi, who, under her bright tan, had blanched. 'Did you know this?'

'I didn't, Quentin. I didn't have any idea.'

'Why should she know anything?' scoffed Aaron. 'She's a girl. She doesn't make decisions.'

'How could you?' Quentin spluttered. 'I mean that literally! Somebody had to sign, to take responsibility. How could you—'

193

'There are papers in this envelope from the Wilshire Heights Funeral Home which is where we had the body sent after the coroner made his report. Roy signed. I witnessed.'

'You knew this the other night when I came to dinner. You didn't mention it.'

Aaron paused momentarily, then went on in a low, menacing voice. 'What were you thinking? That his body would ride home in state like Abraham Lincoln? He was just another ink-slinger, another dime-a-dozen writer. And, I might add, we have absorbed all the costs.'

'Oh, for Chrissake!' cried Gigi. 'Money, money, money!'

'Will you just shut up, Gigi? I've heard enough out of you to last my whole goddamned life.' Aaron turned his attention back to Quentin, articulating carefully, as though Quentin were not a native speaker of English and might need time to process. 'Frank was an employee of Regent Films, a foreigner, here in this country as our employee, and we made the decision. To be helpful to you. There was nothing out of the ordinary.'

'Really, do you make those choices for all of your dead employees?'

'Check out the paperwork, Quentin. It's all there. It's all correctly done, including the twenty thousand dollars in life insurance that will come to the widow in the next few weeks. Now get on the goddamned plane or the ship, or the back of a broom for all I goddamned care, and go back to goddamned England and take goddamned Frank Carson with you.' He smiled.

'There's more,' said Quentin.

'There isn't. I promise you.'

'There is the matter of Frank's papers, his correspondence, his notebooks. Your father-in-law ordered you find it for me.'

'No one orders me to do anything.'

194

'Except the Lotus,' said Gigi.

Aaron's fleshly jowls went red, and the stubble on his cheeks seemed to grow darker by contrast. 'There was no such box or papers. I called the Garden of Allah and checked. Deal with the maids there if you like, but don't suggest that we are keeping something that doesn't belong to us. We treated Frank well. We treated you well. I am sick of your British arrogance. This is Hollywood, not the fucking Empire where you can order around a lot of coolies. You're finished here. You too.' He wagged a finger at Gigi.

Quentin stood. 'I'm not leaving Los Angeles without the second suitcase.'

'There are no papers, no suitcase, no, nothing like that. Maybe he burned it all. Burned it all and then committed suicide.'

'Bloody unlikely the man who was having an affair with Linda St John would want to kill himself.' Quentin spat each word like a pellet. 'She is Regent Films' biggest star. You would do anything to protect her, to protect your investment. Your reputation. Roy doesn't like scandal, doesn't like bad behaviour, and what was this but the worst possible behaviour? Adultery and murder. I think Gilbert Vernon found Frank in bed with his wife, and killed him!'

Aaron laughed. 'Go sleep it off, you arrogant Brit. Who do you think you're talking to? We are Regent Films!'

'Today is Friday. I leave on Tuesday. I'm coming back here on Monday morning to collect that second suitcase with Frank's manuscripts. I want that, and everything else you cleaned out of his flat. All of it. The letters, the bank statements, the—'

'We're finished here! Get out! Mrs Lindstrom!' he cried, and then turned to Gigi. 'If you try to bring this gawky, underfed bastard back on the lot, I'll see to it Roy takes the car away. I will. I swear. He already knows you went to the set yesterday when he ordered you not to, and he's god-damned mad about that. Now get out of here, both of you, and take these stinking ashes with you.'

'I'm not leaving Los Angeles without the second suit-case. This is not over,' said Quentin, trembling as he rose and left the room.

Gigi reached across the desk and took the black velvet box and the large manila envelope. She suggested certain unnatural acts to Aaron, and followed Quentin out of the office, past the formidable Swede, and into the winter sunshine.

'Quentin!' she called after his back, but he was far ahead of her. 'Quentin, wait!' She ran and caught up with him in the small parking lot before the executive offices. He stood beside the MG, his back to her. 'I had no idea, Quentin. It's so terrible! All I knew is I was supposed to drive you around.'

He turned to face her, his hazel eyes bleak. 'And sleep with me?'

'I haven't slept with you.'

'But that was the plan. Fob me off on the pretty girl and maybe I won't notice how we're all being screwed by Regent Films?'

'I'm sorry, Quentin! They didn't tell me anything, I swear!'

'Of course they didn't, Gigi. Look at yourself. You're young, and beautiful and vibrant and shallow, and com-pletely content to be Roy Rosenbaum's stepdaughter and nothing more.'

'What's wrong with that?'

'You won't always be young and vibrant and beautiful.'

'Are you saying I'll always be shallow? Hey, baby, you're the Brit with fishy breath! I'm the Girl of the Golden West, and don't you forget it!'

196

Quentin opened the door and sat in the car, held his peace, and looked straight ahead.

Gigi stalked to the driver's side, pulled the seat forward and placed the black velvet box and the manila envelope on the floor, but she did not get in. She paced back and forth in front of the MG. She reminded him, oddly, of his father lighting his pipe, how he would bring the match to the bowl, and rest it there, never quite lighting the tobacco, letting the match burn down.

At last she got in the car. 'What'll you do if they don't have the suitcase?'

'They have it.'

'If they don't give it to you.'

Quentin took off his hat, ran a hand through his hair. 'I don't have any damned idea. I don't even know why I said that. It's probably been destroyed. Probably his wife's letters have been destroyed. Everything. They probably went into Frank's place and swept him up and out of there, and destroyed everything.'

'What was in the suitcase that was so important?'

'The future. Work that could be published post-humously.'

'You mean the novel Frank was writing about us, I mean, everyone here? I remember him at the Christmas party, standing by the mantel, writing, whisky in one hand, pen in another, having a gay old time making everyone uncomfortable.'

'Yes. Well, Roy wouldn't like that, would he? A novel about what Frank actually thought of all of you?' Quentin's tone was more acid than he'd intended.

'No. Roy wouldn't like that at all, but he wouldn't do anything dishonest. Not Roy.'

'Aaron?'

Gigi seemed to deflate, to sag against the leather seat. 'Honestly, I don't know.'

'Does Roy have that kind of power, to get things settled, life and death, so it suits him? Don't look at me like that. It happens all the time. Lord thus-and-so wants this or that hushed up and it gets hushed up. I'm not impugning your great American values.'

'Well, thank you for that, at least. I'm so happy to hear it.' She crossed her arms, and sulked. 'Shall I take you back to the Garden?'

'No, God no. That place makes my skin crawl. Answer my question. Does Roy have that kind of power?'

'I don't know. Probably. Maybe. The studios rule, and men like Roy are … They have a lot of power. But I know Roy, and I trust him.'

'I don't. They have made a fool of me.'

Gigi was thoughtful for a while. 'It would have been the same no matter who came for him, Quentin. Or even if no one had come. It doesn't reflect on you, personally.'

'That doesn't help. I have bollocksed this badly.'

She put the key in the ignition. 'Are you hungry?'

'If I eat anything I'll be sick. I feel sick anyway.'

'Where do you want to go?'

'Home. Home to London. But I have days and days left. And the four-day crossing after that …' He raised his glasses up and pinched the bridge of his nose. 'It's really all too much to bear. I've failed. Worse, I've been used, and I know it, and so will everyone else.'

Gigi sighed. 'Me too. Played for a chump. They probably gave me this car and told me to look after you to keep you, I don't know, busy. Maybe I was supposed to go to bed with you. I guess they think I'm irresistible,' she added, but he did not respond. They sat in silence, save for the some nearby twittering birds in the hibiscus bushes. 'Would you like to learn to drive?'

'What?'

'I could teach you.'

Quentin put his glasses back on. 'What in God's name are you talking about?'

'This is a British car, baby. I could teach you to drive, and then when you go home to London you'll know how.'

'Look, Gigi, I can't afford a car. I'm a junior partner in a literary agency, peddling the lowly or troublesome writers my father can't be bothered with.'

'Francis Carson was an important writer. You represent him.'

'I don't. He is my father's client. The truth is, I never even talked to him. I only saw him once.'

'If he wasn't your friend, why did you come?'

'I made a promise to his wife. I said I would act in her stead, in her interest, that I would bring him home. Somehow I thought it would be dignified. And now, what is he? A box of ashes,' he said sourly. 'I don't have the second suitcase. I don't have Claire's letters. I don't even know the name of his bank. And I'm taking him home in what looks like a chocolate box.'

'You have twenty thousand dollars for her.'

'Yes, but for the firm, for our agency? Nothing. No posthumous work. My father will certainly think I have failed, and spent a lot of bloody money into the bargain. Miss Sherrill will never let me forget it.'

'Who is Miss Sherrill?'

'The other partner. She hates me. Who can blame her? Nepotism, you know. Father's firm. I join, and presto! I'm a partner, following in Father's footsteps.' He gave a low, dismal chuckle.

'What's so funny?'

'Oh, there's an old music-hall tune, "Following In Father's Footsteps". About a drunk. There's no other work I could have done, no other profession I could have taken up.'

'What did you want to do?'

199

'Nothing. It's pathetic.' He turned to her candidly. 'I never had a passion for anything at all. I like to read, that's all.'

'We're more alike than you know, Quentin.'

'I suppose we are. I apologize for calling you shallow.'

'No apology necessary. I am shallow.'

'But very pretty.'

She reached over and touched his arm. 'Look, let me teach you how to drive, and at least you'd have that when you go back.'

'You never give up, do you? You're just like an old dog with a slipper. Once you get your teeth into something, you never let go. Look at what I'm wearing. You put me in these clothes!' He held his arms out.

'You look great.' She turned the ignition and pulled the choke. The motor leapt to life; the car hummed. 'And no, I never do give up. Do you want to learn to drive? It's a useful skill. Really.'

'I've never even tried.'

'It's easy. It's like a little dance you do with your feet, clutch, gas, and then your hand on the gearshift, first, second, third. We can't go back to the studio till Monday anyway. Do you want to learn or not? I know just the place to teach you. Plenty of room. No cops.'

'Where?'

'Mexico. Baja. Come on. What have you got to lose?'

Perhaps it was not a serious question, but Quentin took it seriously. Pondered it. Not only there, in that moment, in the dappled sunshine, and on the road going south to Mexico, but later, that weekend, and later still, years later, he would wonder what he had to lose. The answers changed over time, but whatever he lost was certainly worth the cost for what he gained.

PART III

CHAPTER THIRTEEN

RETURN OF THE NATIVE

THE CAB'S HEADLAMPS barely dented the broth of fog and soot and night as the driver inched along, chatting about the weather which, in his 'umble opinion, was getting worse every year. Flattened with fatigue, Quentin could only grunt in reply. At Quentin's home, the cabbie kindly helped him haul the two suitcases to his front step, where the door was locked.

'Worse luck,' said the cabbie cheerfully. 'The old ball-and-chain's locked you out, has she?'

'I suppose she has.' Hardly worth it to explain that he was arriving home five days sooner than anyone expected. None of his family knew he had bought a Pan American ticket in Los Angeles, booked flights all the way to London, a transcontinental to New York and thence transatlantic to London. Riding with Gigi Fischer had made him less afraid of flying, though he had hardly slept in days.

Slivering sleety bits of rain beat down as Quentin rummaged about in his Burberry pockets for his keys. He found his Mexican sunglasses, but not the key. He opened the leather case, knelt and muddled through its contents, finding the key at the bottom. The house he entered was dark, and chill. He left the bags by the door, and dropped his hat on the umbrella stand. Louisa Partridge's words came to him. *The cab left me off in front of the house in Chiswick. My key still fit in the door. I opened it, and Herbert was exactly where I had left him. As if nothing had changed.* He walked, peering into each room, like a guest, or a ghost. Chintz chairs in the sitting room faced each other across a tea table. The wireless stood silent. His own chair sat by the window with the stacks of manuscripts on a table nearby, their pages hanging out, like white tongues lolling. He glanced into the dining room, its sturdy oak table and empty chairs, the purple African violets on one window-sill, the aspidistra in the other. The narrow passage to the kitchen where the smell of Effie's fags still lingered, and the tap dripped with a metronome's precision. Everything was exactly the same. Except for Quentin.

Quentin Castle came home a changed man, though not as changed as Frank Carson, whose ashes were in the black velvet box. With Gigi at the wheel of the MG, they sped through southern California and crossed the border into Tijuana. Beyond Tijuana's galaxy of septic stench and piñata colours, a ribbon of pocked road separated low, dry hills from the pounding surf of the Pacific. She pulled over, got out of the MG, and said it was his turn to drive. Before he took the wheel, he took her in his arms and kissed her. In those three days in Mexico he learned how to drive a car, to feel the wheel beneath his right hand, the throttle of the gearshift in his left as he leaned the MG into curves and swerved around potholes in the Mexican roads, or over the beaches of Baja. He drove to the Jacaranda Café in Ensenada, where lacy purple blossoms fell, to the Rosarita Beach Hotel where he danced with Gigi on the hotel patio to tinny and repetitive Mexican music. They walked from the hotel, barefoot, and stood before the waves crashing into foaming flounces on the smooth sand beach marred by trash, empty beer bottles and used condoms like tiny, spent jellyfish. He tasted for the first time tequila and tortillas and jalapeños, and guacamole made from the weird, soft avocados, limes and cilantro, tastes he had never even imagined. He learned how to make love in a way he had never imagined.

Quentin stripped off his clothes, stepping out of them, leaving them where they fell on the bathroom floor instead of methodically hanging them. He used the toilet and washed his face and hands, brushed his teeth without looking in the mirror. In the bedroom the lamp by Florence's side of the bed was on, and she had fallen asleep reading her Barbara Cartland novel, her head to one side, her breath heavy and soft. The room itself was in total disarray; a nightgown lay in a heap on the floor. Other clothes, stockings, dressing gown, knickers, a slip, a blouse, were strewn about, almost happily, it seemed to Quentin. He had no idea she was so untidy. It was endearing, to think she had a secret side of herself when he was not there. A single lipsticked cigarette butt lay in the ashtray by the bed.

She roused slowly. 'Quentin? Quentin, is that you?'

'Yes, dear.'

'Quentin, you're home so soon! I didn't expect …'

'I know, Florence. I missed you.' He went to the bed and she flung the satiny quilt back, and opened her arms to him, to warm him, to comfort him. He went to her and drank in with gratitude the scent of her, powder and perfume and sweat. Sustenance.

Miss Marr, Miss Sherrill and Monica were nearly as surprised to see him in the office late the next morning as Florence had been the night before. They commented on how different he looked, though words failed them. He was certainly browner or pinker or something. They offered him a cup of tea, and exclamations of alarm.

'You flew from New York to London! Wasn't it terrifying?'

'I tried to think of it as a modern adventure.'

'And was it?' asked Miss Sherrill.

'Yes.' He put his leather case down and took off his Burberry, hung it on the rack with all the others, still damp, their human miasmas mixing in the heat of the nearby radiator. He took the Cunard ticket from his pocket and gave it to Miss Marr. 'Get us a refund, will you, please?'

'I shouldn't think they'd give us a refund just because you changed your mind, Quentin.'

'Miss Marr, I do not doubt that you can do anything you really want to achieve.'

Miss Marr's sallow face flushed, and she patted her hairpins.

'Would you please tell me when my father comes in,' he said, knowing full well that Albert's entrances were always known to the entire office.

'You mean Mr Castle don't know you're back either?' asked Monica.

In fact he did not. What Quentin had to tell his father, as with what he had to tell Claire Carson – the failure of his mission, the failure of this fool's errand – could only be said face to face. This morning he had told Florence nothing of substance. She was content with a bowdlerized version of the goings on at the Garden of Allah, and thrilled to hear of his long chat with Linda St John (that's how he told it, a long, cordial, on-set conversation) and disappointed he hadn't got an autograph. Florence cared nothing for the death of Francis Carson, whose remains she assumed were decently in the capable hands of London undertakers, and not in her own front hall.

'I got in very late last night,' Quentin said to Miss Sherrill, Miss Marr and Monica. 'By the way, has there been any word on Mrs Partridge's new book?'

'They all three came back,' said Miss Marr. 'Chatto and Windus, John Murray, The Bodley Head. They're all on your desk.'

And so they were. All three manuscripts returned. The three declines for Louisa Partridge's *Apricot Olive Lemon* he laid out side by side on the blotter. All stale phrases ... *lovely that Castle had thought of them ... should Mrs Partridge wish to write something along the lines of her classic ... happy to* ... He skimmed through the other letters stacked on his desk. Nothing of interest, save for one letter in a strong, hasty hand.

Harrington Hall nr Woodstock

15 February 1950

Dear Quentin,

The outpouring of grief and sympathy and offers of help when people have learned of Frank's death has left me humbled and anxious, contrite and comforted all in the same moment. I cannot begin to describe, certainly not in the midst of everything obliged of me, how I truly feel. I dash this off to let you know that when you return from California, we won't be at Harrington Hall.

We are just moving into north Oxford, Summertown, Polstead Road. Prof. Ellsworth, a longtime admirer of Frank's work (he used to come out here to talk literature with Frank, to catch the pearls of wisdom as they dropped from Frank's lips; that was Frank's description of their afternoons), has offered to sublet their place on Polstead Road for three years while he will be teaching in America. Very modest terms. I think there is a telephone there, but I don't know. I'll call your office if there is. I'm in such a rush, packing, no, not packing, really just throwing what I want to take into crates and boxes. I'll come back and go through the rest. I've no time to find a new tenant. I don't care, really, I plan to sell Harrington Hall as soon as I can, and you cannot imagine my joy at being out of here and moving into town. The animals, of course, are a problem. The dogs Pooh and Tigger are good farm dogs and someone will take them, and the pigs and chickens and ducks, they'll go, but no one wants the horse. It is good for nothing. We only kept it to amuse the children. I fear I'll have to have it knackered. Cats always fend for themselves. You can't imagine everything, large and small, I have to deal with.

Thank you for bringing Frank home, Quentin. I am so grateful for your seeing to everything.

And I'm grateful to your father too for advancing money. I look forward to seeing you.

Yours in haste,
Claire Carson

PS I have quit smoking. Just quit. I never again want to need something as badly as I wanted a cigarette in those days before you came here.

He read it twice, and then called his mother. Margaret too wanted to know all about Linda St John. She demanded to know what drove him to the foolhardy extreme of a transcontinental *and* a transatlantic flight. Quentin listened to her with forbearance and affection while he again reread Claire's letter. Tomorrow. He would see her tomorrow. North Oxford. He rang off with Margaret, and made a new file for the cabinet, *Claire Carson*, and put the letter in. His happiness at the thought of seeing Claire again was tainted with anxiety, dreading what he had to tell her.

Quentin removed his glasses, massaged the top of his nose, and stared out the window at the well-known view, the roofs and chimney pots softened by the light, ashy snow. He closed his eyes and saw instead Gigi with a yellow hibiscus tucked behind her ear, and another tucked in the cleavage of the off-shoulder blouse she had bought in Ensenada, leaning together over a table shaded by an umbrella thatched of palm fronds. They would go up to their room and make love. The recollection came to him with a splash of lime and jalapeños, margaritas with salt around the rim of the glass, and the scent of something he could not name, not even in the moment. He opened his eyes and glanced at the carriage clock on his desk. Nearly ten. Two in the morning in Los Angeles. Gigi would be asleep. He could not picture her life at all. Perhaps that was the way of all love affairs. They had nothing to do with the rest of one's life. He could only picture her behind the wheel of the MG, on the beach at Rosarita, the sunny streets of Ensenada, the hotel bar, their tousled bed. *Baja*. He liked the softened sound of it, *Baja*. He liked the hard consonant sound of her name, *Gigi*. He had gone to bed with a woman not his wife. He knew he should be stricken with guilt. Going to bed with Gigi was a lapse, put mildly, a sin, put boldly, a breach of faith, a broken vow by any standard, but Quentin felt no special regret, indeed Quentin felt only pleasure at the memory of Gigi. She seemed to him like a vivid character in a novel, like Elsie Rose in *Some of These Days*, an indelible, though unreal memory, a bright experience woven like a brilliant seam across the otherwise neutral fabric of one's life. Gigi was appetite, he told himself, not sustenance.

'Hello, all!' Albert Castle's voice echoed through the office.

'Your son is back,' said Miss Marr, loud enough that her voice would carry. 'He'll be in your office directly.'

Quentin took the leather case with him. He wasn't about to carry Francis Carson's mortal remains through the office.

His father shook Quentin's hand genially. 'Transatlantic flight, eh? Florence called Margaret as soon as you left the house this morning. Hours instead of days. They say speed is the wave of the future, or some such rubbish. Why we should all wish to go faster is beyond me. We paid for the Cunard liner.'

'I'm sure Miss Marr can get a refund.'

Albert grunted, though in dissent or doubt Quentin could not tell. 'I've had a wire from Roy Rosenbaum saying what a pleasure it was to meet you,' Albert went on. 'Oh, and he sent along the name of Carson's California bank, and the account numbers.'

'That's more than they would do for me.' Quentin closed the office door and took a seat in one of the leather chairs by the fireplace He did not wish to face his father across the desk. That chair was quite low, and he always felt like a boy in it. 'I got bloody nothing from them.'

'Well, maybe they thought it would be better just to send; you know, more efficient.'

'More efficient than dealing with Mrs Carson's representative while I was there, in Los Angeles? In the office? More efficient than that, Father? And Roy's lying through his bloody teeth about the pleasure to meet me. It was not a pleasure for anyone. Not for them, and certainly not for me. They are corrupt, the lot of them. Brace yourself for what they've done to *Some of These Days*.'

As Albert listened, his efforts to light the pipe became more agitated. 'San Francisco earthquake, indeed! Beastly! Why would Francis do that to his own book?'

'He didn't! Don't you understand? He wrote the first version of the script, but he was one of many. As soon as he finished his version, they handed it over to another writer who moved it to 1906, and made Elsie Rose thirty years younger than she is in the novel.'

'Carson must have been appalled.'

'I was appalled. I can't even begin to imagine what Frank must have felt.' Having worn his clothes and carried his ashes, Quentin could never again think of him as the distant, formal Carson. 'They wanted him to go back to England after he finished, but he didn't. By then, he was bedding Linda St John.'

'No! The actress! He was bedding her? Linda St John! Really!'

'Regularly. I think her husband killed him.'

At that Albert Castle went to the desk, punched the intercom and told Miss Marr to hold all calls. He went to the door of his office and locked it, leaving the key in the hole. He returned to the chairs before the grate and sat opposite his son, cautioned him to keep his voice low, that Miss Marr had the hearing of a cat. 'Murder? How do you know he was murdered?'

'I don't,' Quentin confessed. 'But I think it might be, certainly, it could be.'

'Have you any proof?'

'No. What was I supposed to do? Badger the police? I'm not Hercule Poirot, Father.' Quentin's shoulders sagged. 'I have no proof at all. None. Just a feeling.'

Albert snorted. 'Well, then, you had better not be offering that little observation round town, had you? That had better stay right within these walls. Isn't it bad enough that he's died, but you would have him murdered by a jealous husband like a third-rate crime novel?'

'Sorry. It was just a thought. He was a strong swimmer. Why would he drown in a pool?'

'Will you just shut up, sir!'

'Yes.'

'Let that be an end to it. And the body? Where is that?'

'Here.' His hands trembling, Quentin opened the brief-case and took out the black velvet box and put it on the marble tea table between them. 'Francis Carson.'

Albert's usually cheery countenance went white as he struggled with the meaning of his son's words and the fact of the box. The only other time Quentin had seen his father express such utter dismay, pale disbelief, even horror, was when they received the telegram with news of Robert's death. 'Francis Carson in there? That is…?' Albert wagged his finger at the box. 'How can that be? What happened?'

As Quentin told his story, Albert simply listened and smoked. His father's silence reproached him painfully. However, he left out the part that when, on Monday morning, he and Gigi had pulled up to the Regent Films entrance booth, they were absolutely denied the right to enter. Moreover the guard said the order had come from Mr Rosenbaum himself: Gigi Fischer was not allowed in. The rebuke angered Quentin, but it stung Gigi, first into shock, then into rage that erupted into invective splattered at Aaron, the Lotus, and included Roy as well. She drove around the block, returned and tried another booth, only to be told the same thing more emphatically. Gigi Fischer was banned from Regent Films. Her native ebullience instantly soured into grimness, and her driving became even more heedless and headlong as she propelled the MG to the Garden of Allah where Quentin had a noisy, pointless quarrel with the incompetent manager. The manager steadfastly maintained his staff had washed the deceased's clothes, and packed them into the only suitcase on the premises. If anyone else had been in Frank's villa, the manager absolutely knew nothing of it. Disgusted, Quentin returned to the villa, threw his own things into his suitcase, snapped it shut, and asked Gigi to take him to the airport. Now. Monday. A day early. Their parting was not hostile, but neither was it sweet. They were no longer lovers. The magic of Mexico, that was gone, fled, dissolved, erased. He got out of the car, and they did not kiss goodbye. That much of the story – that and Mexico itself – he did not tell his father.

Albert puffed out clouds of smoke, as the depth, the scope of Quentin's failures, became more and more apparent. When, clearly, there was no second suitcase, no lucrative posthumous possibilities forthcoming, Albert's mood further darkened. 'This whole trip ... the entire ...' Albert blustered, stammered, 'has been ...'

'A snafu,' said Quentin, 'from beginning to end.'

'A what?'

'Disaster. I did the best I could.'

'Yes, and we can all see how well that worked out!' Albert stared at the black velvet box. 'This certainly changes the question of burial, doesn't it? Lady Sybil Dane has been in and out of here, dealing with Enid, mercifully. Oh, fancy Enid's response when she sees ...' He pointed to the box. 'When she hears ...'

Quentin could all too well imagine Miss Sherrill's stinging response. He stared at the match burns in the carpet.

'Lady Sybil's offered Woodlands, the family mausoleum there, for Francis. The wife, the FMB, has agreed.'

'I find that hard to believe. Mrs Carson detests Lady Sybil.'

'That may be, but she's agreed nonetheless. She ... God! I should never have let you go on such a difficult, delicate matter. You've bollocksed the whole thing! You're inexperienced. I should have ... A situation like this ...' He quickly relit his pipe and puffed the unsaid into smoke circling the room. 'Now I shall have to tell the FMB that her husband ...' Again he wagged his finger at the black box, bereft of any words adequate to the moment.

'To call Mrs Carson the FMB seems ungenerous under the circumstances. We want to keep her as a client.'

'Indeed we do, and won't she be pleased to see that you've made a total cock-up of it.'

Quentin burned with shame. A mere foretaste of what he would feel facing Claire. Yet face her he must. 'Whatever blame there is is mine, and I will accept it. But I shall do it face to face.'

'What! Do you think for one minute I will entrust you with this any further? Are you mad?'

'I should be the one to see Mrs Carson. I acted on her behalf.'

'You will do as I say. Francis has been my client since '37.'

'Do you want to hand her this box with his ashes?'

Albert smoked furiously. 'I see what you mean. Quite right. She's moved to north Oxford.'

'I know. I had a letter from her. I'll go tomorrow.'

'Tell her to make an appointment with me, at her convenience, naturally, and we'll discuss what's to be done with Francis's work.'

'I suppose you will renegotiate with Selwyn and Archer for better terms for new editions of Frank's books, especially if his work continues to sell well.'

'Oh, of course I will try. But I rather doubt interest in his work will last. No offence to Francis.' Albert glanced uneasily at the black velvet box. 'There'll be a spasm of appreciation for his work, a year, perhaps, and then it'll be over. Without new work, he'll be forgotten. That's the way it always happens.'

'Sydney Thaxton is still read and admired.'

'Perhaps,' Albert said with a shrug, 'but he is rather an anomaly, and who knows if that will last. I've been at this trade too long, thirty years, and I personally don't believe there is such a thing as deathless prose, or even great authors – oh, Shakespeare aside, of course. There are authors who make a sort of lovely splash, lots of praise and attention, money, and then the fashion changes – don't think it won't – and it's over. Look at Galsworthy, Michael

Arlen, Compton McKenzie, Hugh Walpole, all wonderful writers in their day, sold like mad, lauded, courted up, adored. Still readable, but no one does. Their books are rotting on second-hand barrows. Who reads Sir Walter Scott any more? All those fine leather-bound collections of the *Waverley* novels? Doorstops in Blackpool lodging houses. Speaking of passé authors, what news of Louisa's book? Is it true you sent it out without asking her for revision?'

'It is.'

'To whom?'

'Chatto and Windus, The Bodley Head and Murray.'

'And?' The word hung between them, dripping irony, and Quentin did not reply. 'Of course! Everyone knows it must be poison if Bernard turned it down. Have you told Louisa?'

'Not yet.'

'I shouldn't think she will much like that. Hmmph. Now, go ring your mother. At least she'll be glad you're home.' He rose and returned to his desk.

'I already talked with her.' Quentin placed the large envelope on the table. 'The death certificate, coroner's report. All that.'

'Fine. Go. Take that—' He pointed to the box '—with you.'

'Don't you want to keep the envelope, read the death certificate, or any of it?'

Albert's broad brow wrinkled with genuine perplexity. 'Take the box of ashes. I can't bear to have them near me. Leave the rest. I will look at it. I suppose I must. Come collect it this afternoon at three.'

'There is some good news for Mrs Carson.'

'Really? To go along with her husband's death and cremation?'

Quentin flushed. 'The studio assigned the life insurance policy to the wife, and she gets double because it was an accident.'

'Life insurance policy?'

'They take out policies on the principals in any film, with the studio as the beneficiary, and they let them lapse when the film is done. The film was not done, and the policy had not lapsed, and Regent Films assigned it to Mrs Carson. She will get twenty thousand American dollars.'

Albert repeated this incredible sum breathlessly, adding, 'To think how I fostered his career! I slaved for that thankless drunk! What would he have been without me? Just another scribbler. A schoolmaster getting his petard hoisted by the local ladies! Everything I gave to him! My time, my insight, my hard work!' He brought his fist down on the desk. 'And she gets twenty thousand American dollars? And we haven't got a sixpence, and not so much as a posthumous scrap to offer.' Albert put the pipe down and fanned the smoke away. 'Please, just leave me to think on all of this. Off with you.'

Quentin took this schoolboy's dismissal without visibly flinching, though inwardly he was more crushed than seething. He had been shown up, proven to be an inexperienced lout, weak, inept, unworthy of the trust he had insisted on assuming, a bungling novice who had been sent to do a professional's job.

He closed the door behind him, and stared across the office expanse. Miss Marr, answering the phone with her crisp voice, held her pencil poised above her notepad. Monica continued to flail away on her typewriter. Enid Sherrill, without so much as a glance at him, greeted a well-known writer of crime novels, a stout lady in a moulting fur coat. Quentin calculated the distance from his father's office to his own door, not in feet, but miles, even years. Could he cross that room and become a man again? Could he ever deserve the partnership? Would it always be a gift unearned?

CHAPTER FOURTEEN

THE INCONVENIENT WIFE

QUENTIN SPENT THE journey to Oxford considering how, quite, he would tell Claire Carson that her husband's ashes were in a black velvet box. He was still wincing from the barely veiled disdain in the eyes of Miss Marr and Miss Sherrill, even Monica, when word had quickly percolated round the office. *Failure, Lout, Incompetent* roiled, unspoken, around the firm.

He stepped off the train into the thick, chill fog that lay swathed over Oxford, and elected to walk to Summertown rather than take a cab, or the bus. Despite the winter weather Oxford seemed cheerful compared to London. No rubble among these stones, people on the street seemed less bent, intent and harried. Pretty girls in twos and threes laughed in passing, and mothers tugged at little children who still regarded passers-by with something like healthy curiosity. He smiled to see the students on bicycles, their black gowns flying out behind them, the ageing dons in their regalia. Were dons ever young? Oxford was resistant to change, and perhaps that was its great secret, one past merely grafted over another, as with geologic strata, change so slow one strata oozed into the next. There were differences, of course, but they were not immediately discernible. Nostalgia enveloped him as he passed by his old college, St John's. His university years seemed part of his own geologic past, as though they had happened to someone else a hundred years ago.

Indeed, a hundred years before, the colleges slowly deemed their dons could marry, and the town changed forever in response. Summertown, north Oxford, prospered, populated with women and children, with new shops to serve these households, with schools to educate these children, and the families of cooks and housemaids and delivery boys who served these solid late-Victorian homes. Moving up the Woodstock Road, north Oxford had a very different air from the monastic confines of the colleges themselves. The streets still retained something of the era of Alice Liddell and Rhoda Broughton, of all the women who, over time, had eroded the ingrown, deeply masculine Oxonian way of life. The streets with their pleasing density of brick homes still exuded a late-Victorian mixture of high spirits and propriety. Quentin imagined families like the Ramsays of Virginia Woolf's *To the Lighthouse* living in them, with all those scampering, rambunctious children. Thick black drainage pipes criss-crossed the fronts, like gnarled veins on aged hands. Many homes had been carved into flats. Occasionally one of these houses had an unkempt appearance, but most testified to comfort and correctness.

When he reached Polstead Road, he was happy to see that Claire's did too. The brick house with its neo-Gothic touches was set back from the street, a small spate of lawn, some border shrubs and a gravelled drive with room for perhaps three cars; one of them was her Humber. His eye was drawn to the top floor where a swathe of windows filled with brilliant red geraniums, pressing up against the glass, contrasted wildly with the nutmeg-brown brick, and the mossy shingles on the roof. The red geraniums clamoured against the windows, streaking them with condensation, making a bright statement against the grey day.

A row of bells stood beside the front door; he rang the one that had a hasty *Carson* taped over it. No answer. He left Frank's suitcase there by the door, though he kept his own leather case, and strolled to the front and waited.

He saw her walking, bundled against the chill, head down, her mind clearly elsewhere. She wore the same long black skirt, an odd, floppy velvet hat and a maroon coat. She was very nearly at the gate before she saw him. A smile wreathed her face. He took her hand in his, pleased to see she still wore his gloves. 'Claire.' He said her name with some pleasure. 'Claire. I'm happy to see you.'

'Oh, Quentin, you're looking so well! So ... I don't know ... different somehow! I'm just back from walking the girls to school. It's just round the corner. Squirrel School, isn't that the silliest name you ever heard? But it's a wonderful school, really charming.' He followed her up the three flights, letting the pleasures of her voice float over him. 'And the girls are going to learn so much, and make friends and be so happy. They're not happy at the moment. They did not want to move. You can imagine, all the freedoms they had out at Harrington, and here, well, the top floor is ours, and that's it. It's a flat after all.'

'They feel constrained,' he offered.

'Yes, and leaving Pooh and Tigger behind, that was traumatic, and I'm afraid they're still angry with me about the horse.'

'The horse?'

'You know, that old grey nag. They loved that horse. The knackers came for it. But what else could I do?' She opened the door and ushered him into a spacious room where boxes and crates were haphazardly stacked on and around the furniture; chaos seemed to reign amid vases of

219

drooping flower arrangements, some of them enormous unto garish. Potted geraniums filled the front windows. 'This place belongs to Avery Ellsworth who teaches at, well, I can't remember now, I get all the Oxford colleges confused. He's gone to America, to Columbia? Columbus? I don't know. He's always so admired Frank's work. He used to come out to Harrington just to talk to him, and then when he heard, he knew we couldn't afford to go on living there, he insisted we move into Oxford and live here, nominal rent. We have the place for three years! It's such a godsend! He considered it a privilege to contribute. He really said that! I know what you're thinking, Quentin: has Claire really forgiven all those toadies fawning over Frank? And the answer is yes! Really, I'm not being a snide cat about it. I mean it. All those people I so despised, they've been so kind to us, and I am grateful. I've had my share of humble pie.'

'Yes,' he said, knowing full well he would be heaping his own plate very soon with that same dish. 'How goes the not smoking?'

'Terrible, but I haven't lapsed. Not yet anyway. When your life's in a total uproar, it's easier to quit; no daily routines, no habits. Take off your coat, and sit down, and put it anywhere. I'll make us a cuppa.' She draped her maroon coat on a hook, the hat too. She wore a thick, knitted sweater the colour of straw, probably one of Frank's, he thought; it was too big for her and she kept pushing up the sleeves. Her hair was pulled away from her face, tied up high on her head, much of it escaping and framing her face. 'Please, put yourself at ease, though I suppose it's difficult with all this mess and upheaval, and all these famous floral tributes. Stale condolences. God, I despise all that stinking convention. And look at them! They're dying, aren't they? More dead and dying everywhere. Who invented such customs?'

'I don't think I know.'

A warm bit of laughter escaped her. 'You are so serious, Quentin. So solid and rooted. You make me feel embarrassed. Of course I should be grateful people thought so well of Frank.'

'I told you that you would not be alone.'

'I'm just not one for gesture. That was Frank's province.' She talked to him from the tiny kitchen – the getting used to living in a small flat after the huge Harrington Hall, Professor Ellsworth having left their ration tickets for her, his wife's passion for the geraniums, and the hope that Claire wouldn't kill them – while Quentin wandered among the boxes and drooping floral tributes. The scent of dying lilies lay heavy on the air. He glanced at the cards (one of which read *With Deepest Sympathies, Albert Castle and Enid Sherrill*) and stepped over children's toys. The chairs were deep and overstuffed, like the laps of Victorian nannies, and a copy of Kipling's *The Elephant's Child* lay, face flattened, on the tea table. A small wireless sat on a shelf beside a phonograph and stacks of records. Apparently Professor Ellsworth liked jazz. The pots of long, leggy geraniums sat on boards placed atop the radiators fronting the window. The flowers looked less dramatic from the inside, even a trifle limp. He stood at the windows and peered through them to the grey fog and the black and leafless branches.

'There,' she said, placing a small tea tray on the table between the chairs. The milk jug, cups, and pot were all chipped, like doughty veterans of old battles. 'I'm ready. I think.'

He sat down across from her. 'I tried to write to you from California, but everything I put on paper sounded trite and stupid. I needed to see you,' he said, tucking two truths into one. 'I think I understand what happened to Frank out there.'

'His dying?'

'No, not that, but how he must have ...' He paused, knowing he was speaking of himself, not Frank. 'Nothing could have prepared him for all that glamour, all that ... bright, hard, unforgiving light. He had no allies. No friends. Nowhere to turn with his ambivalence and confusion. Those people are all so gorgeous and desirable, so patently false.'

'Are you talking about those Hollywood tarts? About Linda St John?' she scoffed. 'His latest Hollywood tart. One might even say his last.' She regarded him defiantly. 'I read the papers. Was she with him when he died?'

'He was alone when he died. He was very drunk. He came back from a party at her house – her husband is the director on *Some of These Days*.'

'A husband never stopped Frank. Look at Sybil Dane. He was bedding her in Sir Sanford's own house.'

'After the party the chauffeur drove him to the Garden of Allah and dropped him off. No one saw him fall in the pool. They found him in the morning.'

'I suppose there was a lot of police and all,' she said bitterly.

'Yes. There's a proper coroner's report. Accidental drowning.' He patted the leather case by his side. 'I have all the papers here. The death certificate.' His failures twisted his innards like a sword dual-edged with trite and stupid. Explaining failure was worse than the failure itself. 'I have it all in my case. There is a life insurance policy too.'

'Frank didn't have life insurance.'

'The studio bought it for him. They do it for all the principals on any film. The studio is the beneficiary in these cases, since it's their loss if the person dies. Roy Rosenbaum, the studio head, had the policy assigned over to you. It's double because it was an accident.'

Her eyes grew wide, and her jaw dropped, and when

she heard the phrase 'twenty thousand American dollars', she put her face in her hands and wept. The thick, gold wedding band gleamed on her hand. His once-atrophied instinct for human empathy did not fail him this time. Quentin moved to sit beside her, to put his hand on her shoulder, but she stood abruptly, kicked a nearby box, and eked out a metallic bit of laughter.

'Oh, that Frank, he dwelt in irony, didn't he? I've lost him, lost everything I loved about him, but I'll have twenty thousand American dollars. How ridiculous is that, Quentin? Don't you want to just fall over laughing?' Her eyes filled with tears as she walked among the chaos, moving towards the curtain of red geraniums where she put her hands over her face and wept.

Quentin followed, handed her his own freshly ironed handkerchief, and waited while she wiped her eyes. He took her hand, and led her back to the chair. 'There's more.'

'More money?'

'No. I think they destroyed the second suitcase, the one with his manuscripts. It was gone.'

'Gone where?'

'I don't know. That's the truth. The suitcase I brought you—' He nodded towards the door '—that has only his clothes.' He did not say he had worn some of these clothes. He wondered briefly if the truth shorn and shaped is still the truth. 'Everyone denied there ever was a second suitcase. I did my best, I even did my worst. I threatened them. It was not enough. I failed you. I'm sorry. I'm sorry,' he said again, hoping to hear her say she forgave him.

'But why? Why would they care about a bunch of papers? Drafts?'

'He told lots of people he was going to write a novel about all of them. He was taking notes. Did you know that?'

'I suppose.'

'Perhaps they just wanted everything scrubbed clean and no trace of him, the scandal. When I came to the Garden of Allah the place was cleaned out, and there was nothing of Frank left. Your letters, letters from my father, everything, gone. The rent was paid for the rest of the month, and I stayed there those few days.'

'You stayed in Frank's place?' Her blue eyes widened. 'Didn't you think that was strange?'

'I did. It seems even stranger on reflection, doesn't it? They said they would take care of everything ...' His throat constricted, and would not clear.

'And tell me who "they" are.'

'The studio. Regent Films. Roy Rosenbaum and his son-in-law, Aaron Reichart. Before I got there, the studio took care of everything. I regret to say ... they did ... I'm sorry to ... they ...'

'Oh, please just get it out, and don't be so bloody English!'

He reached into his leather case and took out the black velvet box and placed it on the low table. 'I'm sorry, Claire.' She stared at it, mouth agape, unable to speak or understand. 'This is how I found him.'

'What?'

'Frank.'

'Frank?'

He nodded meaningfully towards the box.

'That's Frank! That's Frank's...!'

'His ashes.'

'They ... they had him *cremated*? They did that without ...'

'Yes. They did it without asking your permission, or anyone's authority, and all I can tell you is that ...'

She burst into long, gasping sobs. He moved to kneel at her chair with his arms around her, and let her weep against his shoulder, her cheek against his as he murmured

224

her name again and again.

Finally she sat back, and wiped her eyes, not with the handkerchief but with the heel of her hand. 'They are dirty bastards, aren't they?'

'They are.' They both stood. She put her hands on his shoulders; he reached up and held them. She searched his face, and he brushed a lock of tawny hair away from her face. Adulterous cad that he was, he wanted to kiss her lips, to drown in the depths of her blue eyes. Though he did not succumb to these impulses, he blamed – or thanked – Frank Carson for having them at all.

'Excuse me, I need a moment.' She left the room, and he heard a door slam, and her long, prostrate sobs.

Quentin stared at the black velvet box. Claire's tears had totally vitiated that spasm of outrage he had felt in Aaron Reichart's office when he had tried and failed to get justice for Frank. Frank didn't deserve justice anyway. Why should Quentin be here absorbing the sorrow, the anguish that Frank Carson had wrought? Why should Quentin be powerless to make right what Frank had done wrong? Quentin stared at the black velvet box. Damn you, Frank. 'It's your damn fault, you stupid bugger.' It was Frank's fault he had met Claire in the first place, Frank's fault he'd met Gigi, went to bed with Gigi. Frank's own fault too that he didn't regret his sins. He recognized, with a dyspeptic twinge, that he and Frank would be somehow fundamentally forever linked. Friends and nemeses. Fellow sinners. Fellow bloody fools.

He heard the toilet flush and the taps run and thumping, as if boxes were being dropped. He wanted to go to her, but didn't. This was not a failure of empathy, but respect. Twenty minutes passed. He went into the small hall, to the one door that was closed, and knocked. She came to the door. She had washed her face, refreshed her hair, and changed clothes. She wore boots, trousers, and a black sweater that intensified her pallor and her tragic blue eyes.

'If we stay here, I will fall to pieces, and that won't do anyone any good. If we stay here I won't be able to live without a cigarette. Let's walk. We have hours before the children are out of school.' She put on her maroon coat and floppy velvet hat, and took her keys and together they walked down the stairs and towards the river.

Winter's eventual defeat lay hinted at everywhere, tiny shoots of green, snowdrops here and there, crocuses in narrow front gardens, the stubs of early bulbs pushing up, a forsythia branch glowing a tenuous yellow. The trees remained stark. Frail sunshine had burnt off most of the fog, though it still lay in lavish banners across the river Cherwell itself. He was unaccustomed to walking beside such a tall woman with such a firm stride.

'Talk to me, Quentin. Tell me anything that isn't Frank Carson. I need to breathe apart from him, apart from his death. Tell me something about yourself.'

For the second time in less than a week, Quentin Castle opened up his life to a sympathetic woman. Unburdening himself to Gigi required that he be specific; her sunlit past was so totally different from his, she required elaborate explanations. Claire was easier. Though she was some five years older than he, she had lived in the country where he had lived, lived through events that he had lived through. The grey-green river itself offered a watery narrative thread as he told her something of his Oxford years as they walked the paths.

'You speak as if it's all ancient history, Quentin,' she chided him, 'as if you're an old man looking back. Your whole life is in front of you!'

'Not really. I sometimes think I was born old. I'm not like Frank, or you, not one of those people who are or become what they want to be, who take risks, and rue

226

them or not, they're shaped by what they dared to be. I love to read novels about people like that, about all their gnashing and uncertainty, their struggles, like the characters in *The Moth and the Star*, or *Some of These Days*, but I have no especial gifts, no driving passions. From the time I was a schoolboy, I always knew the job I would have, even perhaps the woman I would marry.'

'Tell me about your wife. You and I are such good friends and I don't even know her name.'

'Florence,' he said, pleased that Claire, too, believed they were good friends.

'Is she pretty?'

'Very.'

'How did you meet?'

'I can't remember a time I didn't know her.' He talked at length about Florence, their long affection, their lovely wedding last June.

'We got an invitation to your wedding, but Frank was in California, and I wasn't about to go alone, though I must admit I was tempted to, just to see the people from the office that Frank described – long-nosed nasty Miss Marr, and eagle-eyed Miss Sherrill. Frank did such funny imitations of all of them. He would have me and the children in stitches when he came back from London. He used to do an imitation of your father with his pipe, telling a story about a second-best umbrella, and that old humbug, Thaxton.'

Quentin felt a twinge of bruised loyalty for his father. Albert would not like it that Frank had used him to comic effect. 'Why do you think Thaxton a humbug?'

'Oh, Frank thought he was just a mediocre writer with a streak of luck. Nothing more. Frank judged other writers harshly.'

'Most writers do. From what I know, or what I've heard, it's a friendless profession. The greater your gifts, the fewer your friends.'

227

'That was certainly true of Frank. But I don't want to think about him. Tell me about your gifts.'

'I told you. I have none. Robert had all the gifts.'

By the time they sat down to lunch in a tiny unpopulated fish and chip café in the central market, he had told her all about Robert, his vibrant life, his distant death; he had told her about his mother, Margaret, and the telegram that stayed on the mantel for five years, the blackout curtains still in the windows. The dreary lunch they ordered brought to mind Louisa Partridge, and her insistence that the British diet was killing the Britons. Even Claire knew *The Book of British Housekeeping*, though she dismissed it as total tripe, and hated its berating tone.

'Louisa thinks the same thing,' he explained. 'She's completely repudiated that book. This new book, *Apricot Olive Lemon*, is something entirely different. Entirely new. I was totally confounded by it. I still am.' He floundered about for fifteen minutes trying to describe the book while greasy steam condensed on the café windows. Finally he gave it up, confessing, 'I don't know what to do next. All three publishers returned the book to me. Everyone knows that Selwyn and Archer have made piles of money off her. Why would Bernard decline if the book didn't somehow ...'

'Stink.'

'I suppose,' he said miserably. 'Louisa will blame me if it doesn't sell. She thinks it's a masterpiece. She won't revise.' He picked up a chip with his fingers; the newspaper they were wrapped in was bleary with grease. 'This is the very sort of food the new book rails against.'

'Perhaps you're presenting it in the wrong way.'

'That's obvious.'

'You say it's a cookery book.'

'Not exactly. There are recipes, but it's like being on holiday, and then looking up from the page, and here you are in London again. It's unsettling. She says the book is about appetite, not sustenance.'

Claire mopped her fingers on a paper napkin. 'Well, no doubt the people you sent it to are eating fish and chips just like we are. Maybe you have to translate it into experience for them.'

'What do you mean?'

'Translate the words into experience. Think how long we've lived this way, Quentin, the shortages, the queues, the austerity, the rubble, the sense of loss. Since 1939. Ten years. Maybe to get them to understand her book, you have to offer them not just something to read but something to experience.' In the distance college bells tolled. 'Oh, look at the time!' Claire glanced at her watch. 'We must get back. The girls will be coming home from school. Michael stays all day, but they don't.'

They caught a crowded bus up Banbury Road, and stood clinging to the pole, their hands touching, their shoulders brushing as the bus lurched. They jumped off and walked swiftly up Polstead Road. Assorted school-children and mothers were already moving up the sidewalks.

'Quickly,' said Claire, dashing up the stairs. 'They mustn't see that box!'

Once in the flat, she ran to the table and picked the black velvet box up, and took it down the hall. He heard childish voices and feet clamouring up the stairs. The door burst open and Mary and Catherine tumbled in. Catherine was the stronger, sturdier of the two, with her father's dark hair and eyes but Mary was fair like Claire. They both regarded him suspiciously. They did not say hello.

Claire came out, brushing tears from her face; she took off her own coat and hat and helped them with theirs and scolded them for making so much noise on the stairs. 'You remember Mr Castle, don't you?'

'No,' they said in unison, and ran off.

'I'm sorry, Quentin. They're very rude.'

'I think the word is hoyden, and that's not so very bad.'

'I put the box in my room. On the desk overlooking the back garden.'

'What will you tell them, the children?'

'The truth. I'll have to. What else is there, finally? But not just yet. Not just now. They're all still so angry, dazed, leaving Harrington, losing the pets, the horse. They haven't yet absorbed the loss of Frank. He was gone for such a long time. Oh God, how can I describe cremation to a 7-year-old and a 5-year-old? How can I possibly explain that their father's body is in that box? Frank! So physical, so full of life! Reduced to ashes?' She gulped back tears, and wiped her nose. 'And Michael! How can I tell him? It's worse for Michael. He's older and he understands the finality of death. He's been beastly ever since we moved. He reminds me of my old Granny Dunstan. He's said hateful things to me. He hates Oxford, hates his school, hates everything. And now, to see the box! Imagine, if I am that undone to see Frank in a box, ashes ...'

'Claire, I'm sorry, I should have written, warned you. I—'

'Oh, how could it make any difference?'

The telephone rang, jangled insistently, and Claire answered it. Her back was to him, and her replies were short and succinct. 'Yes, it's true, they cremated him.' A long tract of silence. 'Please, calm down. No, I don't know why ... Yes, I have the box with his ashes.' Silence. 'There is no rush now.' More silence that seemed to Quentin to be interminable. 'Shall we talk later? No. Yes. I understand. No. No marble urn. No. Absolutely not. I'm going to put his ashes in the carpet bag I brought from America, Sybil. There's an end to it. Yes, I'm very clear on that. I don't need time to ... Look, can we discuss this later? I have someone here.' She hung up, turned and faced him. 'Sybil Dane.'

'My father said you'd agreed to have Frank buried at Woodlands. I didn't believe it.'

'Well, it's true.'

'But why, Claire?'

'The schoolmaster's son to lie among the nobles, the landed mighty? It would make Frank happy, the silly sod. Of course these glorious dead aren't Sanford Dane's family. He bought Woodlands off some poor busted-up aristocrat whose family had owned the place for three or four hundred years. That's what Frank thought he was doing buying Harrington Hall. It's all such rot.' She moved among the boxes, picking up toys, righting nothing. 'But it mattered to Frank.'

'But to have him buried there at Woodlands where you were so unhappy? Every time you want to see him, you'll have to return there.'

'See him? There'll be no more seeing him! He's gone. I won't be taking my children to lay flowers on marble head-stones. I'm not the sort of person to be making pilgrimages to graves, laying wreaths. Stone angels, the old family burial ground? I don't give a damn about any of that. I'm an American. Life matters to me. I have my children, and I am going to look after them. If Sybil wants to immolate herself on Frank Carson's grave, let her, to throw herself over the family mausoleum, let her.'

'Is that really why you agreed?'

'It's nothing to me.'

'You sound very bitter, Claire.' He picked up his case to leave. 'You despise her. Don't you?'

'I don't despise anyone any more. I haven't that luxury.'

'With the life insurance money, you could make your own choices.'

'I have made them.'

He put his hat on. 'Anything you need from me, you

231

have but to ask.'

'Thank you, Quentin.'

'I'm sorry I so failed you in California.'

'It wasn't your fault they cremated him. You did what I asked. You brought him home.' But she did not offer him her hand, or say she forgave him, or that she hoped to see him again, and he walked down the stairs and out into the cold February afternoon with a heavy heart, and the conviction that this failure was one he would rue for the rest of his life.

CHAPTER FIFTEEN

AUSTERITY AND DESIRE

THE CHELSEA STREET where Louisa Partridge lived had had its bohemian heyday with the likes of Rossetti, Oscar Wilde and other late-Victorians. Even more raffish repute lay a few years in the future when Mick Jagger, Marianne Faithfull, Keith Richards, Twiggy and their ephemeral entourages descended. But when Quentin Castle found her door, in late February 1950, he was disappointed. He expected to find Louisa Partridge in a space as exotic as her hat, her snake earrings and alligator handbag, but it was modest, very narrow, squeezed in on either side by more imposing homes of bankers, or wealthy businessmen. Unlike their immaculate steps, Louisa's were crowded with pots of herbs, now in sad, frozen states of disrepute, grey, drooping, bitten by the February cold.

'Coming,' she called in her cawing, unlovely voice. 'Ah, Quentin.'

The hall was not broad enough for two people shoulder to shoulder, particularly as the hooks on the wall bulged with an assortment of coats, a brilliant-red poncho, an American army jacket. She enquired how he had come, and when he said the bus, she replied, 'I suppose you're one of those who sit up on the top, aren't you? One of those "He who is tired of London is tired of life" types?'

'I suppose I am.' He did not know what else to say.

She took his Burberry. 'Follow me.' She wore grey woollen trousers and a shirt of some thick weave with a colourful fringe and tassels at the bottom. Her bangles made a noise as they passed a door on the right, and she flung his coat without a thought on the chair in the tiny sitting room filled with strange and jumbled artefacts. 'I knocked out a wall,' she explained. 'When I moved here, the sitting room was large, and the kitchen was small and squalid. And so I thought, why not change things around? Now the kitchen is big, and the sitting room is small. Of course it meant I had to buy the place, I mean, to knock out the wall, and fortunately, I have my own money, and Herbert has his. We have separate lives altogether, though every Christmas we do the whole grisly Yuletide family bit with the children.'

'It's like no other kitchen I've seen,' Quentin confessed, coming into a long room that was at once functional and marvellous: a large, plain pine table in the centre, one end of which was taken up by a typewriter, a ream of paper on one side, a box of carbon paper on the other. The Aga monopolized one wall, and there were two fridges speckled with postcards taped to them, and a board across the top to serve as shelf. From a high brass rack hung copper pans and kettles, sieves and ladles and cooking instruments he could not begin to name. Shining knives and cleavers were on the wall, clinging to a two-inch-wide metal bracket, and the kitchen dresser held an array of mismatched plates.

'Have a seat. What's your poison?'

'What?'

'That's what my Tallahassee colonel always said. It means what do you want to drink.'

'Coffee, please,' said Quentin, afraid to ask for the conventional cuppa in her demanding presence. 'What is that wonderful smell?'

'Onion tart.'

'You needn't feed me, you know.'

'I want to feed you, Quentin. I like to see people eat as long as it's not rubbish. Onions can be had off any barrow in the street, and this tart takes only two eggs, a bit of butter, and a bit of sugar for the caramelizing, and some bacon. It's not out of the question even in London, especially since the bacon ration got raised last month. We'll have coffee after lunch. Wine with. How about a martini?'

'I confess I've never had one. I just do gin and tonic.'

'Civilized people drink martinis. Are you civilized?'

'I like to think so.'

'You've been to California. That ought to make you civilized.' She turned to a bureau that held several bottles and a cocktail shaker. 'You're back rather sooner than I expected.'

'I flew the whole way.' Their talk turned to travel, air versus ship. Why are these conversations so predictable and tedious, he wondered, even with someone as original as Louisa Partridge? Should he wait for her to bring up the subject of the three declines, or just launch into it? After all, when he called her yesterday, he was the one who had insisted on secrecy. He had his reasons for not wanting to meet her in some public place, a restaurant, say, where no doubt she would find the food appalling, and might well make a scene. And the office? Never. If she disparaged his idea, she would not do so quietly. Not Louisa Partridge. No, he had specifically requested to see her on a Saturday in her own home. 'By the way,' he said, 'the figs were shattering.'

'Shattering?' She looked pleased.

'The figs you gave me. They had the same effect on my parents.'

'You shared them with Albert?'

'And my mother. '

'Of course.'

'And my wife.' He didn't know how to say that his wife had made love to him without checking her calendar under the bed. He just said Florence had loved them too.

'And you?'

'They were ... they seemed to shatter some wall or impediment between me and, well, I don't quite know what. I can't describe it. They were an experience I shall not soon forget.'

'I have more!' She brought a small woven basket from a shelf and there in mauve tissue paper were three more black figs. She took one out, placed it on a saucer and sliced it expertly. Its roly-poly body split evenly and fell in two halves. 'Just look at them,' said Louisa fondly. 'I always think of figs as widows.'

'Widows? That seems odd.'

'Young widows. Look at them, clad in black, but inside they teem with possibility, swarm with these pale-pink seeds connected by tiny green threads.'

'I suppose that's true,' he said, unable to keep his thoughts away from a certain widow who, though not clad in black, certainly seemed to Quentin to suggest possibilities he tried not to imagine. 'But it's still very odd.'

'I am odd. Haven't you guessed?' She gave one of her jagged laughs. 'Now, the olive oil. Tell me, what did you think of that?'

'I ... I can't describe it. I tasted it, of course, and I brought it home, but I hid it in a cupboard.'

'But you must use it!'

'Oh, I shall. I hid it because I didn't want Effie using it.'

'Who is Effie?'

'A maid-of–all-work who comes every day. Her wages were Rosamund's wedding present to us.'

'So like Rosamund,' she clucked in an unflattering way. 'Finish that martini. Lunch is nearly ready. Oh, and by the way, there's your letter. On the dresser. Take it.'

He hoped it was not the one he had mailed from Mexico, but it was. It had been opened, and replaced in its envelope with the Mexican stamp he had bought at the hotel. He slid it into his pocket. He instinctively felt he ought to make some sort of social apology for writing a letter by turns chaotic and confessional, but he also instinctively knew that Louisa would scoff at social apologies. 'Why are you returning it to me?'

'Because you'll need it. Oh, not today or tomorrow, or really, who knows when, but one day you will want to remember everything that's in that letter.'

'I might not,' he said, colouring.

'Fine. Destroy it if you like, it's yours to decide. Honestly, I thought that's why you wanted to come here today. To ask for it back. It just arrived this morning.'

He hoped she hadn't read it, but she informed him that she had. 'Most impressive.'

'I'm not a writer.'

'No, but it was passionate and headstrong, and that's always impressive.'

'And utterly unlike me.'

'Yes, all the more reason that you must keep it, I should think.'

'Why?'

'One day you'll need that letter to remind you that this was a beginning. A harbinger. Next to panache, harbinger is one of my favourite words. I like the way it tastes. I like the way they both taste, but harbinger seems to me one of those salty words with layers of possibility.'

'A harbinger of what?'

'I don't know you well enough to answer that. I hardly know you at all. But I feel there's a sort of *simpatico* between us. Don't you?'

'I do, or I would not have written you such a letter.'

'Exactly.'

'I don't know what I was trying to say, really. I was in a sort of fog, and though it was only a week ago, it feels as though I am at a great distance.'

'There's the past for you!' Louisa said. 'Always inconvenient. Either failing to be retrieved, or so close, so vivid, it makes you cringe.'

Quentin did cringe a bit, remembering the rest of the letter, the contrast of austerity and desire, and how, in going to Mexico with Gigi, he had flung off austerity like a dirty shirt and embraced desire. 'Perhaps,' he ventured, 'you are one of the three strange angels in the D. H. Lawrence poem, "The Song Of A Man Who Has Come Through".'

'Well, I'd certainly be a damned strange angel, wouldn't I? I prefer to think of myself as a retired demon, but you mentioned that poem in your letter. He was a marvellous poet, wasn't he? A much better poet than a novelist. All that emotion! Who can bear to read it? Page after page!'

'People do.'

'Not over lunch.' She took the onion tart from the oven, snapped a tablecloth out, put down some cutlery, rumpled napkins, and battered plates. The oniony fragrance wafted up to him, and he breathed deeply. She smiled and cut him a large wedge. The taste of the tart was a revelation, and he said so. The proud, harsh lines of her face relaxed, pleased at the compliment. In two mismated (but genuine Waterford crystal) glasses, she poured them each a splash of wine which she described as swill, but there was nothing else to be had. 'What shall we toast to?' she asked.

'Expect great change?' he replied, easing, feeling the martini's tingle.

Louisa Partridge lifted her glass to his, and lowered her voice. 'Why are we meeting in secret?'

Quentin collected himself, began in a businesslike way, repeating what he'd said on the telephone about the three declines.

'I know all that,' she interrupted. 'What can't wait? Why are we meeting on Saturday? Besides, sod them all, Chatto, Windus, John Murray, and The Bodley Head. Have they no insight, no sense of adventure at all?'

'Only pirates make money from adventure, Louisa. Publishers are conservative men.'

'What next, then? I'm assuming you have some ideas.'

'I do, actually. I have had some thoughts, unconventional, but interesting. I thought they might appeal to you.'

'Is it immoral, illegal or likely to frighten the horses?'

'I don't think so,' he faltered.

'Then out with it.'

'I've come to have a new vision of *Apricot Olive Lemon*. You see, Louisa, when I first read the book, I didn't know how to approach it. My letters to those editors were all wrong. Now I understand, it has to be read, for now, like a novel.'

'I didn't make it up.'

'No, of course not. But when one reads a novel, one does so from a happy distance. You know, the adventures of whomever, whose life and bad judgement the reader watches from afar, the romance, the penalties, all that, without ever having that experience oneself. Think of Lawrence, or a writer like Frank Carson. They're exhilarating to read, but who would want to actually live like those characters? All that lyricism and emotion.'

'No one has the energy to live like that, investing everything with such significance.'

'Exactly! But while the reader is in the pages, everything is invested with such significance, and the very best novels become one's own experience. One carries them around in one's head and heart, like memory.'

'But my book is not fiction!'

'No, but now, this moment in time, it has to be read like a novel. That's what Bernard failed to realize. That's what I failed to realize. The book is about appetite, not sustenance.'

'Yes. I told you that.'

'Bernard didn't know the difference.'

Louisa's brow furrowed, but her eyes lit with interest.

'Neither did Chatto or Windus, or John Murray, or The Bodley Head. Neither did I until ...' He took a bite and considered his words, keeping to the kernel, but not the whole plant, which is to say, not mentioning his insights gained in Mexico. 'A man wouldn't know the difference if he hadn't had experience that made it clear. Sustenance, that is, the way we live now, that's easy to describe. But appetite? A man who did not know the difference couldn't possibly recognize appetite. It would be a grave error to confuse them, or believe they could ever be the same thing. You see?'

'Keep talking.'

'People expect sustenance of Louisa Partridge. *The Book of British Housekeeping* was sustenance. But *Apricot Olive Lemon* describes something we do not know, like fiction, like Frank Carson's novels.'

'Lyricism and emotion? I doubt that, Quentin!'

'Think again, Louisa. All those lovely lemons and apricots, saffron and rice and Sicilian olive oil, all that rosemary and garlic, and cinnamon and honey, what are they but fiction? But one day, people will be able to read it as a cookbook. We will move beyond this....'

'What exactly are you trying to say?'

He groped for words. 'In my office you quoted Rupert Brooke, remember? That we had all buried some part or another of ourselves far away. For my parents' generation, even mine, everything we endured during the war is fresh and raw, and likely to stay that way, but right behind me

240

there is a whole generation who may be in the schoolroom now, but in five years, say, they will be out in the world. For them, the anguish of the war, the losses, the tears, scars, the terrible price we paid, all that will be dulled. It won't be fresh and raw. And for people born today, 1950, or next, or in ten years' time, there will be a sort of creeping amnesia. Finally, only people like my parents, say, will still care – every day of their lives – that Robert died at El Alamein. They are the people who will never escape that past, any more than my mother's brother who lived through Verdun escaped Verdun, which he never did.'

'Oh, don't I know it! My uncle was gassed in the trenches. He couldn't work, and he had to move in with us, and he would wake in the night, screaming his bloody guts out. Scared my brother and me within an inch of our lives first few times we heard him.'

'And then?'

'And then, it was just old Uncle Walter, foaming at the mouth, we used to say. That's the way it happens, isn't it? The horrifying becomes commonplace.'

'And yet, when I was in California, Louisa, no one would ever guess there had ever been a war.'

'Yes.' She lit up a cigarette. 'The Americans are not alone. A year ago I was in Italy with my daughter. I was astonished. I wanted to throttle the Italians, to cry out, to shake them by their national shoulders! How dare you drink aperitifs in your sunny squares, you happy bastards! How dare you have your beautiful women and fat babies, your noisy little scooters and your wine and opera? How dare you have your lovers strolling arm in arm, lost in one another? How dare you? We won the war, you happy bastards! You lost! Here, in London, we have rubble everywhere, and we're crushed under it! The basic necessities of life are meted out to us with ration tickets. For us life has slowed to an ugly crawl, and we're all of

241

us, rich and poor, urban and rural, relentlessly grim and pinched and grey.'

'You see, we recognize sustenance, but your book asks people to imagine appetite! You understand now why Bernard turned the book down, why those other three did as well? Like a novel, your book describes experience they have not had, not yet, appetite for things not just food, but a world that is bright and warm and gay, and for want of a better word, opulent, a world of desire. But it will not always be fiction. Life will not always be pinched and austere.'

'Tell that to those narrow, pettifogging editors.'

'We can't tell them. We have to show them.'

A slow, conspiratorial smile spread over her face. 'I am going to like this.'

Quentin's idea – which, he stressed, she should not tell anyone else in the firm; he certainly wasn't going to tell anyone in the firm that he was contemplating something so outside the bounds of standard practice – was nothing short of brilliant. At least that's what Louisa Partridge called it, bloody brilliant.

Quentin would choose three or four editors from likely houses, and Louisa would invite them all to lunch one afternoon in March. Louisa would cook for them. It must be magical, Quentin insisted, and everything from the book *Apricot Olive Lemon*. It must suggest a not-distant, not-dismal future. 'You invite them for lunch, and you and I will be wonderfully charming and witty. You will be anyway. I'll do my best. We will absolutely not mention *Apricot Olive Lemon*.'

'Why not?'

'We're not asking them to buy the book. We're telling them a story. When they read the manuscript, they'll see it, they'll understand.'

'But maybe they'll bring it up. Four publishers have

turned it down, so it must be poison.'

'Or nectar.' Quentin finished off his second piece of onion tart. 'Don't worry. These men subscribe to a code of civility. They will want to talk about *The Book of British Housekeeping*, that wonderful tome that everyone knows and loves.'

'Except me.'

'You must promise not to be savage about it. Think of it as a relic, Louisa. You wouldn't savage a relic.'

'I would.' She smashed out her cigarette. 'I'm something of a relic myself. They might not come.' She poured his coffee from an instrument he had never seen, explaining, 'This is how they make coffee in Africa.'

'You still have a good deal of cachet. They'll come.'

'Will you tell them the others will be here?'

Quentin sipped his coffee. 'We'll let them be surprised.'

'Well, don't invite all the old men. There must be one or two hungry young editors out there.'

'Good idea. And when they leave, we'll give them each a copy of the manuscript. A parting gift. And we'll let them quarrel over who will publish it.'

'I like the way you think.'

The strategy hatched that Saturday afternoon earned Quentin Castle the cryptic dedication of Louisa Partridge's *Apricot Olive Lemon*. It read:

For Quentin Castle.
For Quentin knows what and Quentin knows why.

Florence was not amused. Albert said it sounded indecent. Rosamund thought it egregious bad taste. Margaret thought it cheeky, which it was, since Louisa lifted it wholesale from a book given to her by her Tallahassee colonel, Don Marquis's *Archie and Mehitabel Poems*, a brash book of free verse ostensibly written by a cockroach.

The Garden of Allah

Thursday 16 February 1950

Dear Louisa,

A writer such as yourself can put paper in the machine and write, but I cannot simply put my thoughts in some sort of free-form expression, I must write TO someone. A letter. So I shall write to you, as, of my acquaintance, you alone, a person who has felt her life upended more than once. I should think you might understand what I am trying to convey, my thoughts, unsettled as they are, confused and contradictory, in a word, ambivalent.

I have come from the land of austerity and stepped into the land of desire, Louisa. I am native to austerity, and find desire both attractive and repellant. Repellant in that excess offends me. I think. However, I wonder if I have actually ever met, experienced excess. Can one recognize excess in theory? This in itself is a conundrum. And desire? Not merely sexual desire, though I include that, but some larger overall aching desire. Can desire be theoretical? I am charmed here by the very things I disdain. I am torn, confused, unsettled, ambivalent about my duty to the agency. To Mrs Carson. To my father. (Quite apart from the agency.) To myself even. And then, to Frank Carson, that adulterous, egotistical destructive bastard, but I am his only ally, Louisa.

Frank Carson and I both came from the land of austerity and walked into the land of desire. Could he have been as confused as I? Could he have got lost, unmoored, and finally just succumbed to the excess all around him, the desire, the artifice, the illusion, the condescension? Could all that have driven him, or made him stupidly plunge to a watery death? Or did something else befall him?

Would that I had some wise counsel, Louisa. But all I had tonight was a fortune cookie. They gave them out at the Chinese restaurant. A bit of cheap wisdom on a scrap of paper. Mine said Expect Great Change. I am not equal to Great Change. I do not like it. I am a man of regular habits and practices. I know this of myself, and yet, I hear, battering at my brain - like the sparrow who flung itself against the grey wired glass - the lines from the D. H Lawrence poem, 'Song Of A Man Who Has Come Through' and the line about the three strange angels. Admit them. Admit them.

Louisa, am I making any sense at all?

This letter – or at least this much of it – was in the pocket of an old double-breasted suit thrust at the back of an unused closet, and it went to the jumble sale in 2000, undiscovered. With it there was a tiny scrap of paper that had all but disintegrated, on which, half a century earlier, the faded words that had promised great change could no longer be discerned.

CHAPTER SIXTEEN

EVERYBODY BACK ON THEIR HEADS

THE FOLLOWING DAY, Sunday, as though he had never gone to California at all, Quentin sat in his parents' sitting room, bound by the gravity of the planets-in-their-orbits luncheon. By tacit agreement, the conversation was local, evasive, and no one brought up Francis Carson, his death or his work. And yet, Quentin felt Frank's presence vividly, a ghost, leaning against the mantel, full of mocking bonhomie, underscoring his own famous charm, contrasting it with Quentin's weaknesses, which were so manifest his own family forbore to mention them.

Returning to work on Monday Quentin found that gossip had percolated everywhere, far beyond Castle Literary. Colleagues and competitors, publishers and writers might ring Quentin up on some pretext or another, only to enquire sotto voce if it were true, what they'd heard, that Carson had come home in a box like the scrapings of a grate. Everyone seemed to know; some seemed to blame Quentin, not perhaps for Carson's death, but for allowing him to be cremated. He had few defences. He wished more than ever that Robert were alive so he could follow his example, or that he had something of Louisa's imperious aptitude, but he did not. Everyone back on their heads. He truly felt that he had waded into a room full of shit and coffee break was over.

On Wednesday, 1 March , he came late to the office, and found atop the post on his desk a bright picture postcard, a beach dotted with umbrellas, Santa Monica, California, and on the side, a note from Gigi, typical Gigi, completely lacking in all discretion.

Sorry our time together ended up so grim. Not yr fault. Not mine either. Hey! I'm taking yr advice, baby. Setting myself up as an agent. Anyone can do it. All I need is a phone, a business card, and letterhead, right? For my 1st client I called Don. The guy who 2 timed me. I told Don I owed him. He called me nasty names, but I said I'd work for free, and he agreed. He's an OK writer. If I can place one of his scripts, think what I cd do with a really good writer! I have built-in connections. People are afraid to be rude to me because of RR. I'm still mad about being banned from the studio. Anyway, wish me luck. I've moved out of the Moroccan Mausoleum and into one of RR's rentals. Home and office. You'll be hearing from me, Mr. muy hombre! Adios and a little Margarita on the side! GGF

Quentin literally groaned each time he read this. Of course Miss Marr – and probably Miss Sherrill, no doubt Monica and his father – had read it, parsing together its more cryptic references. He was about to bolt for the London Library, anything to escape their collective disapproval, when the intercom buzzed and Miss Marr, in an aggrieved tone, said, 'You must come out here now. You have a visitor.'

He opened his door to find the outer office frozen in a sort of tableau: Miss Sherrill emerging from the small staffroom and loo at the back, a stunned look on her face, Miss Marr wearing a particularly pruney expression, Monica turning round, mouth agape, and Albert, his face draped with wounded shock. Claire Carson stood behind the low gate.

'Claire!' Quentin cried, then modulated his voice to a professional register. 'Mrs Carson! I didn't expect you.'

She wore her maroon coat, floppy velvet hat, a long, thick-knitted scarf of rainbow hues, and trousers. That probably accounted for Miss Marr's disdain. What she said next accounted for Albert's outrage and Miss Sherrill's shock. 'I should have been more specific, Quentin. I asked for Mr Castle and your father came out to see me, and I have been explaining to him, to them—' She glanced uneasily round the office '—that I meant you. That you and I will be working together now. You will be representing Frank's work.'

The look on his father's face so pained Quentin that his reflexes dictated he must defer, at the very least, say they should work together. But he did not. Whatever he ended up paying for his arrogance – oh yes, arrogance is how they would see it, Albert and Enid – he would pay the price. He went to the low gate and opened it. He shook her gloved hand (his gloves) and she held close a parcel tied with string. 'This way, Claire.' He nodded uneasily to office staff and led Claire to his office. He did not dare look at his father.

'So this is where you spend your days,' she said, sitting in the battered armchair. 'Very Pickwickian, if you ask me. Frank would have liked it.'

'He was never here. He is – was – my father's client.' He quickly hid Gigi's postcard, and sat across from her, thinking that he for once understood the phrase to feast one's eyes. She radiated a kind of tonic quality that enlivened everything around her, and she brightened the grey confines of his native habitat. The room seemed happier with her in it, even the wan African violets seemed to turn merrily in their small pots.

'Is that Robert's picture? Handsome. Do you have a picture of Florence?' From a drawer he produced a framed snapshot of Florence in front of Dove Cottage. Claire pronounced her lovely, and said all women should be lovely on their honeymoon. She laughed and added in a low voice, 'Frank and I never had a proper honeymoon. We had a baby before we even got married.'

This casual admission of Michael's illegitimacy so shocked him, he had to clear his throat before he asked how he could help her.

'I've come begging a favour.'

'Anything.'

'I'm meeting Sybil Dane for lunch to talk over the arrangements for Frank's burial, or entombment or whatever it is now, whatever we have to call it, and even though I said I was prepared to be nice to everyone I once detested, I'm not equal to Sybil. I can't go through with it.'

'You mean, burying Frank, or rather, placing his ashes at Woodlands?'

'No. Lunch. I need an ally for lunch.'

'Ah,' he said, perplexed.

'I'm supposed to meet Sybil at the Savoy. That's why I wore trousers. I'm hoping they won't let me in. I can't bear the thought of sitting in that woman's presence and listening to her rattle on. She's embraced this mourning, this funeral, like Medea, or Medusa, or whoever that was, tearing out her snaky hair. She's planning a vast, public spectacle, Quentin, two services, one for the family and one for Frank's so-called friends, and a huge reception at Woodlands afterwards. So gruesome! I told her I just wanted something small and private, a farewell, but she's absolutely intent on a great public show of … grief?

Adulation? I can't endure it, even though I said I would.'

'Lady Sybil has no right to say how Frank ought to be buried. Change your mind.'

'It's not that simple.' Discomfort knotted her features.

'Is it money? Please, be candid with me. If you need something immediately, we'll advance it. You have, or you will have, the twenty thousand American dollars. You are not beholden to her.'

Claire stared at her hands in her lap, the left one atop the right, the thick gold wedding band gleaming. 'Actually, I am beholden to Sybil. I didn't tell you everything last week when you came to Oxford. The truth is, I made a sort of bargain with her, with them, really, Sybil and her husband, Sir Sanford.'

'The newspaper magnate.'

'Yes. I don't quite know how it happened, but it has, and now ... now I have to go to lunch with Sybil, and talk about all this face to face, and it makes me want to scream.'

'What kind of bargain?'

Colour rose to her face. 'Sybil and her husband are paying for Dragon School for Michael, the finest, the most elite school in Oxford for my son, all the fees, uniforms, sports, everything. The fees are astronomical. Not only that, but Sir Sanford got him admitted immediately. The day after we moved to Oxford, somehow it was all beautifully and quickly settled, and Michael goes to school there.'

The stark exchange shocked Quentin even more than her admission that Michael was born out of wedlock. He said, 'I see,' though he did not see at all.

'Michael hates the Dragon School naturally. He's full of anger and confusion. He's full of rage, really. I've told him, you'll get no sympathy from me, my lad. Hate it all you like, but being educated there will serve you for life. I'm not being a snob about it. It's a fact of life here.'

So that he should be absolutely clear, Quentin said, 'They pay for the Dragon School for your son's education, and in return, they – she – gets your husband's ashes?'

'What good are his ashes to me? I loved the man, not a box of ...' Then, deflated, she added, 'Yes. Sybil gets Frank's ashes in her mausoleum. I would do it again.' Claire struck a note of bruised bravado that was, at least in Quentin's experience, unlike her. 'Whatever happens after this, it's on me. I will protect my children. I will see to it they have opportunities and possibilities. I never want them to say, "Oh, if only Da hadn't died, it would all be different." I suppose you think I'm an awful hypocrite.'

'No,' he lied baldly. 'As you've said, you are an American, and not likely to be laying wreaths on graves.' He glanced down at the day's appointments. He was supposed to lunch with an author of sporting books and later, an appointment with a journalist just back from the Soviet Union. He punched the intercom and asked Miss Marr to cancel everything for the rest of the day. 'I'm going to lunch with Mrs Carson.' The disapproval from the main office seemed to seep under the door, a rust-coloured, septic pool congealing at his feet. He turned back to Claire. 'Of course I'll be your ally. I'll always be your ally.'

'There's something else. Before we go.' She handed him the parcel, and pulled the string. 'I've gone back out to Harrington several times, to pack, to collect what I couldn't get in the first rush of moving out. I've found some really astonishing stuff, Quentin. Go on, open it.'

He pulled out a thick sheaf of typed carbon pages. His fingers went instantly blue. 'What is it?'

'That suitcase of Frank's, the one that was lost, well, he's been writing so long now it wasn't big enough for all his drafts. I found all this material, Quentin, you see? It was there, at Harrington all the time! I found the carbon I made of *An Inconvenient Wife*! Can you imagine?'

Her favourite phrase, *can you imagine*, always struck him as both challenge and invitation. 'But it wasn't finished, was it? Was it finished?'

'No.' Her blue eyes met his candidly, searching his face. 'Not yet. But it will be. Soon. As soon as I find the rest of it.'

'I see.'

'Do you?'

'Yes. I see.' He wasn't quite sure that he did, so he said very carefully, 'Shall we give it to Monica to retype?'

'Oh no. It's not ready yet.' She took the pages back, laid them on the paper, wrapped and tied the string neatly. 'I have so much to do. I have boxes yet to go through. There's still, oh, scads of stuff at Harrington that I have to deal with before I can sell the place, but I wanted you to see this much of it. So you'd know it exists, and there's enough for a posthumous novel. Maybe two. Frank's work needn't die with him.'

'My father will be delighted.'

'Only you're Frank's agent now, remember?'

'Oh. Yes.'

'And when I've found it all and put it in order – I don't know when that will be, there's so much to do – but when it is, you'll come to Oxford and collect it, won't you? I don't think we can trust the Royal Mail with the only copy.'

He smiled in spite of himself. She wanted to see him again. He agreed that anything that important should be hand-carried to London. He rose and opened the door for her, meeting, as he expected, Miss Marr's disapproval, though Quentin could not tell if it stemmed from Claire's choosing Quentin over Albert, or the fact that she wore trousers.

As they walked towards the Savoy, Quentin's mind scurried over everything he could remember of Lady Sybil Dane. He had met her, briefly introduced he remembered, at Selwyn and Archer's elaborate cocktail party for *Hay Days*. Claire, clearly, had not deigned to come; he would have remembered her, no matter how numerous the crowd. But since Carson's wife wasn't there, Lady Sybil had rather carried the day as Francis's consort, especially since the book was dedicated to her. He remembered watching her, thinking that she was accepting accolades as though she'd written *Hay Days* herself. He remembered too that Lady Sybil Dane created around herself the impression, even the conviction, of beauty, though in fact her youth had long fled, and she had an olive complexion, an outstanding nose, short legs, and an undifferentiated waist. To compensate, she wore flowing clothes in peacock colours, blues, greens, and glints of gold. Her conviction of her own worth also remained unimpugned despite unflattering portrayals in any number of anecdotes, stories, novels and a few juicy memoirs over these past thirty years.

He asked Claire several questions, and while her replies were tainted with dislike, Sybil's story emerged: her unlikely pilgrimage from penniless bohemian to mistress of the vast Woodlands manor. In the mid twenties, at some avant garde gallery opening, Sybil, then an aspiring writer, aspiring actress, aspiring artist, artists' model, and all-round poseur, captured the attention of the recently widowed Sir Sanford Dane, a man thirty years her senior. Having lived a life of unrelenting propriety with his first wife, Sybil blew into Sir Sanford's milieu like the wind off the sea. (His grown children thought her a foul miasma and remained unreconciled.) He could have kept her as his mistress, but he was besotted, and married her. Sir Sanford remained enchanted with her and she remained enchanted with his fortune, an empire in newspapers. Sybil built her own little empire of literary magazines, small presses, and funded gallery showings for her variegated coteries of taste and expression, writers, painters, poets, critics, many of whom she slept with. (Sir Sanford adopted her casual approach to fidelity.) She preferred men, but she was known to be eclectic, and she was never exclusionary for more than a few months at a time.

'Except possibly for Frank,' Claire conceded as they approached the Savoy. 'She might have actually loved him.'

Quentin thought to himself that Linda might actually have loved him, and Claire certainly had loved him, and he wondered how three such different women could have been so devoted to (as Gigi would say) a two-timing bastard.

'Their affair went on the whole time we lived at Woodlands, naturally. She gave us, the family, a suite of rooms on the fourth floor to live in, mostly so the children and I would be out of sight, and she gave Frank her whole vast library to write in. Sybil convinced him he could do no wrong, that every word that fell from his pen was golden. I refused even to type it. Never mind, Sybil typed it. We finally left Woodlands before the war ended, and took a cottage by the sea. We froze there, but I had him to myself again. Selwyn and Archer gave him that fine fat advance, everyone thinking *Hay Days* would be another *Some of These Days*. Frank bought Harrington Hall and, well, the rest you know. I ended up there alone with the children and the menagerie, and the place falling down around our ears.'

'How did Frank take the failure of *Hay Days*?'

'Badly. It accelerated his drinking. He blamed Sybil. He was angry with her. I kept reminding him of his own stupidity. That was probably a mistake. We had terrible rows. Then, I don't know how, or exactly when, but he reconnected with Sybil in London. At some point, she gave him the key to her flat. He brought other women there, I'm sure of it. Served her right. When he went to America, honestly, at first I was glad. At least Sybil wouldn't have him any more. I was certain when he came home, we could ... we would ...we always had ...' They were nearing the Savoy; she stopped walking, and turned to him, and again for a man unaccustomed to reading women's eyes, he saw the pain submerged in her pride. 'You see, yet another of Frank's stories of a desperate woman and an errant man. I was so inconvenient, he not only didn't come home, he quit writing to me at all.'

'You are not inconvenient to me,' he said, taking her arm.

The Savoy maitre d', noting that the lady was in trousers, was about to pluck a few choice phrases from a repertoire of rejection until Quentin said Lady Sybil Dane expected them. All was well.

Quentin followed Claire, admiring the way she sailed through the Savoy, wearing her unconventional trousers, and floppy velvet hat, confident, uncaring, perhaps even unaware of how beautiful and unique she was amid this sea of overdressed privilege. Quentin remembered Gigi Fischer striding into Schwab's, consciously creating an effect. For Claire, the effect she created was effortless, a spontaneous expression of who she was. He wished he had met her in a Broadstairs pub fifteen years before.

Lady Sybil Dane too exuded an air of singularity, wearing deep, unbecoming mourning. Though she was now at least fifty, her great dark eyes, her jet-black hair had not deserted her. She was clearly surprised to see Claire with a man until Claire introduced him as Frank's literary agent, Quentin Castle.

'Oh,' said Sybil in her gravelly voice, waving her cigarette.

'You might have confused me with my father, Albert,' said Quentin politely.

'I rather doubt that,' replied Sybil, letting her

unimpressed appraisal of Quentin bubble beneath her words. 'You are the junior partner, the one who went to California.' She folded her menu and turned to Claire. 'I hear the veal is very good.'

Hoping he could quell the flush of shame rising in his cheeks, Quentin ordered a civilized martini. Claire asked for a gin and tonic. Lady Sybil gave her attention entirely to Claire, insisting on driving her back to Oxford after lunch, and hopes that grief had not sapped all her strength. Not until their meals arrived did Sybil Dane turn again to Quentin. 'Your father has been renowned for his literary taste for thirty years, so you have a lot to live up to.' Her tone left no doubt that she thought him unequal to the task.

And yet within five years Albert Castle desperately wanted to retire, though he told no one, not even Margaret, the true reason he wished to retreat from the firm he had founded and sustained, the business he had loved. His son – the weak-eyed son who never seemed to have much promise or any charm or even ability, the son, in short, who was Not Robert – had eclipsed the father.

Quentin's handling of the estate of Francis Carson was shrewd and exemplary. The posthumous novel *The Inconvenient Wife* reinstated the writer's reputation that had been diminished by *Hay Days*. Published in 1954, *The Inconvenient Wife* sold well, sold internationally, and save for the grumbling of younger, more astringent critics, the book reaped elegiac, even ecstatic reviews. All that glory reflected on Quentin. And yet Albert had instigated, nurtured, fostered, advanced Carson's talents when no one had heard of him. Albert could hardly bear it. Even worse, Louisa Partridge, once Albert's lover, treated him as one would a friend's old, nasty dog: a pat on the head, a kind hello, but one wouldn't want to get too close. She reserved her respect and affection for Quentin.

Albert finally did retire in 1956. Quentin moved into his father's spacious office, sparking a colossal fight with Enid Sherrill, who departed Castle Ltd. She started her own agency, taking all her authors with her.

Quentin was glad to see her go. Castle Literary Ltd flourished. Not only did they still have the cachet of tradition, but Quentin proved himself – quite apart from his father – a man with daring literary instincts. Quentin took on, advocated for adventurous writers whose colonial experience of Empire was searingly different from, say, Kipling's. The voices, the views of these writers undercut the old imperial complacency and upended literary criticism, enlarged the scope of writers in English. Moreover, Quentin was envied for his lucrative contacts with American film producers (and American film agents, like Georgina Fischer). But it was the story of *Apricot Olive Lemon* that raised him to fame, a story that came to have the same smoothness as Thaxton and the Second-Best Umbrella, as it was told over and over, by writers drinking pints at pubs, by other agents over bad red at wine bars, over martinis at editors' luncheons, and later – decades later – fodder for chatter among young editorial assistants riding in lifts to ozone levels of glassy office buildings in sterile corporate parks. The story testified not simply to Quentin's acumen, but to his audacity. Who else would have thought of so unconventional a plan, and made a fortune for the author and the agent?

The four editors who came to lunch at Louisa's that day walked into a honeyed snare. Louisa created an enchanting moment: for that afternoon these four men were transported to the proverbial Other Country, the realm one visits in fiction. All four responded as they should have and made Louisa offers, very low, given the experimental nature of the book, and of course, the prevalent austerity everywhere. Quentin for his part negotiated up, not for the immediate offer, but for the percentage. A young editor finally agreed to Quentin's terms for a twenty per cent royalty rate (unheard of then or now) for Louisa. The book was published in the spring of 1951; critical reception was mixed. Some brayed that Louisa Partridge was a traitor to *The Book of British Housekeeping*, which they still admired. Some saw it as ludicrous, and quoted the recipes only to poke fun at them. ('Vermouth to moisten the stuffing for a roasted chicken? Preposterous.') But some, an eclectic, influential few saw it for what it was: the first clarion call to a post-war world. Louisa's tart, sharp, clean prose, her evocations of culinary experience-yet-to-come struck some as an antidote not simply to the grey pall of 1951 Britain, but an antidote to both gloom and nostalgia. *Apricot Olive Lemon* sold slowly at first, but it sold well, and it picked up momentum. The book did not reflect, it predicted. It has never been out of print, from that day to this. It was followed by six more volumes, all selling well and rapturously reviewed, and countless collections of essays, minor journalism and myriad magazine pieces, but nothing as seminal and important as *Apricot Olive Lemon*. In 1964 Louisa Partridge was awarded an OBE. Her dear friend, and longtime literary agent, Quentin Castle, escorted her to the ceremony.

CHAPTER SEVENTEEN

FOOTPATH TO FOLLY

ALBERT, AS THE head of Castle Literary Ltd, received the black-bordered invitation to the memorial service for the late Francis Carson, at ten in the morning, Monday, 6 March 1950 at the Woodlands parish church. Luncheon at Woodlands to follow. Albert intended to go alone, but Miss Sherrill reminded him that Mrs Carson might look askance, even take offence if Quentin were not there. The firm wished to keep Carson's estate. Grumbling, Albert could see the wisdom in this. Then Miss Sherrill announced that she too would be going. Albert objected, but Miss Sherrill asked no man's permission.

They drove to Oxfordshire the night before, Albert at the wheel of his trusty Morris. Miss Marr was able to book only two rooms at the local inn, a dreary place with dusty stuffed pheasants on high shelves. The three ate an abysmal supper in a dining room where the walls were dotted with hunting scenes featuring lots of bloody animals. The stuffy, low-ceilinged chamber Quentin shared with his father was also decorated with paintings of bloody animals. Quentin's stomach troubled him all night, and Albert snored like a bellows, so much so that

Quentin more than once had to get out of his own bed, go to his father and shake his shoulder to shut him up.

Breakfast was, if anything, worse than the supper. Quentin took dry toast and tea. As they were about to leave for the church, Miss Sherrill could not find the gloves to go with her navy-blue suit. She fussed and flapped, unhinged because no lady could go to a church without gloves. She returned to her room and insisted they search the car. Quentin swore under his breath. By the time she found the errant gloves, and they drove to the church, and parked the car, they were very nearly late. They stood in the doorway while the organist filled the church with lugubrious music, and wondered where they might sit. The pews were packed.

In that back row many bottoms squeezed more tightly together so Quentin, Albert and Enid could sit. Since the church was unheated, the close-pressed human warmth was not unwelcome. From his place at the back, and across a sea of black, Quentin could only see the hats of Claire and Lady Sybil where they sat with Sir Sanford, and pre-sumably, the three children in the front pew, reserved for the family.

The vicar stepped into the pulpit, raised his hands, prayed, and addressed them as brothers and sisters; he began with praise for the deceased, farewell to one beloved of all, our brother, Francis, with copious references to his genius, his goodness, his many merits. Quentin found the whole exercise excruciating. Though he had been uncom-plainingly raised C of E all his life, he was suddenly impatient, irritated beyond endurance by the well-known phrases and responses, by the rhetorical lauding of a man who, for all the good he had written, had strewn many lives with pain. Quentin's included. When required, Quentin stood and sat, and sang with the rest of them, but bereave-ment for Francis Carson, like sleep the night before, eluded him. His mind wandered, and his stomach was upset. The vicar laced his remarks with biblical references reminding everyone there would come the day when death would be as nothing, and love would triumph over all; he invoked the ubiquitous Corinthians, verse 13. Oh God, Quentin thought, was ever there a set of verses so often abused? And yet, to Quentin's surprise, these words of comfort and farewell clearly moved people in the congregation. He heard snuffling, and many dabbed their eyes with hankies, including, of all people, Enid Sherrill. Disdainfully Quentin Castle spent the service reflecting uncharitably on Frank Carson, though acknowledging his own hypocrisy: how else would Quentin have met Claire? How else would he have met Gigi? He knew that in some fundamental way both of these women had exerted a lunar tug upon his life, though quite what that tug was, he did not know. Expect great change? They had brought him great change whether he liked it or not, wanted it or not. He had not wanted it. And yet, he cherished it. He thought of love and death, and bits of Donne, the master of love and death, floated through his mind, chased away when, beside him, his father moved uneasily with a gas pain which he then discreetly released. Quentin turned his head. At the last amen, Quentin rose with the rest of them to sing the final hymn, 'Abide With Me', while the front rows filed out first.

Michael Carson led, perhaps in his eagerness to escape. As he walked up the aisle Michael shot Quentin a look of resentment, detestation, so pure, intense and unguarded it could only have been on the face of a boy. Catherine and Mary, in lovely new dresses of dark-blue taffeta, held hands and seemed pleased by the novelty of the experience. Quentin assumed they had grown up heathen and probably church itself seemed a place to play-act. Sir Sanford, corpulent, bald, adorned with medals, looked pleased rather than saddened, probably happy for Sybil's sake, at the turnout. On his arm, Lady Sybil Dane, her black hair sleek under a smart hat, her black clothing belted at her thick waist, her dark eyes downcast, looked every inch the grieving mistress, if not the widow. She carried a tiny bouquet of snowdrops tied with a black ribbon. Claire followed behind them. In a simple sheath she looked like a tall black flower, regal, Quentin thought, like a black iris. Her veiled hat concealed her bright hair, which was tucked up high and tight in a French roll. She too carried white snowdrops in black ribbon. As she passed him, she raised the slight veil, and in those few seconds, her blue eyes were bleak and eloquent with pain.

A long cortege of cars drove up to Woodlands, the Danes' grand, many-winged Georgian mansion, the golden stone glowing in the cold noon light. Overworked servants greeted them, directing guests to ascend the broad staircase. As they handed off their coats and hats, Quentin and Albert and Enid mingled with the publishing professions, with Frank's European and American publishers and translators, with other writers, artists, critics, the entire editorial staff of Selwyn and Archer, editors from other houses, editors of defunct arts journals, and assorted other literati and hangers-on, nearly all of them men (the few women were of the mothy-sweater sort, indifferent to their looks and tetchy on their politics). The hall was vast and Quentin's gaze was drawn to the high overhead dome where fat, glowing cherubs cavorted with nymphs, their flesh so opulent, their breasts seemed to hang pendulous from the gilt dome, their rosy nipples like jewels. All along the walls hung massive works of Elizabethan and seventeenth-century art, portraits, landscapes and scenes of antique grandeur, portrayals of classical myth and literature, all in thick gilded frames, all this grandeur now gracing the home of Sir Sanford Dane, once a scrappy Manchester lad.

Miss Sherrill remarked as they walked up the vast marble staircase that one didn't see too many houses of this splendor so well maintained any more. At the open doors of the elaborate gold and green drawing room with its six Venetian chandeliers illuminating gilded furniture, stood uniformed waiters bearing trays of drinks. No further enticement was necessary. For writers and artists free drinks and free food were cause for celebration, no matter who had to die.

Theirs was a genial profession, and Albert Castle, certainly, was known to be amiable, affable even in these sombre circumstances. Albert became more delightful the more he drank, the more they all drank. Miss Sherrill, who drank only sherry, and that in sips, staked herself beside Albert like a pole to a patch of runner beans. Over years of social occasions when Albert waxed indiscreet, Miss Sherrill had evolved a quick, almost invisible jab to which he responded like Pavlov's dog. Her elbow was at the ready as they stood in a small clutch of compatriots and competitors. The whole high-ceilinged room echoed with a respectful drone broken here and there with bits of stifled laughter. It was, after all, a sad occasion.

Quentin stationed himself quite alone, in a far corner before a phalanx of enormous potted palms. Perhaps if need be, like Tarzan, he could run into the jungle. But first he took a drink from a passing waiter who carried trays of sherry and whisky. Quentin bolted his first whisky, and felt its burn and its tingling in his veins almost immediately. He signalled the waiter for another.

From where he stood Quentin could look across the room at Claire and Sybil and Michael, who remained stationary while people swarmed around them. He watched as Sybil introduced Michael to everyone, her arm draped protectively on his shoulders. Michael looked miserable, twitching as though his fine suit of clothes itched, or perhaps to shrug off Sybil's protective hand. Get used to it, lad, thought Quentin; she is paying your school fees, and she's got you now. He watched Claire nod, smile, nod, smile, moving like an iris in the wind, responding to outside forces, the effort clearly taxing her patience, perhaps her strength, but not her innate dignity. The spontaneity he always so prized in her was utterly eclipsed. Oh Frank, Quentin thought, what an ass you were. What kind of fool trades Claire Carson for Mavis Ryan? For Sybil Dane?

'A sad loss, eh, Castle?' said the managing editor from Selwyn and Archer.

'Are we here to bury Caesar or to praise him?' Quentin replied.

'I hear they've turned the film *Some of These Days* into some sort of farce.'

'Have you?'

'Well, I heard it from your father. You went there, you saw it.'

'I went, I saw, but I did not conquer,' Quentin said with ironic gravity.

'Tell me, is Linda St John really that beautiful?'

Quentin snatched yet another Scotch from the tray of a passing waiter. 'What does it matter?'

'Must have been a jolly old shock to you to see they'd cremated him.'

'Oh, will you just bloody shut up!'

The editor moved away, but Quentin was joined at his jungle outpost by others of the publishing fraternity, each of whom had sympathies and opinions. Quentin had neither. He drank, and listened, unamused, to anecdotes of Francis Carson's capacity for alcohol, and his gifts with inciting women into bed. The stories were legion. Time for another whisky.

The two Carson girls were playing hide and seek

among the guests, and wreaking hell among the waiters with their darting, shrieking back and forth. The youngest, Mary, barrelled into Quentin's knees. He knelt and caught her, and the collision spilled a bit of his drink on her blue taffeta dress.

She stared at him intently. 'I hate you!' and she was off again.

'Does no one discipline those children?' asked an agent from Watt. 'They're heathens.'

'They're little girls,' snapped Quentin, 'and you should be damn glad they're happy.'

The voices in the room were louder now; laughter was more frequent, the occasional guffaw so loud it echoed up and rattled the Venetian chandeliers. Political discussions too broke out here and there, grew heated as various left-wing factions argued finer points of socialism and the Soviet Union. Thick banners of cigarette smoke wafted up. Quentin wondered if Lady Sybil and Sir Sanford had quite anticipated the effect of all this whisky before lunch on a crowd of people of the ink- slinging trades.

An agent from another rival firm planted himself at Quentin's side. 'I hear there is a posthumous novel.'

'Really?' said Quentin.

'So the wife has control of everything now. Be staying with the old firm, will she?'

'Where did you go to subtlety school?'

The man laughed good-naturedly and took himself off with one of his own authors, leaving Quentin to the comfort of Sir Sanford Dane's fine Scotch. The meandering crowds shuttled and obscured his view of Claire, still rooted between Sybil and Sir Sanford.

Michael Carson, squirming finally from under Sybil's embrace, bolted, and found his way to Quentin. 'I don't s'pose you'd give us a sip of that whisky, would you?'

'What? You're only ten.'

'I'm disgusted.' The boy crossed his arms over his chest grimly.

Quentin regarded him with affectionate understanding. Michael was pudgy and unlovely, though he had not seemed so when Quentin first met him. At Harrington Hall he had seemed quite the man of the place. Perhaps because at Harrington Hall he was in his own element. Here, he was in the Danes' element. Quentin wondered how many years would pass before Michael Carson found his own element again. But all he said was, 'It'll all be over soon.'

'It'll never be the same.'

'No,' Quentin conceded, 'it'll never be the same. How do you like Dragon School?'

'I hate it. And that won't be over soon. That'll go on for bloody years.'

'Yes.' Quentin watched Lady Sybil Dane accepting the sympathies of an especially voluble writer. 'That's likely to go on quite a long time.'

Claire, too, eventually managed to break away from the reception line. She had taken off the veiled hat, and her bright hair wound tight atop her head made her look like a candle moving across a sea of darkness. When people accosted her, she swayed towards them, listening, nodding, shaking hands, accepting air kisses, back pats and praise for her late husband. Some were friends from their old Chelsea days, some the very critics who had reamed *Hay Days*, some from Sir Sanford's papers who had praised it, some were translators, and some had no discernible connection with Francis Carson and were here for the spectacle, the food and drink. When she could disentangle herself, she gave a wan smile to Quentin and Michael. Each thought the smile was for him alone. Her progress towards them was slow, but they both knew she was coming. Each thought to him alone.

When she at last stood before them she placed a gloved

hand lightly on Michael's head, and handed Quentin the snowdrop bouquet. 'Please get rid of this for me, will you? Sybil's idea of … something. Too bizarre. Like a wedding with the dead.'

He took the bouquet, and dropped it in the potted palm behind him. He sent Michael off to get his mother a drink. 'See you don't spill some,' he added, assuming the boy would drink half before he got back to Claire.

'I should have put Frank's ashes on the bookshelf, and left him there,' said Claire, peeling off the black gloves. Quentin held his hand out for the gloves, and then tossed them into the potted palm as well. This amused her.

'Sybil looks terrible,' he offered, happy to heap abuse on their hostess.

'Mourning doesn't suit her. She looks much better in flowing peacock robes.'

'But here she is the star of a play. I think it's called *The Beloved Mistress.*'

'As opposed to the inconvenient wife.'

'Exactly.'

'I'm afraid I've made a grave error, Quentin.'

'You mean burying him here, all that? All this?' He waved his arm around to the lively, literary crowd; voices were louder now, laughter more persistent; even the vicar and the organist were jolly under the amber influence of whisky and sherry. 'I agree with you, Mrs Carson. This was an error of the gravest sort.'

'I thought I was past all the pain associated with this place, and I'm not. Frank seems to me more present here than he ever did at Harrington, as though he better belonged here with her than with me.'

'Well, he's here now,' said Quentin, 'forever.'

'Yes, I have stupidly delivered Frank into the hands of my enemy. I certainly shan't be coming back, I can tell you that. Sybil's car came for us yesterday, chauffeur and all, making a big bloody fuss on Polstead Road, and once here, servants led us to a lovely suite of rooms on the second floor. *Can I do this for you, madam? Can I do that?* Revolting. The girls thought it was all great fun, tea in that massive library. Michael was a complete ass, sulking through everything. And then we had to sit through that awful service at the mausoleum.'

'Last night? What was that we just sat through?'

'That was the public one. Last night they put my old carpet bag with Frank's ashes into the marble tomb and sealed it up. Just us, Sybil, Sir Sanford, the vicar and a string quartet. The girls went berserk, no one could calm them. They screamed the whole way back here, and Michael was roaring through the place, slamming doors, and swearing like a trooper, and then the servants insisted I leave the children and go down to dinner with Sybil and Sir Sanford. They awaited me. Can you imagine how ghastly that was?'

'I can, but I'd rather not.'

'The whole day, beginning to end, was just unspeakably awful.'

'Worse than what we just sat through? What we're doing here now?'

They watched as Sybil moved through the crowds, collecting condolences as if sympathy could be minted into small bright coins to be showered upon her outstretched hands. She looked both tragic and joyous, and Quentin noticed that someone had brought her a glass of champagne which the waiters were now circulating.

'Is that champagne?' asked Claire. 'What is she celebrating?'

'She's won,' he observed.

Michael joined them and thrust a half-filled glass into his mother's hand.

'Oh, Michael, thank you for the drink, dear.' She

smoothed his hair away from his eyes.

'I'm famished,' he said. 'When'll we eat?'

'Whenever Lady Sybil finishes holding court,' said Quentin.

'That'll be forever,' he grumbled.

'Yes,' Quentin agreed, 'she will not be finished for a very long time. Years, I should think. Perhaps we should all get used to it.'

'Why are you being unkind?' asked Claire. 'It's not like you.'

'I'm angry.'

'At?'

'Everyone. Forgive me. I'm a stupid sod.'

'Ha ha ha!' Michael crowed. 'You said it, you sod!'

'Michael! Go find the girls and go into the kitchen,' said Claire. 'The cook there will remember you. Tell her you're hungry and she'll feed you. Go on. Tell her Lady Sybil said you were to be fed anything you like.' She turned back to Quentin when he left. 'You're not a stupid sod.'

'A cad, then.'

'No.'

'You don't know the half of it,' he muttered.

'Are you angry with me?'

'Of course I'm angry with you. I'm an aspidistra, the kind you despise, all tidy and contained in its little pot behind respectable lace curtains, and I never knew it till I met you.'

Her blue eyes widened. 'And what are you now?'

'A bloody fool. Drunk too, but no longer the potted aspidistra. No, madam—' He set his empty glass in the potted palm '—I'm an ass, I know, but a newly minted one, and now that I know I'm not an aspidistra, I am truly an ass, a fool, and I can say I could take you away from all this. No, really, I have a chariot outside. A Morris chariot. I could say your chariot awaits, madam. I can drive now.'

269

'And where would we go?'

'Mexico. Baja.'

'Mexico! Is this part of the play?'

'You mean *The Beloved Mistress*, that play? No. This play is called *The Fool's Confession*, written by some lesser talent, some dreary hack. Me. I am the fool. My lines are: Time's winged chariot awaits you, and I am at its help, I mean, helm. The grave's a fine and private place, but none I think do there embrace,' he went on, knowing his tongue had been unhinged by alcohol, and flinging himself into folly nonetheless. 'I could say that Frank is gone, but I am here, and I love you, Claire. I loved you from the moment I first saw you. Sorry to muddy up the whole bloody farewell, but on a day like this one thinks of love and death, and nothing else. At least I can think of nothing else. Love and death. I'm afraid I will always love you, and I have to say it before I die.'

She was momentarily quiet. 'Why afraid?'

'Because love is an uncharted territory for me, wholly and completely new. What I feel for you I've never experienced before. I keep thinking of old McVicar, up on some peak where the air is cold and thin, and he can hardly breathe. He knows he's looking at undiscovered country, and his heart must have constricted with excitement, knowing that everything he's seen before is small, diminished now that he's seen this. That nothing will ever seem quite so grand or fine as this, and he could reach out his hand, and ...' Quentin reached out his hand, and Claire took it. He snatched it back. 'I've had too much to drink. You can ignore me if you want. You should. In any case, I'm hopeless. I mean, I haven't any hope that you ... And I couldn't expect you to. I don't expect it, but I don't want to die without saying it. I'm a fool. Forgive me.'

She placed her hand lightly on his arm. 'I don't need to forgive you. I want to be with you. Will you come to me,

Quentin? Will you?'

He focused his attention on her eyes, forced himself to look only into their blue depths, and for a man with so little experience reading women's eyes, he saw there clearly, truth plain, love unsullied. 'When? Whenever.'

'Shall I come to you?'

'Yes. Where? Tomorrow? Shall I come to Oxford tomorrow?'

'Today. Now. There is a suite of rooms on the fourth floor, north wing. Where we used to live. They're empty. The whole wing is empty. Meet me there. There's a small lift. You'll find it at the back of the central staircase. Take the lift and go to the fourth floor and turn to your right. The second door on your right.'

'Now, Claire? Do you mean it?'

'Now. I'll follow.' Her blue eyes gazed into his, and an expectant smile tugged at her lips.

She turned and left him, taken up by the soggy embrace of a writer from the old days in Chelsea.

The fourth floor was preternaturally quiet, abandoned, no sounds floated up. The room itself was furnished only with a high, hard, canopied bed of ancient origins, a rug rolled up leaving the heavy wood floor bare, and a portrait of a glowering be-wigged clergyman pointing at a Bible. He was the very embodiment of austerity, save for his heavy, fleshy jowls. Quentin stood at the window, waiting for her, fearful she wouldn't come, half wondering if he had dreamed her words, looking out over gardens, and beyond the woodlands for which the place was named, swathed in fog. From this window he could see the distant folly, an airy gazebo in marble with fine columns and a domed top. He smiled to himself. Footpath to folly. He was ready to tread that footpath, dance down it, embrace folly in all its glory and consequence.

*

He came down in the lift, mercifully passing no one except an overburdened housemaid who ignored him. The green and gold drawing room was empty, save for a corpulent editor drunkenly passed out on a settee. A waiter collecting glasses directed him to where luncheon was being served at the other end of the wing, a different drawing room, this one in blue and gold.

Quentin had roused his every appetite and now he needed sustenance. He was positively starving. The many tables were, most of them, only half full; people had trains to catch. Quentin seated himself with a couple who introduced themselves as neighbours of Sir Sanford and Lady Sybil, lord and lady names Quentin didn't bother to remember. They were delighted to meet Francis Carson's literary agent. A tired-looking waiter offered him food which he ate, not knowing or caring what it was. Another waiter offered some wine. Quentin declined anything to drink.

He wanted nothing to blur the moment, nothing that might soften the tingling awareness that shot through his body, head to toe in sweet little jolts. He needed every ounce of concentration to play his role. Calling on all his skill in undergraduate amateur theatrics – which, at long last were not useless – Quentin Castle put on the performance of his life: to persuade this fatuous couple and others in this unsuspecting audience, including his father and Miss Sherrill, that he was the same man who had sat in the church that morning. However, Quentin was absolutely not that man, and never would be again. That man had never known the passion Quentin had experienced, the madness, the sheer act of devouring and being devoured in another, of reaching with his body what his heart and soul and spirit had always longed for, exulted in, wanted to proclaim. Instead he asked the Danes' neighbour if she might pass him the salt.

Quentin Castle and Claire Carson had made love in their own fine and private place, on that ancient bed and in full view of the disapproving cleric whose expression darkened with every endearment, with every piece of clothing that fell to the floor. Quentin and Claire had no time for languor, or long lovers' talks, no time for the lilt and ease, exploration, tease, but here, now, swift, stolen, delicious, tender and intense. Quentin's every corpuscle seemed to rejoice, his flesh – and hers – seemed transcendent when Claire's lips slid down his chest, when he brought his mouth to her nipples, across the creamy expanse of her torso, that she had rolled over him, sat astride him, head back, eyes closed, mouth open, making little sounds that fell on his ears like grace notes. *I love you, Quentin* wreathed his heart in happiness. *I love you, Claire, I love you....* And when he held her tousled hair in his hands, his cheek to hers, and urged her, body and soul, to meet him, that final jolt of joy, to be with him, and in him, and part of him forever.

Lord and Lady Whoever-they-were spoke highly of the Danes' tennis courts. Quentin listened, bringing his napkin to his lips to inhale the smell of her still on his fingers. He played his role to perfection so that these people should never guess he had rested his head against Claire's belly, and risen from that bed, laughed and given the American kiss-off to the grim, be-jowled cleric pointing to the Bible and promising hellfire. Quentin and Claire could have come together and perished right there, in flames, and been happy. Quentin knelt before his lover, and kissed her pliant thighs before he rolled each stocking up her long legs. She had begged him to go downstairs first, pressing herself to his chest, impressing herself there forever, and brushing his lips with words of love so sweet he could still taste them, words far more confectionery than the elegant fruit-studded cake placed gleaming on a dish before him.

When finally Claire came down to lunch, Quentin dared not look at her. She made her way to the table where the Danes and Bernard and some left-wing journalists sat. She asked them to excuse her absence, that she was overcome with emotion, that she had a headache. Sir Sanford patted her hand, and said everyone understood. She gave her attention to a journalist, a woman with frowsy hair and nicotine-stained fingers who hoped to publish something posthumous of Frank's. Claire said all such requests had to go through the agent, and pointed out Quentin to her.

A fine and private play indeed. *The Fool's Confession* became *The Beloved Mistress*. They acted their parts well.

The last scene: at the end of that very long day, and after a lavish tea (also garnished with alcohol for those who wished to imbibe), when only those few people who had cars remained. Quentin, his father and Miss Sherrill were among the last to leave. Their car was brought round, and they collected their coats in the high and airy hall. Albert was clearly very drunk, and Miss Sherrill very tired. Quentin was very grateful to Lady Sybil Dane – she would never know for what – and offered his formal farewells to Claire.

'Yes, goodbye, Quentin, and thank you for all your help.'

'You're most welcome.'

'Can you come to Oxford, do you think? One day later this week to talk about the book? Or shall I come to London?' she said, pressing his hand.

Quentin could only gulp and nod, and be grateful he had his Burberry on, such was the surge he felt from the mere pressure of her hand. 'I'll come to Oxford.'

'Francis didn't mention any new book to me, a'tall,' Albert sulked, 'and I'm his agent. I take it as a damned insult.'

'An oversight, Albert,' Enid soothed.

'He wrote like mad these past few years,' said Claire, speaking to anyone nearby, including their hostess, 'since we moved to our lovely country place. Harrington Hall was so good for him creatively. He was so hard-working and productive.'

'But he wasn't always able to write there,' said Sybil, 'what with all the distractions. Sometimes he had to come to London just for the peace of it.'

'Peace indeed!' snapped Albert. Enid delivered him one of her practised jabs. Albert, muted, gazed up at the cavorting nymphs in the dome.

Lady Sybil turned to Quentin. 'Was he writing in Los Angeles?'

'Yes. All the time. Every day. Every night at the Garden of Allah. He had his own typewriter there.' Quentin was such a happy actor he wanted to say Frank had fallen head first into his typewriter and drowned there in a sea of inky ribbons and a swathe of keys, letters imprinted across his face.

'I have all his many letters from California.' Sybil's dark eyes shone. 'He was so dispirited at what they'd done to *Some of These Days*. I buoyed him as best I could. I'm so delighted there will be one last novel.' Her brightly ringed hand splayed across her breast. '*An Inconvenient Wife*, though I'm sure the title was a figure of speech,' she added with a look of consummate pity for the widow.

'I'm sure you were a great help to him, Lady Sybil, an asset,' said Enid Sherrill. She turned to Claire and offered a prim smile. 'Though we all know you were his muse, Mrs Carson.' She cast an odd, knowing, unsettling look to Quentin and announced that they should leave now.

'We should too,' said Claire. 'Could your driver take us back to Oxford now?'

'You should spend one more night,' Sybil protested.

'The children can go riding in the morning. We have ponies.'

'Thank you, no. Ah, here are the children.' She smiled to see them accompanied by Sir Sanford Dane. 'Go get your things. We're leaving.'

'No need,' said Sir Sanford, a manly hand on Michael's shoulder. 'The servants will bring them down.'

'Can you say goodbye to Mr Castle?' Claire asked the children. 'This is Mr Castle's father, and this is Miss Sherrill. Can you say goodbye to them? Please.' Her last word tattered into shreds of desperation as she met their stubborn faces. 'Please.' The girls finally did as she asked. Michael hung back, grim and defiant. 'Don't disappoint me, Michael.'

Albert, the ever-cordial, stepped forward and forced the issue for young Michael. Albert patted his shoulder, called him a fine young man just like his father. Michael was forced to shake hands. And on that insincere note, Albert, Quentin and Miss Sherrill went outside where their car was waiting, already warmed up.

'I'll drive,' said Quentin.

'Can you drive?' asked Albert and Miss Sherrill together.

'I learned in California.'

Albert was only too happy to cede the wheel. Miss Sherrill got in the back seat and fell asleep immediately, as did Albert in the front. While Albert's snores were punctuated with farts, Quentin drove, eyes alight, the joy he felt all but parting the darkness falling before him. He was loved. He loved and was loved. Love and death. That's all there is. One's guaranteed. One you must risk.

CHAPTER EIGHTEEN

THE EAGLE AND THE MOLE

MARGARET FLUNG OPEN the door, and stood framed by the light, her lips pursed, her arms crossed over her dressing gown, watching as Quentin helped his father stagger out of the Morris. Margaret expressed some surprise that Quentin could drive even before she chastised Albert for his drinking, and wrapped her arm round his shoulders, and helped him up the steps. Her back to them, she said that given the hour, Quentin should take Miss Sherrill home and return the Morris on Sunday when he and Florence and Rosamund came for lunch.

He wanted to cry out, *The planets have dropped out of their orbits!* He wanted to announce that he would *not* lead fat Rosamund up the steps on Sunday, *not* extol the cabbage soup! Never again! Given what he now knew, of discovery, of returning and rejoicing in love, he was, for the first time in his life, a whole man. A whole man could not live a half life. In fact he might have said all this, but Margaret closed the door. Quentin returned to the Morris.

Miss Sherrill, fully alert, had moved to the passenger seat beside him. 'We've suffered two calamities in a month,' she said as soon as he had put it in reverse and backed out of the drive. 'McVicar's heirs will almost certainly leave us.'

'How do you know that? He only died ... what? A month ago?'

'It does not look good for us. The family will fight it out in the courts, and it will take a long time, but it really doesn't matter who wins. They are all rather sour on your father of late.'

'Why?'

'I'd rather not go into it.' Miss Sherrill was silent, as though she had an elaborate menu in her hand and could not choose. Finally she said, 'Francis Carson will be a lucrative client especially for the next few years. The posthumous novel will help. What is it called again?'

'An Inconvenient Wife,' he offered, thinking that the title described Florence.

'Well, good or bad, it will get attention and it will sell. We cannot lose him.'

'Mrs Carson won't be leaving us.'

'Are you resting on the laurels you brought home from California?' she said, the sharp rasp of sarcasm grating on his ears.

'I wasn't altogether successful,' he admitted, 'but I did bring him home.'

'Well, his wife is your client now, and his work will be your responsibility. Albert feels the loss, you know.' The motor, and the unspoken, hummed between them. 'Your father is a good man, but he can be very foolish. I should certainly hope you will not be making his same mistakes.'

'What sort of mistakes?'

'Louisa Partridge, for one.'

His high spirits got the best of him, and he laughed out loud, assuring her he was not having an affair with Mrs Partridge.

'Think this quite funny, do you? It would be a dangerous error for you to take up with Mrs Carson. There, I've said it.' She folded her gloved hands over her handbag.

Quentin strangled the high-spirited laughter that begged to erupt. He pretended instead to burp, then retorted, 'I'm not taking up with her, as you so genteelly put it, but what makes you think that I would?'

'She's vulnerable now. If it was hard for her when he was alive – and I've certainly heard enough Francis Carson stories to assume that life with him was hard – it will be twice as difficult now that he's gone. She has no one but that surly boy. She's in need. I gather from watching her today she detests most of her husband's friends. Who can blame her? They're all wastrels. She was the one carrying all the responsibility, not just for the children, but for Carson, getting him to write at all these past few years. All that genius and he threw it away on drink, on women, on any sort of excuse that would keep him from working. The stupid sod. Oh, and that Sybil Dane is good for nothing except feathering her own silly nest. Hmmph.' Enid had absorbed this exact expression from Albert. 'Carson was a gifted fool. Charming, I suppose, but he squandered his gifts in his all too brief life.'

'You sound as though you pitied him.'

'Today, I actually did. There, in the church. He might have written books better than *Some of These Days*. It was a fine novel, but not superlative. He might have grown with maturity. He might have done something quite extraordinary had he lived. Now he will never write anything again, his wife's alone and his children are without a father.'

'She's not alone. She has the firm. Our firm. We can extend her some extra courtesies.'

'Whatever you are about with her, please do not call it courtesy. You are not gifted, but you are not a total fool either, so let us be plain.'

'Thank you, Miss Sherrill,' he replied, downshifting, 'your estimates of my abilities are so appreciated.'

'Don't patronize me, Quentin. I was working for this firm when you were a mewling babe. This firm is my life, the reputation we have built, and I shall not be made to look after you as I have looked after your father for nearly thirty years, this scrape and that, this forgotten bit of business, and that, this detail overlooked and that. Why do you think we're losing McVicar?'

He did not want to hear the stories behind that statement. He took the offensive. 'Are you saying that the success of Castle Literary is entirely due to you?'

'Not entirely. But the longevity of many of our relationships, yes. It's simply not possible for Albert, for anyone, to dally with people's affections and their work, and then to walk away with impunity.'

'I'm not my father. I do not dally with affections, and I'm grateful for all you've done for the firm.'

'Oh, shut up, will you? Anyone could see you are in love with her. You're mad for her, and she is mad for you.'

'Anyone?'

'All right, not anyone. I could. It can't last, Quentin. It won't, and the firm will suffer. Our reputation will suffer. You personally will suffer, and I do not speak of your marriage to Florence. I'm not about to lecture you on sin. I do not care a fig for sin. Whatever you may do with your personal life – including that woman in California, a pretty bit of business, that! Imagine every postal clerk between here and there knowing ...'

'Knowing what?'

'Never mind. I care nothing for any of that. The firm—' She took a deep emphatic breath '—the firm is my responsibility. Your recklessness will cost us Carson's estate.'

Quentin was rather pleased to be thought reckless, but he suppressed a smile. 'I assure you, Claire, Mrs Carson, won't leave us.'

'Won't leave you, you mean.'

'Yes, that's exactly what I mean.'

'She could be using you.'

'What for?'

'To forward Carson's posthumous career, and ensure her own well-being. Her children's well-being.'

'She is not using me.'

'The boy detests you,' Enid observed. 'The girls are flibbertigibbets, probably like their father, but the boy is not, and he detests you. He is important to his mother, and she to him. He will be more important as he grows older, and you will find him resistant to your charm. If you had charm, which you do not.'

Quentin thought of the look on Michael's face as he had walked up the aisle. 'He'll get over it. He's angry now. He's lost his father.'

'He lost his father a long time ago. Carson hadn't even been home in almost a year. That boy has only had his mother, and he's desperate for her attention.'

'He's desperate to be thought the man of the house.'

'My point. He's a grim, determined child.'

'Claire says Michael reminds her of her dour old Grandmother Dunstan.'

'I care nothing for Mrs Carson's relatives. You are jeopardizing my life's work, Quentin! You are treading a dangerous path, young man.'

'A footpath to folly?' he asked lightly, suppressing a smile.

'Are you really so stupid as to think this is funny? Our reputation is at stake. Will you heed me on this?'

'Miss Sherrill, I am not a schoolboy to be lectured. I know you think I do not deserve to be a partner in this firm, but I assure you I am. I work hard. I am not bedding the clients, using or being used by them. Please say no more on this. Which is your address?' He ground the gears to downshift as he dawdled along her street.

'Will you heed me on this?' she insisted.

'Miss Sherrill, I value your judgement, and experience, but my heart is my own.'

'You personally will suffer for this. It cannot bode well. I have been in this business for nearly thirty years and I have seen it all.'

'Enid, you are a gallant woman in a man's profession. I salute you.' And he did, with something of cheery bravado that Robert might have done.

'Here is my flat. Don't get out. I'm perfectly capable of walking myself to my door.' She took her small suitcase from the back seat and without another word, left him.

He drove all over Bloomsbury. Never having had a car, Quentin had never considered the complications, frustrations of where to park the damn thing. This late at night every possible kerbside slot filled. He was tempted to drive back to his parents' place, leave the Morris in their drive and stay the night there, but the thought of the St Ives watercolours, of having to sleep in Robert's shrine of a room, of breathing the dust-choked air of a long, stale marriage, a dismal yoke of years and custom, was too terrible. And his own stale marriage? Quentin would step from that as one would peel off filthy clothes and stand naked, clean in a summer rain. He would undo the past. He had married Florence in a surfeit of ignorance. What was it Louisa had said of marrying Herbert Partridge? *I didn't love him, but I didn't not love him. I was married off before I had any idea what the world might hold.* The same was true for him. He and Florence knew nothing of life or love when they wed. They had simply fallen into what was expected of them, and called it love. His marriage to Florence was a mere legal fiction. Adultery? Quentin did not feel remorse. On the contrary, he felt clean and alive and refreshed. Not simply as he had à la his *petite affaire de corps* with Gigi, but a positive burst of gratitude and plentitude and beauty engulfed him. In that transfiguring light, all else paled. Oh, to be given this experience now! He was still young. It wasn't too late for him. His marriage to Florence was an obstacle, an impediment. Nothing more. Divorce would be temporarily unpleasant. Fine. Whatever it cost, he would pay. Whatever he had to give up, so be it. 'If this be folly, then fate lead on!' he cried, quoting someone or another, ecstatic to see another car pulling out so he could have the parking place. However, squeezing the Morris in was more difficult than he'd imagined, and took a long time. Gigi had taught him many things, but not how to park on a crowded London street.

His brief, lovely romp with Gigi had awakened in him desire, as one might feel hunger or thirst. Claire did not sate his desire; she fanned it. With Claire desire seemed to Quentin suddenly limitless and profound. If it hadn't been for Gigi, he might never have had the courage for Claire. Gigi did not love him. Claire did. Claire returned his love. *I love you, Quentin. We have, we love each other.* 'We have each other, Claire,' he whispered as he finally forced the car awkwardly into the space.

He was perhaps three quarters of a mile from his house, and the chilly walk through the night-time neighbourhood was odd. The occasional dog barked. A distant cat mewed briefly. Lights were off. Drapes firmly drawn. Milk bottles on the step. All the little lives tucked up within. He walked past them all, pitying them, pitying everyone from Mrs Rackwell to Linda St John. He pitied his father's eternal philandering, and his mother's stoic avoidance of the unpleasant. He pitied Enid Sherrill, whose love affair with an entity, a firm, would never pulsate under her dry, thin hand. He pitied plain Monica and prim Miss Marr, whose lips had probably never brushed another's. He pitied fat Rosamund, who had not been fondled in thirty years. He pitied his own wife, who hadn't the wit to live, or be, or even imagine beyond the small, pre-etched grooves of their life. He pitied everyone who did not know what he had known this day. He walked more quickly, breathing the damp cold, wishing like hell Robert were alive. Robert would have understood this feeling. He did not wish that Frank Carson were alive, but Frank too would understand because at last Quentin understood what Frank Carson knew. Quentin had always believed that writers like Carson and Lawrence dwelt in hyperbole. But it wasn't. It was the truth. An act of love so elemental, so commonly human, could in fact be transcendent, could change a man or woman, could alter everything, and everyone. Two people stood, naked, hand in hand forever, and the rest of the world fell away. Quentin did not pretend to be Frank Carson – he was not, could not be a wild poetic presence – but thunder to Claire's lightning? Yes! Quentin could be that. Frank Carson might have been the proverbial eagle. But Quentin Castle was no longer the mole living underground. At long last he had come up, come out, soared in the sunshine. Claire Carson was that reigning sun. 'Claire Castle,' he corrected himself. He would get a divorce, and marry her, and they would be inseparable. Grow old together. He laughed out loud, happy at the thought.

At his own house he was surprised to see the sitting-room light on. He did not call out, but removed his hat and coat, put down his small overnight case beside the umbrella stand, and opened the sitting-room door. Florence was asleep in the chair, a book in her lap. Her mouth was open and her hair in pin curls. He took the book from her hands. *Some of These Days*. He was touched;

she usually read Barbara Cartland, and took no interest in his authors. He kissed her forehead fraternally.

She woke with a start and a smile. 'Quentin, you're very late. I worried. Your mother called some time ago. After you brought your father home.'

'I had to take Miss Sherrill home, and then I couldn't find a place to park the bloody car.'

Surprise lit her face. 'I didn't know you could drive.'

'It's not so very hard. A little dance you do with the clutch and the accelerator and the gearshift, that's all. Let's go to bed. Thank you for waiting up. It was kind of you.' His pity for her made him gentle.

'Well, don't you want to tell me all about Woodlands? Your mother said—'

'Tomorrow,' he replied, offering her his hand. 'Tomorrow.'

Not having slept well, Quentin was still up early the next morning. Earlier than usual. He got the milk, snatching the bottles from the pelting rain. He made a pot of tea, but he only scanned *The Times* in the most rudderless fashion, waiting to hear Effie at the back door. And soon enough, she came in, her tread heavy, her expression ever the same, slack jaw, resentful scowl tightening her brow. She brought with her the odour of wet cigarette smoke. Quentin felt sorry for her too; he was suffering a paroxysm of universal pity for the blighted and unloved, even those as blighted and unlovely as Effie.

'I see you're at it again, sir. You know Mrs Castle don't like you in the kitchen.'

'Effie.' He rose, removed her coat and hat from the hooks, placed her hat on her head at a jaunty angle and gave her odorous coat a good shaking-out. 'Today you are taking a holiday.'

'A wot?'

'Have you never heard of a holiday, Effie?'

'Not on a Tuesday, I ain't.'

He held her coat as though she were a duchess. 'Well, this Wednesday, you have a holiday. We shan't be needing your services today. You're off. You'll be paid, but you're free.'

'What does Mrs Castle think?'

'That you deserve a paid holiday. Go do something daring, Effie. Go get into trouble.'

She stepped away from her own coat. 'Are you making advances on me?'

'I swear I'm not, but someone should. You'd be the better for it. Now, off you go.' Quentin held the door for her. She backed towards it, and once through she said she'd be back tomorrow and there had better not be any funny stuff.

It won't be funny, Quentin thought as he went upstairs. He bathed and shaved and dressed, and returned to the kitchen to make breakfast. He found Louisa's bottle of olive oil high in the cupboard where he had stashed it. He poured some in the fry pan and lit the gas. A single, tired-looking onion lolled in a bowl, and he chopped that fine, and when the pan smoked, he put the onion in. The fragrance wafted upstairs, and soon Florence came down, her pin curls out, her hair tumbled about her pink face and a quizzical expression in her eyes.

'Where's Effie?'

'Gone for the day. I gave her a holiday.'

'Isn't that rather extraordinary? I might need her. There's the ironing.'

'Well, we don't need her today. I don't even like her, but we certainly can get by one day without her. We deserve one day to ourselves.'

'But it's Wednesday.'

'What does that matter?'

She looked pleased. 'What are you going to do with those onions?'

'Put them in with powdered eggs, I guess. That's all we have.'

She went to the fridge and reached into the back, withdrawing two eggs. 'I was saving them to ask Effie to make a cake.'

'A cake made by Effie is a waste of two eggs. Go on, take the paper and the teapot into the dining room, I'll bring breakfast in. The eggs will cook quickly.'

'What's come over you, Quentin? Are you—'

'I am excellent. That is the absolute truth.'

'I have to ask, Quentin. It's crossed my mind. You seem strange. You've been rather, well, different, ever since you got back from California, and I hate to ask, but I suppose I should. Was there a girl in California?'

'Linda St John. Love at first sight.' He chided himself for his high spirits and humour, knowing what he was about to inflict. He ought to be gloomy but he was jubilant. 'Why do you ask?'

'Something Mummy said. She said you seemed quite unlike yourself at lunch on Sunday.'

'Really? I wouldn't have thought Fair Rosamund would pay me any mind at all.'

Florence frowned, unsure what he might mean. She went on, 'Mummy says you might have had a driver while you were in California, and it might have been a girl, someone to chauffeur you about. She always had a driver when she went to garden shows in America.'

'And did she have affairs with her drivers?'

'Quentin! What a terrible thing to say.'

'Your mother should stick to her herbaceous borders. Now, go on. Off with you. I'm about to make you the Louisa Partridge special.'

'More figs?' She looked at him flirtatiously.

He gave a small compliant laugh, though he knew he was about to break his wife's heart. He was a cur. A total cur.

At breakfast Florence talked about *Some of These Days*, how she wanted to like it, but couldn't really. Elsie Rose, throwing herself into that love affair when she knew it was wrong. 'I haven't finished the book, but I'm certain there's no happy ending. And the writing is so ... so ...'

'Lyrical and full of emotion. Yes, all that's out of favour now.' Quentin bolted his eggs and onions, enjoying both the appetite and sustenance. 'But it could come back. It probably will. We can't always live like this.'

'Like what?'

He gazed out the window where the rain streaking down rendered the rubble across the street into a sort of impressionist study in grey, highlighted by the pale aspidistra and the African violet. 'In such austerity.'

'Are you talking about rationing, Quentin?'

'No. Finish your eggs and onions. What do you think of them?'

'Interesting, but a bit weird, don't you think? Are you done? Shall I wash up?'

'No, you stay here and have a cigarette.'

'Not just now, thanks.'

He took the dishes into the kitchen, threw them in the sink, cursed himself again for being a dog. His heart was thumping; he could feel it in his throat. If he spent one more night in this house with this woman, he would crumble into dust, implode, explode. Something dire.

When he went back into the dining room, she was leafing through the paper, but she seemed to sense his urgency and folded it. She smiled. 'Tea?'

'Yes. Thanks. I mean no. No, thank you. Florence, dear.' He sat across from her. 'There are important things, important days that are ahead of us, our whole lives, really, and what I'm trying to say ...' He knew very well what he was trying to say, but the look of rapt affection on her face stole his words. Damn! He should have said yes to the girl in California. It would have been so much easier. Perhaps Florence would accuse him again of having slept with another woman when he was in California, then he could say yes. Yes, he had been unfaithful. There would be a scene, of some sort, tears, unpleasant things said, but it would all be over in, say, half an hour. Hour at most. He wasn't really sure how long scenes like that lasted. He had only read about them in novels. 'Florence, it's change that we all have to make, of some sort. Nothing stays static, does it?'

'I suppose not.'

Be a man about this, he regaled himself. You are a whole man at last. The eagle and the mole. Act like the eagle. 'I'm trying to say that everything's about to change. Everything. My whole life. And yours.' How could he explain to Florence that Claire had touched his life, his soul from the very beginning? If he had never seen Claire Carson again after that first time, he would never forget her until the day he died. How could he explain that one woman's blue eyes had changed him forever, and now that he knew she loved him, his life was forever altered? He could not do that. Too complex. But he could admit to Gigi and Mexico. He could admit to being a faithless cad in California. Admit to infidelity. Florence would have an accusatory fit, and expect him to beg her forgiveness. Then he wouldn't. He wouldn't ask for anything at all, except a divorce.

'What is it, Quentin?'

He gulped. 'It's hard to say.'

'Yes, it is.' She nodded, bit her lip and she seemed to tear up.

'It's something we should have spoken of when I came back from California. The truth is—'

'You're right, dear. Of course it's life-changing and exciting. Oh, Quentin.'

'Don't cry. I mean, of course you must cry if you feel like. You must do just exactly as you like,' he said as she picked up her napkin and wept into it. 'I will take care of you. You mustn't doubt that. It's true, Florence—'

'Oh yes, it is true! Quentin, dear, dear Quentin,' Florence choked with emotion. 'You've guessed, haven't you?'

His lips parted, but no words came out. Could it be? Could he be so fortunate that Florence had fallen in love with someone else? That she too was willing to admit their marriage last June had been a foolish, youthful mistake, that they had more or less fallen into marriage, ignorant of love or life, that divorce was very modern, lots of people did it, lots of people, and moved on with their lives? He studied her more intently. He read her eyes, her expectant expression. No. He was not that fortunate.

'You see, I've known, well, I guessed,' she added. 'And then ... I've just been waiting for the perfect moment, and here, you knew all along, didn't you?'

'Not all along, no ...'

'I haven't felt well, but that will pass. That's what the doctor said.'

'You've been to a doctor?'

'Yes, dear; you see, I wanted to be absolutely certain before I told you, but you're so sweet, you guessed. And you couldn't wait for me. And I was so silly to think there had to be a right moment. But you chose it, Quentin, and I'm so so happy. So happy. And so happy you're happy.' She rose and walked to him, placed her arms around his shoulders, and her cheek to his.

Other lips than Quentin's formed words. These other lips seemed to be working in some sort of happy, happy unison, ringing with her voice to create the impression

that Quentin Castle was happy, that he was responding, replying to his wife's chatting about the baby due in
November and perhaps they ought to move, to a proper
house, perhaps nearer to their parents, not right away, of
course, but think about it, and her having told Rosamund
and Margaret and her dear schoolfriend Amelia, who was
the bridesmaid at their wedding – he remembered Amelia,
didn't he? – and swearing all of them to the most solemn
secrecy until she told her husband....

Whatever these other lips were doing, Quentin Castle
watched the rain shimmer down the window. He watched
the African violets pucker and pale, and go grey before his
eyes. He watched the aspidistra turn, really rotate so that it
faced him and regarded him with the pity he had so lately
bestowed upon the rest of the human race.

'So I'm grateful to Louisa Partridge.'

Other lips forsook him and she said it twice and he
finally croaked out, 'What's Louisa got to do with it?'

'It was those figs, so luscious, so earthy. I forgot to check
the calendar that night. The night that Francis Carson
died. How can you forget that night?'

'I shall never be able to forget that night.'

'Nor I. We'll name it Robert if it's a boy. Would you like
that?'

'Yes.'

'Can Margaret tell Albert now? She's been beside
herself. Can I go ring her, and tell her to tell Albert?'

'Yes.'

'I'll be right back and we'll have the whole day to ourselves, won't we? A holiday.'

'No. Sorry. Can't. The old family firm, you know. Off I
go. Cheerio.' He rose and allowed himself to be kissed. He
patted her back. Then she went to make her telephone call.

Quentin somehow propelled himself up the stairs,
listening to her voice echoing from the phone alcove. He

took his glasses off. Mechanically he brushed his teeth and smoothed his hair and washed the smell of onions from his hands. After he had turned away from the mirror, he put his glasses back on. When he went downstairs, Florence was in the front hall by the door.

'Must you go in right now?' She kissed him, and fondled his tie. Her peach-coloured dressing gown slightly open, the arc of her white breast bright in the grey morning light falling from the transom. 'What about our holiday?' she added coyly. 'You did let Effie go for the day.'

The thought of Effie was somehow intolerable, though he forbade himself to say so. Instead he burbled and bobbled about things he had forgotten at the office. A mistake. He should never have ...

'Well, stay for a bit, dear, anyway. I want to hear all about yesterday. Margaret says your father is not feeling well – overindulged, I expect. She has called Miss Marr, and cancelled his morning appointments. She said the memorial at Woodlands was vulgar beyond belief.'

'Yes. Vulgar beyond belief.' He took his hat and slid his arms into the Burberry. 'I'll tell you later.'

'When you come home this evening.' She gave him a light connubial kiss on the cheek and said he had made her the happiest little wife in the world. She handed him the second-best umbrella, explaining she would need the best one later when she went to type for her mother.

He took his leather case, and opened the door to the pounding rain, stepped into the street, opened the umbrella and bent under it, bobbing like the rest of the black-clad populace, men making their way to the Russell Square tube station to go down, down, down into the bowels of the city that had ingested many little lives like his.

PART IV

CHAPTER NINETEEN

SONS AND LOVERS

QUENTIN JUMPED OUT of the cab in Greek Street in the midst of a summer downpour.

She had invited him, no, summoned him to The Gay Hussar in Soho, the small, chic restaurant much frequented by the literary and political trades. The note, written on her personal letterhead, offered no gentle *could we meet*, or *please RSVP*, simply the date and time, one o'clock, Monday 8 August, 1960, yes, just as if he might show up a year late. He was fifteen minutes late; in her eyes, no doubt, a breach of courtesy.

'Good afternoon, Mr Castle. We gave Madame your favourite table when she told us she was meeting you,' said Anton, whipping out a clean white napkin.

Quentin took the hint, pressing it gently over his face, the water dripping from his dark hair and quickly cleaning off his glasses. He was no longer a gaunt young man; his height and broad shoulders carried his weight well, though his face was more memorable than handsome, the high thin nose like a mountain ridge, a man in the prime of life, at the top of his profession, respected, even feared by his peers, prosperous, confident, secure, no longer the sort of person who let others finish his sentences. All true, but the very sight of Enid Sherrill reduced him to feeling like the juvenile lead in a bad play, wheezy, adenoidal and gauche. 'Please bring me a double martini,' he said to the waiter as he handed back the napkin.

He assumed that Enid Sherrill had planned to put him ill at ease even if he had been on time. Enid already had her menu face down, her cocktail before her and her first cigarette lit. She was hatless, her hair dull and cut short, and she wore a navy-blue suit enlivened by brass buttons. Her eyebrows were finely arched and pencilled in with a firm hand, dark against her pale skin. Her lipstick looked like a tiny red seam between her sharp nose and her sharp chin. She was thinner than ever. She removed her cat's eye glasses.

'How good to see you again,' he offered after his flustered, mumbled apologies and excuses, and took his seat. 'You only used to drink sherry.'

'That was when I had your father to look after. Someone had to stay sober.'

'Ah.' He opened the menu.

Though it was August, both he and Miss Sherrill nodded to a few of their passing compatriots and competitors, publishers, editors, other agents in The Gay Hussar, some of whom regarded them quizzically. As well they might, thought Quentin. Enid's leaving Castle Literary and opening her own firm had provided the insular world of London publishing with a good deal of gossip in 1956, including the rumour that Quentin had evicted her. This never happened. She left of her own accord after Quentin moved into his father's office. The transition was rocky, their parting acrimonious, but Quentin was satisfied. Enid left Castle Literary to start her own firm, which had not exactly prospered. Their paths had seldom crossed, save for Albert's funeral the last year, where Enid had been kind to Margaret and Florence and Rosamund, but only civil to Quentin.

'I hope all goes well with you, Miss Sherrill.'

'It does, but that's not why I'm here. The usual,' she said to the waiter who brought Quentin's martini.

'Yes, madam,' the waiter replied without a blink, 'and that would be the ...'

'The asparagus and bacon salad for a starter, and the duck.'

The waiter made a great ado that he had not remembered, and Quentin knew she did not eat here often enough to know the waiter, or to have a usual. She was grandstanding, but why? The waiter did in fact know Quentin's usual. He left them, and Quentin made some remark about the food at The Gay Hussar, paprika and so on. Past that, it was her show and he was prepared to sit in silence and drink till she led.

'Miss Marr tells me Castle Literary prospers,' she offered, billowing out a plume of smoke.

This surprised him. Did she often see Miss Marr? 'Yes. Everyone in the building is doing quite well. Last year Number 11 collectively hired a day porter.'

'Collectively is a rather suspect expression in these Cold War days.'

Had the old girl gone anti-Commie bats? 'He is a sergeant who fought with my brother at El Alamein. Poor Mrs Rackwell died last March and we now have a Jamaican charlady who sings at night.'

'I suppose Rackwell finally killed her.'

'Actually, they found her on the floor at the foot of the stairwell one morning when the first people came to work. Her heart just gave out.' Of all the tenants at Number 11, Quentin alone had gone to her shabby funeral, stunned, disgusted, really, to see old Rackwell sobbing, supported on either side by young women, daughters, presumably.

Quentin sat through the service, but left without offering Rackwell any morsel of sympathy for his loss. He regretted going at all. Quentin polished off his martini while Miss Sherrill nattered on-and-dreary-dull-on, professional gossip mostly. He was annoyed with her tone of carping superiority, remembering it all too well from his early days with the firm. In the guise of a sparrow, Enid Sherrill clothed the instincts of a hawk.

'And I see Louisa Partridge is her own little publishing factory,' said Enid, stubbing out her cigarette energetically. 'She alone must be filling your firm's coffers.'

'Yes.' Might she be hinting she'd like to quit her own foundering firm and return to Castle? Preposterous. He had crammed three young agents into what was once Enid's office. The thought of having her nearby gave him heartburn just to think of it. 'Louisa's bought a house, a villa, in the hills above Fiesole.'

'I'm surprised you're not with her. On holiday. I mean, it is August and you and she are such great friends.'

'I bought a country place in St Ives. The family is there now. I've only just returned to London.'

'I remember your mother loved St Ives. Years ago—' She lit another cigarette with a small silver lighter '—when Robert was a boy. How is dear Margaret? Still mourning Albert?' She nodded to the waiter who placed their dishes before them.

'It's only been a year. She's used to mourning.'

'And Florence and the children?'

'Fine. You saw them at my father's funeral last summer.'

Using her fork she poked about in her *Spargelsalat* as though looking for bugs. 'I fear I was rather rude to you at Albert's funeral, Quentin. I felt his loss terribly, and I was more upset than I should have expected to be. We were together for a very long time, you know. Thirty years.'

'I know.'

'I was angry. I thought if Albert had gone on working, he might have lived longer. He ought not to have retired.'

'If this is an apology, Miss Sherrill, please consider it accepted.'

'Yes, well ...' She finished her cocktail, leaving the cherry to loll in the glass. 'Albert ought to have been pleased with what you've brought to the firm. His taste was not unerring, but I doubt he would have had the vision to take on those colonial writers whose work you are championing.'

'You do my father a disservice, Miss Sherrill. In his day he was equally daring. Sydney Thaxton might have been a genius, but his work was difficult to place, and he was constantly changing, and that alone cost him the loyalty of publishers. My father protected Thaxton, and advanced his work even after his death.'

'And you have done the same for Francis Carson. Can it really be ten years since he died? How fortunate that he left so much work behind. *An Inconvenient Wife* resurrected his reputation, and the second one ... what's it called?'

'*September Street.*'

'Yes, just out last spring, conquered the critics, save for Kingsley Amis and his ilk.'

'There are always nay-sayers,' he replied. He had the terrible feeling that he was about to be grilled here and served up like the Hungarian foie gras and caramelized onions on his plate.

'Rather prominent ones in this case, but who's to care when the sales, British and American, are going so well? You must be pleased with yourself. And I hear it's picked up a very nice little film offer. Was that through your friend?'

'My friend?'

'Fifi or something.'

'Gigi Fischer. She is a very reputable film agent.' He stopped with that.

'After what the Americans did to *Some of These Days*, I'm surprised Mrs Carson agreed to a film.'

'I got a No Bollocks clause inserted into the contract,' he offered by way of a joke.

'I must say I thought *September Street* rather threadbare – I mean the story, not the writing. The writing was some of Carson's best. But the story, you know? Orphaned girl sent to live with her bedridden, hideous old grandmother and her lecherous uncle. He has his wicked way with her against her will. She falls in love with a local lout, and it all goes wrong. They could have called it *Tess of Broadstairs*.'

What in God's name was Enid up to? Quentin signalled for another martini, not caring that in drinking this much at lunch she would no doubt accuse him of *Following in Father's Footsteps* as the old song had it. His wrist began to itch. Hives. He scratched discreetly under his watchband.

'I'll come to the point, Quentin. I've asked you here because I do not want there to be any misunderstanding between us. Whatever you, personally, may think of me, I shall never let it be said that Enid Sherrill acted out of spite. I wish to be quite clear from the beginning.'

Spite? The skin all along his arm prickled. 'What are you talking about, Enid?'

'Lady Sybil Dane. You remember Francis Carson's memorial service, no doubt.'

'I am not likely to forget that day.'

'She has approached me to represent her book. No, more than that, I have taken her on as a client. There, it's said, isn't it?'

'She's written a book?'

'Yes, a memoir of those war years that she spent with Carson.'

'He lived at Woodlands with his wife and children too.'

'True, but as you might expect ... well, it is Sybil's memoir, and Mrs Carson, I'm sorry to say, comes off as something of a cow, certainly bovine, good for carnal reasons and bearing children. An American of earthy appetites and no real understanding.'

'And what is Lady Sybil's role?'

Enid Sherrill stubbed out her cigarette, and gave him a look she had practised on Quentin since he first entered the agency, silently accusing him of crashing stupidity, of being so dim-witted that he should feel the top of his head for donkey's ears. 'Naturally Lady Sybil and Francis Carson were free spirits who had deep, distinguished, literary discussions when they were not rollicking in the lovely green meadows and by idyllic springs, making love in the folly. She was his saviour and muse, she fostered his talent, and he loved her deeply. Don't be an ass,' she harumphed in Albert's old manner.

'Why am I here?' he asked, hoping to truss up a bit of dignity.

'I wanted to tell you myself that I have taken Lady Sybil on as a client. Which I have just done. I shall see her book through its first printing, and then retire. Majorca, I think. Someplace warm.'

'How nice for you.'

'Don't patronize me. I'm certain Lady Sybil brought the book to me to spite the Castles, knowing that you and I had quarrelled bitterly.'

'It wasn't bitter for me, Miss Sherrill.'

'It was for me,' she replied, taking a bite.

'Miss Sherrill, Enid, I am finding all this rather hard to take in!'

'I, on the other hand, have thought it through. That's why I asked you to lunch.'

The waiter brought their main courses, whisked the other plates away, did his usual fanfare with the pepper, clicked his Hungarian heels and left them, but not before Quentin asked for a bottle of wine.

'None for me,' said Miss Sherrill. She cut her food into tiny bites which she ate quickly. 'There will be a lot of gossip, Quentin, spicy tittering among the ink-slinging trades, the very people who crowded Woodlands ten years ago to drink Sir Sanford's single malt, and bid a garish farewell to the late Francis Carson. How well I remember.' She emitted a heavy stage-sigh. 'When Lady Sybil's book comes out, people will choose sides. There will be those who think Lady Sybil Dane is a self-serving hag, and those who will be glad to see the late Francis Carson get something of a come-down.'

'A come-down?'

'Well, she paints herself as his muse, his nurse, his confidante, his soulmate, his lover, naturally. As if without her, without her love and devotion, and dedication, he could not possibly have written a word of his masterpiece, *Hay Days*. I'd call that a come-down.'

'Yes, I see what you mean.'

'*Hay Days* was mediocre at best, Lady Sybil's memoir is better than Carson's *Hay Days*, I don't mean the writing, her writing is execrable, but the story is far livelier, not to say prurient.' One little bite followed another between her thin, over-red lips. 'The Land Girls are mostly gone from the story, Francis sleeps with no one but Sybil, and presumably his wife since one of their daughters was born there, I believe.'

'Yes. Catherine in '44.'

'In any event, there's quite a bit of ecstatic, not to say athletic, sexual goings-on.'

'And does Lady Sybil include all the other men and women she slept with?'

'No need to be catty with me, Quentin. I am representing the book. I do not pretend to like it. However, in

302

answer to your question, the answer is no. Mostly the book is the great lady's great love affair with the great novelist.'

'I suppose,' he said, thinking back to that day at Woodlands, 'that her book could be called *The Beloved Mistress.*'

'That's not the title, but yes. I myself am dismayed by her lack of discretion, but it will be published. She's still quite powerful, you know, though she has nothing to do with her late husband's newspaper empire. When Sir Sanford died, his children got the empire. She got the money and the house, much to the frothing rage of the rest of the family.'

Quentin's digestion roiled. 'Why am I here, Enid?'

'I did not want you to think I acted out of spite. If I did not take on Lady Sybil's book, someone else would have.'

'Yes.'

'I am hoping it will make a great deal of money for my retirement.'

'You did not act out of spite. Fine. Why am I here?'

Enid drank her water. 'I assume you still see something of Francis Carson's wife. She is your client.'

'Yes,' he replied, feeling like a prisoner in chains replying to a be-wigged, black-robed judge.

'You should prepare her for this. It will not be pretty. It is an unfortunate book. Whatever one might say of Francis Carson – if I may offer a personal opinion – there was always about him a fundamental brightness, a need for applause that was part of his charm, until he got disgustingly drunk, of course. But short of that, he cast a sort of glow and people were happy to warm themselves in it. All of Carson's charm, his zest, that sense of spectacle and high spirits is lost in Sybil's book, and he comes off looking rather like her little lapdog, a Peke with a pen, you might say.'

'God, is it really that bad?'

'It is. Francis Carson emerges from these pages looking like a fool. Lady Sybil writes as though she's defending a genius, that *Hay Days* was his masterpiece, a misunderstood masterpiece, its reputation clouded because of his being a conscientious objector. Oh, and she has much to say about that too, about his witch of a Quaker mum, and dear old failed-intellectual father whose literary aspirations were the heartbreaking basis for *The Moth and the Star*. Francis's schoolmaster father enjoyed caning his students till they bled and whimpered. He enjoyed beating Francis too, for that matter, took a real pleasure in all that pain. Albert told me Francis lived in fear of his father, of both his parents, for years. Francis could never quite squeeze out from under his father's baleful glare until Claire came into his life. She gave him courage he did not have on his own. A powerful woman.' Enid chewed thoughtfully. 'Albert feared Claire Carson. He disliked all writers' wives, of course, but he actually feared her. Did you know that?'

'No. He didn't like Americans. He called her the FMB. The Foul-Mouthed Beauty.'

'Or bitch. One tends to denigrate what one fears.'

'I should never have thought he feared or respected her.'

'Well, he did. Albert knew that were it not for his wife, Carson would still be in Broadstairs teaching nasty boys and bedding local matrons. She is a remarkable woman, but I'm sure you know that.'

'I'm surprised to hear you say something nice about her, Miss Sherrill.'

'You've always misunderstood me. My feelings about Mrs Carson when I spoke to you the night of the memorial service were candid, but they were not personal. I cared not one whit for adultery, if that's what it was – mind you, I am not asking. I thought only for the good of the firm. I am no longer a part of that firm, and I can allow myself the luxury of personal feelings.'

'Had you always lived without them?' he asked, suddenly curious. 'Without personal feelings?'

'My life has no bearing here. I'm trying to give you a notion of what this book will do to Francis Carson's reputation, and to his wife, his family.'

'Thank you. I mean it, I'm grateful for the warning.'

'You should know –' She took a deep breath, as though plunging underwater '—it's dedicated to the boy, though he's not really a boy any more, is he? Twenty or twenty-one.'

'Michael.'

'Yes.'

Grim premonition gnawed at him. Quentin bolted his wine. 'Sybil Dane always brewed a lethal cocktail, equal parts flattery and seduction, with a fine bright cherry of her wealth gleaming at the centre. Frank succumbed to it, and so did Michael.'

'How could he resist?' Enid remarked. 'He's living it up at Oxford, I can't remember which college, but trust me, he stays on there thanks to her money. And, of course, there were all those holidays abroad with her and Sir Sanford, the yacht. Even after Sir Sanford died, well, there were still holidays abroad, only not on the yacht. One of Dane's sons got the yacht, but Sybil bought a flat in Paris, and she rents a villa at Lake Como in the summers. That's where they are now in August. She and Michael.'

'How do you know all that?' He took a long drink.

'How do you think? She adores talking about him. Sybil entertains Michael and all his young friends with extravagant weekends at Woodlands. She has invited me to come as well.'

'And will you?'

'God, no. I can't bear the woman. He is estranged from his mother, isn't he?'

Quentin nodded. 'Michael broke his mother's heart. Again and again. But the last, the worst, the day after he left school – with Lady Sybil's chauffeur waiting for him at the door – he packed a bag, left Claire's house for good, and moved to Woodlands. Claire and Michael have scarcely spoken since, in now two or three years. You can't imagine how it pains her.' He fought the urge to confess more, but he knew if he started, the whole would come tumbling out, and that this unsympathetic woman had no wish to hear his truths. He was already in her debt for this forewarning; his pride would not allow him to ask for her pity or understanding. 'Dedicating the book to Michael is Sybil's final blow to Claire.'

Miss Sherrill finished her lunch, or as much as she was prepared to eat, and laid her knife and fork decidedly on the plate. 'It may not be the final blow, Quentin, that is what I am trying to tell you. It's worse. The dedication reads *To Michael Carson, ami de mon coeur*. Yes, as well you might go rather pale.'

'What does that mean, exactly?'

'He figures in the book.'

'Michael is the son Sybil never had.'

'And he has taken the place of his father.'

'Surely not in her bed!' Quentin burst out, embarrassed to see he had collected a few oblique glances in the restaurant.

Again she harrumphed in a way that recalled Albert Castle. 'At her age, she's probably sixty, it's flattering to Lady Sybil to be thought of as something of a siren. That is why I wanted to meet with you. You had best brace Mrs Carson for this book. She will be pained. Hurt. By the way, Lady Sybil says outright in her book that Michael was born before his parents were married. If that's libel, it will have to be edited out, but perhaps it's true.'

'That bastard!'

306

'Yes, well. Enough said.' Enid lit a cigarette. 'There's a good deal of that sort of thing, more innuendo, probably, less fact.'

'Is it too late to talk with her, Lady Sybil, I mean, maybe to convince her to—'

Again Enid gave him the look that suggested he should feel about for donkey's ears. 'Can you imagine Sybil Dane listening to such a plea? Agreeing to it?'

'No. It would only give her pleasure.'

'Exactly. I'm sure they've already taken pleasure in the pain they know they will inflict. They're that sort of people.'

'They?'

'Michael too. He's like Lady Sybil in that regard.'

'You've met him?'

'Oh yes. He might look like his father, but he has nothing of Francis Carson's charm. I've seen enough of young Michael to get his measure. And I shall have to see more, no doubt. In becoming Lady Sybil's agent, I've left myself at her beck and call. She loves to take up one's time, and once she gets her talons in, it's difficult to extract oneself. She's insufferable.' She signalled the waiter. 'I must be going.'

'Dessert?' asked the waiter, touting the poppy-seed strudel.

They both said no thank you in unison, and she laid money in the dish. A good deal of money. One did not want to be seen counting sixpences at The Gay Hussar.

Quentin swallowed his pride in an audible gulp. 'Might I ask to see a copy of the manuscript,' he ventured, 'please?'

'I have one with me.'

His face fell, and he stumbled about in inadequate thanks. 'You astonish me, Enid! Would you have given it to me even if I hadn't asked?'

'Yes. I have it with me. That's why I asked to meet you.

To give it to you.'

'To give it to me,' he repeated, dumbfounded.

'It's a second carbon, so blurry here and there, but you will understand.'

'I – I don't know what to say. Thank you. I don't know what to say.'

'I have a favour to ask of you as well. It's nothing to do with the carbon copy, I bring you that of my own free will and because I dislike Sybil and what she is up to, though I shall certainly represent her book. I need the money. No, here's my question, Quentin. When I retire next year may I tell my authors that Castle Literary will take them back? I know they're a rather rag-tag bunch, certainly by Castle standards, but they were loyal to me when I left the firm, and I fear another agent might not …' Her voice trailed off.

'Absolutely, Enid. I will take them all back. Naturally,' he added, knowing full well that had she requested this before this very moment, he would have turned her down.

She pulled from the bag beside her a fat parcel, wrapped in paper and bound with string. 'Like chops from a butcher shop,' she noted with some asperity. 'It will have to be edited down for publication, for libel. Perhaps the most egregious parts will come out, but I doubt the overall tone will change.'

'This is very kind of you. Thank you again.' He sought something stronger, but words eluded him. 'On behalf of the firm.'

She gave a paltry laugh. 'Oh, the firm!'

'And Mrs Carson.'

She put her glasses back on and watched the summer rain sluice down the windows. Then she turned back to him, smoke escaping from her thin red lips.

'You are still in love with her, I take it.'

'I am,' he said, surprised at how the simple admission relaxed him, how the simple, spoken truth could create such a feeling of release, relief. He might have waxed on about their ten-year love affair and the happiness Claire had brought him if Miss Sherrill hadn't cut him off.

'Then speak for yourself, Quentin. Not for the firm.'

'Thank you, personally. I'm grateful. Thank you on Claire's behalf.' He thrashed awkwardly as she no doubt meant him to. But then he gathered such gravitas he had earned at thirty-five. 'You are a gallant woman, Enid, and kind, and I'm sorry if I misjudged you.'

'Oh, you didn't misjudge how I felt about you, Quentin. The minute you came into the firm, I knew what would happen. I knew he would always love you better than he loved me.'

'My father?'

'Of course your father! Who else? You are surprised that he loved you? Or are you surprised that he loved me?' When Quentin did not reply, she went on. 'Well, perhaps he didn't love me, but I loved him. I couldn't marry him, of course, but I wanted a partnership, a different sort of marriage, you might say. I told him if he didn't make me a partner, I would leave him. That story you've heard, no doubt.'

'Yes.'

'I got the partnership, but it was ... what's the term, pyrrhic? A pyrrhic victory. Albert could not be intimate with an equal, and by the time he took up with Louisa Partridge, our affair was over, but our partnership continued.'

'Yet you remained dedicated to the firm, and to him,' said Quentin, suddenly seeing the past bathed in a new light.

'He and Castle Literary were my life's work. All I shall have to show for my life's work.' Behind her cat's eye glasses her eyes filled with mirth, a quality Quentin could not remember seeing in all the years he had known her.

'In truth, I loved dear old fascinating, fornicating, Gilbert-and-Sullivan-spouting, tipsy, misadventurous, unfaithful Albert.'

'I would not have guessed.'

Some vestige of a smile tugged at her thin lips, as she rose and picked up her handbag. 'Of course not. I am not indiscreet. That was Albert's failing. Don't let it be yours as well.'

CHAPTER TWENTY

LE VOLEUR DU TEMPS

IF EVER, TRULY, there were a time-torn man, Quentin Castle was he. His time was torn, but his heart was not. He might count as a faithless husband, but he was a constant lover, even though he had meant to give Claire up, tried to give her up.

The day after Florence's announcement of the impending baby, guilt-racked, and miserable, he cancelled his few appointments, told Miss Marr he was going to the London Library to read, and took the train to Oxford. *I mustn't ... we cannot ...* rang in his head and his heart on the train, on the bus to Polstead Road. *I mustn't ... we cannot* even when Claire flung open the door and flew into his arms, pulled him inside. *I mustn't ... we cannot* as she loosened his tie and pressed him against the closed door, and his hands slid over her body beneath a wrapper secured only with a silken tie. *I mustn't ... we cannot ... I can't ...* he murmured against her soft lips, and full breasts, and after that, even though *I mustn't, we cannot, could not. Florence,* they were pulling each other's clothes off, as they stumbled backward towards the bedroom, and though Claire nodded, weeping, *yes, yes, I know, I understand ...* even as they tumbled into bed and stayed there till they heard Mary and Catherine on the stairs coming home from school.

Claire scurried into some trousers and a sweater, ran into the living room, gathered up Quentin's clothes in a flash, and pitched them to him in the bathroom just as the girls tore into the flat. Mary pounded on the bathroom door. Quentin smiled as he opened the door. Mary was the image of Claire, fair hair and flashing blue eyes.

He found Claire in the tiny kitchen, the kettle on, her hair tumbled down around her face, eyes alight, her whole being glowing. He sat at the small table by the window and opened his arms to her. She came to him and he pressed his face against her breasts while she stroked his hair and whispered endearments.

'I just want to walk away from everything, from everyone, and be with you,' he said, breathing in the earthy scent of love. 'I don't care about anything else.'

'Of course you do. And you know you can't walk away. You'd hate yourself.'

'I wouldn't.'

'You would! You're a good, a decent, a fine man, Quentin. What do you think drew me to you from the beginning? Why do you think I love you? You're not false or cruel.'

'I'm false now.'

'But you're not cruel. And you cannot leave your wife and child.'

'What about us? I can't give you up. I can't lose you. I have been blind, deaf and dumb, and lame, ignorant and unknowing, stupidly treading the paths already marked out for me, and suddenly! Suddenly, I'm alive and awake and rejoicing!' He stroked her back and buttocks, wishing they could just retreat to the bedroom again. 'You are everything to me. I want to marry you.'

'No. You don't.'

'I do.'

'I don't want to be married. I want to be loved.'

'But I want both, Claire. You and always you. Only you.'

'You have me. You and only you.' She pulled a flimsy kitchen chair up close to him, and their hands entwined. She still wore her wedding ring, but her blue eyes were bright with love. 'For the first time I know what it is to be loved for who I am, not what I can do or be or make easier for someone, but for myself. I can't lose you either, Quentin. We can have each other. We must.'

'How can we have each other if I am married to Florence?'

'If you left Florence, you would one day hate yourself, and you would hate me.'

'Never.'

'We don't need to be married to love each other, to be true to each other, to keep what we have, our love, and let it strengthen us.'

'Only I would go home to Florence, and you—' He nodded towards her left hand, her wedding ring '—stay married in spirit to Frank.'

'You want me to take it off?'

'Yes,' he said simply. 'I do.'

'All right, then.' She removed the ring which left a pale shadow on her finger. She put it in her pocket. Quentin took his own wedding ring from his hand and went to put it in his vest pocket, but she stopped him. 'You keep yours on, Quentin. Florence and the baby are one part of your life, the honourable part, and I am another.'

'My love for you is every bit as honourable, more so, than what I feel for Florence.'

'Then keep it so, and love me. I don't need you to make an honest woman of me. I don't want to marry anyone. Not even you, dear, and I don't want to be the cause of anyone else's unhappiness, but I do want to be loved.'

'I love you.'

'Then that's all I ask of you. I need you to love me, to love me best and always. Can you do that, dear?'

'I can. I do. I will. I promise.'

'Then I shall love you best and always. I promise.' Her lovely face suffused with joy. 'As long as we love each other ...'

'Best and always. And forever. I promise.'

'And forever,' she repeated as the kettle began its noisy shriek. 'We mustn't lose each other, and we must bear whatever comes. Can you bear it, dear?'

'I can bear anything for you.'

These were, as it turned out, solemn vows. From that day forward, Claire and Quentin had borne everything, and though they had endured struggles, they had not lost each other.

But in that first year – and however ecstatic, fulfilled he was in Claire's arms and the light of her eyes – each time Quentin returned home to Florence, he plunged into an abyss of self-loathing. Rosamund, Albert, Margaret all greeted the prospect of the baby with undiluted joy, and Florence's happiness in her advancing pregnancy was an agonizing reproach to him. He tried to be especially kind to Florence, and she, in return, was pleased, touched, warm, sending him into further paroxysms of guilt. Florence showed him each evening how she was learning to knit. Quentin thought the clicking of the needles would drive him mad.

But after baby Eleanor was born (pink and roly-poly, a font of gurgles and giggles, a delight to all the family) the situation slowly, subtly changed. Florence was so besotted with the baby, she did not seem to begrudge, or even notice, his very long workdays, the days he spent in Oxford. She did not know he was in Oxford. No one did.

For these ten years the London Library had served Quentin as the perfect fiction. (In turn he had served it as a respected trustee.) Twice a week he told Miss Marr, everyone, he was at the London Library, reading, and then he got on the train to Oxford. Claire met him at the station, and drove him home, Polstead Road, and later, to the house she bought on Linton Road, nearer the river.

This was where Quentin Castle lived and breathed and had his being. Mornings they had in bed, and then after school, when the children came home, they would work side by side, reading, writing. The girls warmed to him swiftly, and in time came to adore him, but from the beginning Michael Carson contested Quentin's right to Claire's affection. When, clearly, she wasn't going to give him up, Michael simply stayed at school on days when he knew Quentin would be there. In good weather Quentin and Claire took the girls punting on the river or walked university parks, or went to the pub at Binsey and fed the ducks and swans. In bad weather they would go to the central market, or visit the Ashmolean. With these coltish girls, Mary and Catherine, Quentin was demonstrative and affectionate, as loving and indulgent a father as if they were his own.

Claire and Quentin spiced these ordinary days with time in London when she came to confer with Bernard, editing and publishing, promoting Frank's posthumous work. They might go to a film or the theatre together; they might have dinner with Louisa Partridge who was a willing party to their love affair and offered an excuse for Quentin any time he needed one. In London they were circumspect in others' company, though they prickled with anticipation, knowing they had reserved a hotel room. Once, they could not wait for the hotel and made love on the carpet in front of the fireplace in his office, after hours, the building deserted save for Mrs Rackwell's clanging broom and buckets echoing through the airy corridors of Number 11.

It was not, however, to the office at Number 11, but rather to the London Library that Quentin went after his lunch with Enid Sherrill. The librarian at the desk nodded to him. As with The Gay Hussar, Quentin Castle was a well-known fixture here. In August, however, familiar faces were few; mostly foreign scholars peopled the tables. He saw that some unthinking foreigner had taken his favourite place. Never mind. He found a table with plenty of room, and unwrapped the parcel. *Woodlands War Years.* Turned the page. Yes, there it was:

Dedicated to Michael Carson

ami de mon coeur

Quentin dug about in his pocket for his stomach pills and took two, gulping them down without water. Damn them, Michael and Sybil, damn Frank, damn all of them, all to hell, not only for what this bloody book would do to the future, but for plunging his immediate plans into darkness.

Quentin and Claire were to leave tomorrow for Scotland. Ten days. A real holiday. Their first real holiday together, time untouched by any other obligations. Catherine and Mary were going with the family of school friends to Spain. Quentin's people were at St Ives all summer. Claire and Quentin were free. He had not been to Scotland since his university days, the walking tour of the Hebrides, and Claire had never been. Her dog was kennelled, the Mini ready for the road, Claire's new Leica fed with film, and Quentin's new fishing rod in a handsome sheath. All in readiness. Only now, the Scottish holiday crashed and smashed like crockery breaking, glass shattering in the quiet confines of the London Library. The blue letters on the typescript seemed to blur before him: *ami de mon coeur*. The great Up Your Arse. And worse lay ahead in these pages. The phrase of some forgotten French poet battered at his skull like a bird trapped against a windowpane. *Voleur du temps*. The thief of time. 'That's what you are, Michael,' he whispered, 'the thief of time that Claire and I have together.'

Michael – who had once so fiercely defended Claire – had done his best to pry her from Quentin, inflicting pain and anguish on his mother in any way he could. As a boy he had had rages and sworn, calling her whore and slut while everyone in the Polstead Road house kept their doors shut and their ears open. Once, when he was about twelve, he struck her. Quentin would never forgive him for that. By the time Michael was thirteen – with an uncanny instinct for that powdery rot in relationships that would characterize his adult life – he learned how to inflict abuse via another. Though he disparaged and made fun of Lady Sybil Dane behind her back, he invited her to everything associated with his school life – sports days, plays – and at these events she beamed and applauded, extolled, showered praise. She overshadowed his mother entirely. Lady Sybil invited them both (and any of Michael's friends) to tea at the Randolph Hotel following these events. Having once accepted this invitation, Claire never went again; Michael and Sybil ganged up on her, flouted their affections. In these years Sybil Dane lavished on Michael presents, clothes, and holidays, summers on the Danes' yacht, Christmas skiing in Switzerland, Nice at Easter. On the day her son finally moved out of her home, and into Woodlands, Claire knew she had failed in the first duty a parent has: to protect her child. She had refused to struggle for her son as she had struggled for her husband. Her guilt and sorrow were unrelenting; she mourned the loss of Michael as she had mourned the loss of Frank.

Quentin could not forgive Michael for the pain he inflicted on his mother. For years fierce quarrels over Michael threatened to tear them apart: Claire weeping, Quentin resentful, knowing that however hot her anger, however deep the hurt, eventually she would excuse Michael's cruelty – she always did – on account of his youth, or that he had lost his father, or that he didn't know what he was doing. Quentin did not excuse him. Quentin, in fact, blamed him. Michael was the canker in the rose of their love. What had Enid said ten years ago? *The boy detests you.* A fundamental truth. *The boy detests you.* After Michael left his mother's house and moved outright to Woodlands, Quentin took care not to express relief, gratitude that he was gone, took care not to disparage Michael. Quentin and the girls tried to put themselves between Claire and the pain Michael inflicted, and slowly, Quentin thought they were coming to some success.

And now?

He took off his glasses and massaged the bridge of his thin nose. A bearded reader in an elaborate rose-coloured turban sat down across from him, nodded and opened his books. Quentin unwillingly turned to the first page of *Woodlands War Years*, and stared at the blurry blue carbon. He could not bear to turn to the second page. This memoir would certainly be published (though not by Selwyn and Archer. Of that, Quentin was quite certain, thank you!). But someone would bring it out. Oh yes, and everyone who ever spilled a drop of sherry at a literary cocktail party, or shared a snide confidence over lunch, would be reminded of the dismal failure of *Hay Days*, reminded of Frank's tawdry death in the Garden of Allah swimming pool, reminded that Claire was *An Inconvenient Wife* to a man she could not give up. Claire would be asked to comment. Quentin would find himself both defending and battling the ghost of Francis Carson, the ghost he thought had finally been put to rest with the posthumous *September Street*. The last of Frank. Thank God. But, no, next year Sybil's bloody book would come out. *Ami de mon coeur. Voleur du temps.* 'You bastard,' he snapped, forgetting his turbanned neighbour.

Perhaps his own affair with Claire was somewhere in these pages. Neither Sybil nor Michael would have any reason to protect the lovers. Enid said the book would have to be edited for libel, but their affair was the truth. Well, what of it? There were days when Quentin himself longed to be done with the stupid fiction he had perpetrated for ten years, to smash Florence's little snow-globe of a world. The profound guilt that had once so tormented him was but a bit of ash, the soot of emotions long since burnt up.

His life with Florence seemed like a stage set where everyone knew their lines and repeated them daily, nightly, like a long-standing, dreary play, scarcely changing even when the family moved to a fine new home, five bedrooms, and a huge garden designed by Rosamund. The housekeeping was tended to by Martha (hired after Effie was caught stealing cigarettes), the garden tended by Rosamund's gardener, the children (Bobby born in 1952) tended by a nanny. When they were older Eleanor and Bobby went to good schools, day students so they could be at home each evening. Family life. When Eleanor and Bobby required Quentin's attention, he was attentive, and kind, though not especially demonstrative, following in Father's footsteps there as well; Albert had never been an especially warm parent. Florence made up for any of his lapses, cooing, and gooing, as Quentin saw it, fussing to no end. But what of it? Bobby and Eleanor flourished just like the African violets on the windowsills and the aspidistras in their pots. Florence flourished. She had a new car and a new television, new kitchen appliances every few years. Her accounts at Harrods, Fortnum's, Liberty and other establishments were paid without question. Florence and Quentin evolved a wordless pact. Each knew what was required, and lived up to it.

In addition to his role as the proverbial Good Provider, Quentin was required to rise to certain kinds of occasions. When Florence required some physical manifestation of his affection, say once a month or so, and though they slept in twin beds, he obliged. When family occasions, like the Sunday lunches (now held at their house), demanded his smiling presence he would be present and cordial. For gala occasions, like Rosamund's sixtieth birthday party, he would be a genial host. Florence was granted immunity from his moods (which could be bleak) and in return on those nights when he came home late, his dinner was left in the warming oven, and his absence was never remarked upon. Occasionally he would be gone on weekends for business.

Florence herself had no part and no interest in his business. As his star rose in his profession, her enquiries into his working life diminished, dwindled into the merely perfunctory. She considered his authors (except for Rosamund) raffish and unsuitable company, especially the colonials whose work he championed, and she was never asked to entertain or even to take them out to dinner. Her sole role in the Old Family Firm was the annual Christmas party. Then, like the lady of the manor, she dispensed little, specially chosen, brightly wrapped gifts to Miss Marr, the typists, the accountant, the new young agents, handed out the Christmas crackers, sliced the cake. In short – and save that her husband felt married to another woman – Florence's life was fine and fulsome, and regulated as the tall clock in the front hall, a clock that tolled the hours.

As those hours slipping into the past became days, months, years, new planets assumed new orbits, held in place by a bland but irresistible gravity that tethered Quentin in a soggy thrall to all of them, to the children, to Albert and Margaret and Fair Rosamund, to Florence, who grew more like her mother every day with her little Rosamund-like fits of pouting. Worse, Eleanor and Bobby, like precocious baby apes, repeated her awful euphemisms, emulated her voice, her peculiar whine to achieve their childish whims. It was unseemly, painful to watch his daughter and son growing into dimpled twits, but he hid his general disapproval since no one in the family seemed to care that he disapproved. Florence reigned at home, and Quentin was more or less the junior partner, disenfranchised by choice.

Can you bear it, dear? Claire's plaintive long-ago question rang in his heart as he stared at the blue pages before him now. He could bear it. His long-standing love for Claire permeated his heart, his very life. He sometimes smiled to think that as a young man he had not shown much promise or energy or aptitude, but in loving her, he had grown, deepened, risked much and thus become more than he could have ever imagined. He had been shaped by what he had dared to be, and whom he had dared to love. Though Quentin and Claire could not live together openly, they gave and received the plunging pleasures of satisfied lust, the nourishment of intimacy, deep emotional sustenance, unsullied trust, shared pleasures, secret places to touch, secret codes of affection, pet names; Quentin was Kanga to her Roo. Their love, which began in sexual intensity, grew into an abiding trust in one another. The marriage of true minds. When they were apart, they sustained each other with little love notes in the post, bits of juicy, lascivious teasing, or extravagant dreams and hungers, small jokes to make each other laugh. They seldom used the telephone, certainly never spoke of anything intimate on the telephone, alert always to the click if Miss Marr picked up. *Can you bear it, dear?*

He could bear it. He had borne it. Scotland was to be his reward: weeks ahead, free of Florence and Bobby and Eleanor, the two grandmothers, free of the stultifying obligations, the inane repetitions. Ten days to spend in Scotland to travel with Claire, to sleep side by side for ten nights. He felt in his pocket; yes, there was the small reassuring lump of the ring box, the sapphire solitaire he planned to give her, blue like Highland lakes, blue like her eyes. He had bought it over time at a Bond Street jeweller's, going there to make payments weekly, like visiting an elderly relative. He had bought her earrings and a pendant and a watch at this jeweller's, but this ring he considered an anniversary present. Ten years. He would slide it on her left hand, to commemorate, to celebrate all they had come through. And now that anniversary, those ten days, were to be blasted by Sybil Dane and Michael Carson. *Ami de mon coeur* indeed. Quentin could all but see Michael's smug smile, his face so like his father's.

'Damn you,' he said, not certain to whom he actually spoke. The turbanned man looked up, Quentin shrugged uncomfortably, and stared into the distance. He thrummed his fingers on the pages, picking up the blue from the carbon. Scotland, ruined, laid waste, ravaged. Just as surely as if Michael had been tucked in the boot of the car. As surely as if Sybil rode on the top, her peacock scarves flying out behind her. Or …

'Or … I could …'

The man in the rose-coloured turban scowled.

Or he could take Sybil's typescript back to the office, put it in the safe. No one need be the wiser. He would go to Scotland and say nothing. He need not let Michael steal this precious time. Go to Scotland, he assured himself.

When he returned to London he would read *Woodlands War Years*, and then give the manuscript to Claire. In keeping it from her now, he wasn't lying. Just a delay. And even if it were a lie, it was the first. Ten years of truth, surely that was an accomplishment. Unless, a small nagging voice reminded him, unless he were to count as lies what he had not told her. He had never let her know that he regretted being party to the fraud that was *September Street*. He had never let her know he felt the ghost of Frank Carson – sometimes mocking, sometimes distressed, sometimes forlorn – but certainly vivid, present on nights when he worked late and alone at Number 11. He had never let her know the depth of his anger at Michael.

Well, *voleur du temps*, he all but whispered now, you won't steal this time. He smiled to touch the ring box in his pocket. He wrapped the carbon copy back in its paper, and tied the string, and left the London Library, exonerating himself of all wrongdoing in the name of love.

CHAPTER TWENTY-ONE

HUMAN ARCHITECTURE

INEVITABLY, WHEN QUENTIN registered himself and Claire as Mr and Mrs Castle, the ruddy landlord or doughy landlady would remark with amusement that Castle was a very good name for these parts, Scotland was famous for its castles. Sometimes the landlord nodded approvingly to see Claire's Leica III draped round her neck, remarking that some of the world's great photographers had found their inspiration here. Claire was pleased, but she explained she was a novice, that the Leica, though a professional's camera, was fairly new (a gift to herself with the money from *September Street*) and she was teaching herself to see in a new way.

As the last of the summer rolled out before them like a Scottish twilight, Claire shot roll after roll of film. They tramped the footpaths and climbed the ruins of castles, milled amid ancient standing stones, and looked across pewter-grey lochs to harsh mountains. They rented a small boat and rowed over cobalt waters where Claire snapped pictures, and Quentin, urbanite that he was, made a mess of the fishing pole, nearly losing his glasses into the bargain, and they laughed so hard they frightened all the fish anyway. They lay in the bottom of the boat and watched the clouds waltz overhead.

The August days were long and often rainy, the nights were short and sweet. Claire and Quentin drank the local whiskies, ate the local food, put their heads together and spoke of plans, possibilities, now that *September Street*, the last of Frank Carson's posthumous novels, was published.

Frank's reputation seemed settled if not altogether secure: Quentin had come to share his father's opinion of short-lived literary regard. In these ten years Sydney Thaxton's star had certainly fallen. But quite apart from all that, Quentin was glad to be done with Frank's posthumous work. His own conduct with regard to *September Street* was perhaps unethical and certainly reckless. No one knew but Claire and himself. No one else suspected. All secrets were safe. With that book behind them, Quentin and Claire could move forward. No surprise, she said she didn't want to be chained to a desk again, not for a long time; she wanted away from literature altogether. The Leica, photography, a pastime that had nothing to do with literature, absorbed her energies, but Quentin slowly came to understand that he had misjudged her: the Leica was a passion, not a pastime.

Driving from Fort William to Oban on a day of rare undiluted sunshine, they came to Appin, with Loch Linnhe on their right, as Castle Stalker came into breathtaking view. They gathered a blanket and the small lunch they'd brought and took their picnic to the shores of Loch Linnhe with its view of the proud, isolate tower. They peeled off rain jackets and sweaters, and rolled their shirtsleeves up, faces tilted to the sunshine, nibbled the sandwiches and biscuits, sipped the tea. Claire opened her camera bag, loaded her Leica, and snapped dozens of pictures of the tower encircled by the blue waters of Loch Linnhe. Then she turned to Quentin resting on his elbows, watching her, his long legs crossed, and took several shots of him.

She flung herself beside him on the blanket, kissed him quickly. 'I think at this moment I can safely say, I am absolutely, perfectly happy. I can't even imagine being happier.'

'If you are happy, then I am content in all things.'

'Let's stay here, Appin, for the night, instead of going on to Oban or Glasgow,' Claire suggested. 'Let's find a hotel, stay here and make this moment last even if we have to drive like hell to get back to Oxford tomorrow.'

'We have to be in Oxford when the girls return from Spain.'

'I'll spell you on the driving, I promise. It's so beautiful. Please.'

'You convinced me. I'm putty in your hands.'

Claire let her hand wander up and over his thigh. 'I wouldn't describe you as putty at all.' Her face still had its luminous beauty, though the creases at her eyes had deepened and there were tiny furrows between her brows. The bright honey-blonde hair of her youth had dimmed, darkened to amber. She kissed him, and lay back down at his side, the sun pinking their faces. 'What are you thinking, Kanga? You're too quiet. I know you.'

'You'll think I'm daft.'

'I think that anyway.'

'I'm thinking how nice it is that we can lie here, that you can kiss me, and it doesn't matter who sees us.'

'Would it matter if I jumped on top of you right now?' Claire sat up, though she didn't jump on top of him. She put new film in her Leica. 'I want to capture Castle Stalker just as it is. I want to have this picture to remind me, no matter how old I get, of how happy I am, how beautiful this place is. This is the best of all the castles we've seen, don't you think?'

'I don't know. They all make me a little uneasy.'

'Why?' She brought the camera to her eye.

'I can't help but think of the hands that built them, that lived here or fought here, or died here, and how the ruins remain, but there's nothing to testify to the people.'

'Of course there is, Kanga! The castle itself testifies to them. That's what makes them romantic, that's why I love them. Growing up in Idaho, there was never any sense of the people who had come before you. They didn't leave anything at all, if there were any people, and there probably weren't. There was only the land, the forests and mountains, all overwhelming. That landscape leaves you dwarfed and insignificant. Humans are just too paltry to make any kind of mark on a landscape like that. But castles like this one tell you people weren't overwhelmed. They made a mark. It's still here. This—' She waved her arm around to the blue loch, the ancient stones of Castle Stalker '—was what I thought I'd find when I came to England.'

'Instead of a vicious old granny and a lecherous uncle?'

'Now you're making fun of me.'

'Never.' He sat up and ran an affectionate hand over her hair. 'Did I tell you that Enid thought the writing in *September Street* some of Frank's best?'

'Too bad it wasn't Frank's at all.'

'That's our secret. Besides, you were so much a part of Frank's work that the transition is seamless.' He leaned back on his arms.

'All except *Hay Days*.'

'Oh, that book. Who cares?' He thought of Sybil's wretched memoir lurking like a ghoul in the office safe. He was so glad he had left it there. These ten days had been the best of his life. He revelled in the invigorating sense of change rippling everywhere, certain as the wind rippling the waters of Loch Linnhe, a feeling he had not known since California ten years ago. Expect Great Change. But now he did not fear it. He welcomed it. He had experience, ballast, and a beautiful woman to love. He put a gentle finger to her lips. 'Do not worry, Roo.'

'What else did Enid say?'

'She called it *Tess of Broadstairs*.'

'That was catty. She's jealous that you are doing so splendidly, and she is not. Why did she want to see you anyway?'

'She plans to retire soon, and she asked me to take her authors back. I said I would, of course.'

'That was decent of you, after the splash she made, walking out like she did.'

'It was the least I could do. Let's walk,' he said, offering his hand and pulling her to her feet. He flung his arm around her shoulders and they strolled down towards the brilliant blue loch, awash in sunlight. He felt suddenly light-headed as well as light-hearted. 'Enid Sherrill knows about us. She knew I loved you ten years ago. That night I drove her home from Woodlands.'

'You mean after ... Woodlands?' Claire's eyes were wide with surprise.

He nodded. 'That very night, she asked me if I was in love with you, and I said nothing. Then the other day she asked if I loved you still, and I said yes.'

'That was very unwise of you, Kanga. She'll spread it everywhere. I told you she's a jealous old cow.'

'No, she won't. Enid Sherrill and I understand each other at last. And anyway, I'm not ashamed of loving you.'

'Look over there,' said Claire, pointing into the distance, a family group, three children, shoes off, wading in the icy loch, the five adults clustered nearby at the water's edge, the men wearing hats, the women wearing dresses, two of them holding umbrellas. 'Only the English would use their umbrellas to protect them from sunlight on a day like today! Don't you want to just throttle them, Kanga! It's sunshine! Enjoy it! I want to go over there and break their umbrellas over my knee and hand them back in shards, and say, you should be tearing off your clothes instead of cowering under umbrellas! There should be a law against it!'

'I'm sure there is. Some old ancient Scottish law declaring that you must fall to your knees, naked, at the first sign of sunshine.'

She brought the Leica to her eye and her shutter snapped time and again, a dozen or more shots. 'One of these ought to be good.'

'What is there to see? They're so far away, you can't tell anything about those people.'

'That's the beauty of it,' she said, putting the lens cap back in place. 'I'm not interested in their faces. To me they're just shapes in the distance with the castle as background. It's the way they're standing, the way the women's skirts are blowing, the tilt of the umbrellas. They're human architecture.' She smiled, her merry blue eyes deeper than the loch, brighter than the sky.

Quentin thought his heart might break from a surfeit of tenderness. 'Marry me.'

'What?'

'Marry me. Every time I register us as Mr and Mrs Castle, I think to myself, it ought to be the truth. We should get married, Roo.'

'I feel married to you, Kanga. Isn't that enough?'

'Not for me. Not any longer.'

'Aren't we just as married as we want to be?'

'I'm not. This whole holiday I keep feeling the ground beneath me shifting, as though the old ways of being and doing won't do any more. The thought of going back to the old same routines, I can't bear it. I've changed. I want to change,' Quentin insisted. 'I want to marry you.'

'Why?'

'Ten years of loving you, isn't that reason enough?'

'I didn't mean it like that.' She tucked her arm closer to his and they continued to walk along the loch's mossy edge. 'I just meant why now?'

'Why not now? Let us take what we can from life while we can.'

'You talk as though we're dying.'

'I've never felt so alive as I have these ten days, but I'm afraid that life will slip away from us, and we will have missed the things we ought to have had, if only we had the courage. I want to grow old with you, Roo. I want my dentures in the glass next to yours.'

She laughed at first, then stopped walking, and combed his well-known face with her eyes. 'You're serious, aren't you? You're not joking.'

'I am serious. My father died last year. He was seventy-one. I'm thirty-five, you're forty.'

'What a brute you are to remind me how much younger you are.'

'Not that much.'

'Then you're a brute to remind me that I'm forty.'

'All I'm trying to say, my point is, half our lives might already be spent. What about the next half?'

'Oh, you're being morbid.' She started walking again, away from him.

'No, I'm not. I'm being alive.' He reached out and took her arm. 'I can't bear the thought of returning to a life that's a lie, a stale lie at that. I've had these ten days with you, and I want more. It's that simple.'

'It's not simple. Think of the scandal.'

'That doesn't sound like Claire the brave! Claire the imaginative! Claire the irreverent! Claire who declared her love for a married man! That sounds like an old maid with her head in a tea cosy, like Miss Marr. Scandal? What is there to fear? No, really, Roo. Will I care that Florence's bridge partners will no longer speak to me? That

Rosamund's gardener will think I'm a cad?'

'I wasn't speaking of them. A professional scandal.'

'Do you really think authors will leave the firm because I'm divorced? Has there ever been a literary man who didn't have a messy love life?' They both thought of Frank, but neither said his name. 'Louisa Partridge will be overjoyed. She'll give me the Distinguished Cross. She's always stirring me on to action of one sort or another.'

'To marriage? That doesn't sound like Louisa.'

'Why should I live half a life when I am a whole man? With you I am a whole man.'

'Divorce, Quentin, think on it. Divorce will make you look bad. It will reflect on, well, on your honesty.'

'Don't you understand? I don't care.'

'Your wife will care. Your mother will care. Your children will care.'

'Florence doesn't give a damn as long as everything stays put and in place. And it will. I'll go on supporting them, naturally. I used to feel like a guilty adulterous shit, but now I just feel like a fraud. Living with her, and snatching bits of time with you, like a pickpocket, like a thief. A thief of time,' he added, bristling.

'What if your father had left Margaret for one of his affairs? How would you have felt? You would have judged him harshly.'

'You are not one of my affairs. You are my one true love, and I am yours. My father could not be faithful to anyone. I have been faithful to you, and you to me. What can I say, Roo? Come live with me and be my love.'

'You speak as if the world was well lost for love, like we were young. We're not two kids in the back of a market-garden truck on our way to the rest of our lives. We're middle-aged people and the choices we've already made have shaped us.'

'But there's more to be shaped! We can have a whole life

331

together, not these shreds, these shards of time we've been satisfied with. I'm not satisfied. I want more. I want you.'

'And what of the girls? What will we tell them?'

'We don't have to tell them anything! They know we love each other. I am as much of a father as they have ever had. They know I love them.'

'What of Michael?'

'He's made his choices.' He instantly regretted reminding her that her son had chosen Sybil Dane over his own mother. 'You don't have to answer to Michael. We're done with Michael.'

'I am not done with Michael. He's my son. I can't ever be done with him.'

'I didn't mean forever,' he lied. 'He'll grow up and come round one day.'

'And say he's sorry?'

'Absolutely,' he replied, hating Michael all the more, hating the typescript in the office safe.

'And ask my forgiveness?'

'Of course.'

'Do you really think so, Kanga?'

'Marry me, Roo. I thought this holiday would assuage all my longings, but it hasn't. It's made me hungrier, made me want more, desire more. Sometimes I think I'll shrivel inside if I can't see you, if I can't ...'

She turned and pressed against him; discreetly she let her hand fall below his belt and stroked him. 'You will never shrivel if I can help it.' She kissed him again, and turned back to the loch and the castle.

He flung an arm over her shoulders and they walked on. 'I don't fear anything except living apart from you. I'm stronger than I once was. Aren't you? Haven't we given each other that much? Shouldn't we have the strength of our love?'

'We do, love.' She placed her left hand with its brilliant

blue sapphire at his lips, and then kissed him gently. 'I have your ring, I have your love, I have your trust, and you have mine.'

'Then tell me you'll marry me, and I'll go back to London, and tell Florence it's over.'

'Florence is in St Ives.'

'Fine.'

'Quentin—' She shook her head '—I told you from the beginning ... really, the beginning, when you came to Polstead Road that day and said there wasn't any hope of our ever marrying, I told you I didn't need to marry you to love you. I loved you then, I love you still, Kanga, but I don't want to marry anyone. I will never remarry.'

'Am I being punished for what Frank Carson did to you?'

'Oh, don't sulk. I hate sulking.'

'I'm not! I'm asking a question.'

'Then leave Frank out of this. You always bring him up when you want to quarrel.'

'I don't.'

'You do.'

'All right then. I do. Never mind him. I'll get a divorce and we won't get married. Will that solve it?'

'Oh, you are impossible.'

'Florence and the children can have everything. I'll come live with you and commute to London. It won't be so very different. Two days a week I work at home with you in any event. Look, I have the courage for this! Don't you?'

'What's happened to you? All this fresh air has addled your brains. That, or you're mad.'

'Then I'll be mad. Marry me. Do you want me to get down on one knee?'

'Don't be foolish. Don't you dare!'

'I am foolish.'

'I thought you were brave.'

'Aren't they the same thing?' Quentin insisted. 'Really. It's all the unbrave dullards who live without love. Like those people with umbrellas to protect them from the sunshine. We've been living just like them.' He got down on one knee.

'Please! Get up! We're not like them in the least.'

'But we are! That's how we've lived for ten years. There's sunshine all around us and we've cowered under umbrellas. Maybe we had to then, in the beginning, but not any more. Look, we have sunshine all around us. Let's crack the umbrellas in half and step into the sunlight.' He stood and enfolded her in his arms.

'The sunlight won't last. It never does.' She gave him a noisy kiss on the lips, and turned to go back towards the picnic blanket. 'Let's go find a hotel.'

He followed her, his mood dampened but not destroyed. He would keep at it, erode her objections, like the wind and the rain had worn down all those old standing stones; he would convince her that now was the time for them to free themselves. And, not incidentally, he remembered with a small thump of conscience, to be able to face the slings and arrows of Sybil's book, and Michael's defection together, a united front, as husband and wife.

'One last picture,' she called out, turning towards him.

'I'm not human architecture.'

'Of course not. You're my one true love. Now smile for me.'

For all the thousands, perhaps millions, of photographs Claire Carson took over a twenty-year career, few survived from early on, save for the Umbrellas of Appin, which she always deemed one of her best. It was one of twelve in her first showing at a small Oxford gallery, and among her most famous even years later when she had her much-lauded 1976 exhibit at London's Excelsior gallery. As a photographer, however, Claire Carson had little interest in portraiture, in people or faces, so there were but a handful of family pictures among her effects – these few of Quentin in Scotland among them – when she died in a private plane crash over the eastern Mediterranean in 1979.

PART V

CHAPTER TWENTY-TWO

'SOME OF THESE DAYS'

QUENTIN APPROACHED NUMBER 11 quite early that June morning, so early the day still felt fresh, the air not yet veiled with exhaust fumes. From an open window above an art gallery, someone was playing *A Hard Day's Night*, Side A, as Quentin very well knew from hearing Bobby and Eleanor play that album down to a hiccupping nub. The smell of coffee roasting at the new coffee bar down the street floated over Mayfair, and he nodded to the baker's delivery boy lofting his trays of croissants and muffins. Across the way Chinese waiters unloaded silvery fish for the Ming restaurant. At the architects' firm, Number 12, a sleepy-looking clerk picked up milk bottles gleaming in the early June sunlight. As Quentin opened the door to number 11, Sergeant, the day porter, stepped out, and scooped up the milk bottles in his arms. 'Mr Castle! You're early, sir! Miss Marr's already picked up your post. She's always the earliest.'

Quentin thanked him, and popped up the staircase with his usual alacrity, meeting Miss Marr on the second-floor landing where she rested on her cane. Her grey hair still bore the neat, crimped imprints of last night's curlers. Her dark suit still had cat hairs. Her beige blouse still carried a whiff of yesterday's perspiration She held a purse, a shopping bag and clutched to her narrow chest a large, bound bundle of heavy manuscripts and many letters.

'You should let Sergeant collect the post, and bring it up. That's why we have him.'

'It's my job.'

'Well, let me take those,' he offered, but she clutched them tighter. 'I insist, Miss Marr.' And he really did. He started up the stairs, but then realized she was still resting on this second landing. He came back and took the shopping bag from her. The scent of stale egg salad wafted from it. 'Let's walk together.'

'I like to take my time,' she said with some asperity. 'You go ahead.'

'I'll wait with you.' Walking at her side, and over the metronomic thump of her cane on the steps, the sound echoing down from the skylights, he realized how stooped she was, how he towered over her. He suddenly wondered how old she was. If he was almost forty, she must be sixty or thereabouts. She seemed much older, a dry, hollow husk of a woman.

'I have to come in early. I don't like to be seen to be so slow,' she said, holding the rail with her other hand. 'Gives those new girls ideas, Lucy and Madge and Becky.' These girls were typists; Monica had long since left, and was the mother of three. 'You know every one of 'em thinks she can replace me. The chits.'

'No one can replace you.'

'You say that,' she grumbled, 'but it'll happen one day. Why are you so early today? You don't usually come in till after nine.'

'Well, I have work. And ... I'm expecting someone.'

'Gigi Fischer.'

'Yes.' He flushed slightly, hoping that his face did not betray his anticipation or his anxiety. Though he and Gigi had exchanged frequent letters, telegrams, telex, even transatlantic telephone phone calls in their many business dealings, he had not actually seen her in these fifteen years. Quentin used his key to open Castle Literary Ltd's door. He put the shopping bag and the stack of envelopes on the desk. He started to untie the strings that bound up the post.

Miss Marr took it from his hands. 'We each have our duties, Mr Castle, and the post is mine.' She gave him a look he could only think of, oddly, as triumph. 'I want to bring to your attention that young Mr Pennypacker took a rather over-long lunch on Tuesday.'

'Perhaps he had an appointment.'

'Perhaps he did, Mr Castle, but he did not check it with me. Did he check it with you?'

'I wasn't in on Tuesday.'

'Quite.'

'I'll speak with him.'

'I confirmed yesterday with The Gay Hussar in Soho,' Miss Marr said. 'They are holding your favourite table for you and Miss Fischer. The contracts for Mrs Partridge's new book are typed and on your desk. Do you wish me to hold all your calls when Miss Fischer is here? As I recall,' she added, not taking her eyes from his face, 'you and she were quite close at one time.'

And that's how Quentin knew that Miss Marr had not forgotten Gigi's indiscreet postcard.

Quentin was unprepared for the emotions that washed over him as Gigi Fischer blew into Castle Literary, lilting the very air with expensive French cologne. For a woman of thirty-five, her dress daringly skimmed above her knees, and she had the shapely, tanned, smooth legs to carry it off. High-heeled sandals, and no stockings. Gigi's hair, an auburn colour not found in nature, and cut sleek, fell forward stylishly. Her eyelashes were astonishingly long and unashamedly false. The gems in her rings and her bracelet were large and unashamedly genuine. She was very chic. More than chic. Everything at sharp angles, and not a bit of frou-frou. She was Mod. Fab. These were words Quentin knew from Mary and Catherine Carson, who prided themselves on being Mod and Fab, fresh, new, and absolutely 1965.

Brief, audible surprise rippled among his employees as he walked through the low gate, took her in his arms and kissed her cheek. 'You look beautiful.'

Gigi, ever assessive in matters of style, told him he had aged well. 'You look every inch the British man of letters, except you're taller and better-looking.'

Quentin laughed, and collected himself to play host, and introduce her to the faces to go with names she might already know. 'Gigi Fischer – or do you prefer your married name?'

'Fischer is fine. That stays the same. Married names can change. I'm on my third husband.'

'Miss Georgina Fischer, the famous Los Angeles film agent, this is Miss Adeline Marr. Miss Marr has run this office admirably for many years.'

Miss Marr managed a stiff smile and asked if they would like tea.

'Only if you have a bathroom nearby,' said Gigi. 'Tea always makes me pee like a racehorse.'

Miss Marr blanched. 'Madge,' said Miss Marr, and instantly one of the young typists got up and went into the small room at the back that served as staffroom and loo.

Quentin introduced Gigi to the other new typists, Lucy and Becky, their machines side by side on a long table. Castle Literary's premises were even more crowded, stem to stern, floor-to-ceiling shelves, and every drawer and cupboard crammed with files and books and manuscripts.

There were many more author photographs in the constellation on the wall above Miss Marr's desk, some in colour. He knocked on the door of what had once been Enid Sherrill's sole domain, which now housed Richard, Angela and Liz, and introduced Gigi to them, and did the same in what was once his old narrow office. The new accountant worked at the desk in front of the window; the place in the closet was occupied by the newest, the novice agent, young Gordon Pennypacker.

All that done, Quentin led her into his own office. Gigi had an assessive look round and announced, 'The place looks just as I pictured it.' She put her handbag and a large alligator briefcase on the low table between the leather chairs.

'The desk is neater than it was in my father's time,' Quentin replied, 'but we have a fine literary tradition and I saw no reason to change that.' He sat in one of the leather chairs, leaned back and allowed himself to bask in Gigi's sunny presence.

Gigi wandered to the mantel. 'I never took you for a rock collector.' She lifted a nondescript stone.

'That's from Kilimanjaro, given to my father by John McVicar. No one reads McVicar any more, but he was a renowned adventure writer once.'

'And who is this framed letter from?'

'Sydney Thaxton.'

'Never heard of him.' She pointed to the framed photo of a jaunty soldier. 'Robert?'

'Yes.'

'He was a handsome devil.'

'He was.'

'So are you, you know. I'm serious. You're much better-looking now than you were all those years ago. What's your secret?'

'Prayer.'

'No pictures of the wife and kiddies?' asked Gigi with an arched eyebrow.

'I keep my personal and my professional life separate.' In this office there was no African violet, no aspidistra.

'How are Florence, Eleanor and young Robert?'

'Fine.'

She waited for him to go on, and when he refused to, she gave a trilling laugh. 'Oh, Quentin, you slay me! You always set yourself to a standard no one else would ever try to live up to.'

'What do you mean?'

'Just that I wish I'd been smarter. I know now I didn't recognize a really good man when I met him.'

'You don't mean poor Don, the writer?'

'I mean you, you ass! If I'd had any sense, I would have never let you leave California.'

'I was married, even then. Hard to believe, but true.'

Gigi sighed. 'Oh, yes. I'd forgotten. Oh well, you still changed my life.'

'Every lover likes to be told that.'

'I wouldn't be an agent without you. All those days in Baja, listening to you talk, I thought, why couldn't I do that here in LA? Sure, there were a few such agencies already, mostly run by geezers. Why not try? After all, I was Roy's stepdaughter and people were afraid to treat me like shit. Who would have ever thought that one day a man like Roy would be obsolete, and I would be a powerful agent?'

'I never doubted you. You are still the Girl of the Golden West.'

'You did once call me a shallow twit.'

'I misspoke. Anyway, I think we both changed in Mexico.' He gave her an indulgent grin. 'I still like to say it sometimes. *Baja.*'

Gigi strolled around the office, glanced back, overtly

flirtatious, and knowing. 'We could give it a rerun some afternoon this week, say tomorrow afternoon?'

'Thanks. I'm flattered. But no.'

'An old married man, I take it.'

'That has nothing to do with it. You and I were a golden moment. That kind of magic? No one gets that twice. It would be a mistake to think we could. I am not a man to tempt fate,' he said, though he had been tempting fate with Claire Carson for fifteen years. He thought, idly, that's what makes fate tempting, to have some forbidden, lyrical presence, like Claire, love that both buoys and roots. Magical.

'Quentin?'

'Oh, sorry. Excuse me, Gigi. What were you saying about sainthood? I thought you were Jewish.'

'What does that matter? I'm sacrificing myself.'

'That doesn't sound like you,' he chuckled.

'I'm atoning. For my sins I am now a stepmother, and my teenage stepdaughter, Kathy, just wouldn't let up. Oh, London is just the swingingest place on the planet, next to the surfing club at Malibu, naturally, oh Daddy, we have to go! Phil, my husband, gave in, naturally, though he couldn't be bothered to come. So here I am. Doris is with us, supervising the shopping, and as we speak the girls are using their daddies' money to devastate the boutiques of Carnaby Street, and raise the gross national product of Great Britain. They came with empty suitcases to take home Mary Quant clothes. We have tickets for Lionel Bart's *Oliver*, and something or another from the Royal Shakespeare Company, and we are signed up for the Beatles Tour in Liverpool. Yes, I am being dragged up to Liverpool, of all places, and I have to listen to three girls singing "Yeah Yeah Yeah" and giggling constantly. I have been to see *A Hard Day's Night* three times. I told you, atoning.'

'Three girls?'

'When word got out that I was taking Kathy, my nieces insisted I bring them too.'

'The Lotus's children?'

Gigi nodded and rolled her eyes. 'Doris insists we're all one big happy family. Holidays are gruesome, of course. Some of us are Christian, some are Jewish, no one gives a good goddamn anyway, but—' She shrugged '—it makes Doris happy.'

Madge knocked with the tea tray and put it on the low table between the leather chairs. Quentin poured the tea and passed a cup to Gigi. She lit a cigarette, and he found her an ashtray. One change he had made in Albert's office was to rid the place of pipe stands, pipe cleaners, tobacco tins, ashtrays and wooden matches, though he kept a vase full of matchbooks from expensive London restaurants.

She blew out a plume of smoke. 'The girls can't understand why I hated London so much in '49. I can't explain how it was just so ...'

'I think your expression was "pinched and nasty".'

'Oh, don't hold that against me, Quentin. It was just so dark, somehow, all that ruination amid cheerio, pip pip, weak tea, warm beer, and Eddie with his fishy breath. I heard he married some Australian heiress, by the way, no doubt knee deep in sheep shit and wool money.'

'You should thank him. He did introduce you to the MG.'

'Yes, and I still have that MGT. My first love and wages for my first job.' She winked. 'I also have an MGA, a '58, along with a Porsche, which I think is overrated, and the Triumph. I had to build another garage for all my sports cars, and the mechanic bills are bankrupting me. They're fussy little buggers, the cars. The mechanics too. But what can I do? The damn cars are always breaking down. Roy always said they're worse than poodles.'

'I was sorry to hear about Roy.'

'You probably weren't, but it's nice of you to say so. It was a shock. Five years ago now, hard to believe. He just keeled over from a heart attack. Totally unexpected. I made my peace with Roy. I've always been glad of that, but he and I were never quite the same after the whole Frank Carson fiasco. He always treated me fine, but ...' She smoked reflectively. 'I couldn't ... you know?'

Quentin didn't, but he nodded just the same.

'Professionally, though, I never lost my admiration for Roy. He could see what television was doing to the studios and he fought it, threw money at it – they all did – but finally television won. People worship the one-eyed idol.'

'They're still making movies,' he observed.

'Yes, but the golden age is behind us – and ahead of us! I've got a lot of good scripts on hand, but my main challenge now is to convince someone to care about a couple of Midwest bank robbers in the thirties.'

'If anyone can, you can.'

'Well, you might not be so complimentary when I tell you that the studio that was so excited about producing *September Street* has entirely let the thing lapse. They're not picking up the option again. It's a no go.'

'I'm sorry to hear that. It would have made a fine film. There are other possibilities surely.'

'Of course. A good agent never gives up. I'll continue to look for a film option. However, I've brought you a consolation prize. A gift. Two gifts.' She picked up her alligator briefcase, and drew out a fat, folio-sized envelope, and then another, a good deal thicker. She stacked them on the tea table. 'These are for you. Hand delivered. A gift from Roy in a manner of speaking.'

The envelopes both had the Regent Film logo boldly stamped on them. Quentin frowned.

'When Roy died, Aaron and the Lotus were on safari

347

in Africa – I'm sure they went there to teach the lions how to maul their prey – but they were far away. Doris was distraught, this time for real, a serious mess, and she kept saying there were things we had to do to protect Roy. I said, sure. So I spent days, weeks, really going through Roy's things. I saved a lot of stuff Aaron would have destroyed. Like this.' Gigi put her hand out on one of the envelopes, her polished nails and ruby ring gleaming red. 'Frank Carson's script for *Some of These Days*. The one he actually wrote. After what you went through for him, I thought you deserved to have it. There's a few letters to Roy in there too, some where Frank is ripping Roy a new sphincter, calling him a philistine, and worse, and then the next page, sometimes the next paragraph, snivelling, slathering on the praise, hoping to get Roy to ... well, it's all pretty abject stuff. Nauseating, really.'

'Writers often debase themselves on behalf of their work. The writer who says he won't is lying. The agent's job is to see that they don't have to.'

'Yes, well, Frank didn't have an agent there, did he? He was on his own. He lost this battle, as you know. Poor bastard. Don't even think of trying to publish it.'

Quentin suppressed a laugh to think how swiftly she had read his mind. 'And why not?'

'It isn't his. Or his wife's or yours. It belongs to Regent Films. It says so on the first page.'

'But they no longer exist.'

'True, but they have heirs and assignees and all the rest of it, and though Regent's finished, Aaron has landed on his feet, and he hasn't changed one bit. Dealing with him will cost you more money than you ever dreamed of. So, you can perish that thought.' She drank her tea, and placed the cup in the saucer with an affirmative plink. 'This is a gift, but you have to promise me you won't use it to tarnish Roy's name.'

'Tarnish? That phrase sounds like something from a Victorian novel, not Gigi Fischer.'

'You Brits aren't the only ones with respect. He wasn't a saint, but I'm still loyal to Roy. It's the past, Quentin.'

'You have my word I won't tarnish Roy's name. Did you read Frank's script?'

'I did. Not half bad. Really, quite good, I think. Honestly, if they'd stuck with what he wrote, *Some of These Days* might have been an OK picture. Certainly better than that farce they ended up with. A big, blowsy Hollywood musical about the 1906 earthquake. Whose goddamned idea was that?'

'Whose was it?'

'Whoever it was never fessed up. Everyone tried to walk away from *Some of These Days* but the stink stuck to everyone associated with it. *Some of These Days* was the beginning of the end for Roy and Regent. For everyone. The last I heard Gilbert Vernon was in Vegas booking acts for one of the hotels. Linda finally divorced him, but by then even Louella Parsons didn't care. Linda only did a couple of pictures after *Some of These Days*. She's actually a competent actress, but she'll never work again. Fifteen years past her heyday, and she's a tub of lard compared to what's considered beautiful now. Look at these London girls with their short skirts and clingy sweaters and skinny legs and their big eyes! All madcap runabouts, like extras from *A Hard Day's Night*, or *The Knack*.'

'They are, rather. Over here they call them birds.' He smiled.

'Did you ever see *Some of These Days*?'

Now Quentin had to stand. He walked to the window and opened it and the smell and noise of the street below blew in. 'I was bloody speechless. I could barely sit through it. I didn't think anything could be that bad. Poor Frank. They did that to his book, and he had to die.'

'Listen, baby.' Gigi smashed out her cigarette for emphasis. 'Frank Carson was his own force of nature, all of it destructive. Everyone whose life he touched, at least in Hollywood, got burnt up, or was destroyed. He left rubble behind him, Quentin, ruination and everlasting regret. Frank Carson only did one good thing in his entire life, and that was introduce me to you.'

Quentin laughed out loud. 'His wife and daughters might disagree.'

She placed her hand on the second envelope. 'These are the wife's letters. Why or how these letters got saved when they cleaned out Frank's villa, I don't know. I think Aaron cleaned it out, went through the place with his own fair lawyerly hands, but that's just a guess.'

'The bastard lied to me.'

'Why are you surprised? Aaron is a snake.'

'And the second suitcase? Where is that?'

'There is no second suitcase. Maybe there never was. You only have the wife's word on that, after all.'

'Yes.'

She rested her jewelled hand atop the envelope. 'I assume you'll give these to the wife.'

'They're hers by rights.'

'She also needs to understand that I don't want all that old shit about Frank dredged up. Roy's not around to defend himself—'

'He didn't defend himself then! Of course,' Quentin added, still stung after all these years at their high-handed, lying disdain, 'he didn't need to. He was Roy Rosenbaum, and he could do what he liked.'

'And now he's dead and I don't want Doris upset over something so paltry as the past.'

'If you really thought the past was paltry, you wouldn't care at all.'

'Well, touché, baby, but I mean it. I don't want dirt

stirred up on Roy.'

'I will see to it that Mrs Carson respects your wishes, Gigi.'

'She must have no shame.'

'Who?'

'Frank Carson's wife.'

'That's a rather cruel thing to say about someone you don't know.'

'If I knew her, I might have phrased it differently, but it doesn't change the truth. All that humiliation she endured? All that ...' Gigi's voice trailed off. 'Reading those letters was painful, I mean that, viscerally painful. My God, she must have really loved him! Those letters are desperate and ardent and angry, and heartbreaking crazy.'

'You read them? Really, Gigi? I find that ...'

'I'm Nosy-Nell, sue me. She's a hell of a writer, but I'd never want to love anyone like that.'

'Like what?'

'Like she loved Frank Carson. To give someone that much power over you? To risk everything like she did? This woman abdicated everything there was to give up, gnashed and threatened and splattered herself, heart and soul, guts and pride, all splayed across these pages, and Frank didn't give a shiny shit. Some of her letters weren't even open, if you must know.'

'You opened them?' Quentin heard his own intake of breath. 'Isn't that ...'

'Like I said, sue me. Sure, I opened them. Who's to care?'

'Well, Claire Carson for one!'

'Who's to know? Unless you tell her.' She lit up again, her silver lighter filling the air with the scent of flammable daring. He did not reply, and she shut the lighter with a snap. She inhaled and repeated, 'Frank Carson didn't

351

give a damn about her any more. These letters are *An Inconvenient Wife* all over again.'

'What do you mean?'

'You're not likely to forget a phrase like lightning to someone else's thunder. Wasn't that one of the chapters in *An Inconvenient Wife*?'

'So?'

'It's just odd to me, Quentin, that a book that Frank wrote would sound so much like the letters his wife wrote. I told you, some of them weren't even open.'

'It's just a phrase. He probably said it.'

'Probably. Anyway, their marriage was over. That much is clear. All marriages come to that. No matter if you stay together or not. They're over.'

'What makes you say that?'

Gigi finished her tea, and dabbled her cigarette into the ashtray. 'Phil is my third husband, so I'm something of an expert on—'

The door flung open, and a young woman burst in, her voice ringing. 'I promise you, Miss Marr, Quentin won't care!' Short skirt, clingy sweater, long legs and enormous blue eyes, her fair hair caught in two pigtails framing her face. 'Oh! I didn't know you had company.'

'That is a lie! Liar!' Miss Marr screamed, standing in the doorway, her cane upraised, waving wildly, her eyes burning with rage. 'I told her! I forbade her to—'

The girl kicked the door shut in her face.

'Really, Mary!' Quentin remonstrated, rising, dismayed by Miss Marr's strident fury, so unlike the mousy, taciturn woman he knew. 'You're so rude to poor Miss Marr! You must apologize.'

'She can be such a sour old cow.'

'Nonetheless!'

'Oh, very well, I will. I promise. But I can't just now. I have an audition! It's in—'

'Mary, meet Georgina Fischer. Gigi is a friend of mine from California, a film agent. Gigi, meet Miss Mary Carson.'

'Frank Carson's daughter?' asked Gigi, the question more to Quentin than to the girl.

'I am,' Mary retorted, bristling slightly. 'One of them.'

'Mary and her sister Catherine are both students at RADA, the Royal Academy of Dramatic Arts,' said Quentin before Gigi could respond. Gigi's candour could be dangerous, and he so hoped she wouldn't say something coarse about Frank to a girl who could hardly remember him.

Mary flung her massive handbag on his desk. 'I've an audition, Quentin! Catherine too! They need twins. We're not twins, but we're sisters. Can I change here in the office? I don't mean to chase you out, but you know I can't put my make-up on in the office loo. The light in there is just bloody awful, and someone's always eating their bloody lunch in the staffroom. Please, Quentin, can I have your office for just a bit? To change for the audition? It's for a Richard Lester picture!'

'Really? We were just talking about Richard Lester. *A Hard Day's Night.*'

'Catherine was in that,' she proudly advised Gigi. 'She was one of the girls in the train station, chasing the Beatles before they scooted into the car. She didn't get a credit, of course, but she's there, and she's in another scene too. A crowd scene.'

'That must have been a lot of fun,' Gigi remarked.

'Oh, it was. But these, these are real roles, concubines for the orgies and dancers for the funeral. This film's from a play, a musical, *A Funny Thing Happened to Me on the Way to the Forum.* Buster Keaton is in it! I could actually meet Buster Keaton! Can you imagine, Quentin?'

He laughed to hear her use Claire's favourite expression. Mary and Catherine had their mother's bright presence, her energy and enthusiasm, though neither had quite inherited her beauty. 'I can indeed imagine.'

'They start filming in autumn in Spain, and they're casting now for twins, sisters.'

'It's a great opportunity for you both,' he said.

Mary grew suddenly serious. 'Of course, it's not Ophelia.'

'It will be much more fun than Ophelia.'

'I can't go looking like this! Can I change here?'

'Of course. Gigi and I were just going to lunch.'

'As soon as I use the loo,' said Gigi, stubbing out her cigarette, and gathering her handbag. She turned to Mary, and said with perfect sincerity, 'I met your father several times at my stepfather's house. Frank Carson was brilliant and everyone adored him.'

'Thank you.'

'It was a pleasure to be in his company.' Gigi gave Quentin a look that forewarned him she would question him mercilessly at lunch. 'Back in a flash,' she added on her way out the door.

Quentin took the two envelopes Gigi had brought and put them in a drawer. 'The place is yours, Mary. When are you and Catherine and I going to tea again? It's been a week at least.'

'We'll celebrate when we get the parts.'

'The Ritz,' he promised. 'Concubines at the orgy, dancers at the funeral. Best of luck, ducky.'

Her face lit, pleased. 'Oh, by the way, Quentin, word to the wise, Mum's got her knickers in a knot because you never answered her letter.'

'What letter?'

'She wrote she didn't want to do any more editing, and she's been waiting for you to reply, or call, or something.'

'I never got any such letter.'

'Well, tell her that. She thinks you're sulking. She hates sulking.'

'Why doesn't she want to do any more editing?'

Mary shrugged. 'How should I know? Oh and … Catherine and I … we'd rather you didn't say anything to Mum about the auditions today. We don't want her to know unless we get the parts. She expects a lot of us. Too much, Catherine says.'

'I'm sworn to secrecy.'

'Yes.' She smiled. 'As always.'

'But really, Mary, you two should share more of your lives with your mother. I'm sure she'd like to cheer you on whether you get the parts or not.'

'You like to cheer us on, Quentin. Mum likes it when we win.'

'Well, my lips are sealed.' He started for the door. 'Oh, and be nice to Miss Marr on your way out, will you? Apologize?'

'Yes. Promise. Sorry.'

But by the time Mary Carson had changed her clothes, undone the pigtails and shaken her fair hair free, teased it up, and sprayed it, applied her make-up, pressed on her false eyelashes, and made her lovely exit into what was certainly going to be a role as the concubine at the orgy, the dancer at the funeral and the glorious future she imagined, Miss Marr was not at her desk.

Miss Marr was in the staffroom next to the loo where there was a hotplate, a sink for washing up, a shelf for tea things, a single deep chair, and a tiny table. She was eating her egg salad sandwich. She was alone. Her bread was streaked with blue from the carbon paper stains on her fingers. Her piece of fruit and digestive biscuits were on a saucer. Beside her on the hotplate, the kettle prepared to boil.

Gigi had such an enlivening effect on him that had he been more musical, Quentin himself might have burst into a bit of Gilbert and Sullivan as he climbed the stairs after lunch. He was still basking in being the envy of every man at The Gay Hussar, from the busboys to the peers of the realm, to have on his arm a woman so chic, so clearly unique, smart and savvy as well. His jovial mood evaporated immediately upon seeing Miss Marr, who glared at him. He instantly feared the worst. 'I hope Mary Carson made her apologies, Miss Marr.'

'She did not.'

'Well then, I apologize on her behalf. She behaved very badly indeed. She can be a bit of a hoyden.'

'Is that what you call it, Mr Castle? You are always excusing her. Excusing both of them. They are not little girls any more. They are women.'

'She was unpardonably rude.'

'It's not the first time. She and her sister, both, her mother too, they all treat me as though I am invisible.' Her lower lip trembled slightly.

'You should always be accorded respect,' he offered, but to avoid further exchange on this touchy subject, Quentin moved quickly to his own office and closed the door.

He retrieved the two Regent Films envelopes Gigi had brought, pushed his other obligations aside and set them on the desk. Now his mood soured. He played with the seal on the envelope, opened it, closed it again. Gigi had had no qualms about reading these letters, even – the cheek! – opening ones that Frank had left unread. Quentin had qualms, but they were not of a moral sort. His, he told himself, were more complex. Did these letters threaten the equilibrium of his life?

Five years ago the manuscript of Sybil Dane's *Woodland War Years* had threatened a storm. Quentin and Claire had weathered it. Not without tears, but weathered it nonetheless. He never told her he had kept the manuscript from her. Indeed, he only gave it to her when Enid alerted him that she had found a publisher. Claire's reaction to the manuscript was much as he had feared, passionate, unbounded, devastating. The treachery of her own son! The hideousness of that stinking bitch, Sybil! Quentin offered up a tidy lie to cover his tracks so he could go and stay with her in Oxford for a week. But really, the following year, when *Woodland War Years* was actually published, it was not nearly as incendiary as the manuscript. The truly libellous stuff had been expunged, though the tone remained overwrought, and full of hyperbole for *Hay Days*, for Francis Carson and his muse, Sybil Dane. Some merciful editor had prevailed upon Sybil to take out passages suggesting she might be more than a mentor to her *ami de mon coeur*, Michael Carson. Publication created a flurry of gossip and a handful of mostly dismissive reviews, though the juicier ones noted that Francis Carson had not married his wife till after their son was born. Claire refused to comment, and her response came exclusively through Castle Literary Ltd. Quentin suppressed the urge to remark publicly that he'd always known Michael Carson was a bastard.

But these letters? What storm did they brew? One, he feared, closer to the heart.

Would he discover that Claire had lied to him? That she alone had written *An Inconvenient Wife* beginning to end? She said she had typed it, and Quentin had no reason not to believe her. *September Street*, of course, was another matter altogether. He took off his glasses and pinched the bones of his nose, trying to remember how they had agreed that Claire should write another posthumous Carson novel using her own experience – the orphaned girl, the bedridden grandmother, the lecherous uncle – and pass it off as Frank's. Had they actually agreed? He could not remember. But Quentin could not forget that he had colluded in that fraud, beginning to end.

At the time it had not seemed so very heinous. And no one, not even the negative reviewers, seemed to doubt the novel was pure Francis Carson. Now, five years after its publication, Quentin regretted being so easily complicit. He could be ruined if the fraud were ever found out. He had risked not only his own reputation but the nearly half-century reputation of the firm his father had built. That fear never quite left him. Like his peptic troubles. He opened the drawer, found his stomach pills, and took two to settle himself. 'If you read these letters, you ass,' he advised himself gravely, 'and if it turns out that they are *An Inconvenient Wife* ...'

What else might she have lied about? Why would she not have told him the truth? Oh, maybe not at the time, so soon after Frank died. He could forgive that. He could forgive her just about anything. He loved her. But why had she not eventually confessed the truth of it? If it were the truth that she had written *An Inconvenient Wife* on her own, not Frank at all ...

What would that mean to their union?

They'd been together so long now. They were so close, even if they were not wed. Claire had steadfastly refused to marry him, and he had finally given up, but they had shared so much, their personal lives, their professional lives, raising the girls. He knew he should not read these letters. It would be an invasion. A breach of trust. He put them away and opened Frank's script for *Some of These Days*.

Perhaps an hour later a sharp knock sounded at the door, and a ruddy, stocky young man burst in. 'Miss Marr said you wanted to see me.'

'Well, she misspoke, Pennypacker. I don't. Leave and close the door.'

One by one the typewriters in the outer office fell silent and he heard the staff bidding each other goodnight, the click of the lock when the last of them left. He finished reading the script of *Some of These Days*, and looked up, aware of the ghost of Frank Carson. Present somehow. Here. Friend and nemesis these fifteen years, the enigmatic ghost silently beseeched him, neither mocking nor compassionate, only questioning, perplexed. And that's when Quentin admitted to himself that neither trust nor courtesy kept him from reading Claire's letters. Fear. He feared that if these letters were as desperate, ardent, and shameless as Gigi said, he would know, for certain, that Claire never had, and never would, love him as she had once loved Francis Carson.

The large envelope lay before him. To read or not to read? That was the question. None of it was nobler in the mind, all of it was rancour to the heart. Quentin had anchored his life and his love to Claire, and these letters could leave him unmoored forever. He sat there quietly, facing the greatest risk he had ever taken, feeling something of what McVicar must have felt on scaling the heights that killed him.

Someone, perhaps in the art gallery across the way, put on *A Hard Day's Night* again, and now that the working day was over, they turned it up loud. The music echoed between the buildings, filling old Mayfair with the Mod and Fab. Quentin, his head in his hands, listened. 'If I Fell' warbled out. Hearing the lyrics, the lover's aching questions, he opened the envelope and tumbled the letters across his desk.

CHAPTER TWENTY-THREE

DEATH OF THE SPARROW

OUTSIDE THE OXFORD station she sat behind the wheel of the Mini, deeply engrossed in reading, and did not see him approach the car. When he opened the door, she tossed the paperback in the back seat, which was awash in books and magazines, grocery bags and empty film cans, the usual Claire-chaos. She put her reading glasses atop her head; the girls had talked her into a short haircut three months before and it was growing out. She wore a jaunty summer dress of some light material, green threads like stems through a pink design, sleeveless; her bare arms were tanned from time outside in the garden, and the sapphire ring gleamed on her left hand.

Claire gave him a brief connubial kiss. 'Why do you look so glum, Kanga? I thought Gigi Fischer was in London yesterday. She ought to have cheered you up.'

'I didn't sleep with her if that's what you're asking.'

'I'm not asking.'

'She offered.'

Claire chuckled softly as she put the car in gear and pulled away. 'I'm sure she did. What did you tell her?'

'That it was a golden moment that couldn't be repeated.'

'That was kind of you, poetic, really, but it doesn't explain why you're cranky. I know you, Kanga, and you're hiding something.'

'Mary came by the office yesterday and met Gigi.'

Claire paused at this. 'Did Gigi make some catty remark about Frank?'

'On the contrary, she was the soul of tact.'

'Well, that isn't something anyone usually says about Gigi Fischer, is it?' She glanced over at him, but he was looking straight ahead.

'Mary said you wrote me that you didn't want to be doing any more editing. I never received such a letter. Why not?'

'I have no idea why you didn't get it. It's not the first letter of mine to go missing.'

'That's not what I'm asking. Why have you decided not to edit anything else? And why did you feel you had to write me to say so?'

She shrugged. 'I wanted to be clear. I'm done with the literary life. No more books. I don't have to give a damn about literature or reputation or the critics any longer. I'm concentrating on my own career, on photography.'

'Fine, but why did you feel you had to write, some sort of formal notice?'

'Oh, you're just so cranky today, Kanga. Why make the trip if you're going to be cross?'

'Mary said you thought I was sulking. I'm not.'

'Mary is telling tales out of school. She can be quite the big mouth.'

'She's just a girl, Claire. She's excited.'

'About what?'

'Life, acting, London!' He felt a twinge of guilt for keeping their secrets from Claire.

'You see more of Mary and Catherine than I do. They hardly ever come home.'

'Well, they live in London now. Of course I see them.' Quentin watched the blue-green smear of summer pass by as she drove up the Banbury Road to Summertown; the view was balm to his eyes, though his heart was troubled.

Linton Road was closer to the river Cherwell, and unlike Polstead Road, these solid Victorian-Gothic houses were not, or not yet, carved into flats. Claire's ample three-storey home had tall hedges for privacy from the street. She pulled the Mini behind the hedges and the gravel crunched under her tyres. Claire had bought this fine house with the American insurance money and the sale of Harrington Hall. *An Inconvenient Wife* paid for a substantial remodel, and *September Street* had paid for a darkroom and a studio for Claire.

Quentin used his own key on the door, and stepped into the airy hall. The kitchen had a wide bank of windows looking out into a garden where – though they had laughed themselves silly about getting Rosamund to design it – Claire had lavished time, money and vision to make it beautiful in all seasons. Now, in the high flush of midsummer, the delphiniums stood like tall blue sentinels at the back, apple trees evenly spaced around the perimeter, and flowering laburnum drooped golden flowers. A few chairs and a creaky wicker table sat under a wisteria arbour where the late purple blooms spindled. He put his leather case on the tiled floor, loosed his tie and took off his coat. 'Where's the dog?' he asked, unaccustomed to the silence.

She took two grocery bags to the counter. 'I gave her away. To a good family, don't worry.'

'But why? Mary and Catherine will be devastated!'

'Mary and Catherine live in London now, as you pointed out. I can't be keeping a dog just to amuse them when they come to visit.'

'But I thought you liked the dog. She was company for you.'

'I've had a year here now, alone, since Mary left, and for the first time, really, in my whole life, I'm not responsible for someone else. Not even the dog. I've always had to be looking after someone. Before Michael and Mary and Catherine, it was Frank, before Frank it was grotty Granny, before her I had a bunch of younger siblings. But now, I look around at my life and I think, Claire, you could do something!' She filled the kettle and lit the gas beneath it.

'You already do something.' He pointed to the rows of photographs laid out on the table. Her photographs in frames lined the walls.

'We have to talk about this.' She sat down across from him and took his hands in hers. 'When I ran off with Frank, I was completely prepared to do whatever he wanted, whatever I could do to get his work into the world. I kicked up my heels in the chorus line. I typed all day when I'd been up all night. I was his wife, mistress, muse, editor, proofer, his typist—'

'I know this story, Claire. Get to it.'

'Sorry. What I mean to say is, I lived in his shadow. But now he is long, long gone, and I'm still living in his shadow. I've become a walking reliquary, I'm Frank's memory on the hoof.'

'What are you talking about? Are you sick?'

'I get all these tedious enquiries from academics begging for answers to their long-winded questions, asking for my time and insight.'

'Just tell them to sod off. That's easy.'

'The truth is if I stay here forever, I will actually become the walking font of Francis Carson memorabilia, one of those dotty old Oxford dames.'

'If you stay here?' He thought he had misheard her.

'I see them all the time on the bus, with their sturdy shoes and their stained cardigans—'

'If you stay here?'

'—and their untidy hair and doughy faces, their glasses slipping down their noses, their handbags full of tins of cat food—'

'That could never be you! You are beautiful!'

'I'm not talking about what time does to women. I'm talking about what we do to ourselves.'

'What do women do to themselves?' He was at a loss.

'Look at Florence, a narrow little life spent fussing over bridge games, or jumble sales for worthy causes, perfectly content with life in a teacup, and now and then to peer over the rim.'

'You talk as if you're in danger of becoming a Barbara Pym character. If anything you've been bold. Even reckless.' He regretted that last.

The kettle whistled and she rose, turned it off, and said, 'I'm forty-five. I have years before me. I'll never know what I can accomplish if I don't leave.'

'Leave? Oxford?'

'Not for good and always. I'll keep this house.'

'Where else would you go?' His face lit. 'Would you come to London?'

She ran a hand through her thick tawny hair. 'Mary and Catherine are making their lives in London. They don't need their old mum hanging round.'

Quentin did not like the direction the conversation was taking. 'And Michael? He's in London too, Presiding Secretary of Great Dane Enterprises, as I recall.' He sounded more bitter than he wanted to.

'Please let's not talk about Michael, Kanga. You know how it upsets me. Besides, I don't even like London, and if I moved there, sooner or later someone would find us out.'

'I don't give a damn! I've told you for years I wanted a divorce! I want to marry you.'

'Yes, dear, and I told you, I will never remarry.'

'We could live together.'

'Kanga, I want to find out something about myself that isn't Frank Carson, or Mary or Catherine, or Michael. I don't want to be forever defined by my marriage to Frank.'

Quentin peered at her as if the steam from the kettle had darkened his glasses and impaired his vision. 'Is that really how you think of yourself? Defined by Frank? How can you say that?'

'I am his widow.'

He laughed out loud. 'Oh, that is rich, Roo! Rich and ridiculous! What are you, some Indian widow about to crawl onto the funeral pyre? I never heard such rubbish. His widow. He's been gone for fifteen years! You and I have been together as long as you and Frank. Do I count for nothing?'

'You prove my point! Men always think of their women as satellites. You're doing the same thing. You admire Louisa Partridge because she refused to be defined by the men in her life, not her husband, not her American colonel when he up and left her. And not Bernard when he said no to her book. Louisa said, "Fie on you, Selwyn and Archer!" And she did something else. You admire Gigi Fischer because she stepped out from Roy's shadow, made her own career. She's her own woman, not some man's satellite. Even Enid Sherrill! You took the office she wanted, and so she left, struck out on her own. Don't you see? It's the same thing. I cannot stay here and be Frank's widow for the rest of my life.'

'What about me?'

'I can't stay here forever and be Frank's widow and your mistress.'

He felt the sting physically, as though she had slapped him. He had no retort. He was speechless, and so he rose and went to his leather case, drawing out the two big envelopes. 'Gigi brought these, gave them to me yesterday. They are a gift, of sorts. One is Frank's script for *Some of These*

Days and a lot of letters he wrote to Roy Rosenbaum. And this one—' He laid his hand on the larger envelope '—is full of your letters to Frank. She found them after Roy died.' He knew her well enough to see that she was shaken.

Claire spoke at last. 'Five years it took her to return them?'

'It doesn't pay to question Gigi's instincts or logic.'

'You always knew those Hollywood bastards were lying to you.'

'Yes, much good it did me.'

'And the second suitcase?'

'Was there a second suitcase?'

'What? What do you mean?'

'This is all Gigi found. There was no second suitcase.' He hoped Claire would contest this, or refine the point, but she only commented icily that they were all bastards, every one of that Hollywood lot. 'They are,' he went on, 'but I came today to bring these to you, and to ask why you lied to me. Please don't insult me by asking about what. These letters are *An Inconvenient Wife*. They are the book itself, the very wording.'

'You read them!'

'So did Gigi.'

'I find that intolerable. They belong to me.'

'Gigi said you could sue her if you like.'

'And you?'

'You can't sue me, Claire. I love you, and you love me, and we have been everything to one another. So I am devastated here. I can't understand why you would lie, and tell me you had a carbon of the novel, of most of the novel, when you didn't. When you wrote it yourself.'

'I had his notes. I had a portion that I'd typed. I didn't lie about that. I knew what he was going to do with it. He would have used me for that book, the story of our crumbling marriage. I knew that story as well as he did. I don't

366

see why you're so outraged. I wrote all of *September Street* and you were fine with that little ruse.'

'I was, and I rather wish I'd thought it through more carefully.'

'You regret it?'

He chose not to answer, returning stubbornly to his question. 'Why didn't you trust me enough to tell me the truth about *An Inconvenient Wife*?'

'I did tell you … most of the truth. I showed you the carbon that I had.'

'Which you personally typed on carbon paper.'

'Frank wrote about desperate women clinging to errant men. Look at Elsie Rose in *Some of These Days*. What was she but a woman who was willing to lose everything for a man who didn't even want her? I just continued his strengths in *An Inconvenient Wife*. The same with *September Street*. Tess of Broadstairs. And look! Everyone said that book was Francis Carson at his finest! Frank would never have published anything if not for me! I made it possible for him to write!'

'Perhaps,' Quentin replied, 'but none of this changes the fact that you lied to me.'

'Look, Kanga, it wasn't really a lie, and it certainly didn't hurt anyone. It certainly didn't hurt your firm or your reputation. It made a lot of money. Both books made money. They're still making money.'

'Why didn't you trust me?'

She wilted in front of his eyes. 'It would have been unethical, and you might not have done it.'

'But a few years later, with *September Street*, you assumed I had no ethics.'

'That's not what I mean, and you know it.'

'You assumed I loved you so much I'd do anything for you. Anything you wanted.' The voice of Enid Sherrill grated on his heart. 'Have you used me to further Frank's

367

career?'

He was not at all sure that he could bear the answer, but he didn't need to bear it. Claire came round to him, and knelt between his open knees. Her blue eyes shone with tears and she murmured reassurances one after another as she brushed his hair, and kissed him over and over, removed his glasses, unbuttoned his shirt, unbuckled his belt, and he rose and wrapped her in his arms, his cheek to her hair. He moved against her so she could feel his hardness, and brought his lips down her neck, knowing that her head would tilt back and her mouth would fall open and he would draw down the back zipper of her pink and green summer dress, and it would fall away from her shoulders like the petals of a spent rose, and beneath his hands, her heart would start to pound as they did a kind of tango known only to the two of them down the short hall, into the study and fell onto the accommodating couch.

They picked up their rumpled clothes and slowly put them back on. In the kitchen Claire poured them each a glass of white wine and made plain ham sandwiches. She placed a tray with the bottle, the glasses and the sandwiches on a low wicker table under the dappled shade of the wisteria arbour. The flowers were past their glorious prime, and the wind moved their shadows beneath the vine. They sat in the creaking wicker chairs. Without preamble, her hands in her lap, not looking at him, Claire told him that eight months ago, in the autumn, she had gone to the Ashmolean to listen to a famous photographer speak. She had met a man there. He worked for the Ashmolean. She had got to know him. Got to know him well. Quentin found himself watching the wisteria blossoms tumble from their woody stems, and he wondered why they were each making such a thud when they landed on the grass. Surely something so infinitesimal should make no sound at all.

'He's going on a long dig, two sites, Turkey and Greece. He's asked me to come with him. As a photographer.'

Quentin waved his hand. 'Do you mean to say ... Is this why you got rid of the dog?'

'Yes.'

He stammered, 'Are you telling me you're going with him?'

'Yes. As a photographer.'

'And screwing the boss.'

'Don't be crass.'

'Have you been to bed with him?'

She thought about this, as if waiting for the waning wisteria to float down with an answer wrapped in purple petals. 'Yes.'

With one swift brush of his arm he set the glasses and plates flying and they landed in the grass.

The wine bottle gurgled its last into the lawn. 'What's his bloody name?'

'It doesn't matter.'

'It matters to me.'

'Please, Kanga—'

'Don't call me that! Have there been others? Besides him. Others?'

'I haven't come to this lightly. I am sick of my own life. I want to be part of something larger than this house, than Oxford, than Frank's reputation. I'm—'

'Have. There. Been. Others?'

'No.' She was silent for a long while, and he did not break it, though he thought surely the pounding of his heart was shaking the earth beneath his feet. 'Yes.'

'How many?'

'Two,' she answered after a long silence. 'They didn't matter.'

Quentin reminded himself he had not cried when Robert died. He called on that stoicism, that misplaced manly reserve he had so often regretted having, to keep him dry-eyed and upright, the instinctive, inveterate, inherited stolidity of his people, his mother as she brushed imaginary lint from his lapels. *There there, that's better, there, that fixes it, there there.* 'And this man. This Ashmolean bastard. Does he matter?'

'I'll always love you. My leaving doesn't change that, doesn't change my loving you.'

'It changes everything! This is a complete and utter betrayal of … of …' A betrayal of worlds and time, the past and future, the wind and sun and stars, the moon, and the planets in their orbits. But words failed him; he could not wrap his mind or his lips around so vast a betrayal.

'This is my chance and I'm taking it! I'm forty-five years old, and what would you have of me? That I should spend my last thirty years pondering seed catalogues, doing the occasional edit, waiting for you on Tuesdays and Fridays—'

'I told you years ago I didn't want that! I wanted to get married. You're the one who wants things as they—'

'Pretending that I have a use or a purpose or something important to do in life? A calling.'

'A calling? Are you barking mad? Are you taking up holy orders?'

'I mean a calling like photography, something that will take me out of myself, and place me in the larger world with new people, and new things to learn, to travel, to put my mind and my hand to work in digging up someone else's world, what's left of it.'

'What's left of it….' He gave a harsh, rueful laugh, and there ricocheted painfully through his mind jumbled bits of memory, like flotsam after a wreck, washing up on a beach, broken, shattered. He moved his glasses down, and pinched the top of his nose till it hurt. 'Are you telling me we have reached the end of our tether? That's what you said about Frank the first time I met you. Were you going

370

to leave him?'

'I couldn't. I had three children with him.'

'And you and I have nothing? After fifteen years?'

'We have two books.'

'Ah. Yes, we are the parents of two bastard brats that we've passed off as Frank Carson's.'

'If I'm leaving anyone, it's Frank.'

'God! Will you stop! He's dead! You can't leave him! Don't you see? Don't you know that? Are you mad? He's already gone! I'm alive! Screw Frank! I hate Frank! I'm talking about my heart! Not Frank's work! My heart is broken.' He thumped his chest, which seemed to echo dully as though his heart had already fled.

'I don't want to represent him any more.'

'You don't! I represent him! He's an author and I represent his work!'

'But I represent his life. I always have. I'm sick of it. I want my own life.'

Quentin's vision seemed to blur, though he could swear he wasn't crying, but the pink and green of her summer dress seemed to lift off the wicker chair and spin before his eyes, the green spindling, the pink shrivelling to tiny points, and the voice of Louisa returned to him as she smashed the black fig in half, the fruit rolling open, the green threads and pink seeds, the black-clad widow teeming with possibility. That was Claire. Certainly that's how Claire had seemed to him fifteen years ago, the bright fruit of desire offered to him in a world that was grey with austerity. Shards of verse and lyric battered at his brain without ever coalescing into understanding till the image faded and the pink and green of her dress dissolved into black shadows at her feet.

'I am leaving,' she said. 'I'm sorry you're taking it so hard.'

He stood, unsteadily, but erect. 'How else is there to

bloody take it?'

'You could be more mature and understanding.'

'You're not a girl leaving home. I'm not your father. You can't just walk out on me,' he said, knowing very well that she could, knowing from the letters he had read that her love for him had never had the pitch and intensity, the passion and bravado, the depths of despair and affection she had felt for Francis Carson. After reading her letters to Frank, he knew that her love for him, Quentin, was by contrast staid, secure, sustaining. Sustenance at best. Sustenance she clearly no longer needed. Now she sought appetite. He called on resources he wasn't sure he had. His every inner organ seemed to pucker painfully, and his throat sprouted a lump the size of a pear. 'If you leave with this man, this bearded bastard in a pith helmet, I am severing all contact with you.'

'You can't. There's Frank's work, for one thing.'

'I will hand it over to a younger agent,' he lied, knowing he'd do no such thing.

'Give it to Pennypacker for all I care,' she retorted. 'I won't try to tell you what to do, even though you want me to obey you and stay around just to make you comfortable.'

'Comfortable? Comfortable! Christ almighty, Claire! You can't really think that! To make me *comfortable*? When have you ever made me comfortable? You sound as though you sit around darning my socks, and sugaring my tea. I've loved you because we've prized the same things, and stultifying comfort isn't one of them! I've loved you because you've always had a sense of adventure and freedom, because you were honest about what you felt, because you were candid, because you are bright and expansive, because you knew how to laugh and you knew how to cry, and you knew how to love ...' Sweat beaded at his brow. He continued more calmly. 'We have been together in every meaningful way a man and woman can be, two sides of the same coin for fifteen years. We have loved each other. We have something unique and wonderful.'

'Love shouldn't bind you. It should free you.'

'Oh, Christ! What's happened to your intelligence? You sound so vapid, so shallow! Like reciting from one of those aphorism books Florence keeps beside the toilet!' He drew a deep breath. 'You want to be free? Go. Be fucking free, but don't paste a bunch of tawdry, vulgar sentiments over it and ask me to agree and be happy for you!'

'I hate it when you swear. I'll only be gone a year.'

'A year!' He felt the blood rush from his head.

'I'll come back. This is my home. I will always love you, Kanga—'

'Don't call me that! Never call me that again!'

'Please ... don't make this ...'

'Make it difficult? Are you really asking for my blessing before you go off to Greece with some barrel-chested bastard? Well, you can't have it. You can't.'

'I'll always love you, no matter what you say.'

'And no matter what you do? Really, Claire. Is that supposed to comfort me while you're gone off with someone else?' He choked back a sob, hearing in his heart the fiction of memory, the memory of fiction implanted into his own experience. *Some of these days oh you're gonna miss me honey, some of these daaaaays you gonna be so lonely, just for me only ...* The heartbreak that had drained down Elsie Rose's face, blackened with mascara, smeared across Quentin's mind, and despite the blue light spilling through the wisteria arbour, he saw the grey-green face of Mrs Rackwell and the ignoble pain in her eyes, the sadness that could never be assuaged, and he choked back a bitter laugh to think that he, Quentin Castle, a successful man in the prime of his life, should share his heart-rent grief with two such old bawds as Elsie Rose and Mrs Rackwell. He understood at last the love that drove people to despair without dignity, that made them give up everything, even knowing they had nothing of value to give. Quentin would have given up everything, anything, but he had nothing the woman he loved wanted, nothing she valued or wanted. He sucked air into his collapsing lungs, his collapsing life.

'Please,' she implored, 'try to understand.'

'Understand why you would leave me? Oh, I understand that. You are betraying, false-hearted, and disloyal. You never loved me.'

'Don't say that.'

'I'll say it again,' he vowed, though he didn't. Like a drowning man – he knew suddenly how Frank must have thrashed in the Garden of Allah pool, drowning, casting about for some last hope to keep him alive – he flailed to find his voice. 'If you leave me, leave here and go off with this bastard, whoever he is, if you leave, we are finished forever. You might come back here, but I will not come back to you. There's no waffling and wailing about that. I am quite clear on that.'

She neither agreed nor argued with him. She folded her hands in her lap. She played with the sapphire ring. Time passed in pregnant silence save for some sparrows on the lawn squabbling over the remains of the sandwiches.

At last he said, 'I see. You knew that's what I would say.'

'Of course. To me you are transparent.'

He clutched his own hand so he would not suddenly lash out and shake her senseless, till her teeth chattered, an impulse so foreign to him he seemed suddenly to have become someone else. 'Have you told Michael?' he asked with cruel delight. 'What fun for him. He'll get to call you a whore again, and this time he'll be right.'

'Michael is the Presiding Secretary of Great Dane Enterprises, a wealthy man. Of what possible interest to him would my travels be?'

'He broke your heart, Claire! He and Frank! They left

you! I never left you. I loved you true and faithfully as they never did. I'm here! Think of all we've been to one another! All we've shared! The years, the days and nights. In sickness and in health. For better or for worse. How can you leave me? Is this my reward for all these years we've had together?'

'Who said you get rewards? That anyone gets rewards? If you love me, I am begging you to love me enough to let me go. Let me go and do and discover and have some life for myself that isn't totally wrapped up in you or Frank.'

'ARE YOU BLOODY BLIND? FRANK'S DEAD. How can you not know that? I'm bloody here!'

'Please keep your voice down, Quentin. Everyone will hear you.'

'Almighty God! Claire Carson worried about the neighbours! You're worse than Florence! Quick, where's the vicar? Does he know?'

'Stop it. You're being cruel.'

'And you're not?'

'Why can't we try something new and different?'

He was speechless as if she'd asked him how many angels could dance on the head of a pin. Was this the same woman whose talents and intelligence, and imagination, whose unconventionality added to her beauty? Whose depths only grew more alluring with time? Try something new and different? He'd always believed that Gigi was shallow, but Claire? 'New and different? Are you trading me in for a new pair of shoes? New and different? Am I out of style? Or am I like the old horse you had knackered when you left Harrington Hall? You know, that spavined nag you kept around to amuse everyone till you moved out and moved on? Is it really that fucking simple?'

'I hate it when you swear.'

'You swear all the time. My father used to call you the Foul-Mouthed Bitch.'

'I am going to Greece and Turkey.' She bit her lip. 'I'm taking this chance now that I've got it.'

He collapsed back into the wicker chair that seemed to splinter under his weight. 'When?'

'Next week.'

'Next week! As soon as that!' *Some of these days, you're gonna be soooo lonely, some of these daaaays.* The future swirled before him, murky and uncertain, as drear as the garden before him was bright. With every passing day and year the fundamental juices of his life would parch, in his heart, his groin, his very soul. The future was too dry and terrible to contemplate, but the past was tainted, ravaged beyond any reclamation. She had betrayed him with three different men. Even if she stayed, their love was ruined beyond redemption. An explosion burst in his chest, and he could hardly breathe. His breath came in scraping gusts. He knew what it would be like one day to die. He took off his glasses, and rammed his palms into his eye sockets till colours burst forth. He rose, paced, and laughed bitterly. 'You know your favourite phase, *Can you imagine*? Today you have finally given me something I could not imagine. Is this what writers call irony?'

'Oh, don't give all that tripe about writers. I hate it.'

'When were you going to tell me?'

'I've been trying to tell you for weeks, to have the courage to tell you.' Her blue eyes gleamed with tears.

'Don't you dare cry. What about the girls? I know you haven't told them or I would have heard.'

'I had to tell you first. I thought if I could tell you first, it would be easier to tell them.'

He gulped and snorted and coughed, and retched all at once. 'How very bloody kind of you. Or no, wait. Did you think I'd make it easier for you to tell the girls? That I'd be there, backing you up? Singing the praises of Greece and Turkey?'

'Don't be—'

'Oh, of course! I could be the music-hall bloke in the funny suit and big shoes and the Cockney patter: "Gwon, girls, tell Mum to 'ave a fine old time woile us old chaps stays here and minds things, keeps 'em all proper, makes sure the old royalty cheques are on time, and old Frank's literary knob gets hisself polished.'

'I'll be back in a year.'

'Not to me, you won't.'

The phone rang and rang, harsh, insistent clangs.

'Hear me well, Claire. No matter what you do in Greece or with the rest of your life, you will never have the chance to destroy me again. I know that for certain. Nothing else is clear. But I know that much. I'm telling you this, as a vow. A sacred vow. On my life, Claire, I swear if you leave me now, we are finished forever.'

Claire looked as though she might speak, argue, but finally she rose, and her bare feet made soft sounds as she went into the kitchen to answer the phone. Through the open door and the open window, her voice floated out to him, though he paid it no heed, once he was certain it wasn't the bloody goddamned Ashmolean bastard.

He turned away from the house, and tried to concentrate on the line of apple trees. He seemed to stand at the horizon of his own life, equidistant between what lay behind and what lay ahead, looking back to the known shores from whence he'd come and that amorphous shore that yet lay ahead, death. Between that horizon and this moment he saw only exile: exile from love, from joy, from fulfilment, exile as clearly as if he had sailed away from a country no longer his own.

When she returned to him, her face pale, she searched his eyes. She put her hand on his chest. 'The call is for you.'

'Me?'

Claire licked her lips and whispered, 'It's Miss Marr.'

'Miss Marr? Miss Marr? Calling me here? How does she know I'm here?' He grew faint, his brain pulling away from his skull. His heart beat in his chest, as though flinging itself against the barricade of his ribs, like a sparrow battering against a skylight. 'What does she want?'

'Your wife is looking all over for you.' Claire's voice trembled. 'Your mother's had a stroke. Oh, Quentin!'

He moved through a murk towards the kitchen, resisting the urge to create a path of destruction, overturning chairs and smashing photographs and crockery. He picked up the phone, cleared his throat. 'What is it, Miss Marr?'

'Your mother's had a stroke, Quentin. She's dying. They are taking her to hospital.'

'How did you know I was here?'

'I have always known, Quentin. I've sent young Mr Pennypacker to the London Library to look for you. For the sake of appearances.' Her voice was full of triumph and hiss. 'Did you think I was a fool?'

As the wires crackled in the distance between them, Quentin envisioned Miss Marr as she had appeared yesterday, framed in the doorway, enraged, her cane upraised, discord, brutal envy, soul-shrivelling fury painted all over her plain face and burning in her eyes. How could he not have seen her truly before? How could he have thought her simply sour and dry? The scope of her betrayals threatened to take his breath away. How had he so totally misjudged everything? Everyone. 'Tell them I'm leaving immediately.'

'I shall. Your wife—'

'And you are sacked as of today. As of this moment. You will have three months' wages, but you will not come back tomorrow. Is that clear?'

'I—I—'

He slammed the phone down. Slowly he turned to face Claire. He took in the whole, this final vision: her ash-blonde hair, the blue of her eyes, her tanned arms and bare feet, her lips parted, as though she might speak, offer up some of the conventional phrases she had always so disdained. He could not bear it. In two steps he crossed the floor, took her in his arms, roughly, brought her up against his body with all the strength he possessed, he held her, kissed her, the fierce, last kiss of a man who knows that as much of time and the world is left to him, between here and the grave, whatever else he might do or achieve, or become, this is the end, he is about to go under once and for all, to drown forever, the waters closing over his head as the sky blurred above.

CHAPTER TWENTY-FOUR

SMOKE AND SHADOW

QUENTIN CASTLE KEPT the vow he made that day. He never saw Claire Carson again. As the head of Castle Literary, he oversaw Francis Carson's estate, but Gordon Pennypacker signed all the cheques and letters; on those few occasions when Mrs Carson called the firm with a question, Pennypacker spoke with her. Pennypacker penned the agency's public statement when Claire died in the 1979 plane crash.

However when news of that crash reached Quentin Castle, he collapsed in his office, and had to be taken to hospital; his staff feared he was having a heart attack. Even when released, his grief was disordered, extravagant; he acted like a madman for days, and then he simply fell into a stupor, refusing to speak, refusing food and drink, clutching his personal copy of *Some of These Days* to his chest. His doctors were concerned for him. Florence and his children pitied him. His friends and colleagues feared for him. Louisa, personally, came to the house (she had never met Florence) and took over the cooking. To no avail. Pennypacker delivered the letter from Michael Carson's solicitor, brought it to Quentin's home, and gave it to him.

The letter read that Michael Carson, as the chosen executor to his mother's estate, withdrew his father's work from Castle Literary Ltd; the agreement between Albert and Francis in 1937 was based on a handshake, and this note sufficed to sever the connection. Further instructions would be pending.

Pennypacker began, 'I've heard they've chosen—'

'I've no wish to know. I count on you to handle everything.'

'Of course. Will we see you back at Number 11 soon, sir?'

'Not soon.'

Florence, unequal to her husband's grief, his refusal to eat or speak, or engage, unable to endure the grim and distant looks he gave her and his children, beseeched Louisa Partridge to take him to Italy, to her house in the hills above Fiesole. Louisa concurred immediately. Quentin neither agreed, nor refused. Florence packed his suitcase and Louisa came to collect him. He went without complaint, without enthusiasm. He allowed himself to be moved like a piece of luggage.

Once there he sat in the Tuscan sunshine on Louisa's terrace. He had no appetite, nor sought any sustenance. He stayed alive. He didn't know quite how or why. Though Louisa let him wallow, undisturbed in his despondence, she requested that Pennypacker send new, fresh manuscripts for consideration. She left them by his chair. She knew that at some point the lifelong tug of work – thirty years – would rouse him, the old habits would press, that London would eventually beckon, that he would return, and pick up the reins of his old life. Those basic, stolid qualities of his character would reassert themselves. Eventually.

One afternoon Louisa brought out to him a letter from Mary. She sat across from him until he deigned to open it.

After he read it, he passed it to her.

Mary wrote that Michael had severed any but official correspondence with his sisters. Mary and Catherine each had a letter from him advising that, as executor of their mother's estate, he intended to sell the Linton Road house to be carved into flats. Mary and Catherine would each receive one third of the selling price. On a specified date they could go to the house to take what they wanted. A security guard from Great Dane Enterprises opened the house for them, remained there while they were inside, and locked it when they left. Furniture, clothes, bits of childhood memorabilia, that's all Mary and Catherine found at Linton Road. Michael had already been through the house with movers who, on his instructions, had packed up all the documents, the papers, Claire's vast trove of photographs, boxes and trunks of drafts of their father's novels, notes, letters, invoices, shards and scraps and reams of paper – all of it in total Claire-chaos. Michael had the whole removed to his country home, Woodlands, to the fourth floor where he had lived as a boy. Mary wrote: *I have heard that Michael personally went through everything before he burnt it, Mum's photographs, Da's papers, their letters, your letters, all of it. Everything either one of them had ever created. They say there were bonfires behind the gardener's cottage, and that the pall of smoke hung over Woodlands for days.*

'So,' said Louisa, 'is that the end of it, then? The spite and revenge of an angry boy destroying his parents' lives.'

'He is not a boy.'

'He is still angry, and loveless, stinking rich, and pitiful.'

'I don't pity him.'

'Michael Carson can never destroy the fact that she loved you.'

'Did she?'

382

'I feel certain she did,' Louisa said. She could speak that much in truth. She gave him back his letter and left him there.

He tilted his face to the sun and the Fiesole hills, remembering the joy, the discovery he had known in that fourth-floor room at Woodlands, remembering the framed picture of the be-wigged cleric, the high old bed, the view that looked out to the distant folly and the footpath to folly. Once he had believed that love and death were infinite, and now he knew he was wrong. Only cold death was infinite. Love, like fire, vanishes into smoke and shadow and silence. Ashes crumble. Time rolls on and over, heedless as the wind that blew pale, poisonous oleander blossoms along the flagstones at his feet.

ACKNOWLEDGEMENTS

The author would like to thank Pamela Malpas and Gill Jackson for their support and enthusiasm, and a special thanks to Peggy K. Johnson, the author's ever-best ally.

THREE
STRANGE
ANGELS